LUCKY'S WORLDS:

BEYOND THE WIZARD'S THRESHOLD

BY

Loretta Sylvestre

*Dedicated with love to my ABC boys
(Andre', Brenden, Collin)*

This is a work of fiction. All characters and events in this book are products of the author's imagination or are used fictitiously.

BEYOND THE WIZARD'S THRESHOLD

Copyright©2010 Loretta Sylvestre

All rights reserved, including the right to reproduce this book, or portions thereof in any form.

Edited by Sandy Fetchko
Cover art by Ron Leming
Cover design and layout by Stephen Blundell.

Published November, 2010 in print
Ebook edition published November, 2010

ISBN: 978-0-9829295-7-5

Marion Margaret Press
Headquarters:
1312 16th St
Orange City, FL 32763
Business Office:
PO Box 245
Hebron, NE 68370

email: publisher@marionmargaretpress.com

www.marionmargaretpress.com

Acknowledgments

Many deserve thanks for help and support as Beyond the Wizard's Threshold worked its way from idea to publication. I can't name them all, but here are a few, each special: Darya Kowalski-Ewczynski, Jason Rolfe, Karla Lammers, Tom Beck, Kim Moore, Lillian Goodrich (and family), Papa (of course), Anna Jones, Pauline American Horse, and Jackie Kelly. Special thanks to MMP editors and staff Diana Cacy Hawkins, Sharon Partington, and Sandy Fetchko, and all the other professionals who have helped bring this book into being.

CONTENTS

Prologue: Three Years Ago...
    The Guardian   2
    The Wizard   3
    The Witch-Mortaine   4

Part One: Luccan Lost and Found
    Pale Blue, Wicked Cold   7
    Old Thief, Rhymes with Sherlock   15
    Beyond the Threshold   20
    The M.E.R.L.I.N. and the Wizard's Job   31
    Lucky's Darkest Night   44
    A Magic He Had Believed Forever Lost   56
    The Lion, the Cookie, and the Heart's Desire   63

Part Two: Mystery, Magic, and Twists of Memory
    The Demon Queen's Midnight Carnival   75
    The Boy's Got Magic   80
    Mind Reading and the Power of Wishful Thinking   86
    No Rest for the Wizardly   100
    A Fine Time to Rebel   115
    Stone Knives, Twins, and Strangers   127
    The Wizard's Question   136

Part Three: Revelations
    Who Is He and How Does He Know My Name?   146
    A Lesson from Ophiuchus' Serpent   155
    A Farewell Cup for Uncle Han   164
    A Young Person's Guide to Making Sense of It   175
    Brothers with Blades   182
    Plans and Contingencies   191
    Mordred Brede   203

Part Four: When All Others Fail

In the Light of a New Day	209
Let Auntie Isa Take Care of You	216
And the Witch is Glad	223
Wolves, Wights, and Heroes	228
Black Hearts and Flames	246
Sahlamahn	258
Mannatha	266

Part Five: Finding Home

Luccan, Let Go	282
The Twin Stars of Home	284

"How queer everything is today! And yesterday things went on just as usual....
Let me think: was I the same when I got up this morning?
...But if I'm not the same, the next question is,
'Who in the world am I?'"

—Lewis Carroll, *Through the Looking Glass*

Prologue: Midsummer Three Years Ago...

The Guardian

Midsummer Day had hardly begun to cool in Black Creek Ravine when Hank George took up his station outside the cavern known as The Doorway. His waist-length, iron-grey braids fell heavy in the humid heat, but that didn't account for the way he felt, as though stones weighted his chest and shoulders.

Inside the rock, the luminous halls of the cavern led to a series of tunnels. The Road Between, it was called. Many generations past, the Others had come to Earth by that dark path. Decades later, they'd traveled the same route back to the world that was their home.

A Guardian had watched at the Doorway ever since.

Hank had been watching for more than fifty years. Countless days he'd listened to the ethereal song of the breeze sighing through the cavern. A strange sound always, but never before had it raised hackles on the back of his neck. He sat on the stump outwardly calm, but tension thrummed through his muscles like voltage through power lines. He rose and took a step toward the entry. A blast of air colder than January cut through his thin shirt and blew back his braids. Perhaps anticipation seized him, maybe dread.

Something was coming. Something was about to begin.

The Wizard

Alone in his dilapidated wooden tower, grey-bearded Wizard Thurlock leaned out the west window to survey the hundreds of party-goers making merry in the vale that dipped between the Sister Hills. He tried to laugh at toddlers' antics, dancing couples, and smiling old-folks tapping arthritic feet to the music of fiddles and pipes. He watched Luccan run across the grassy North Rise, where he and L'Aria, his friend-for-life, endeavored to fly their new kites. He tried to enter into the prevailing Midsummer joy.

He failed miserably. This was Luccan's eleventh birthday, the day the boy should have received his cardinal name so that he could begin to gather the strength it would impart. Knowing a little of what his fortune might hold, the Wizard thought surely the youngster would soon need all the strength he could find.

Across the vale stood the neat, sunlit windows and varnished logs of Sisterhold Manor, Luccan's home. Beyond that, in the near distance, Oakridge rose from the hillside like a monument to history. When Luccan was only two hours old, Thurlock had brought him out into the summer dawn and fumbled him into his father's strong but equally fumbling hands. The man had carried his child to the sun-sparked granite on the ridge and whispered a name into his ear, a powerful name known only to them, witnessed solely by the wind.

Now, because of what Thurlock had not done then, disaster threatened—for Luccan, for Sunlands, perhaps for all the world of Ethra. The infant, of course, had forgotten the name. His father had become lost. And the Gods' Breath, fabled dawn wind of the Sunlands, kept its secrets.

The Witch-Mortaine

Privately, Isa thought it would be best to kill the boy and have done. Granted, the recent, strange behavior of time brought opportunity. And true, the boy's unformed powers might boost her own—in the service of her master, of course—if she could subvert them.

Yes. She would bow to the wishes of the Ice-Lord, Mahl, and alter her course. The boy would live, long enough at least to determine if he could be put to use. If the costs in time and effort grew too vast, the boy's death would destroy the enemy's hopes, and Mahl would be appeased.

She took stock of her image in the looking glass. The light filtering through the icy walls of her keep lit her eyes with blue fire and emphasized her long bones and sharp angles. The reflection pleased her. Gone was the soft-faced girl of ages past, the girl who had been a fool. Staring back from the silvered glass was a woman of power, a Witch who could wait for reward.

Yes. She would sow seeds now for the Sunlands' defeat. Later, when she reaped vengeance against the one man who mattered, the fruit would be that much sweeter.

From glass shelves holding bottles, boxes, and vials, she gathered the bits she would need for the spell.

Midsummer stood on the cusp. The moment for cold, hard magic had come.

Three years later...

PART ONE: Luccan Lost and Found

1. Pale Blue, Wicked Cold

When Lucky stepped off the asphalt at the end of 12th Street and into the weeds, it was twilight, a time of day that stretched long on June twenty-first—or so you'd expect. He only made it halfway across the mile wide strip of open land that separates Valley City from Black Creek Ravine when night surprised him. It had fallen way too fast.

"All I did was blink," he said to no one, and tried to laugh it off. But dark had taken hold of him, creeping up his spine, cold like something witched from its grave. He told himself to handle it, to hang just a little bit longer. "It's been a creepy day, that's all, and it's almost over."

The day in question, his fourteenth birthday, had staggered by, every hour weighted by his sincere wish that it would move along. Now, the wind moaned in the pines farther on, and the moon hung like a blood-red bubble between the rock spires known as Death of the Gods. Frogs and crickets went stone silent just ahead of his step, and webs appeared out of nowhere, as if hungry spiders by the thousands rode in on moonlight to stretch traps in the grass.

He stopped and put his hands on his hips, leaning forward like a runner out of breath. Either pumping his too-bony knees high enough to clear the tall grass left him winded, or else the night had him spooked. He wasn't sure which.

After a moment, he pushed his hair out of his eyes and marched on. Before he'd gone ten more steps, Maizie, the big yellow mongrel he'd raised into a best friend, started barking. He slowed, scanning the grasses and the trees looming ahead. She'd seen, heard, or smelled something that didn't belong—Lucky was sure of it. She never barked just because he was coming home. She hardly ever barked at all.

"Chill," he told himself, and walked on. Seconds later, his oversized mutt bounced out of the trees like a big ball of animated sunshine. She greeted him with her whining, toothy grin just like every night and this time he really did laugh, despite his mood.

"Okay girl." He dropped a bag of groceries trying to fend off her slopping tongue, and roughed her thick yellow fur. Her tail mowed the weeds flat in a circle around him, and for those few seconds he didn't feel quite so cursed with dark.

But she bounded off toward home, and as he picked up his spilled pouches of ramen noodles—precious even though he'd found them on sale at six for a dollar—the shroud dropped around him once more. He didn't even try to shake it off. Hefting his grocery bags, he forged ahead through the whispering weeds on the edge of the wood.

In the pines, he answered an owl's challenging *who*. "It's just me," he said, and felt pretty silly. But when he emerged from the trees and caught sight of his shack, chill prickled over his scalp like a tattoo needle made of ice. He stopped dead and stood there for a few minutes—weeks, whatevers—shoving his hair back repeatedly and shifting foot to foot. Had he somehow come to the wrong place?

For the comfort the sound of his voice might offer, he answered his question out loud. "Don't be stupid, Lucky. You know your way home by now."

Homeless and raveled to his wit's end, he'd happened on the half-century-old shed almost a year ago and camped there one jumpy night. Come the following dawn he'd swept away bugs and started pounding loose nails and mending split planks, and in a few weeks he'd transformed the place into a cozy hideout. Ever since, he'd shared the ten-by-twelve space with Maizie and a family of finches in the eaves, and he'd come to think of it as the one secure place on Earth.

The shack squatted on the cliff at the end of the flats and leaned out into Black Creek's infamous gorge. Ordinarily, that didn't trouble him. But tonight a mist rose from the Ravine and pearled silver in the moonlight, twisting and twining like ghost-flesh. The strange, swarming fog cut the cabin's black hulk off from everything beyond, as if the place that should have been his refuge hunkered at the edge of oblivion, the brink of the world.

He accused himself of thinking too much and snapped a leash on his imagination. After he forced a deep breath, he swept his hands through his hair and stepped forward. Maizie stayed close and quiet at his heels as he strode to the door.

"See," he said, glancing at Maizie as he pushed open the shed's door. "It's exactly the way we left it." Blankets, toothbrush, half-empty bag of kibble, everything remained in place. Nothing was moved, nothing mussed, nothing touched. "Nothing's wrong."

It was a lie, he knew it, and it hurt like ice in his bones. His security had been breached, his bunker exposed. His sanctuary had ceased to be safe.

He sat down hard on the shelf he called his bed, hung his wearied head in bruised hands, and stared at his knees. In the dim light he saw not those scarred joints but a replay of the day's events. He would have liked to pinpoint the moment when things had gone from bad to worse. He wanted to figure out why the day had been a nightmare. Perhaps not his worst Midsummer, but close.

The morning had started with a dream about a key, one of a handful of inexplicable objects which were all that remained of his childhood. A woman with golden hair and eyes shaped like his but green, rather than coppery brown. A woman he'd dreamed about before. She pushed the key into his palm and flung him some cryptic advice. She vanished then, shrieking, and some cold, dark thing took her place. Lucky screamed himself awake and smacked his head on the shelf overhead, leaving a lump the size of a duck's egg to decorate his forehead.

It throbbed, purple by the time he reached the bus stop at 12th and Main an hour later.

He sat down to wait for the number sixty-eight bus, wishing for shade. With his arm draped over the back of the bench and his feet sprawled out nonchalant, he hoped he looked cool despite the heat wafting from the asphalt. When an old man trundled up wearing grey sweats and combat boots, he ignored the fact that the stranger looked weird, even for downtown.

Polite as always, he said, "Excuse me sir. Do you know the time?"

"Time? Excellent question." He fished in a jacket pocket Lucky never would have guessed existed and brought out a pink paper bag, opening it to show crullers with maple frosting melting in the heat. Lucky inhaled deeply but tactfully refused the offer and the man set the bag on the bench between them. It rolled itself up ... which couldn't possibly be true.

The stranger said, "I've brought enough for both of us."

It seemed an unlikely thing for him to say to someone he'd never met, and Lucky debated whether to respond.

Suddenly the man brandished a huge yellow umbrella and flourished it open over their heads just in time for rain to begin falling from the still cloudless sky. "Eight forty-six." Out of the impossible pocket, he pulled a large clock bearing hands but no face. Inside the glass housing, gears whirred and clicked, but they didn't quite mesh.

Lucky forced his gaze away, leaned elbows on knees, and cradled his throbbing head.

"Not feeling quite yourself today?"

Lucky ignored him. The street had gone too quiet. He ran a hand through his hair to clear his line of sight. One car, a hulking Ford Crown Victoria, idled at the stoplight. By some trick of the light, its white paint reflected blood red, and the windows were tinted a blue so dark the driver looked like a ghost.

Strange.

Without warning, the old man dropped the umbrella in front of Lucky's face. When he snapped it shut the white car vanished, the traffic returned, and the rain ceased.

Most fourteen-year-olds don't have a workday routine, but Lucky did, and after the day had gotten off to such a rotten and perplexing start, he had tried to get it back on track. The routine consisted of finding customers (mostly criminals), doing their chores (mostly laundry), and avoiding police, social workers, and the truancy patrol (mostly easy).

If a bad dream, a crack on the head, and a strange old man hadn't been trouble enough, the day also proved bad for business. Police had run a crackdown on petty vice the night before. Most of Lucky's usual employers were locked up.

He scraped for work all day, and finally in desperation went out to the Langdon brothers' bungalow to see if they could use some help cleaning up after last night's party. The brothers, Benny and Johnny, were always flush with cash and they partied every night. They'd have a humongous mess. They always did, because they and all their friends courted insanity.

"There's barf in the green bathroom," Benny said, standing in the center of the cyclone-struck kitchen with eyes mostly closed against the sun beating down from the skylight. He rifled his blonde hair, shaking out a rain of blue glitter. "Did you bring gloves?"

Of course he did. After a year in the laundry-and-chores business he'd learned to come prepared for yuck. Still, other things had to be considered. The Langdons' sprawling house was always sliding into chaos, and despite their "a deal's a deal" intentions, working for them was risky business.

"Pay me now."

"Half," Benny said, patting at his jeans pockets. His brow scrunched in a puzzled look, and then cleared as he apparently clicked on a mental link. "Oh, yeah, my cash is in my jacket. Wait a minute and I'll find it." He started to work his way around the room, shifting bottles, cans, and pizza boxes on the counter and kicking at piles of litter on the floor.

Silent, dark-eyed Johnny picked up a Frisbee-shaped object—ketchup leaking, pickles poking out the sides—and found a stash of limp bills on the table beneath it. He pinched a twenty and a five in his fingernails and held them out. His sour face dared Lucky to object.

Lucky needed groceries. Maizie needed a flea collar. He rinsed and blotted the bills, folded them in a paper towel, and stuck the packet in the hip pocket of his cut-off cargo pants. Three hours later, he congratulated himself for having had the foresight to insist on the advance.

The job had gone fine until he'd disturbed one of the Langdons' friends, a burly woman with a black Mohawk and serpent tattoos for bracelets. She took offense when the vacuum cleaner probed too close to the closed door she'd been lurking behind. He was blocks away and still running when his shoe broke and he fell down an embankment. At the dusty bottom of a dry wash, he laid low in the snagged litter and tumbleweeds and took the opportunity to catch his breath and give the predator time to lose interest.

Fifteen minutes later, give or take, he climbed up to street level and picked his way through a forest of sticker bushes and signs telling him who to vote for and what herbal remedy could help him lose twenty-five pounds fast. The wild-woman had gone, but the blue-glassed Crown Victoria crept by just then, like an omen.

"I hate omens." Omens were never normal. Everywhere he'd ventured all day, he'd encountered that same car with its bug-eye windows, through which he could just make out the driver's wild-haired, haggard, hook-nosed profile.

Later, as the sun began to sink, with his broken sole slapping the pavement, he trudged from the 12th and Main bus stop to the Quick-Shoppe on the same corner, calculating what he could buy and what he and Maizie would have to do without. It had been a long day. He now sported enough bruises for the Guinness book, a headache thumping like a boom box, and a rare but heartfelt nasty mood that did not improve when he saw the Crown Victoria cooling in the parking lot.

The store's sixties-vintage automatic doors tried his patience, but eventually huffed open and admitted him to the familiar glow of fluorescents and the rattle, beep, and clink of the aging market's interior. He accepted a cart from a teenage bagger with a pimple, a salon haircut, and brand name cross-trainers. And a real job. And a future full of everything Lucky could not look forward to, such as a driver's license, high-school graduation, and a scolding from a loving parent if he stayed out too late on Friday.

Envy smoldered uncomfortably in his gut until it cut loose with a sharp jerk, as if someone reached in and gave his personality a twist. After that, for the first time ever, being mean felt good. Really good.

He almost ran down a five-year-old with his cart and he didn't even say he was sorry. A lady reached for the best, juiciest apple, and he snatched it right out of her hand. He knocked down a rack of Cuddle Soft toilet paper and laughed as the rolls bounced under an old lady's bedroom slippers, tripping her up. He felt alive, energized, and it lasted right up to the moment when the tall, horrid woman cut off his progress down the pasta aisle.

When he'd seen her beak nose and frayed hair, he'd known instantly she was the shadow behind the Ford's blue windows. He'd been peering at her from the far end of the aisle, letting his thick hair fall forward to hide his gaze.

"Those have got to be the ugliest eyes I've ever seen," he'd said, but only under his breath. She couldn't have heard, but suddenly she closed the distance and stopped, legs planted wide and hands on hips, less than two feet away. She stared and he drew back, horrified. What he'd said was true.

Her eyes *were* ugly, indescribably so; pale, pale blue, bloodshot, and wicked cold. Their chill bellied over his skin like snakes of ice and froze him to the spot. His throat closed as she slowly reached out a sharp-fingered hand toward his neck.

"Hate," she said, in a voice that could have crushed stone. "Anger. It's good, isn't it? Powerful—that's how it feels." She laughed, a slithering sound, and then whispered. "Don't let anyone fool you, child. Everyone loves power."

Her claw-fingered hand was an inch from his bare neck and creeping closer. Part of him insisted, *this is not really happening in the grocery store,* but the rest of him panicked. She seemed strong, a giant, a glacier.

She could kill me with a squeeze, he thought, and imagined the sound of neck bones crunching.

Her hand stopped.

She leaned close to his face and whispered again, but this time softened her voice into a lure. "You know, boy, you could feel that kind of power all the time, every minute. Come with me, Luc—"

A crash and the shatter of glass cut off her words and broke the hold of her gaze. Lucky turned toward the sound and found the floor and his bare shins splattered with red. The sight of glass shards poking through that shining liquid shifted his heart into high gear. Finally, after a couple of time-warped seconds, the scent of garlic and basil got the message through to his brain. Not blood, spaghetti sauce.

He looked up from the mess on the floor, and relief gave way to confusion. All he saw was a yellow disk. An umbrella. No, THE umbrella, and the same old man he'd met that morning at the bus stop. Incredibly, he stood there in the pasta aisle like a silver-haired swordsman, holding the umbrella by its round golden handle and thrusting its pointed end at the woman. Lucky stayed rooted to the spot, mouth open, staring while those two strange creatures sparred.

The old man lunged forward, back straight and arm outstretched, strong as iron. The umbrella fluttered and spun and cool relief blew over Lucky like the west wind. In a flowing voice, steady and calm, the stranger said, "Isa, you shall not succeed."

"And you will stop me, I suppose?" She followed the flinty words with a laugh.

Silence rolled in. No one moved.

In a voice barely audible yet strong enough to bust that stretched silence wide open, the old man said, "A word has been spoken, Isa, a Command. I'm yet strong enough to enforce it."

The woman shrilled her response. *"You will not keep him!"* Lights flashed, thunder cracked and the air thickened with smoke and sulfur. Then the Quick-Shoppe went as dark as the back of the moon.

2. Old Thief, Rhymes With Sherlock

The morning after his birthday, Lucky flopped on the bus bench next to a bottle in a brown paper bag and nudged a trio of cigarette butts from the curb to the gutter, moving them a few inches farther from his too long, too sensitive nose. Last night, after his dark walk home with the groceries—which he had managed to buy despite the fright at the Quick-Shoppe—he'd spent half the night sorting through his possessions, trying to figure out what had been taken and decode the reason why. He had discovered the what, but the why had left him mystified.

He'd slept three hours starting at dawn, the whole time riding runaway nightmares. It left him feeling slow and moving like a slug on sand. By the time he got to the bus stop, ten o'clock had come and gone.

He stood, unfolding his tired limbs into long straight lines as Valley City Transit sixty-eight hissed to a stop and engulfed the gutter's trash fumes in a diesel cloud. The doors folded open and he boarded, carrying his shoes. The left sole still hung loose from yesterday's chase, and he'd brought along some dollar store Power Glue to fix it. The driver frowned, but he knew Lucky and let him board with bare feet even though it was against the rules.

"Thanks, Rob." Lucky said, and stepped down the corrugated rubber aisle to claim a seat.

The lumps and rips in the vinyl weren't comfortable, but they scratched at the backs of his knees the way they did every day—normal, and that's what he liked. If he could, he would collect normal like some kids collect Magic Cards or game gear, but normal had a talent for avoiding him. When the bus door rattled open for boarding a few blocks down the line, he had a premonition.

It's going to be him.

Sure enough the bent-kneed old man he'd met twice yesterday clambered aboard. He waved at the fare counter, and the gears inside whirred and ticked while coins multiplied, and Rob said "thanks" just as if he was paid that way daily. In heavy black boots, the man tromped up the aisle passing empty seats, and slid in smiling next to Lucky.

This time he carried a canvas bag. From it he produced—among less remarkable things—an amber colored dinner plate, a hovering light with no visible housing, and his ever-present yellow umbrella. Lucky did his best to stare out the window, but this time when the old man proffered a crinkled pink bag filled with maple bars, his resolve broke. Silently cursing his bottomless stomach, passion for maple, and recent pledge never again to be rude, he accepted the pastry with sticky fingers and thanks.

Brakes hissed, and the bus slowed so quickly that Lucky skidded off the seat, folded into the space in front of it, and slammed his sore head against the back of the next seat forward. He recovered dignity and donut to find Rob shaking a fist at a familiar white Ford. Cutting across lanes, the car dodged suddenly in front of the bus and squealed into a right turn, barreling down on a young woman laboring to pull onto the curb a candy-striped stroller holding a baby in pink and an orange bear.

Lucky's seatmate scowled. Eyes flashing, he jabbed his umbrella toward the corner and muttered some foreign words with lots of 'th' and 's' sounds. A ray of light, which Lucky preferred not to notice, shot from umbrella's tip. Stroller, teddy, baby, and mom vanished with a pop, reappearing in the same instant safe among the sand drifts on the sidewalk. The speeding car mowed down only the plastic bags and bottle caps it raised under its wheels.

The old man said, "When will she learn? The high laws apply everywhere, even to her."

Lucky wanted to scream, *What just happened here*? Instead he swallowed a forgotten bite of maple bar and asked, "Pardon?"

"Thurlock," the greybeard said, answering neither of Lucky's questions. "Rhymes with Sherlock." Then, when Lucky deciphered what he meant and politely offered his own name, the old codger rolled his eyes and said, "I know who you are, boy. We've met."

Lucky thought he referred to some other time, some meeting more normal than yesterday's strange encounters, but if so he didn't remember the occasion. That came as no surprise. He didn't remember the first four-fifths of his life.

He shoved both hands through his hair and winced as he made contact with the sore spots. Explaining his weird life raised too great a challenge, so instead he closed his eyes, leaned his head against the cool window, and faked an out-like-a-light sleep. When the bus slowed for his stop in the city's low-end suburbs, he jumped off as it rolled, not saying even good-bye.

He landed on a square of dead grass outside a chain link fence enclosing more of the same, in a blaze of hot sun. Shame, hotter still, burned his face. He'd been rude despite his new rule against it and he couldn't think of any excuse. Strange as the old man seemed, troubling as that was, he had shared his maple bars. Lucky turned quickly to wave belated thanks, but Thurlock wasn't looking at him; the bus window framed his profile.

A sharp light glanced off the chrome of a parked van and struck the old man's straw hat as he settled it on his silver head. There, the beam glinted off a small, metal object which Lucky recognized instantly. He owned it. As far as he knew it had no value to anyone except himself. Yet last night, searching his burgled shack, he'd found that this little trinket had disappeared.

"My key!" He shouted as if the words would magically stop the bus, but of course they didn't. Mind set, he dug his newly fixed shoes into the turf and took out after thief and treasure at a dead run.

Less than an hour later, sweat trickled down his ribs, the late morning sun burned his neck, and a fat black fly buzzed his ear. He ignored it all and crouched behind a juniper shrub, spying on the old thief. He had a nagging sense that the old man just didn't belong in Valley City, and neither did the house into which he'd vanished.

Except for the wooden tower jagging five stories skyward like a giant thumb, the building would have been ordinary if it had stood across town in the fields past Martinez Bridge—just another rundown farmhouse. Here at the end of a road known for hired help, Land Rovers, and swimming pools, the tower appeared no more misfit than the rest of the ramshackle place.

Misfit. Yes, that was a good description of the old man he'd chased into that hideout, too. But then he had to smile. *As if I have room to talk.* He could count on his fingers the things that made him forever an outcast. Things like being the only kid in Valley City with no last name, like not knowing whether he had brothers or sisters or even parents, like living in an abandoned shed teetering on the brink of Black Creek Ravine, the spookiest place in at least three counties.

Probably, nobody else in town would have chased a weird old man three miles uphill to reclaim an odd bit of metal, either. Lucky laughed, despite his aching head and the sting of sweat in his eyes, remembering how Thurlock had sped through the suburbs on his crooked legs.

Definitely, I'm the only one around fast enough to keep up.

He hadn't yet caught his breath from the long uphill run, but already the silver-haired thief came back outside looking well cooled and refreshed. Again, the old man mumbled foreign words—though they seemed vaguely familiar—and held his hat in his hand, looking everywhere except at Lucky's shrub. He tugged at his grizzly beard for a moment then stepped forward and placed the hat on the peeling porch rail. Bit by bit, he turned and tilted it until sudden sunlight flared like lightning from the stolen key.

The broad porch sagged everywhere except where the steps held up a direct path to the door. There in the corner, on the once-white two-by-four that might or might not keep a person from falling into the unkempt but lush pansies below, lay Lucky's golden key. Tied to Thurlock's hatband by its silken yellow cord, it drew Lucky's eyes as if magnetized.

The slender key had an odd-shape and would fit in the palm of his hand, perfectly concealed. Lucky knew that because he'd palmed it every day for the last three years, studying the feel of it and imagining what it might do for him, the way Aladdin might have handled his lamp, the way Scrooge might have counted his coins.

Yes, the key was precious to him, but he had trouble holding on to the idea that anyone had stolen it—especially this old man, Thurlock. He tried to picture him creaking through the shack's plank door in the half-light, stepping so lightly he disturbed not even dust, going straight to the cardboard box that held Lucky's few treasures—souvenirs of a life long gone—and taking the key.

Only the key. Strange though it seemed, that had to mean he'd been searching for precisely that singular object. *Why?* he asked himself. *Was he after it? Or was he after me?*

3. Beyond The Threshold

Another half-hour passed and still Lucky crouched behind the juniper, sun pounding his shoulders. His legs—always longer these days than the last time he looked—scrunched into two big cramps. He stood up, hoping to relieve them, and turned sideways to the sun, trying to make himself narrow enough to be concealed by the scraggly bush.

As lanky as he'd grown, hiding shouldn't have been tough to pull off, but when Thurlock came out again, he looked right at Lucky's hiding place. While Lucky stood scared-rabbit still, another man came out of the house. In contrast to the grey-eyed, ruddy-faced old thief, he had brown-skin like Lucky, and dark hair. He wore a tee shirt and jeans, but stood ramrod straight and moved easy, like a man who'd become used to being strong enough for any task. Broad-shouldered but not heavy, he stood so tall his head barely cleared the top of the doorjamb.

Thurlock, the bent, shrunken-seeming geezer, was even taller.

That's impossible. But maybe not. Lucky remembered the showdown at the Quick-Shoppe.

The two men stood together in the shade, speaking in low tones. Then, Thurlock's volume rose and in a voice as smooth as tacks in a blender he said something that caught Lucky's attention because it included the word 'boy' and ended with the word 'stubborn.'

"Blood pressure, sir," the younger man was saying, as he stepped off the porch in shiny boots that seemed altogether too hot for the day after Midsummer. He used one of those same boots to level the weeds in front of the door to a tool shed across the yard. While he worked the door open, he raised his voice and added, "Breathe."

"My blood pressure is fine, Han." Thurlock's face went baked-tomato red and he crossed his arms in a huff, but his chest rose and fell through several deep breaths. When he passed through the door to go back inside, he must have ducked because the beam couldn't really have arched itself up to let him pass.

Lucky blinked hard, trying to clear his eyes. "Too little sleep," he muttered, "too much sun."

That sun threw even more heat as it began to drop toward the southwest. No true wind rose to cool the sweat trickling down Lucky's limbs, but skirls of hot air twisted over the foothills and dusted the tarred street. A grey cat ambled off the porch and hunched in a patch of milkweed just inside the once-white picket fence, staring out at Lucky through the slats. The man Thurlock had called Han, white tee shirt darkening with sweat, rode the back of an industrial strength lawnmower, balancing left and right to steer—a charioteer slaying weeds.

The house, floating in a sea of overgrown lawn, didn't appear foreboding. It was large but loosely assembled, with one thing hooked to the next as if every room was an afterthought. And the skinny square tower poked up stories higher than the rest, looking like it would fall any minute.

The front door, on the other hand, a massive panel carved with unknown symbols, fitted with black iron hinges, and a golden doorknob *did look* foreboding. It no more fit on this decrepit house than the house fit in this posh neighborhood, or than combat boots fit on an old man with grey sweats and weird clocks.

But there the door was, regardless, and if there was anything Lucky was sure of, standing there peeking through the juniper fronds, it was that he did not want to knock on it. What's more, he wanted to get his key without having to face Thurlock. Despite a thousand questions he might have asked the old geezer, he hoped he would *never* have to meet him eye to eye again. He wanted to grab the key, get away, and wake up tomorrow with everything back the way it had been the day before yesterday. It seemed unlikely, but he made up his mind to give it his best try.

At the far end of the oversized lot, the fence butted up against a steep rocky hill. A dry-wash gully ran down the slope, roughly in a line with the south wall of the house. Where that wall ended, it met the porch rail upon which perched the hat, with the key. Creosote bushes and broom filled the gully, which ought to provide good cover for a sneak-up. If he climbed around to the back of the hill and came down that crevasse, he wouldn't be seen. From the fence, it would be only seven or eight strides to the house. He could sprint across, and then sidle up to the porch, staying hidden behind the overgrown shrubbery along the wall.

A perfect plan.

If he timed it right Han would be mowing on the other side of the yard. Lucky could dash in, pluck the key, and be gone before anyone knew he was there.

I can do it, he thought, *I know I can—as long as no one, like maybe Thurlock, looks out the window. But if someone does see me... Well, I'm a fast runner and it's downhill.*

He went for it.

When he'd made his plan, he'd pictured himself skillfully slithering down the gully, perhaps belly-crawling like a soldier in an old war movie, but it didn't happen like that. He tripped on a root at the top, and tumbled, scrabbled, and slid all the way to the fence. He slammed to a stop against it, sucking breath through his teeth and every inch of his bare arms and legs burning.

As it did a thousand times every day, his hair flopped over his face. He pushed it out of the way to squint at the windows, but the panes stared back empty. He couldn't believe he'd gone unseen after the racket he'd made, but no one came out asking after his health or shouting, *"Up against the wall and keep your hands where I can see them."*

He took a deep breath and got on with it, pacing back uphill. When he had a good start, he flew into a hurdler's leap. He almost cleared the fence, but his trailing knee scraped across the sharp end of a picket. It took fortitude to ignore the injury, but he kept silent and galloped to the side of the house where he slipped between the wall and the bushes.

There, he met with thorns and another opportunity to practice not screaming in pain. By the time he'd extracted the stickers from his skin and freed his clothes he fully expected to be busted. *Surely, the old coot saw the bushes shaking.* But Thurlock didn't appear and neither did anyone else, so Lucky snuck onward until he reached the corner where the house joined the porch. A dense, pink, mulberry squatted there, and he lurked behind it for several minutes, quietly bleeding and recognizing the flaw in his plan.

The rail was too high for him to reach with a jump, and he saw nothing strong enough to climb.

Can I knock the hat down with a rock? No. With my luck, I'll break the window. Sneaking up the stairs—or else running up them full tilt—would be risky, but he couldn't think of any other plan.

The open front door sat dead center behind the four steps to the porch. If the door itself didn't prove a fatal trap, once on the porch he'd have to cross in front of a crystal clear, unobstructed picture window. Anyone, like maybe the bizarre and frightening old thief Thurlock, might be on the other side of the pane looking out.

But there was no other way, so with courage wound up tight, he popped out from behind the mulberry, ran around to the front, and started a dash up the steps. He could just about taste victory, feel his hand close around that strange and wonderful key.

He hadn't given a single thought to his shoe. The one he'd fixed only hours ago on the bus. If he *had* thought about it, he would have had every reason to believe that the Power Glue would hold.

Yet, in the very moment when he was bounding to the second step the sole flapped loose, folded under, and created a drag strong enough to stop his foot instantly, leaving his head to fly forward on momentum. Simple physics, laws governing bodies in motion, predicted a sharp crack of the chin on hard steps. Instead, he stopped midair, hanging by the back of the belt. The position gave him a clear view of what was behind him near the ground. Two jean-clad legs and spit-polished black boots.

Han.

Lucky's heart revved, ready for fight or flight. No flight without fighting first so he started in kicking and flailing, making contact mostly with air. In the process he got a look at the top stair, and standing there were two combat boots topped by grey sweats. *Thurlock.* Lucky went all out with the war effort, then, and made one heck of a lot of noise. For once, he was hoping to attract attention.

Of course no one came.

"Stop kicking, please, and reach your feet toward the ground." The voice came from behind him, above the blue jeans. Han, the owner of that voice, sounded very calm, which was not comforting. The flailing didn't seem to be working, though, so Lucky hung limp, trying to think up a new plan.

"You're nearly as tall as I am these days," Han said, and then laughed. *Laughed!* "And even though you're still scrawny, you're heavy. I'm trying to keep you from getting hurt, but I can't hold you here all day."

What does he mean, these days? Who are these guys? Sudden change of plans: I can live without the key. He did reach his toes toward the ground as if to cooperate. But as soon as Han let go, he swiveled and crouched like a sprinter on the starting block, ready to flee.

"Don't run," Thurlock said in a flat tone, and then mumbled something into his hand.

Lucky found himself standing stock-still, which was humiliating, but his mouth ran on, making an idiot of itself. "You wouldn't have caught me if my shoe wasn't broke."

Thurlock lifted one brow.

Lucky's head pounded worse than ever after hanging upside down. Sick to his stomach, he grabbed the porch rail to steady himself and it gave him splinters. Too bright sun, too hot day, too dry air. Everything out of order, falling apart, plain wrong.

And now this crazy old man is laughing at me.

He swatted away the liver-spotted hand Thurlock put under his elbow as he swayed, and shouted, "You took my key you ... you old thief. But you know what, mister, you can keep it. *Keep it.* I don't want anything to do with it or you. And stop following me around!"

"You're right of course." Thurlock's grey eyes peered over the top of his spectacles, studying Lucky, and he tugged at his grey beard. "You are absolutely right. It would be wrong, dangerous even, for me or Han Shieth, here—" He paused to gesture toward the younger man, "—to threaten you in any way. Fortunately we know about that, even though you most likely don't. Let me assure you, Lucky, we don't even dream of harming you."

He pulled his spectacles off, stuck them in the pocket of his yellow tee shirt, and turned away to slump against the porch rail, leaning on his elbow. "It's been a long couple of days."

Feeling as spent as the old man looked, Lucky sighed and pushed his hair out of his eyes, then spoke quietly. "I probably should have knocked on the door. Maybe you didn't even steal the key. Maybe you found it." His legs started to shake and a breath later Han took hold of his arm, helping him stand. He ignored that. "Maybe I did the wrong thing, but it was all I could think to do. When I got off the bus, I looked back at you and saw that you had my key on your hat, and I had to get it back."

"Yes." Thurlock brightened. "Therein is the hope, young man."

"Listen," Lucky said. "I don't know what's going on, and I don't know how you got the key, and I don't know why you or anyone else would want it. It's useless, as far as I can tell, so why it matters I can't say, and it probably doesn't make any sense to you, but it is important. It's important to me. I've had it since ... a long time. Please, just give it back. I'm sorry I was rude." Out of breath, he stopped.

Han stepped toward the door. "Shall I make some tea, sir?"

"Yes, please. I'm absolutely parched." Thurlock still sagged against the rail, but the idea of refreshment seemed to perk him up. "Iced and sweet?"

"Of course. And, sir, might I remind you that the lad is bleeding? Perhaps it would be good to move things along?" He went into the dark house, as silent as the cat that followed him. He left the door standing open.

"Well then, Lucky," Thurlock started, "here's how I see it." He moved away from the rail and began to pace back and forth in front of the doorway, hands clasped behind his back. "Certainly, the key is yours. And to clear up the mystery for you, I have it because Lemon Martinez stole it, on my orders." He broke off mid-pace, scratching his beard, and gave Lucky a direct stare. "He's very good at that sort of thing, you know."

"Lemon?"

"Martinez, yes, the cat. You'd be surprised at his skill. Of course Han trained him, and he's the best there is. At training animals, that is, not stealing. The stealing was more like a dormant talent. You see we found him under Martinez Bridge—"

"Master Thurlock." Han's voice carried from deep inside the house. "You might want to get to the point, sir?"

Thurlock looked at Lucky and rolled his eyes. "Thank you, Han." Pacing again, he said, "He's right. The point is definitely what I need to get to. I have a tendency to ramble on, you see—"

"The point sir," Han reminded.

"The point is," said Thurlock, "well, the point is ..." He stopped pacing and put both his hands on Lucky's tired shoulders. "I'm sorry you've been upset. I took the key because it was important to bring you here. Kidnapping you wouldn't encourage you to feel comfortable, and you wouldn't have accepted an invitation. You probably would have dug an escape tunnel all the way to the South China Sea just to avoid my house."

Thurlock gazed evenly at him. His cheek twitched; probably a tic, but it looked like pain, a wince repeated over and over again. It made Thurlock's next words seem important, maybe even urgent.

"I have erred. I've frightened you and that was never my intent. I assure you neither I nor Han are serial killers or anything else that's going through your head." Lucky didn't have to decide whether to try to deny that he was thinking any such thing, because Thurlock kept talking. "You can leave, if you want, with your key. If you go, I'll watch over you as best I can, and—"

"Watch over me?"

"—and I'll never again force you or trick you into coming here. You never need come back, if you wish it that way. Or—" Thurlock shifted his gaze and though he didn't move, his grey eyes closed in on Lucky's until it felt as if they stood nose to nose. "—Or you can open your eyes, and look into mine, and let yourself see with that part of you that you trust even though you don't understand it, the part that knows when something is important, when something is true."

Lucky knew what Thurlock meant. He was aware of that extra sense; he used it often. When he was younger, he'd told Grandpa Hank that it was like he had a special antenna, and they'd started calling it the Antenna of Truth, as a joke. But how did Thurlock know?

"I'll tell you something, if you'll listen."

Lucky swallowed, feeling cold feet walking up his spine.

"I know that yesterday was the third anniversary of the first day in your life that you can clearly remember. I know precisely where, through a cave in Black Creek Ravine, you emerged from a past that has ever since been lost to you. I know what—or I should say who—put you there."

"Tell me!"

"I don't think I'd better, just yet."

"That's not fair."

"Never a truer word said, I'm afraid, but remembering is something you'll have to do yourself. If you want help, though, I'm your man."

"What would happen if you told me?" Lucky was almost afraid to ask. He suffered a disturbing image of a cartoon Alice beleaguered in Wonderland, and feared that suddenly everything might change again just because he spoke.

"Let's say it isn't a good gamble. The odds are against us, and what we would risk is too precious." Thurlock smiled—an expression at least as sad as any Lucky had seen. "What we would risk," he said, "is you. We might lose you, and that would be a tragedy far beyond our personal grief."

He stepped to where the straw hat rested on the railing, detached the key with its silken yellow cord, and held it out to Lucky in his left hand, palm down. "This is the Key of Behliseth, and it's yours."

He looked directly at Lucky, never blinking, and Lucky couldn't help staring back.

"In your heart," Thurlock said, "you know this world isn't your home. What was done to you three years ago upset a delicate balance. That threatens our world and this one, too. It's urgent that you unlock the mystery of your past. You have the power to do it, and the courage. Call upon it."

Lucky stared, his mind awash like he held a sack full of riddles. One thing he understood. Thurlock offered him the prize he wanted more than anything else. He had a chance to reclaim the memories of a lost childhood. The prospect frightened him, but when it came down to it, he had only one option.

He raised his hand and turned the palm up beneath Thurlock's, slow motion, like swimming through water thicker than blood. He recalled his Midsummer morning dream. This was how she had stood, the woman with green eyes, holding out the key. And this was how he had felt, reaching for it; like the whole world, even the air, was trying to keep him from it.

His skin quaked when Thurlock took hold of his hand, and he gasped, wide-eyed. The old man's grip was strong, warm, and unbelievably familiar. When Thurlock took his hand away, Lucky closed his palm around the Key of Behliseth.

It shivered like something alive.

"Come in for tea," Thurlock said, and disappeared into the house.

The invitation rang in Lucky's ears, and the idea of an ice-cold drink teased his dry throat.

He stepped closer, but stopped. Sunlight angled under the porch roof and brushed past his arm, illuminating the half-open door. Carved into the oak panel, a crowned horseman thrust a sword into an exploding sky. His fingers close, but never quite touching the wood, Lucky traced the detail on the sword's hilt. He could have done it with his eyes closed.

Every day, he ran his fingers over this same strange symbol etched into a stash of coins and a solid amber knife, kept hidden in his cardboard treasure box at home. A disc surrounded by twelve sharp rays to represent the sun.

Lucky had supposed the heavy coins, which had acquired the subtle glint of long-aged precious metal, might be valuable. When he found himself alone and broke, he'd squandered hours at Valley City Library searching reference books, checking Amazon and E-bay and following mazes of links, Googling every coin-collector on the web. He'd gleaned not so much as a picture of a coin like his, no alphabet to match the runes, and no trace of the twelve-rayed sun.

On the door of Thurlock's house that symbol shone, and Lucky's eyes swept upward, following the sword's thrust to the six-foot lintel. Pungent cedar, fresh cut. Droplets of sap wept from the familiar runes inscribed across it. This creation seemed far too new for this falling-down house.

If I step through this door, I'll never come back ...
Uh-huh. Get real.

He shook his head and his battered skull hurt, but he almost welcomed the pain. At least it felt normal, like the sweat trickling down the back of his knee, and the blue-backed fly hurling itself against the windowpane. Everything else had gone strange and silent. No traffic, no birds, no children playing in the distance.

As if the world is waiting ...
Right. Ridiculous.

Gravel crunched on pavement down the block, loud in the silent afternoon. The white Crown Victoria with its blind blue windows crept up the road, and the sight struck Lucky like an ice bullet, dead center in his chest.

He turned to face the doorway, a portal that had somehow reshaped itself to let Thurlock pass. No way could he ever step through any door that might do such a thing. Yet, he balled his fists and straightened his shoulders. Fighting triple the usual gravity, he lifted his right foot and watched it travel across the threshold. He let it fall on the other side like an anchor, and then followed it into Thurlock's house.

Beyond the threshold, in an ordinary living room, yellow afternoon sun bathed two overstuffed chairs and an oversized stone hearth. A worn, once-purple rug covered an equally worn wooden floor. The breeze billowed gauze curtains at the windows and wandered to the dining room. There it stirred music from the prisms of a massive chandelier, which in turn cast rainbows over the round, age-beaten table beneath it. In the middle of the scarred top rested a copper tray with glasses, spoons, sugar, and lemon so fragrant Lucky almost sneezed.

Han came from the kitchen carrying a crystal pitcher of red-gold tea with chattering ice. Thurlock stepped out of a dark hallway and stood beside Han. His silver hair returned the sun's shine like white gold and he smiled, holding out his hand toward Lucky, beckoning. When the two men spoke, Lucky heard a chorus of voices from every corner. "Welcome," they all said. "Welcome, Luccan."

4. The M.E.R.L.I.N. and the Wizard's Job

Luccan stood rooted to the spot in front of the door, so still that Han thought he must be in shock. Han set the pitcher next to the tray, took the lad by the elbow, and led him to a chair at the old table where sunlight and cool breeze could reach him. Once seated, Luccan fidgeted, shaking his leg, popping his knuckles, and repeatedly shoving his hair back. That last gesture, Han remembered, had already been a habit by his fourth birthday.

While pouring Luccan a glass of tea he covertly looked the boy over, cataloging changes. He chewed his lip, wondering where the boy's lofty stature had come from. Luccan had already grown taller than either parent. His eyes were like his mother, Liliana's, but brown instead of green. Han smiled inside, noticing that Luccan had inherited his mother's straight nose too, but about two sizes too large. It could be hoped the rest of him would catch up. In the meantime, *thank the gods*, it was offset by the coarse mane falling over his brow. His father had likely given him that thick hair, but Luccan's grew straight as string and had a red-brown, bloodstone color all its own.

Even as a toddler, he'd battled that heavy hair, which had refused to stay contained no matter how often it was tied. It fell in his eyes whenever he bent to study a rock or a bug. It blew wild in the breeze when he threw his head back, laughing. And he was always laughing then. But a lot had happened since he'd been a carefree boy splashing through puddles, monkeying up trees, and racing over the fields around his home.

Now, Han laid a hand on Luccan's shoulder meaning to offer comfort, but the lad stiffened in alarm, so he took his hand back and went about offering comfort in other ways. In the kitchen, he filled a basin with warm water and scooped crushed ice into a checked-cloth ice bag. He collected soft cloths from the linen closet, and then visited the medicine chest for band-aids and salve.

He returned to Luccan's side with the supplies, but as he set about tending to the boy's injuries the amazing truth of the situation struck him, almost stealing his breath.

Of course, Han already understood the facts. He'd served as the Wizard's Shield Man—also gardener, cook, and housekeeper—long enough to know that time could not be counted on to move at the same rate, or even in the same direction, from one world or moment to the next. But for him, the past year spent with Thurlock in Earth had seemed only as swift or slow as any he'd lived in Ethra.

That was deceptive

Luccan had just turned eleven when the Witch-Mortaine Isa banished him. Now his fourteenth birthday had just passed, but thirty years had flown in Ethra. Liliana had endured three decades clinging to hope for her only child and Han had spent thirty years searching for him. He'd followed Thurlock from world to world, time to time, going stoically into the vortices, never letting on that he shook inside every time they stepped across a Portal-of-Naught, never giving up.

At last the gamble had paid off. Here in the flesh sat Luccan. Han gave him the ice bag, and the lad tilted back his head, closed his eyes, rested the bag on the purple lump on his forehead, and blew out a relieved-sounding sigh. Han smiled, and set to work extracting thorns, bathing wounds, and covering them with soothing salve.

He breathed a prayer to whoever might hear. *He's safe at last. Let him stay that way.*

Immediately the chandelier began to shake and spin and the grind, whir, and clack of magical technology swelled around them until the whole room shook.

Oh thanks. It's always nice to know the gods are listening.

Luccan started to stand, ready to flee, and lacking time for subtlety Han put both hands on his shoulders and held him down. Eyes round as copper moons, Luccan stared at the chaos spinning in the glass of what he probably thought was a window.

Han couldn't blame him. The M.E.R.L.I.N. device looked strange enough doing nothing at all. How many Earthborn's had a six-foot-diameter round window looking out on a brick wall just inches away?

But the M.E.R.L.I.N. was no ordinary window. The Wizards in Research and Development at the University of Nedhra had done something new with magic, creating a device that mimicked Earth's technology. When activated, the amber panes around the edge flashed, the central pane gyrated, and the whole thing pulsed and thrummed until one of its pre-enchanted functions locked in.

Even someone with limited magical talent, someone like Han, could operate some of M.E.R.L.I.N.'s functions—retrieving messages, creating reminders, calling home. But this time, it was the vortex tool, the Portal, which sprang into life.

Someone approached—either someone who wielded a Wizard's power or something else entirely. And they were coming through uninvited and unannounced.

Han sent a mental call of alarm upstairs to the Wizard and shifted into something like a fighting stance, keeping one big hand on Luccan's shoulder to weight him down in the chair. But almost immediately the clashing sounds sorted themselves into a lilting melody, a magical song Han knew all too well. The soaking wet, petite figure and sassy, slightly crooked features of a familiar face took shape.

Han stood up straight, rolled his eyes and puffed out an exaggerated breath. "L'Aria, what are you doing here?"

Han had to admit, her eye-rolling skills were far superior to his own, and when she'd finished demonstrating that, she flashed defiance out of her black irises in a way he never could have managed.

"I want to see *him*." She pointed at Luccan and gave her dripping sable hair a flippant toss. "So?"

Han shook his head and laughed, exasperated, but then he noticed that Luccan seemed on the verge of wild panic, eyes all but bulging out of their sockets. L'Aria's right lower leg emerged into the dining room, water dripping off of it and pooling on the floor. Han held Luccan in his chair with both hands by main force. At the same time, he donned his 'I-am-the-Captain-of-this-army' look, and said, "Spitfire, Go back. Get away from the M.E.R.L.I.N., now."

Though 99.9 percent of the Ethran population would have complied instantly, it was no safe bet that L'Aria would obey, instantly or ever. She'd defied Han since her toddling days, mouthing off, fuming at him, and thoroughly earning the Spitfire nickname. Besides, it could be argued that the girl had every right to be in the middle of things where Luccan was concerned.

As the only child of the strangest, most enigmatic man in Ethra, everyone had always known L'Aria was unique. But on the night of Luccan's disappearance it had become clear how important she was to Ethra's future, and how closely her fate was tied to Luccan's. That night, she'd fallen into a stupor and couldn't be roused even by Thurlock. Finally, her father, the legendary Tiro, had carried her away to Greenwood Forest. Neither had been seen again for twenty-nine years.

Last year, the day after Thurlock and Han had come to Earth, she'd shown up alone at the Sisterhold, still a girl! Every Wizard, Witch, and Scholar ran to the scrolls. Histories, prophecies, and theories papered walls and tables and even floors in studies and classrooms around the globe.

But it was Rosishan, the least scholarly of all the great Witches, who'd figured it out. L'Aria's fate was inextricably tied to Luccan's. Luccan had aged in Earth years, and so had she. Born at spring equinox forty-one Ethran years ago, this year she'd turned thirteen.

Now, Rosishan showed up at L'Aria's end of the Portal connection, grabbed hold of the girl's elbow, and yanked her not-too-gently back to Ethra. Usually Rose, whose attitude matched L'Aria's, sparked only Han's ire, but at that moment he could have kissed her. Linked to Luccan or not, this seemed a bad time for her brand of trouble.

As he began to breathe easier, the M.E.R.L.I.N.'s glass cleared to show, once again, only the bricks outside. He experimented with lightening his hold on Luccan's shoulders, and when the lad stayed put Han stepped around and peered into his face. Luccan's eyes were still a bit glazed, but he breathed evenly and healthy color had begun to return.

Moving only his eyes, Luccan glanced up. "Merlin?"

"M-E-R-L-I-N. It stands for Magic for the Evocation and Reorientation of the Ley-lines Interweaving Naught."

"Uh ..."

"It's useful."

"Useful?"

"For instance, yesterday we used it to find you."

"Lucky me."

Han smiled at Luccan's nervous pun, but it made him wonder. Certainly, Thurlock's power and skill brought them to Luccan, but maybe luck had worked in their favor, too. Han was no expert, but converging time streams seemed beyond predicting, let alone controlling.

Thurlock had been so excited when he told Han about it on Midsummer Eve that he'd slipped into the language of Earth's sciences, which he'd studied admiringly since the moment they arrived.

"It's an anomaly," he'd said, and his aged eyes sparkled.

"Anomaly?"

"A rare event, unexplainable. The time streams of Ethra and Earth will become, for a bit, isochronous, and they'll quadrate at Midsummer."

"Sir?"

"They'll flow together and Midsummer will coincide, here and there."

The coinciding Midsummer had indeed arrived yesterday, bright and early, but Thurlock's sparkle had dissolved into pique. He wasn't a morning person. He'd stood in a swath of early sunlight that cut across the dining room, blew out a surly breath, and muttered, "May as well begin."

He activated M.E.R.L.I.N. with a flick of his wrist, read his stored reminders, mumbled, let in the cat, yawned, and checked his M-mail for letters from home.

A tinny female voice said, "There are zero messages in your inbox."

"Of course," he scowled and yanked the belt of his robe tighter. Half-hearted sparks escaped from the tips of his gnarled fingers.

"Blood pressure, sir," Han called from the kitchen.

Thurlock took the prescribed deep breaths, and washed down the aspirin Han had supplied with a long swallow from his mug. "Good tea," he said.

Even if he hadn't palmed his eyes and leaned on the back of a chair, his quiet tone would have alarmed Han. The old man looked tired, and not the kind of tired that could be cured with a charmed forty winks. A tired Wizard could make mistakes. Han worried—he considered it part of his job—but he did it silently, while chewing his lip, watching the Wizard out of the corner of his eye, and breaking eggs for breakfast.

Even fatigued, Thurlock made the hardest parts of his job look easy. He brought up M.E.R.L.I.N.'s locator function with a strong word and an almost invisible gesture. "Find," he commanded, "Luccan Elieth Perdhro." It was as much of Luccan's whole name as anyone living knew, and Thurlock routinely invoked it to guide this spell. In his deep-chested baritone, he added, "*Suth Chiell.*"

Those were old words, from a language long unused. A title, it meant 'Sun Child,' and it belonged to Luccan. Including the title in the invocation would bring the search to the eyes of Behlishan, the god of light. The god who made the title more than words. The god who held the Wizard Thurlock in service, and had for a thousand years.

Day after day since they'd arrived in Earth a year ago, the Wizard had stood in that spot and repeated the routine. Day after day, the locator pane failed even to flicker. This time, the Wizard spoke and M.E.R.L.I.N. pulsed into brilliant life.

Thurlock's petulance vanished. His spine straightened and his shoulders widened and suddenly everything about him transmitted a single message—*power*. Double-time, Han lifted the bacon from the pan and turned off the burners, clothed himself in Warrior strength, and stepped out to take up his watch at the Wizard's left hand.

Just as Luccan's dilapidated shack appeared in M.E.R.L.I.N.'s screen, a dark cloud mushroomed in the east of the viewer, and a brooding weight fell on Thurlock and Han.

Han broadened his stance, shifted his weight and set his mind for a fight.

Thurlock held up an open hand to summon his staff. When the yellow umbrella slapped into his grasp, he blinked at it, confused, then said, "Oh, of course."

As deftly as if his staff had always worn an umbrella disguise, he swooshed it open, pointed it toward the east, and set it spinning so fast that the blur of yellow silk became a second sun. The chandelier overhead responded with showers of tiny lights, and M.E.R.L.I.N.'s viewer flooded with golden brilliance. "By Behlishan's light," he intoned, "Witch-Mortaine, you may not follow here."

The cloud stilled, frozen in place.

The Wizard added gently, "Be gone, Isa."

A crack of thunder answered. Instantly, the pressure lifted. The roiling cloud shrank back toward its source at the eastern end of Black Creek Ravine, Isa's Tower of glass and ice. With a final flash of blue fire, the dark cloud vanished.

Thurlock shook his head. "My fault," he sighed, and then looked to Han for a report.

"Secure, sir," Han said, then smiled. "Nice move with the umbrella."

Thurlock chuckled, dipped his head in a mock bow, and set to work weaving a protection of guardian spells, misleaders, and wards. "Which I should have done first," he said.

They found Luccan at home with a yellow dog curled at his feet, the two of them ensconced in makeshift comforts. The shack's décor included two threadbare rugs, a frayed poster of horses galloping over grasslands, and a cracked mirror. Shelves housed books, trinkets, candles, and a single setting of chipped white dinnerware. A broad, low bench had been converted to a bed, made up with limp feather pillows and an old quilt of dim patchwork colors.

Order and cleanliness ruled the small space. Clothes were neatly folded, canned goods and dog food stowed. A broom and dustpan leaned in the corner. Hand and dish soaps, comb, toothpaste, toothbrush, and floss all marched in neat single file alongside a green plastic tub. A workbench ran the length of the wall opposite the bed, and Luccan sat there on a three-legged stool, bent over some task.

While he took in the scene, Han had held his breath. Now he breathed, "Luccan."

Thurlock looked at him sidelong. No other person alive would have known Han well enough to hear the emotion behind that quietly spoken name. He reached over to pat Han's arm, saying, "Easy, my friend," and it helped Han order his heart back to regular rhythm.

"It's amazing, sir." Han knew Thurlock would understand that he spoke of the way Luccan had made the shack into a home. By no means a fine place, but well tended. And, miraculously, its threshold was warded.

The boy's dog rose to her haunches and growled at the spot near the door where, so to speak, Han and Thurlock stood watching. Luccan turned to see what the dog growled at, then abruptly froze, his eyes narrowed with suspicion.

"Behl's teeth," Thurlock cursed, "I think he senses us." He shut M.E.R.L.I.N. down quickly and turned to face Han, saying nothing for a moment. Then his brows arched and his eyes twinkled. He smiled and spoke quietly. "As an Earthborn might put it, wow!"

Han laughed, and Thurlock sank onto the nearest chair and picked up his teacup.

"Wait," Han motioned, "I'll get you some hot water." While he waited, Thurlock talked. "We have to bring him here; it's the only way we can keep him safe. And we'd best do it quickly." By the time Han came from the kitchen with the kettle and his own coffee, the Wizard's expression had turned grave.

He didn't have to explain. Han, a military man, understood the danger of letting time pass while one's enemy advanced. They tossed ideas back and forth as to how it might be done, considering and dismissing everything from cookies to kidnapping. Other notions exhausted, Han went out on a limb. "It's a bit ... shady, sir, but we could trick the lad."

A long silence stretched between them. When Han's nerves got the best of him, he went back to the kitchen to finish preparing breakfast. As he put down a final plate of toast and pulled out his chair, Thurlock locked eyes with him, tugging thoughtfully at his beard. "Did you have something in mind?"

Han looked at Lemon Martinez, aiming a thought in the cat's direction: *I may have a job for you. Are you willing?*

Lemon looked back at him from the porch rail outside the east window, flicking his tail. *What's in it for me?*

The chance to serve the cause of justice—

Like I care!

—and possibly save a life—

Don't make me repeat myself.

—and ply your sticky-fingered trade, and play with something shiny.

Lemon yawned, curling his tongue and flopped onto his side. *Fun idea, Warrior, but on the other hand I could nap.*

Han gave the cat a sly, sideways look. *I'll sneak you into Thurlock's closet.*

Lemon popped up, eyes wide and lit with greed. *Deal!*

"Stop! That's enough cat-talk." Thurlock hated to be reminded that, powerful Wizard though he was, he could not read minds, cat or otherwise.

"Just tell me your plan," he said.

Han chewed his lip to quench his smile. "Lemon has skills, sir. They might be useful."

"Thievery?"

"Well, breaking and entering ..."

There was another uncomfortable lull in the conversation, during which Thurlock made a number of faces and spread blackberry jam on his toast. Finally, he said, "We wouldn't actually be stealing."

"No, sir."

He pursed his lips. "Whatever we take, we'd give it back."

"Yes, sir."

In minutes they worked out a simple plan. The cat would sneak in to Luccan's shack and steal the Key of Behliseth. Thurlock said that of the things Luccan had from home, losing that would trouble him the most. "Even if he doesn't know why," he added, "he'll want it back."

The Wizard's eyes grew distant.

Han said, "There's jam in your beard, sir."

"Jam? Oh, jam, thank you." Dabbing absently, Thurlock smiled. "And the Key is made to order for a cat burglar—he can carry it easily by the cord. He can crawl under the eaves without breaking anything, and perhaps avoid scaring Luccan unduly by tripping his wards—"

"Sir, how could Luccan have set wards?"

Thurlock laughed. "My best guess? Raw magic. He's done it with a wish, unaware."

"That would take considerable talent."

"Considerable at the least. And that talent bodes well for Luccan's future and ours unless Isa gets to him first."

Han spoke loudly to be heard over the clatter as he stacked thick china mugs and plates, clearing the table. "Too bad we don't own a truck, sir. Lemon and I could be a stone's throw from the lad's shack in minutes."

Thurlock growled his pat answer to every plug Han put in for embracing Earth's transportation technology. "No hang gliders, no motorcycles, *no truck!*" He shoved his chair in for emphasis and added, "Even that lawnmower of yours is dangerous."

"Sir, even Isa drives."

"Since when do we envy the Witch-Mortaine?"

"Speaking only for me, since the day she bought herself a big white Ford."

They couldn't take the bus because Lemon refused to be caged, and no way would the cat travel by the M.E.R.L.I.N.'s magic. He consented to live in a magical house; he'd followed them home willingly enough after they'd found him under the Old Martinez bridge huddling amidst his stolen goods, but he spent most of his time outdoors. Aside from sleeping on Thurlock's pajamas, he shunned anything magical.

So Han donned manly running shorts and a pair of perfectly white shoes and lifted the grey-eyed, grey-furred Lemon Martinez to his shoulders like a fluffy, purring towel. The morning wouldn't stay cool for long and it would be a twelve-mile run to Luccan's shack. He was anxious to get started but on the way out he stopped, having noticed Thurlock's furrowed brow.

"That's not your average cat," the Wizard said.

Han smiled, waiting.

"I'll be going to that part of town, too." He stepped over to the M.E.R.L.I.N. "I'll make contact. If he remembers me, it'll make everything easier. And if not ... It seems wise. Isa has found him. She'll be after him, too."

***

Wizarding is a tough job, even for the very best, and once Luccan was safely inside the door, exhaustion had nearly knocked Thurlock off his feet. Han, looking out for him as always, had sent him upstairs to his tower, saying, "Rest, sir," with that ridiculous formality that didn't hide his concern. Thurlock had gone, but Wizards recuperate quickly if they know what they're doing, and after ten minutes under the quilt and five more in the shower, he was up and ready.

To some, Thurlock's tower room might have seemed strange and cluttered, but to him it was home and he took it with him wherever he went. In it was his four-poster bed, stacked with pillows and covered with the purple-and-gold quilt his sister had made for him centuries ago. The bookshelves and two fat chairs before the stone hearth always beckoned. A rough wooden table shoved against the wall never failed to hold a cornucopia of oddments. At the moment, it bore stacks of clean and dirty dishes, three jigsaw puzzles in worn boxes, very small things, hidden devices, and five huge socks.

He sat at that crowded table and sighed in a not-so-very-wizardly manner. He was anxious to talk to Luccan, but first he should call the boy's mother.

He didn't want to do it.

He dreaded it.

She could be a difficult woman. He tried to think of a reason to put it off, but Wizards, at least good ones, absolutely cannot lie—even to themselves, and he eventually came to admit that such a reason did not exist.

He scooted his chair closer to the table and extracted from the heap a dinner-plate sized disk of amber and glass. No one would have known by looking, but this little portable thing was a cousin to the big M.E.R.L.I.N. downstairs. He held the disk up, watched his reflection scratch its beard, sighed again, and gave in to his mind's penchant for wandering and self-doubt.

If I'd spent more time Wizarding and less time dragging Han through the vortices, I could have found Luccan long ago.

He'd lately realized he should have focused his search on Earth from day one. Ethra and Earth had a common origin, were nearly parallel, and occupied roughly the same space, so they wandered in and out of each other's time streams. Far from stupid, the Witch-Mortaine had understood that relationship and exploited it on Luccan's eleventh birthday.

And what is it that makes eleven such a dangerous age?

On the day Thurlock turned eleven, he'd come home through Midwinter snow on leave from his apprenticeship. A scrawny boy with more power in his hands than he could safely handle, he nearly fried his mother meaning only to warm her a bit. From that day forward her once lustrous hair stuck out in a frizzled mass. A thousand years later the shame still burned.

But his mother, Behl bless her, never held it against him, and he could look back and laugh. Not so in Luccan's case. And no one could find humor in the violence of Han's eleventh birthday.

Thurlock shook his head. A thousand years of Wizardry hadn't been long enough for him to solve the puzzles and answer the why. What made him think he'd do it this afternoon?

Besides, one thing he *had* learned in the last ten centuries was that if a man has to make a phone call to the temperamental mother of a missing child—a mother who also happens to be a highly skilled Witch, a Captain of the cavalry, and a powerhouse politician—it was best all around just to do it.

5. The Story of Lucky's Darkest Night

Thurlock came downstairs sooner than Lucky expected and before he'd fully recovered from the shock of having seen the girl come through the M.E.R.L.I.N.

"You have nothing to fear from Han," he boomed from the stairwell.

After Lucky picked himself up and reoccupied the chair he'd knocked over jumping at the sound of the Wizard's voice, he noticed the old man seemed refreshed. He smelled of soap, and his silver curls were brushed, gathered, and tied. His back was straight, his eyes were bright, and his step was spry. He had exchanged sweats and combat boots for long, swirling grey robes and soft sandals. In sweats, Lucky had thought he looked silly. In robes, he looked ... *um ... well ... magnificent.*

"And, you have nothing to fear from me." He sat down at the table two chairs from Lucky, and pointed at the window that wasn't a window. "The M.E.R.L.I.N., there, is a device, technology, a tool. As for L'Aria, she's willful and surprising, but when it comes down to it she's just an ordinary girl."

Pouring Thurlock a fresh glass of tea, Han coughed. "Ordinary, sir?"

"Point taken. Still, a girl, nothing more frightening."

To Lucky, for whom *every* girl had recently become a bit frightening, that statement begged argument, but he said nothing and didn't move. Ever since he'd come into this house his abs had been clenched so tight he could have done an infomercial for Fit-Machine. He knew he would have to talk to Thurlock; he wanted what the old man offered, wanted his life back. But some caveman part of him preferred to crouch in a corner and hide, invisible. So after the tea and Band-aids, he'd refused all Han's offers of further comfort. Even food. Even a chance to nap, though every bone and bruise begged him to accept.

Han loaded three spoons of sugar into Thurlock's tea and stirred it in, the ice in the glass tinkling like tiny bells. He handed the tea to the old man with an easy, familiar smile, and Thurlock accepted it with a nod, a sparkling eye, and a grin. Despite his reticence, watching the friendly exchange made Lucky feel lonely to be left out. When Thurlock turned and included him in his smile, Lucky's heart spun with joy.

Then Thurlock looked at Lucky and said, "I want—"

Though he spoke for some time and surely must have completed at least that first sentence, Lucky heard not another word. His briefly spinning heart wobbled and flopped down around his navel, and cold dread took over, leaving him with just one question. *What does Thurlock want?*

"—I believe I speak for Han as well." As Thurlock finished his speech, he turned to Han with a questioning look.

Han didn't answer. He chewed his lip, watching Lucky, "What's the matter, lad?"

"What?"

The old man raised his eyebrows, and then spoke slowly. "I was saying, Luccan, that I want you to know we're glad you're here."

"Oh, that's what you want. I mean, uh ... Thank you, sir. Thank you very much."

"Luccan," Thurlock said, "is there something you want to ask me?"

Yes, definitely. There were questions, one in particular, which had howled for an answer ever since Lucky stepped into this house. "No," he said, and then clutched his stomach against a sudden pain.

"Are you sure?" Thurlock seemed amused, not worried.

"Yes," he lied again, and shielded his eyes from the stab of too-bright light from the chandelier.

"I think you have a question."

"No sir, really," he said, choking the words out despite the burning coal that seemed to be stuck in his throat.

With no sound but Lucky's labored breathing, the silence grew until Han sighed and broke the new-formed ice. "Are you hungry now, Luccan?"

Of course I am! I haven't eaten anything all day but a maple bar. "No, please," Lucky said and doubled over in his chair. Then he added, "I think I'm sick," which was true, so the pain eased up a bit.

Either Han's upper lip itched or else he was trying not to laugh. Fortunately for Lucky, he was able to answer all Han's next questions truthfully. He asked if Lucky would rest a while ("no"), if he wanted to borrow a fresh shirt ("no"), if there was something left undone in tending to his injuries ("no").

"Do you want an aspirin?"

Lucky's contrite glance met Han's golden-brown eyes for the smallest fraction of a second. He hoped Han could see the apology; he hated to be rude. But he said nothing at all.

"I hate to do this, Luccan," Thurlock said, "but I think it's for the best." He mumbled something and then, in precisely the tone he'd used that afternoon when ordering Lucky not to run, he said, "Ask it."

Lucky's own voice startled him. "Did you know Hank George?"

"Hank George? Why?"

"You know my name."

Thurlock smiled and nodded, clearly pleased. "Yes we do, though we weren't sure you remembered it. Pretty foxy of you, boy. You never gave a hint of recognition." He tilted his head sideways and pursed his lips. "Do you remember anything else?"

Lucky scratched his head rather violently, which he often did when he was trying to ignore an irritation. He noticed that the bump wasn't quite so sensitive; thanks to Han's ice bag, he supposed. But he was ticked. Thurlock had forced him to ask, and now he responded only with his own questions.

He answered anyway, but couldn't help sounding curt. "I don't remember much. A big house, fields, and water, a lake or something. I try to think about when I was little, and I can feel people around me, but I can't see their faces. I remembered my name, and I told Grandpa Hank. I've never told anyone else."

Lucky found it strange that Thurlock and Han knew his name, but they knew much more than that. He picked absently at a scratch in the tabletop, a chill breath prickling the back of his neck. These two men had power over him.

"Don't pick at that, Lucky, you're making it worse." Han had at last taken a seat at the table. "Why," he asked, "did you not tell anyone else?" His expression was thoughtful, as if he expected a certain answer, perhaps testing a theory.

Lucky looked back at Han, and dropped his head into his hands. Too much was happening, too fast. He'd survived through the last year always at the edge of disaster. He'd gotten pretty good at sniffing out danger, and this situation reeked of it. But did the threat come from these men, or from elsewhere? Or maybe both?

A year ago he wouldn't have had to worry. Grandpa Hank had still been doing the worrying for him, as he had since the day Lucky had crawled out of the cave so shaken he could hardly stand. Hank George had been there, and he'd taken Lucky in. For two years, living in Grandpa's old log cabin, Lucky had a life that was perhaps eccentric, but almost normal.

Hank treated Lucky well and taught him about the world. Since boys with no identity couldn't go to school, Hank gave lessons at home. And when Lucky had finished chores and lessons, sometimes they'd watch TV on Hank's old set with the rabbit ears. Hank had paid Lucky to stand and hold the antenna, because that way they got channels they otherwise couldn't get—from other countries even, from across the ocean. Hank's nephew Henry would come sometimes from Sacramento, where he worked as a firefighter. On those days, they'd all swim in the creek, or read out loud by the fire, or maybe Henry would take Lucky for a ride on his black and chrome Harley.

Incredibly, after losing everything—parents, home, even the knowledge of who he was—Lucky had been happy. They'd laughed, Lucky and Grandpa Hank, a lot. And every once in a while when Lucky was feeling down, Grandpa would sit with him and pat his shoulder even though Lucky refused to cry. "There, now, Luccan, ease up," he'd whisper. "You'll feel better." And Lucky would feel better, like magic.

Since Lucky came out of the cave on Midsummer, they chose to call that day his birthday. Last year on that day, Lucky had stumbled out of the cool shade of his bedroom into the morning sun that streamed into the cabin's great room. He spotted Hank in the kitchen, tying his long steel-colored braids behind his back to keep them out of the gas flame while he cooked. "Morning, Grandpa," Lucky mumbled, and then sat down at the pine-slab table.

"Hey, Lucky," Hank said, and then greeted him with the same words he used every morning. "What do you remember, today?" But that day was special. Hank had made Lucky a birthday cake—a stack of pancakes, maple syrup, and a big glob of whipped cream, bristling with fourteen flaming candles. They'd sat at the table and Hank had read the Wizard of Id comic out loud from yesterday's Valley Independent, and they'd laughed and gotten sticky together eating the birthday breakfast.

Afterward, Hank said, "Do your chores up early. Henry said he'd come down for your birthday. We'll go to the lake." Then Grandpa Hank left to walk the high trails along the Ravine, as he had each day for fifty years or more, but this time he didn't come back.

Somehow, he'd fallen from the path he knew so well and smashed his brains on the rocks in Black Creek's bed. Lucky had heard about it on the television, but even then he hadn't believed Hank had simply fallen. *He died because of me*, Lucky had thought, and although he had no idea why, he knew it was true.

He ran away from the cabin before Henry had time to get there from the city. He never went back, and never saw Henry again. He'd heard a few times about a tall Native man around town looking for him. But Lucky didn't want Henry close to him. He didn't want to be close to anyone. He wouldn't risk someone getting hurt because of him. Never again.

But now, sitting in Thurlock's kitchen, the situation was different. *This time, I'm the one taking the risk; I'm the one that might get hurt.* Thurlock and Han probably didn't mean him harm, but at the heart of all the strangeness he sensed some unfathomable, extraordinary power.

Cut and run! His cautious mind and street-kid instincts screamed. But he couldn't; the Antenna of Truth was going crazy, and it told him that none of this was chance and not much was choice. This was deep water, swift current. He, Lucky—no, Luccan—was in it "fins and gills" as Hank George would have said, and he was going to have to swim.

Thurlock broke into Lucky's thoughts. "Will you answer, Luccan? I won't Command it."

"That's nice of you, sir." Lucky tried unsuccessfully not to sound sarcastic, but Thurlock only raised an eyebrow and chuckled. Annoyed, Lucky demanded, "How do you do that, anyway?"

"Well, as you mentioned, I know your name, at least enough of it to accomplish a Command."

It made no sense at all, but Lucky had a heart-racing feeling that he'd been told something important. He stared. Thurlock scratched at his beard, donned spectacles as if about to read fine print, and looked at Lucky over the wire rims. "By the way," he said attempting to sounds casual. "Do you remember any more of them?"

"More of what?"

"Your names, of course."

Lucky didn't, but when he shook his head he wasn't saying no, he was expressing bewilderment.

Nevertheless, Thurlock said, "Ah, too bad then ... or perhaps not."

Lucky decided to pretend the conversation had never jagged off on that whole tangent. He pointed his gaze at Han and answered the question he'd been asked. "Hank George ... I met him when ... when I came ... lost ... well, the first day I can remember. He didn't ask my name, but I told him, and he said that I should keep it to myself. 'You never know', he told me, 'who might be looking for your name, or what they might do with it.'"

"Smart man," Thurlock said.

"He started calling me Lucky. He said it sounded enough like my name that I would feel like me, but different enough someone else wouldn't recognize it. And he teased me," Lucky smiled. "He said I needed all the help I could get, and if everybody called me Lucky maybe the spirits would believe it."

Thurlock and Han laughed, but then Han sobered, biting his lower lip into a serious line. The gold in his eyes shimmered, his gaze intense, but not hard. "How did you come to meet this man?"

Lucky had never told the strange story of the day he met Hank. Even when Grandpa had still been alive he'd tried not to think about it. Sitting at Thurlock's table, now, he felt a knot deep in his belly come undone and set that hard tale loose.

***

"I remember everything about that night," Lucky began. He knew right away that before the night was over he would tell Thurlock and Han all of it, tastes and smells and sounds, the brush of the breeze over his arm, the trickle of rain—not tears—down his cheeks. But first, he told them about Hank.

He recalled the sound of Hank George's drum, his knuckled hand holding the curved beater, the way the painted hide stretched over the drum's 'bones'. He told them about Hank's song, and about how he made him feel safe. The love and gratitude he harbored for Grandpa Hank came together glowing in the center of his chest. He took a deep breath and let his first ever telling of the story of his darkest night pour straight from his heart.

"I don't know what would have happened," he began, "if Hank had not been there. Maybe I would have died. I told him once that the only thing that made my name 'Lucky' true was that he had been there that first night. He said that wasn't so, that wasn't luck. He'd been there because of a promise he'd made, and a habit of keeping it. He called himself the Guardian."

As Lucky spoke, the last of the prism-scattered rainbows in Thurlock's house stretched thin, dimmed, and disappeared. Dark crept in. Their faces donned veils of shadow. They could have been anywhere. They could have been in that cave where, three years and one day ago, Lucky awoke.

"It was cold, dark, wet. At first I couldn't see anything at all, but then I realized that to one side there was a glow, so dim I had to stare to be sure it was there." He had heard water, waves on rocks, maybe, and something splashing.

"I pictured some horrible creature, and that was the first thought that made enough sense to scare me. After that, I was terrified every single minute, even after Grandpa Hank had me safe. It only lasted one night, I know that now. But then it was all I knew, all I remembered of life. Forever.

"It scared me even to move, but finally I stood up and crept toward the glow. I found a passage, and I followed it." He'd clung to the walls even though they cut his hands, crawled where the ceiling dropped, slithered over slime that stank like rotten eggs.

He clenched his fists where they lay on Thurlock's scratched tabletop, and raised his eyes to meet Han's. "The whole way, I kept saying 'No, I can't do it.' Eventually, though, I did. I reached the end of the tightest, slimiest, smelliest tunnel, and I had to close my eyes, the light was so bright."

He'd expected to emerge into daylight, but found himself standing in a cavern. Its glimmering ceiling soared overhead, so high that it did seem like starlight, but brighter than stars ever should be. The air moved like breath, carrying whispered chimes.

"It felt like I'd blundered into a giant's tomb." Hank was there, and Lucky had been afraid of him, too. "But as soon as he got me out he started taking care of me. He never stopped until he died."

After a silence, Han rose and made a circuit of the three front rooms in Thurlock's house, turning on small lights over the mantle piece, next to the sideboard, on the stove. Their allied glows pushed back the dark. He closed the windows too, shutting out a surprising chill, and drew down the shades. Thurlock went to the door to call in the cat, the sound of his voice rising warm above dampening night. Han gave Lemon some milk and Thurlock some tea—hot this time.

51

To Lucky he said, "Would you like a glass of milk, lad?" Perhaps he knew that Lucky was set to refuse, because he quickly added, "It's chocolate; Thurlock won't drink the white kind." Lucky accepted, returning Han's smile, and the sweet milk soothed and cooled him. Thurlock asked if he was too tired to go on, but he felt refreshed enough, and the rest of the tale pushed like something solid at the back of his teeth, wanting out.

It had not been quite dusk when Hank brought him out of the cave and for a few minutes the sun had warmed him, but when night fell it turned cold despite the season. Lucky had shivered so hard he'd barely been able to stand. Suddenly remembering, he laughed, and then explained when he saw Thurlock's questioning smile. "Hank got an axe, and I thought he was going to kill me, but he just split firewood."

He recalled the warmth of the fire, and how completely lost he'd been. He'd sat wrapped in Hank George's old quilt, quenched his awful thirst with the water Hank dipped for him, and eaten the hot stew Hank had cooked over the fire. But he'd still felt empty and confused, and the more Hank quizzed him, the more hopeless he became.

Grandpa had told him later that he'd hated having to question him, asking the same things over and over, hammering away. He'd done it, he said, to be absolutely sure he was right about who—and what—Lucky was.

"I couldn't answer anything except the one question he didn't ask. Finally I shouted it out. 'My name is Luccan, that's all I know.'"

He drew away from that room in Thurlock's house, fell back to that night three years ago and that bright fire in front of the cave. He was there, drowsing, watching the smoke as it tumbled and twisted up to the darkening sky, leaving holes for stars to peak through, coloring the moon like ink and filling that long, long night with fragrance. He heard Hank George speak, saying things that for three years since he'd tried hard to forget.

"*You are one of the Others.*"

With those words echoing from the past, the story Lucky was telling took complete hold of him. Entranced, he walked to Thurlock's living room as if he was home and sat in one of the two threadbare armchairs, bare feet digging into a soft, thick rug. Han followed in much the same state, said nothing, just stood until Thurlock gently pushed him into the other armchair. On the windowsill, Lemon made tiny movements of his paws and whiskers, dreaming.

Lucky saw those things at the edges of his vision as he stared into the grate, the cold empty heart of a massive wall of river-rounded stone. He was only distantly astonished when, at a small gesture from Thurlock, flames sprang up in that hollow like sudden blooms. The old man then fetched a straight-backed chair from the table, set it facing the fire between Lucky and Han, and sat silent and wakeful, waiting as the glass clock ticked on the mantle. Lucky closed his eyes, feeling Thurlock's flames warm his face.

When he opened them, time had fallen away and it was Hank George's wood fire three years past that he watched. Then, he'd been a child, bewildered and unable to believe. Now, digging the truths Hank George knew out of the past for the first time, telling the tale aloud in a house where magic happened, he began to believe.

***

"I'm worried about you, boy. In the old stories the Others came because there was something bad happening in their world, but they came of their own accord. You're alone. You seem to have lost yourself on the way. Someone sent you, and I'll bet dollars to donuts they didn't have your best interests at heart."

Hank had put his back to the flames and faced Lucky. He'd said, "Listen, now," and his voice, soft as old leather until that moment, had gone sharp.

"You're lucky to be alive, I'd say. There's some kind of darkness following you. Until you know its nature, young cousin, you'd better hang on tight to your name and anything else you brought with you, and be on your guard. As long as I'm alive I'll do what I can to keep you safe.

"But I don't know," he said. "I don't know if that will be enough."

***

Had Hank George truly spoken these words? Sometimes Lucky wondered, thought that perhaps he had only dreamed it, hypnotized by fire, and food, and the soft, safe night that wrapped him like a blanket. And now, this room enfolded him the same way, Wizard's flame shielding him against harm. He glanced around the room, like coming up from deep sleep to the surface. Strange, but real, he assured himself. Then he slid back down to the dream.

***

"Ever since the Others came and stayed with us for a time, some children were born with this." Hank pulled his tee shirt back from his brown shoulder and turned it so Lucky could see. "The Mark of the Others," he called it. But in each generation, fewer and fewer newborns were marked. "In my generation," Hank had said, "only my sister and I bore the Mark. My nephew Henry is the last."

***

Lucky opened his mouth to tell more but, suddenly exhausted, he only said, "I'm done." He leaned his head back and his eyes fell closed.

Han took a deep breath and broke his silence. "It's as the prophecy says, isn't it, sir?"

"Without question."

Lucky snapped his eyes open, feeling like he'd just woke up and oddly disoriented, like a goldfish dropped in the rum punch. He looked from Han to the Thurlock. "Prophecy?"

"This time in our worlds' story was foretold a thousand years ago."

Lucky waited, sure the Wizard would say more, but all Thurlock did was to pull thoughtfully at his beard. Finally, he blurted, "What does it say you have to do?"

"Do?"

"The prophecy ..."

"Oh," Thurlock chuckled. "Prophecies don't work that way. They tell you some of what will be, but they never tell you what to do about it. Mostly useless, really."

"Then why did Han bring it up?"

"It's not important." Thurlock walked over and put his back to the fire as he spoke.

Han walked to the window. "Interesting, though," he said.

"What about the Mark, then?"

"The Mark, yes," said Thurlock, turning to the hearth to motion the flames higher. "That's interesting too, wouldn't you say, Han?"

"Very much so, sir," Han answered, opening the window to fan cool air into the room.

The Wizard paced silently before the fire, hands clasped at his back. Then, decisively, he pivoted to face Han. "Would you be so good as to take your shirt off, please?"

"Certainly, sir."

Lucky's mouth flapped open, but he had no time to form a question or run from the room. Thurlock took two huge strides over to Han, mumbled, "Pardon me," and pulled back Han's thin, ribbed undershirt to reveal a tawny, well-muscled shoulder branded with a mark as wide across as the length of a man's thumb. At its center burned an almost perfect disk; twelve rays exploded around it. As light as cream where Grandpa's had been almost black, it was the polar opposite of Hank's Mark of the Others.

"Our world is called Ethra, Luccan, Behlis Ethra." Thurlock's voice was a whisper, yet it echoed from the hearth and set flames dancing. "This," he said, "is the Mark of the Sun."

6. A Magic He Believed Forever Lost

The Tower walls, glass colored blue like deep ice, stole the last of the day's light from dusk. A man with heavy chestnut curls and a scarred face limped along the crow's walk, circling round and round. His steps fell as listless as his greasy hair, and his mangled left hand drug along the thin rail that separated the pinnacle from the clouds it speared. The cold steel burned, and he pulled the nearly useless limb against his body, trying to rub life into it with his better hand.

He stopped, facing the black stone columns the Earthborns called Death of the Gods. He swayed, feeling for a moment that if he stared long enough he might fall through the empty space between those columns. Shaking his head, he turned to face west. He found the view of Valley City, sprawled across the dusty floor of Cirque Basin, much less disturbing.

The waking metropolis lay confined in a round valley, walled in by the ring of peaks known as the Noose, crags that jutted up like teeth to guard the basin that was once the fiery throat of a volcano. Black Creek Ravine, an uninhabited crack in the crater's floor, split the valley and its city into halves.

In places, cliffs bound the creek in a deep, narrow channel. Elsewhere the walls rose in crumbling slopes, folds of smooth basalt, or bore shelves that supported groves and meadows. The deep, wide parts of the gorge taunted Hench with lush, living greens—stark contrast to the desert valley and bony peaks surrounding it.

At the dry, eastern end of the Ravine, the creek gushed from underground caverns, tumbling between the pillars of Death of the Gods as if they were giant gateposts. On the north bank, time-chiseled palisades loomed forty feet above the watercourse, but on the south side a low rise at the bank sloped into a sunken plain.

The Witch-Mortaine's tower rose from that boulder-strewn plain, rooted between high ridges and veiled in spells.

At this hour, the entire crater lay in shadow, but even in the half-light and with only one eye Hench's vision was sharp. He could see cars sliding along the city's roads, trailing columns of red and white like snakes of light. He imagined the people piloting them, tired Earthborns who wished they'd already arrived wherever they were going.

He wondered about their lives. Did they have any kind of magic? Had they ever had it? Had any of them possessed magic and love and a good life and lost it all? He wondered whether their cars would pile up in a panicked crash if they but once saw through the magical veils and glimpsed the deadly crystal beauty of the spire from which he gazed.

He worked his shoulders into a painful shrug, wishing that he could rid himself of the black shadow that weighed them down, a shadow he himself had created out of anger and hate. He shook his head in persistent disbelief that it had overtaken him so easily, so fast.

He'd committed himself to vengeance, and the shadow had been born, a larval vampire that fed on his spirit, consumed his strength and joy. It grew stronger with every cruel choice and every time he lashed out, burning with rage. It fouled his every step, turned even his best intentions to evil end, drained him of substance as surely as if it had torn his heart and bled him dry. The remains had become a joke, fool to a fiendish Witch, tool in the hands of the person he most hated.

He leaned against the rail, half-wishing the steel would vanish and let him go. The wind thrummed against the glass and steel of the spire, but he ignored it. Whatever shame Earth's night winds might hiss into his ear, they couldn't carry the single word he should not have forgotten. Only the Gods' Breath knew that name, and he had little hope ever to stand again in that sweet dawn wind of the Ethran Sunlands.

"Hench!" The Witch Isa shrilled her summons into the darkling sky, and though it was not his name and thus had no real power over him, it was hard to ignore. She well knew that he would answer to that demeaning tag, or any other slur she cared to impose.

"Hench," she growled again, "I want you in here now."

He held his feet to their places, and stretched his small moment of defiance as far as it would go. Leaning out across the rail, he looked down past the once living land that surrounded the Tower's base, poisoned now to ash and ice and dust. A fathomless moat guarded the structure, empty and falling away to black death. It would be a long drop if a man were to jump.

"Hench," the screech came a third time, "NOW!"

He lingered a scant moment longer until a cloud came between him and the hope of silence with which that black abyss taunted. He sighed, clothed himself in servility, and bent to open the hatch leading into the Witch-Mortaine's lair.

Isa's chamber was as cold as polar ice. The caustic-blue glass of the Tower's shell, a foot and a half thick, formed the floor and one wall; white stone had been chiseled square and stacked to build the others. Hewn of blue-veined marble, the Witch's bed remained hard and bare. Hench entered through a steel door and limped into the room. The sound of his steps returned in echoes from the dungeons below.

Isa spun on her blue-slippered heel, face twisted with anger. "You took your time, thrall."

Hench dropped his eyes lest they enrage her further, but resisted the temptation to throw up a shielding arm and cower. With the intuition of a whipped hound, he gauged her mood. The crystal flash of her pale eyes made it plain that she was at the end of her small patience, but he was safe enough for the moment. She held no weapon, wouldn't spend her other magic on him except in dire need, and she'd never touch him with her bare hands. After all, the same hallowed blood still ran in his veins.

Still, he used her formal title, and bowed from the waist. "I'm sorry, Witch-Mortaine Isa." He wasn't pretending. He'd borne too much pain at the wrong end of her favorite weapon—a whip with myriad glass-tipped tails—to deliberately court her displeasure. His guide in every choice was knowledge, scarred into flesh and memory, of the agonies Isa was all too willing to inflict. He might risk a small, secret defiance, but never open rebellion.

"Of course you're sorry, fool." Isa paced back and forth, sharp steps rattling the rows of bottles and vials on her worktable, shaky as it was on a slim pedestal of steel. She slammed a hand down on that table and turned her gaunt face toward Hench. He looked in her direction, but kept his one-eyed gaze from meeting her eyes. He watched instead the shadows of her jewel colored potions quaking after her blow. He concentrated on stillness, a hunter's skill he still owned.

These days, it often made no difference what he did or said. She was frustrated, and she took it out on him. She had spent a year, by Earth's time, searching for a boy she herself had banished to this world. Despite her powers and her foul god and her alliances with the evils of Earth, she had not been able to find the child.

Isa drew in a long breath, her bony chest heaving, and the dissatisfaction in it belied her words. "Your duties will change. The boy has been found."

For one shred of a second, when she said "the boy," Hench thought he heard another sound whispered around the edges. A name? He wanted to hold onto the moment, pursue the phantom memory, but he saw the Witch narrow her eyes, studying him. His face must have registered the shock. Quickly, he buried the reaction and all emotion beyond her reach.

Except fear—he let that show. She liked to see it.

"Look at me," she snapped, and he did, but by then his eye was as empty as death. She strode a step closer and leveled her deadly regard at him, snarling. "What is about to happen, is the reason you've been kept alive, little man." She pivoted abruptly to face the empty center of the chamber, raised her hands high, and lifted her voice in the visceral language of her god, the Ice-Lord Mahl.

Dark-Chant threatened to bury his thoughts in ice and the god's presence, the void that was his essence, bore down on him. He fell to his knees.

When finally the sound stopped and the cold weight receded he stayed down, head bowed to the floor, sucking in desperate breaths. Too late, he heard the whine of the Witch's scourge slicing air, and then barbed tails cut through the leather on his back, shredding his skin. That one blow, which channeled the Ice-Lord's touch, drained all remaining warmth from his body, turned the beat of his heart to icy shivers, impaled his thoughts on blinding blue-white light.

Isa spat an order to rise and he struggled to put his feet under him and obey, but strength refused to flow to his damaged left leg. He toppled.

"Stand, slave," she snarled again. "Or perhaps you'd like a taste of real pain today?"

"Mortaine Isa," he begged, buying time. "Please, no." At last he found his feet. Cautiously, fleetingly he raised his eye to hers.

A moment later—completely calm—she said, "Very well, Hench. Be thankful. Worthless as you are, Mahl has favored you." Her thoughtful gaze felt strangely unthreatening. It was a face of the Witch that Hench had never seen and apprehension gripped him like pincers. "Behold," she said, "his gift."

In the center of the chamber, where there had been nothing before Isa's Dark-Chant, stood a bulky, irregular shape covered with a cloth of glowing, graveyard blue. Isa pulled the cover away and revealed a granite stone. Hench chanced a look at the Witch, not knowing what it meant.

"Put your hands on the rock," Isa said, more quietly than he had ever heard her speak.

"Mistress?"

"Do it."

"Yes," he said and limped toward it, afraid of what it might be, what new persecution the stone might hold, but certain about what the Witch would do if he didn't obey. His weak, wasted left hand fell onto the rock, and he drew in a sharp, surprised breath. He felt a current there, the faint flow of magic. Did he recognize it?

Anxious, he placed his right hand deliberately, palm down over the curve of the stone. An instant later the magic hidden in the stone recognized him and the current grew strong. Tears threatened. This was a magic he had believed forever lost.

"You know what it is? You can feel it?"

"Yes, Mortaine."

She paced as she spoke, like a lecturing professor. "The Black Blade, the Obsidian Knife, the Dark Twin. *Fool!* You had it in your hands. But you threw it away twenty-seven years ago, from the Heights of Gahabriohl into the depths of Mardhral." She stopped and spun to face him. "Why?"

He hedged. "The magic in it was no longer useful to me."

"Hah!" Her laugh was sharp, cut short, but it echoed against the glass and steel of the tower. "Well, be that as it may, Hench, I have reason to believe that you can still use it. My Master believes that makes you a person of interest, potentially useful in the upcoming struggle over our precious boy."

She smiled, but looked like she had swallowed something bitter. Hench had the unexpected notion that she was doing something not entirely of her own choosing. He guarded his face, keeping that realization, and a flare of hatred, secret.

She turned her gaze away and again raised her arms. "Hold fast to the stone, fool," she said flatly, and then she started Dark-Chant once more.

This time he didn't fall. He knelt and embraced the stone, shivering as the magic of the Blade coursed through him, both dread and welcome. The blue granite in his arms grew icier with every repetition of the chant, but when the stone shattered, though pebbles battered his flesh, his arms wrapped around the Knife. Silence fell over the chamber like snow.

"Go, Hench, get to your place." The Witch's voice, trembled, breaking the stillness. "Take that thing from my presence."

"Mistress." He stood and bowed his head in her direction, his voice small, but clear.

He exited the steel door and lurched down a flight of narrow stairs. Musty, small, no more than a forgotten corner, he'd furnished his quarters with cast-off comforts: torn mattress, lumpy pillow, worn grey rug. It wasn't a home, and the feeling it gave of safety was false, but it had become his den, and he inhaled its dusty air gratefully. He sank onto the mattress and pulled a frayed blanket over him, warm and soft against the cold, bloody wounds of the lash.

Curled around the Blade he slept, unafraid of its edge.

7. The Lion, the Cookie, and the Heart's Desire

Thurlock sat in the faded brocade of the armchair Lucky had deserted, his sandals flung aside. He glanced up from massaging his feet as Han stepped into the room from the stairwell. "He's sleeping?"

Han nodded and tossed a chunk of wood into the fireplace, then watched as the flames caught along its split edge. Magic flames were well and good, but the scent of cedar and the crackle of wood fire spoke to Han of home. He opened the damper to let the heat escape. It wasn't the season for a fire, but the air cooled enough in the foothills at night, and the flames calmed him.

"Thanks for making him comfortable," Thurlock said. "I'm relieved he chose to stay."

"It's not surprising. Once his belly was full of those burgers and fries of yours he could hardly keep his eyes open." Han smiled, taking a seat in the other armchair. "But he did talk to me, sir, a little, and that surprised me."

"And pleased you, I see."

Han didn't miss the teasing twinkle in the old man's eyes. He smiled. "He's worried about his dog, and his things. I told him I'd go with him in the morning to get them. That's alright?"

Thurlock nodded, but stroked his beard thoughtfully. "I wish we could just keep him here until we can get him home. I fear we've woken the sleeping lion."

"Lion, sir?"

"Earthborns have such wonderful sayings don't you think? Lions disturbed from dreams get nasty. In this case the lion is the Witch. She knows we've got him. She won't be slow to respond."

Han hesitated, but then spoke his mind. "I think it might be a mistake, sir, to keep him here against his will." He drew in a breath to continue, but then stopped to chew his lip, thinking how best to frame what he had observed in Luccan's character. "He's skittish as a colt," he said finally, "and he's used to being on his own, making his own choices."

"And he wants to think he can trust us, but he doesn't." Thurlock ran tired hands through his grey hair, freeing it of its leather bond. "So, we'll take the path of least peril. Better to have you go with him than have him leave on his own. Perhaps I'll follow, if I don't have to go home tomorrow. We'll need to take steps for his safety in case he gets separated from us both."

Han nodded. "I thought of that, sir. I gave him our phone number."

Thurlock studied his attaché with a worried frown. "We don't have a phone, Han."

Han lit up with a jack-o-lantern grin. "Luccan doesn't know that."

After a few seconds, Thurlock's puzzled frown disappeared and he nodded, laughing. "Oh, I see. Good thinking, then." He chuckled some more and added. "Yes, that'll do for now. I'll throw what protection I can on him, too. He won't be safe, but he'll be safer, at least."

The topic having turned to safety, Han confided something that had troubled him since yesterday morning. "Sir, Luccan's shack ... He was living right on the edge of that ravine."

"And?"

"Well, it's a troubling place. I mean, I know there's the Portal down there in the cave, but it's more than that."

Han recalled the day, soon after they'd arrived in Earth, when Thurlock brought home an armload of books from a local library and dumped them on the table. *"A little history,"* he'd said. *"A little geography. It never hurts to be informed."*

Han preferred to get information first hand, but the Wizard was the boss. He'd cracked the books and he'd found tales about the Ravine that he wasn't likely to forget. "You remember those stories about what happened when this place was settled? Unexplained deaths, disappearances, and ... uh ... the homesteads ..." He was having trouble getting the words out. They threatened to launch his most horrible memories.

Thurlock understood his distress. He leaned forward and patted Han's arm. "They were burned, yes," he said.

The plain words blunted the spear of memory, and Han felt tension ease out of his shoulders.

"The place has a bad reputation," Thurlock was saying. "And you're right. There's more to that ravine than meets the eye. It's more than the presence of the Portal entrance; the worlds are closely intertwined there. It's my guess that the place has been targeted off and on for centuries by Ethrans with less than neighborly motives and enough power to make it count."

Lost in thought for several seconds, he tugged at his beard. "That's why the locals stay away as far as they can," he said. "I'd lay odds they don't even look down when they drive over one of the bridges." He gave his beard a couple more pats, and then turned to Han. "Why did you bring it up?"

"Why would he choose to live there?"

Thurlock smiled. "Because he's a smart cookie."

"Sir?"

"It's another figure of speech, Han. What I mean is that I imagine he felt quite safe in that shack and near the ravine in general. It gave him what he needed most—a place where people wouldn't notice him. He couldn't afford the attention of the authorities. He wouldn't be able to tell them even his name; who knows where he would land? And, he wouldn't want to be noticed by the criminal element either—"

"But he works for them."

Thurlock cocked an inquiring eyebrow.

"That's what he talked about, sir, while we were putting sheets on the bed. He told me how he's been getting by since Hank George died. He watched the other people on the streets, especially the kids. He saw the things they did to survive—stealing, panhandling, and, well, other things." Han looked up to meet the Wizard's steady grey gaze. "He said that of all the possibilities, stealing was the only one he figured he might be able to do. So he tried it."

Thurlock grimaced and shook his head. "It didn't go well, I presume?"

"Every time he laid his hand on something that belonged to someone else he heard a horrible ringing in his ears and his head hurt. It wouldn't stop until he put the thing down. And then, once, somebody caught him."

"He tried to lie about it?"

"That's right."

"Sick?"

"Vomited on the man's boots."

"Oh," said Thurlock, rolling his eyes and getting suddenly to his feet. "That's worse than what happened to me the time I tried it. At least I made it outside." At this Han burst out laughing. Thurlock put an indignant hand on his hip, glowered at Han, and said, "It wasn't funny at all."

After a renewed bout of laughter died down enough for Han to speak he said, still chortling. "You *tried to lie*, sir?"

"Don't act so surprised. Everyone lies at least once; it's only that a person with the old blood doesn't try it a second time. Or at least most of us don't. By the Lights of Heaven, I worried the boy was going to kill himself with half-truths tonight."

"He's willful, isn't he?"

"A bit of an understatement, I'd say. But considering who his mother is—"

"Some can lie, though." The statement silenced them both. There were important exceptions.

"Yes, of course," Thurlock acknowledged, "if they've turned away from the light."

Han moved closer to the hearth. "I'm sorry, sir. You're right—you trying to lie, that isn't funny."

"Nonsense, my friend. It wasn't funny then, but—case in point—I have to be honest. Thinking about it now, it's hilarious."

Han smiled again. "In any event, sir, Luccan's experiment turned out to be a good thing. The man made him clean up the mess and he did a good job, so the guy hired him to do some other cleaning, and laundry. He was a small time con, and he told his friends, so our Luccan ended up with his own little business, doing laundry and what-not for criminals." Han gave Thurlock a puzzled look. "He said they were almost always honest with him, sir, paid him as much as they said they would or sometimes more."

"Ah, well there you go. That's one of the supreme puzzles. It's easy—sometimes at least—to tell whether something someone has done is right or wrong. It's not so easy, though, to judge a person good or bad. But at least the story shows us Luccan is resourceful."

"And honest."

Thurlock laid his head back, closed his eyes, and almost in a whisper added, "Poor kid." He heaved a sigh and changed the subject. "I suppose I'd better try again to call his mother."

"Be brave, sir."

"Cut it out."

Han fought down the corners of his mouth, "Seriously, what can she do from a world away?"

Thurlock shot a look at Han, eyebrows arched. "You call her, then."

"Not my job, sir. Good night." Han straightened the welcome mat one last time and closed the door behind him.

"Coward," Thurlock accused, and heard Han laughing. The boards of the porch made not a squeak or a thump under his careful feet.

By the time the door clicked shut, Thurlock had set the M.E.R.L.I.N. spinning, and he smiled despite his mood as a soft Sunlands night settled into view. Moonlight cast a silver sheen on the log-and-thatch bulk of Sisterhold Manor, and a few of the windows in its broad face winked with yellow light. He froze the viewer with a raised hand, wishing he could linger.

"Get on with it, old man," he said, laughing at himself, and directed the viewer forward.

When it showed him the gold-varnished door, he imagined knocking with the brass stag knocker, lifting the latch, and stepping into the familiar old house. The Lady Grace Liliana sat at her dressing table in a room painted summer sky blue, with white lace panels at the window that fluttered in the breeze. A candle's flame cast gold on the polished floor and set Lili's pale complexion aglow, but her eyelids drooped over tired eyes. Her golden hair hung loose, shining, and her fingers toyed with the smooth-worn handle of her boar-bristle hairbrush.

"Just finished your nightly one-hundred beauty strokes?"

Liliana eyed him through the M.E.R.L.I.N. that doubled as her mirror. "He's with you," she said. "I'm coming tonight."

"That's not wise, Liliana." Thurlock slumped in his chair at the dining table. "I know you're anxious, you've waited thirty years." He looked away from the M.E.R.L.I.N. to avoid her gaze, and poked his yellow-umbrella staff listlessly at the chandelier.

"Yet he's still a boy."

Thurlock nodded. "More or less. For him it's been three years. He's fourteen."

"He needs his mother."

"He needs his mother—as we all need his mother—to stay put where she is and keep things in order in his home world. Which reminds me, what happened with L'Aria this afternoon?"

"I wasn't here." She wore a look of distaste, but as she turned her attention away from the girl, her expression changed to a worried frown. "I went up to Northvale. Strange things are happening again. I was going to ask you to come home tomorrow. A lot of people are upset." She paused and the frown changed again to displeasure. "And L'Aria's run off again."

Thurlock ignored Lili's well-known dislike for her ward. "Strange things?"

"Deaths. And no, I didn't find out anything useful. The circumstances are very much like the Greenwood incidents a few years ago, dead trees and missing blood. Of course, we all know who the likely culprit was then."

"Likely, but not convicted."

"True, and he's dead now, so they say. But then, we haven't found his corpse."

"Nor shall we, if what we surmise is true. Mardhral Canyon makes a deep grave."

She was quiet, methodically rearranging the creams, lotions, and scents on her dressing table. Bringing a bottle down with a sharp crack on the hard wood, she said, "But that's not what this call is about. How soon will you be bringing Luccan home?"

"When he's ready, and I've determined that it's safe." Thurlock, annoyed, batted the chandelier with his umbrella and the fixture started to swing.

"Put that staff down, Uncle, you're making me nervous. Why can't Luccan come home? You said he has the Key and the Amber Knife. And he has enough magic! I'm sure of it."

"It's highly likely that he does, considering his birthright." Thurlock abruptly dropped the umbrella on the table. It set loose a shower of sparks. "Nix," he said, arresting the flow.

He sat up straight and scowled into the M.E.R.L.I.N. "Whether he has magic or not, he can't use it. Yes, he has the Key of Behliseth and the Amber Blade, but those are only tools. He'll get into trouble if he tries to use them with neither skill nor knowledge." He saw scorn in Lili's green eyes. "And don't call me Uncle, Niece. You only do that when you want something."

"Why can't he use his magic? He was born to it."

"I've told you this before, Liliana, but I'll tell you again." His words were terse. "If he tries to travel through the Vortices—or even if we try to bring him through—when he doesn't have a clear idea who he is or where he's going, he could end up anywhere in a thousand worlds. Or worse, everywhere in a thousand worlds."

He pressed the heels of his hands to his eyes, leaning on his elbows. "For Behl's sake," he said, frustration leading him to take that sacred name in vain. "He only remembers one of his names. Worst case scenario, he could end up nowhere at all."

"And why is it that he only has one of his names, Uncle?" She drummed her long nails on the golden wood, and didn't bother to keep the accusation from her tone.

"You know the answer."

"Well if you'd listened to me then. 'As thee send, return to thee, good or ill, by rule of three ...'"

"Stop quoting me the primer, Lili! By the gods' teeth, I've been a Wizard for a thousand years. I've heard the rule of three a time or two."

"Well then you should have known what would happen if you let that man hold Luccan's Cardinal Name. With the things he'd already done, nothing could have stopped ruin from falling on his fool, stubborn head."

"You're wrong, child. I shouldn't have known. One can't *know* what will happen inside another soul." He stopped. It was hard enough, he decided, to defend himself against self-reproach. *By Behl's curly whiskers, I don't have to answer to my great-great-great niece.*

"What if—"

"Drop it, Lili." Thurlock leaned into his hands again and started to massage his temples.

"Take some aspirin."

"Aspirin?"

"For the headache. Uncle Thurlock, I'm Luccan's mother. I know what's best for him, and I know him. He'll be fine in the vortices. You can give him his other names to help."

"I can give him the third, as soon as he asks for it. If he shows a single clear indicator that he's ready to grow into his title, I can give him that, too. The second name, he'll probably remember on his own—it was never a secret. If he doesn't, you can give it to him when the time comes, since it came from you anyway. His cardinal name remains a problem, and as you're well aware, it's the one that counts."

"I thought you said there's a way you can call it back from the wind? And, you said some people remember it on their own."

"There is a way, but I don't know what it is. And some people do, but he hasn't. I asked."

"You've been working on this for thirty years."

"No, dear, I have not." He let his hands fall from his face and let his words fall quiet. "I've been divining Portals and surfing Naught trying to find where the Witch-Mortaine beached your son's craft. How much time for research do you think that left?"

Lili narrowed her eyes, and though Thurlock had never considered green a hot color, at that moment, he half expected her pupils to burst into flame. "Let me talk to him. I'll remind him who he is."

"No, Lili." Thurlock spoke firmly despite his weariness. "He'll want to believe anything we can tell him about his past, especially you, since you're his mother." He resisted the urge to add, *poor child*. "He'll convince himself that he remembers. A false memory, or even a vague one, will serve him no better in the vortices than no memory at all."

Thurlock slapped his open palm down on the table, emphasizing his next words. "True, clear, desire of the heart, Liliana, that's the *only* magic that works beyond the Portals, you know that. He has to have the real memories. Without his true name, it's the only way. We'll wait. We'll give it time."

"L'Aria went through."

"L'Aria knows who she is. And for that matter, she didn't use the vortices, not the way we do. She used her song."

"Bring him home. If Isa could banish him, surely the great Thurlock can get him back."

"First," he said, his voice scarcely louder than a whisper as he rose from his chair and began to pace, robes swishing, cheek twitching. "First, the power that the Witch-Mortaine employs is not available to me. Second, if it was, I would not partake. Third, although you might feel better, how will it help Luccan or Ethra if he comes home reduced *once again* to a blank slate?"

He stopped and turned to her, the muscles of his jaw working through his impatience. "When she banished him," he said, keeping his voice deliberately small, "he lost his identity because he never had it in the first place. That hasn't changed."

"I'm his mother." She'd risen to her feet too, and now she leaned toward the eye of M.E.R.L.I.N. Her features were set, and the words she hurled had barbs. "Since his father is dead, or at least gone, I alone decide for my son. He comes home now."

Adding together magical ability and political clout, Liliana amounted to one of the most powerful people in all of Ethra. Yet, Thurlock looked her in the eye and spoke with confidence. "In matters concerning Luccan, the authority is mine. The law is clear."

Liliana's jaw muscles tightened as she struggled for control. "I'll take it to the Council."

"I am the Council."

"You are one of the Council, as I am."

Thurlock simply pursed his lips and acknowledged her with the tiniest nod.

Without warning, she broke into sobs and sat again at her table. Thurlock could barely discern her words through her tears and the hands she held up to hide them. "He's my son, Uncle, my only child."

Lili's threats hadn't touched him, but her tears did. Thurlock's ire fled and his own voice grew thick. He reached across the table, as if to reach into another world to take his niece's hand. "Liliana, dear, please don't cry. Be glad that we've found him."

"I am, of course," she said, dabbing the tears with a soft white handkerchief. "It's just ... with him so close ... it's harder. Can you understand?"

He ignored her question because no right answer could ever exist. "Maybe it will help a little," he said, "if I tell you that I believe things will happen fast, now. I'm worried about what you say is going on there in the North, and everyday here I discover some alarming development. Still, with reasonable luck, Luccan could be home within the month."

He hesitated before conceding a final point. He didn't want to give her future ammunition, but he longed to see her comforted. Sighing, he gave in. "And, if things here get to the point that your way seems the lesser risk I'll give him what information I can and try to bring him home."

"Keep him safe." Lili's steady eyes demanded his pledge.

"I'll do my best."

After saying farewell, he broke the link, shut down the M.E.R.L.I.N., and addressed the silent room, echoing words spoken three years ago by a once-powerful man of Earth.

"My best," he repeated, "but, Behlishan help me, I don't know if that's enough."

PART TWO: Mystery, Magic, and Twists of Memory

8. The Demon Queen's Midnight Carnival

Hench had not dreamed the return of the Black Knife. He'd proven that an hour ago when Isa's summons woke him from exhausted sleep still clutching the Blade to his chest.

This will change things, he'd thought then, but so far all remained the same.

He still limped; Isa still raged. She had ordered him out into the wild dark that hung in the Ravine at night, and he'd gone. Now he crouched at the entrance to a shallow cave, melting into the shadows of cracked rocks and craggy oaks. Bile rose in his throat when he thought of the role he and the Blade were to play in tonight's ritual. Still he waited in obedient silence for the Witch to give him his cue.

The Witch's new disciples came, twenty-seven of them from different corners of the night. Moonset had passed and Hench almost laughed at the way they startled one another, coming out of the darkness in their black robes and cowls. They were ridiculous. But not everyone. One man stood tall and deep chested, with hair so black it shone blue even in the night. He called himself Mordred Brede.

Isa, or the Demon Queen, as she styled herself to these Earthborn acolytes, waited for them at the end of the clearing nearest Hench in the open. Her blue robes shone in the night, and a loose hood concealed her face. With her scavenger's features hidden, she looked regal. When her followers had gathered, she spoke. They listened, rapt.

"Disciples of the Demon Queen," she began, and opened her arms in a theatrical flourish, fanning her draped sleeves wide like wings. "Tonight you who are chosen will receive your first revelation, partake of your first communion, and do your first service of obeisance."

She clapped her hands once and the empty center of the clearing burst into blue flame. Twenty-seven gasps sounded, and twenty-seven black robes backed quickly away, broadening the circle around that center. Only Mordred held his ground. The flames shot higher, obeying Isa's gesture, and then settled into the guise of a viper. Hissing blue breath, the burning serpent coiled at the disciples' feet.

Carnival tricks. Earthborns are easily impressed.

At her summons Hench came forth from the dark, a crippled mystery in a black cowl, and set a three-legged steel cauldron over the blue fire, flames cold enough to burn. He stepped quickly away and the cauldron filled with clear viscous liquid. Isa's witch-fire chilled the summer air to stinging cold, and on the ground a ring of frost formed around the flames and then spread outward in a wave. Every toadstool, weed, and bug in its path shriveled so that for a time the night was filled with snaps and pops and infinitesimal screams. Soon, the entire clearing was floored in frozen earth, silent.

Thin-winged insects hummed into the bright circle expecting heat froze in the icy air, and fell away into the cold, bubbling cauldron. Bats plummeted, their wings cracked to ice, mammal screams frozen in their tiny throats. Spiders spun in on tethers of silk drawn to the smell of a thousand deaths, and found their own. The liquid went red, then black, and that was the color of the smoke that plumed up and out to form a dome of impenetrable sky.

The rite that followed was sophistry, no more than theatre. Isa was playwright, director, and star. She worked her audience until they were marionettes, puppets on cruel, barbed, strings. Her glass-tipped scourge writhed in her hand, and when she struck, Hench's agony became the Disciples' fear. They partook of that fear like a sacrament. They baptized themselves in delicious dread of the dark, bitter power they saw and foolishly thought they understood.

Hateful people with empty lives. Who else would have come? They coveted the power Isa showed them, too blind to see the illusion, a mask hiding something that would consume them. They gave themselves over, willing slaves.

Theatrics aside, Isa truly did command dreadful magic. When the time was right, when the disciples' lust for power had risen to frenzy, she gave the night air the slightest magical tweak. A gesture, a whisper, a tiny twist in a single synapse in each of twenty-seven brains, and she owned them. All but Mordred.

Now the show is over. Hench's chest tightened in dread. The Witch would test her new slaves. Their part was small. The rite they would perform would be meaningless, darkly comical, if it were not for Hench and the Black Blade. Yet they would inflict real harm.

Still working the crowd, Isa changed the face she wore. She clasped her hands behind her back and paced like a concerned teacher, a professor contemplating commencement and students set loose to prove the worth of their lessons.

"I wish you well, but I will not stay. You must complete this ritual on your own, united. It is a test of your value as a Disciple of the Demon Queen. I will leave my apprentice, Mordred, to observe and deal with any ... problems. Hench, my thrall, will be the blood-letter. His Knife is more than it seems. Trust that you do not want to meet that Blade, so when the moment comes for blood, do not hesitate with your own dirks.   "Fare well in your service tonight."

She turned and walked to the edge of the clearing. The blue flames blazed skyward then died away completely, a magician's trick but well performed. Hench stared along with the others at the spot where, an instant before, she had stood. In her place lay a yellow dog, the boy's dog Isa had said. The tools he would use were laid out beside her limp form—rough twine, Black Knife, crystal chalice for blood.

He did as the Witch commanded. He made precise, perfect cuts, drew the dog's blood, and said the words that would bend the Knife's magic to this purpose. He used the Knife this way even as it protested in his hands, and then he used the Blade's opposite magic to stop the blood and close the wound. He preserved the dog's life but as Isa had required, he took possession of her soul.

After he finished, he sat at the edge of the clearing while the Earthborns completed their empty, hideous ritual, Mordred moving in their midst. Hench's eyes followed their dance, but he didn't see. He didn't hear their chant. The smell of their burning blood meant nothing. Every shred of his awareness fixed on two sensations, the dog's pain and the agony of the Blade.

Something in him broke. In the hour before dawn when some animals wake to hunger and move to hunt, he stumbled away, dragging his lame leg. He went as an animal goes, feral and deadly, to quell his hunger and slake his terrible thirst.

***

Born a sacrifice, laid at first breath upon the consecrated ice of the Blue Floe in Ethra's far North, Isa was no stranger to pain. Unique among centuries of children born to that fate, she had clung to life in that heartless cold until Queen Hilgaardre, Mahl's high priestess, had intervened, taking her as heir. But Hilgaardre's heart harbored secrets, and in the end she'd sent Isa south mounted on Ahrion, the Queen's moon-white winged mount, in the care of an old groom.

Years later Isa had forsaken the old man's kindness and the Queen's ill-guided mercy and returned to the Ice-Lord, seeking access to his endless power—a path fraught every step with pain. She knew what to expect now from her Master's wrath. She had failed him before.

When she had banished the boy, she had not succeeded in separating him from the Key of Behliseth. A critical error. It would have made it so much easier to teach him hate, to shape his ambitions, to darken and subvert the power he would unleash when he claimed the Key and used it. And her spell had gone further awry, she had lost him in the vortices. It had taken her three years to find him, and the infernal Wizard had reached him first.

She had been punished, and punished again, and again and each time it diminished her, damaged her until she had little life or power of her own left. She was Mahl's tool, his shadow, his servant. Serving him had become her only life, her only path to power, or to the revenge she so desperately needed.

Now she had failed him again, lost the pathetic slave and his Knife. Mahl would punish her and endure it she must. Endure it she would. That was one thing Isa knew how to do.

His touch inflicted agony, the infinite anguish of discreet cells dragged from their beds into the purposeful void of the Ice-Lord's maw. Yet, in surviving his bitter attention she had come to know Mahl more thoroughly, perhaps, than anyone ever had. His power was all-consuming, his form vast, but alone he could not tilt the scales that balanced the powers of gods.

He would not destroy her; he needed her mind, her voice, and her human hands. Once his shapeless fury over the lost slave was spent, she would offer another. Mordred Brede, an uncommon Earthborn ripe with magic and rotten with greed. She, the only living Witch-Mortaine, would mold him with her own hand. He would be a worthy weapon.

Then it would be time to take the boy, to bend, break, or crush him. One way or another, the power locked inside the child must be theirs.

9. The Boy's Got Magic

The shadows were still long, the grass was still damp, and the sun was still climbing when Lucky ran across the field toward his shack. He felt a little guilty for having run off from Thurlock's house three quarters of an hour ago without saying anything to anyone. He'd agreed, last night, when Han offered to come with him this morning to get Maizie. It had seemed a safe idea, then.

And he'd felt safe enough when he first woke up. The sash window had been open but the shade drawn, the air fresh and the light coming through colored like caramel. The bed was cloud-soft, and the white sheets still crackled, and he felt drowsy, cocooned in patchwork. Even though he knew he needed to go take care of Maizie, he was so comfortable he almost turned over and went back to sleep.

Last night he'd decided to stay for no better reason than because he hadn't wanted to leave. Han had taken him up the narrow stairs, showed him the room, and made sure he knew where to find what he might need. They'd talked in an easy way that felt natural even though he wasn't used to it. Before he left Han said, "Sweet dreams, lad," and the ordinary words had fallen over him like a spell.

When he woke to bright summer morning the charm remained. The room and the bed and the light seemed so normal Lucky almost felt guilty. But then his brain cells woke up.

Who am I fooling? I spent the night in the house of an old man from another world who makes magic fire.

As if the bed itself was burning, Lucky bounded out of it, put on his clothes (laundered by Han), slid into his shoes (glued by Han), and pulled his Key (strung on a chain by Han) over his neck. He put a leg out the window and stepped into the thick branches of a very old, conveniently placed maple. Pulling the other leg out behind him he whispered, "I wish I was invisible," and descended. He hit the ground running, vaulted the fence, and beat feet down the road.

On the way to his shack, he pondered Thurlock's flames. Also Han's Mark, Hank's stories, the weird lady at the Quick-Shoppe and, of all things, the cat that stole his key.

If someone had been saying out loud the things he was thinking, he would have wanted to cover his ears with his hands and say "la la la la la," very loudly. He decided to think about something else, and his stomach growled a suggestion, but food didn't prove to be a safe topic. It reminded him of the two burgers and paper sack full of fries he'd eaten last night, more than he'd ever eaten at one meal and absolutely wonderful—but he'd expected Thurlock to conjure them like his flames.

"Luccan," the old man had said, "we do things the hard way unless we have a very good reason." Then he'd left to go buy the burgers, laughing all the way out the door, and Lucky was left to cope with the idea that for a moment, magic had seemed not only possible, but normal.

Now, jogging across the field, Lucky tried out the word that seemed best to describe Thurlock. "Wizard." The sound of it was enough to push a little jet of adrenaline through his veins. He ran faster.

***

Han bounded up the narrow steps and burst through the side door, making an uncharacteristic amount of noise. Three paces took him through the big, farm-style kitchen and around the corner to the stairway, where he began to ascend the steps three at a time. He stopped at the door to the room where Lucky had slept and listened, hoping his instincts were wrong.

Without knocking, he opened the door. He took one look and shouted. "Thurlock!"

"I'm right here," Thurlock said, and indeed he stood behind Han, no more than a foot away, shaking his head in disbelief.

"How could he have done it, sir? Your wards ... my talent ... and I've been watching since before dawn. How did he get past it all?"

The Wizard snorted, and then he said, "Behl's sweet whiskers, man. It's obvious isn't it?"

Han chewed his lip, but he didn't speak, and Thurlock supplied the answer himself.

"Magic, Han Shieth. The boy's got magic—rivers of it. Deep enough to drown him in a sea of trouble, and he hasn't even begun to learn to swim."

**

Through five or perhaps ten of the longest minutes in his life, Lucky waited for Maizie. He called over and over, whistled, went to the doorstep and rattled the kibble in her bowl. No raspy bark. No tail beating the brush, no bright eyes and sloppy tongue. No dog. He stepped onto the path that snaked through mesquite, around rocks, and under pines before it descended into the gorge, thinking that if Maizie was scared she'd head for the Ravine to find a bunker.

While he jogged that zigzag trail, dodging thorns, scaring up small birds, and leaping a sunning King Snake, he tried to recall what Grandpa Hank taught him about tracking. At the time, he'd approached the lessons as a game, but now he hoped he remembered enough to use the skills. He slowed to scan the ground, and a few steps into the pines, he found a clear paw print in damp earth. He continued, sweeping his eyes side to side, checked the ground before putting a foot down every time. At intervals, he stopped and called out.

Any minute, he insisted, *she'll come running.*

As the trail descended into the gorge the going got tricky, both rough and steep. He concentrated on finding places for his hands and feet that wouldn't crumble, until he heard a growl—vicious and close. His head snapped up and he saw, ten feet away and level with his gaze, two blood-rimmed brown eyes. Familiar brown eyes.

He checked the dog's markings. There was the white half-inch at the tip of her tail, the white 'necklace' of fur half-hidden in the gold, the pink freckle on her black nose. But that snarl, the bared teeth, and those bloodthirsty eyes, none of that belonged to the dog he loved.

She sprang suddenly and he jumped without thinking or planning or even looking where he was going. When he landed, the shale cracked, and he tumbled down the rocky slope. He came to a hard stop, bashing his left shoulder against a black finger of basalt sticking up like a guardrail at the edge of a narrow shelf of rock. New bruises throbbed, scratches burned, and when he sat up, the world started to spin.

When it rolled to a stop, he was shocked to find that his legs dangled off the edge of the rock ledge, swinging in open air and pointing toward a long fall to the creek bed below. He scooted carefully away from the edge and put his back against the steep slope.

Maizie snarled again, the sound no less threatening, but farther away and coming from a different direction. Then she cried, the sound of a dog in pain. He knew she was dangerous; he remembered the way she'd lunged at him. But that cry was full of agony, and he couldn't bear to stand by and do nothing. Whatever had happened, she was hurt. She needed him. He reined in his heart, ordered his thoughts to line up single file, and shut panic away. He had to figure out how to help his best friend.

He scanned the slope above him in the direction of Maizie's cries. He focused on each of the shadowed places behind boulders and scrub brush until he spotted her hidden under an overhanging ledge, further obscured by brush. A jerking movement, a spasm of pain, had drawn his eye, but in the midst of it she bared her teeth and snapped at the air in his direction. Her eyes burned like twin fires.

Despite his good intentions, he had to force his feet to stay put, resisting a massive urge to run. He blew out a stiff breath and shoved his hair back off his face. He managed to bite back fear, muddle through indecision, and now he had to swallow pride. He wrestled with it until Maizie howled as if someone had raked coals over her back, then he said three words that were at least as familiar on his tongue as ancient Greek.

"I need help."

He climbed out of the Ravine and ran through the green shade under the pines. He ignored the blast of heat that assaulted him in the open field and raced for the phone booth outside the Quick-Shoppe. His breath caught up with him while he dug in his pocket for a quarter and the phone number Han had given him last night, all the while trying to remember why he didn't have a cell phone.

Turning his back to the glare off the parked cars outside the booth, he laid the scrap of paper on the chrome shelf, took the bulky receiver off the hook, and punched in the number. *Han can help,* he was thinking, *Han will come. Han, Han, Han ...* It rolled through his brain like a chant.

Han picked up before the phone rang. "Luccan?"

"Han!"

"I'm coming lad," he said, not asking what Lucky wanted, where he was, or what was wrong. "Go back down into the Ravine; but stay away from the dog." Han's voice came over the line clear and steady as rain on a lake, calming Lucky despite his astonishment. "Don't go to your shack; we don't know who else might be around. When I get there, we'll get Maizie. Hide. I'll find you."

Before he hung up, Han said, "I'll be there before you know it," and no sooner had Lucky settled down half buried in duff in the hollow between a boulder and a nurse log than his spit-shined boots approached. "It's safe, lad," he called. "Come on out."

Lucky surprised himself, and surely Han, by burying his face in Han's shoulder and clinging like duct tape. The quiet man hugged him back, patted his shoulder, and Lucky didn't cry, thank goodness, but the words, "Thank you" had trouble getting out.

"Certainly, Luccan," was all Han said. Nothing could have been more reassuring.

The trek back to Maizie's hiding place was tough, what with the burn of cuts and bruises and a heart beating fast from dread. Once they'd found her, Han climbed up the slope and squatted a few feet away, locking his eyes on hers. He kept still and he didn't speak, but as she gazed back at him the fire in her eyes cooled. Her growl died away, her hackles laid flat, and finally she sighed into sleep.

"Will she be okay?"

Han hopped down to the ledge where Lucky waited before he answered, "I can't say for sure. I can't tell what's wrong."

Lucky had so many worries and questions that he didn't know where to begin, and it must have shown.

Han rested his hand briefly on Lucky's arm. "Take it easy, lad," he comforted. "As I said, I don't know what's wrong, but I don't think it's rabies, or any disease. She's got a little cut on her leg, but it's healed, mostly, and not hurting her. No other injuries. So the—"

Panic waved giant red flags inches from Lucky's eyeballs. Han hadn't touched Maizie. He'd never gotten within three feet. "How do you know all that?"

The few seconds that passed while Han chewed his lip seemed like a month. Finally, he looked at Lucky sideways and said, "I have a way with animals?"

Lucky's eyebrows went up, but he said nothing.

Another silent month crept by, then Han shrugged. "Alright, I can read their minds."

Lucky choked.

Han patted his back until the cough died to a raspy breath and said, "We'll talk about it later. Right now, let's get Maizie home."

10. Mind Reading and the Power of Wishful Thinking

Going back, Lucky and Han kept to the pines. Once past Heart Lake at the west end of the Ravine, they turned south to make an easy, gradual climb to the place where the Wizard's unlikely house hung in a bony hollow of the dry-grass hills. They only stopped twice to rest, and by the time they reached the leaning fence Lucky's step had begun to falter. Sweat soaked the back of Han's shirt, but despite his ungainly four-legged burden, he remained strong.

To Lucky's surprise, they didn't go around to Thurlock's front steps, where Lemon Martinez eyed them from the porch rail. "He isn't home," Han said, and carried Maizie around to a little house in the back corner of the yard, a building Lucky hadn't even noticed yesterday. It sported a neat coat of white paint, a clean-swept porch, and windows that winked with half-drawn shades.

Inside Han's quarters, as he called them, waited a sparse, cool, clean space, free of frills and solid, just like the man who occupied them. A blanket of security dropped over Lucky as soon as the door thunked shut behind him. He followed Han through the small front room with its one recliner to the bedroom, where the spread draped so neatly that every fringe hung just so. They ducked through a lowly door and entered a shed with cloudy windows and a floor of hard-packed dirt.

The enclosure smelled of new-sawn wood and harbored a pen fashioned from two-by-fours and chicken wire. There, on a bed of clean straw, Han at last laid Maizie down. In the Ravine, he'd lulled her to sleep with stillness and quiet presence.

Now, he knelt to examine her and sent Lucky to get blankets from the bedroom closet. Once she'd been settled and given a dose of liquid from a brown bottle, Han turned to Lucky and pledged to do his best to get her well.

"That's not an empty promise," he said, "I really am good with animals." His smile seemed kind but possibly a little sheepish, and though Lucky's thanks were sincere, the words rekindled the question he'd left smoldering all morning.

Before he could speak, Han said, "Lunch," and led the way to his tiny kitchen. He gestured for Lucky to sit at one of the two chairs at the pine-board table, and went to scrub his hands. Soaping up, he said, "Now's a good time to ask, lad."

Lucky opened his mouth, but then closed it to think. He watched Han take a loaf of white bread out of a roll-top breadbox, and packets of meat and cheese out of his tiny, must-be-an-antique refrigerator, and then toss the loot onto the spotless cream tile of the countertop. He turned his back toward Lucky, as transparent as a brick wall.

He can read the animals' minds he said… Lucky raised his hands to smooth back his sweat-damp hair. *So what about people? Can he—?*

"Yes, sometimes," Han said. Suddenly. Without being asked. Startling Lucky and causing him to box his own ears and swallow his tongue.

After coughing it back up, he asked, "H-h-how did you know what I was thinking?"

"I don't know how I do it, precisely. I was born with the talent, which is normal enough in Ethra, though not exactly common even there. When I was old enough to understand my gift, I worked at developing it." He turned to face Lucky, a teasing smile in his eyes. "Think of it like this. Many people here in Earth can ride a bike, but only a few have the skills to do stunts."

"What about you? How good are you?"

"If it were bike riding, I'd win all the competitions."

Han tried to explain mind reading and Lucky tried to listen, but he didn't exactly have an open mind on the subject.

"It's just not right," he said. "You're invading everybody's privacy."

"That's not how it works. I can't just know everything you're thinking." Judging by the set of his shoulders and the way he smacked mayo onto the bread, he found he idea insulting.

"Listen," he said. "Just like any inborn magic, it works two ways. The first way is self-protection, so if someone is close by, I hear what they think about me, which is not always pleasant. The second way, the strongest way, my ability works is to protect others, if someone I have a connection with, like you, calls to me in their thoughts. That, I'll pick up even from a distance, unless some other strong magic is in the way."

"The phone call?"

"Yes."

Han turned his starched back again, and continued to build their sliced-ham sandwiches with the precision of an engineer. The activity must have worked out some mental kinks. By the time he turned back around, put their plates on the table, and took a seat across from Lucky, his shoulders had softened and the kindness was back in his eyes.

He poured Lucky milk (white), drank his coffee (cold), and worried about why he couldn't figure out Maizie's ailments (aloud). He polished off two sandwiches in four bites—a feat Lucky admired but couldn't quite duplicate—and then sat back, scratched his T-shirted chest, and yawned.

Ridiculously normal, for a mind reader.

Minutes later, he disappeared into the bedroom leaving Lucky at loose ends in the tiny house. Closing the door between them he said, "Lad, don't touch anything you don't fully understand."

So, Lucky didn't touch the unstrung bow leaning in the corner by the redbrick hearth; runes were carved into it. And he didn't touch the arrows, some of which were fletched with feathers that had markings like the flame decals on street rods, and stood in a quiver made of skin with big, shiny scales. A shield that hung on the wall had been made of similar skin—one huge scale with a mean-looking spike in the center that appeared to have grown there. Lucky left it alone. He didn't even think about touching the pale metal sword that also hung on the wall, or the scabbard—fashioned either from gold that looked like wood, or from wood that looked like gold.

To keep his hands from trouble, he did the dishes, but that didn't occupy much of his mind, so he while he worked, he also thought. Of course, what he thought about doggedly, even after he ordered himself to stop, was the mind reader, Han. And the Wizard Thurlock. And what had happened to Maizie, and ... *And why can't my life ever be normal?*

As he put the last of the silverware in the drainer, pulled the plug, and swished the cloth around the sink, Han came up behind him on silent steps and said, "Ah," apparently pleased.

He startled Lucky nearly out of his pants. Either he didn't notice that Lucky was having respiratory failure, or he had faith that Lucky would recover on his own, because he went on talking as if Lucky wasn't clutching his chest. "You did the dishes. Thoughtful. I can't think of the last time someone did a chore for me."

He grabbed his shirt off the back of the chair. "Thurlock is home," he said, pointing toward the door with a toss of his head. "Let's go talk to him about Maizie."

Before they covered half the distance across the yard, Thurlock came striding up, robes swirling in a tailwind. He scowled. Just in case that expression was directed at him, Lucky stood behind Han, where he felt a bit safer, but the old man ignored him.

"We'd better talk, Han," he said. "I've got some important intelligence from home. Seems those killings up north were the tip of the iceberg, literally. Rumors are about Drakes—Blues, mind you—prowling into Sunlands territory on the heels of a creeping boreal freeze that's turned the whole Northern Marsh to frozen mud."

"What will the clans do for food," Han asked, "and trade goods?"

"We've already sent relief goods North, we're bringing back some of the able bodied to work the harvest so they can take wages and supplies home, and some of the basket weavers were thrilled at the prospect of a shipment of Rainbow Grass from the south coast. But—"

Thurlock stopped and looked into the west where an inflated orange sun fell toward the needle-sharp tops of the Ring. He pulled almost frantically at his beard, and then suddenly swung his lion-mane head around to look directly at Han, eyes burning as if the sun had kindled them.

"It's the Drakes, you see. The Blues. The clans up north still remember the Northern Peril. For all that it was two-thousand years ago, and most of Ethra thinks of it only as fireside legend, their Sooth Keepers still know it as history. The leaders have fallen back on their old ways, now, to keep panic down."

"Sacrifice?"

The things Thurlock said seemed unreal to Lucky, like a fantasy movie. But Han's one word question and the look on his face sent fear grating down Lucky's spine. Thurlock must have noticed. He stopped short and leaned around Han to make eye contact with Lucky.

He tossed his hands up in a gesture of apology. "I'm forgetting that we have important things to think about right here," he said. "I'm sorry, Luccan. Did you find your dog? Is she alright?"

"Um, no sir ..." Lucky trailed off, not sure where to go from there.

Han gave Lucky's shoulder a squeeze. "The boy's dog is not alright, sir. We were—"

A blue flash and a clap of thunder bullied its way through Han's words, demanding attention.

"That's odd." Thurlock mused in scholarly fashion while heavy drops began to spatter off his spectacle lenses. He was looking up at a very large, very dark, mass that had gathered in the sky and now shadowed the hills to the north and west. "I don't remember seeing that cloud—"

Han ran back out from the cottage's covered stoop, where he and Lucky had already taken shelter, took hold of Thurlock's elbow and tugged at him. "Perhaps, sir, you should wonder about it inside, out of the rain."

From under the low peaked roof, Lucky watched the thunderhead roll in. Like a giant locomotive, it pulled a thick bank of clouds behind it, crushing the evening sun under its sparking wheels. He sucked in a breath of alarm and started to turn toward Han's little house. But in that same breath, the rain stopped and the air went cold; so cold that Lucky's thoughts froze.

Forgetting his intention to run inside, he hunkered down, crossed his arms over the goose bumps prickling his chest, and started shivering. Lightning flashed again, this time kicking up a gust of wind that struck him hard enough to steal his breath.

A crackling sound assaulted his ears and the metal Key sparked, flashed, and burned like a hot iron against the frigid skin of his chest. He ripped the chain over his head, dropped the Key to the worn boards of the stoop, and kicked it away, gagging on the stink of sulfur and what he guessed might be his own burnt flesh.

Recovering, he said, "That's no ordinary storm." And then a horrible thought reared up, as clear and undeniable as the voice of a god. *It's here for me. Whatever it is, it's come for me!*

Han came back out the door bearing sword and shield and said, "You're right, it's not ordinary." He stopped, taking in Lucky's shell-shocked appearance, and the key smoking on the ground. "Luccan," he said, but Thurlock slammed out the door behind him and interrupted.

"Never mind, Han, go. I've got the boy." He stepped in front of Lucky, grasped him by the shoulders and pushed him back a single step, standing between him and the storm. Holding onto Lucky's arm, he stooped for the discarded key, all the while muttering under his breath. "Here," he said, his voice quiet but stronger, somehow, than the dry thunder or the wind.

Lucky felt as if he'd just woken from a nightmare, but then the Wizard dropped the key over his neck and put his hand over it, cooling it, and calming Lucky's heart.

"Come with me."

Lucky anchored his eyes on the calm grey center of Thurlock's gaze. He nodded and took a step at the Wizard's side. At that moment, thunder cracked so loud that the ground quaked and shivered. Lucky made a small sound and put his head down, covering it with his arms. But still, he heard Thurlock speak softly.

"It won't touch you, Luccan. Come now."

Lucky couldn't remember how he made his legs work, but he stayed on top of them as he followed the Wizard, all the while clutching the sleeve of the man's grey robes like a lifeline.

Inside Thurlock's house, he relaxed the moment the oak door whisked quietly shut behind him. He grabbed hold of his key, which still offered comfort though it grew stranger every day, and he felt certain that everything would be alright. Like a nosy patron at a street fair, he watched Han and Thurlock go about the house like actors preparing for a show.

Han strode to the door and swung it open, closing it again behind a frazzled, wet Lemon Martinez, who jumped to the top of the armchair and hung on like a bull-rider as another wave of thunder rocked the room. Then, Han made a circuit of the ground floor, securing windows and doors. Lucky still stood a few paces clear of the door, and Han didn't bother with instructions. Taking him by the arm, he pulled him to the foot of the stairs, took a deliberate place in front of him midway between the front door and the stairway, and turned to face the door.

He placed the sword's point on the ground in front of him and wrapped both hands on the hilt. He broadened his stance, and flexed his knees, and fixed his attention on the doorway. He'd strapped his shield to his left forearm, and the spike at its center protruded in front of him, as if set to impale an oncoming foe.

Light shimmered on the shield's iridescent disk and sparks crackled over its surface like miniature lightning. The display of usually hidden force drew Lucky's attention and he had a nagging feeling that he was forgetting something.

But it wasn't until thunder crashed again outside that he remembered to feel afraid.

Thurlock had been standing in the dining room, looking off into the distance, and speaking quietly to himself as if rehearsing a monologue. Now he moved to plant himself, quite precisely as if there was a stage mark, a few feet to Han's right. He began to sway and gesture, like a magical Tai Chi master.

Lucky's eyes felt stretched, taking it all in. His heart thumped and he started to sweat, despite the way the afternoon had cooled. It had grown much too dark for the time of day, and Lucky realized, that as Thurlock and Han gathered up defenses, the storm prepared its assault.

The noise outside rumbled and rolled and cracked constantly, and beyond the windows thick mist tumbled in the wind, flashing with inner lightning. The notion entered Lucky's brain that they were inside the storm, that it had descended on the house and swallowed it whole. Or maybe the house had flown up into the black cloud's heart like Dorothy Gale on her way to Oz. And if he were to go to the door and step out, he would fall a turbulent mile before finding ground.

When he looked again at Thurlock, the old man had changed. He'd grown so tall, wide-shouldered, and menacing that Lucky was afraid he'd break right through the roof. All of this—Han's weapons, the mounting storm, the mystery of Thurlock—all of it added to his fright, notching up his heartbeat another click.

Thurlock continued his Wizard's dance, pointing his furled yellow umbrella here and there with his right hand, and all the while murmuring strange words, sending those 's' and 'th' sounds winging to every corner. A light began to build; a glow sheathed the umbrella and brightened until it shone like a miniature sun with the Wizard's right hand at its center.

Lucky thought, *that's no ordinary umbrella,* and in precisely that instant thunder slammed like solid stone against all the walls of the house at once. The chandelier's prisms rang against each other and the windows shook in their frames like prisoners rattling bars. Even the stones in the hearth shuffled loose in the dust of disintegrating mortar.

Lemon Martinez yowled, and the sound shredded what was left of Lucky's calm. By the time the thunderclap began to die away, his whole body thrummed with fear like a taut cable in a wind. Han, who yet stood rock still, said, "Mister Martinez," in a firm voice, and the cat settled onto his haunches, looking annoyed but manageable.

"Luccan," Han said, "be calm, lad. The power behind this storm feeds on fear." He turned with confident grace to meet Lucky's eye and stood like a bulwark, the picture of unyielding strength. Encouraged, Lucky nodded and drew himself up to stand a little straighter, and when Han's mouth quirked into a tiny smile, he very nearly smiled back.

Maizie howled, and despite his new resolve not give in to fear, all the hairs on his arms stood up at once, like tiny prairie dogs sniffing the wind. Her howls grew wilder and soon they were the frenzied shrieks of a dog gone completely mad. Lucky's knees melted. He looked at Han and the Warrior spoke, but Lucky couldn't hear the words over the blood beating in his ears.

Thunder exploded again, and this time light slammed into him, striking him in the center of the forehead and exploding like a paintball. For a time he wasn't sure if his eyes were open or closed—all he could see was a sharp black afterimage on a blinding blue ground, like the negative of photographed lightning. When that cleared, it was as though he saw with a new kind of eye.

Nothing remained unchanged. The span of time over which that vision held, perhaps a dozen breaths, would measure in seconds, Lucky knew. But every heartbeat inside it stretched into a small eternity, every pulse was forever enough for him to see a brand new world, both wonderful and horrifying.

Faces roiled in the storm. Rotting, red-eyed things writhed in anguish, remains of things that were once alive. Caustic, nuclear eyes glowed in the faces of other creatures, things that had surely never been anything but the monstrous, fanged beings they seemed now. Blue light snaked in under the door, and inside it Lucky saw the shape of a hooded, demon-eyed serpent.

It reared up to strike at the Wizard, but Thurlock raised a shielding palm. "Avert," he said, and a blaze of gold enveloped him, painfully bright. Thurlock stood at the core of that golden blaze, a pillar of pure light, more than a man. If he had sported wings, Lucky would have called him an angel.

The light-snake assaulted the golden armor around the Wizard, testing it, and Thurlock's umbrella swooshed out and clicked open. He held it at the end of his outstretched arm and executed a triple spin worthy of the Winter Olympics. Lucky saw the yellow fabric disk like a noon sun against deep night, but he also saw through the tool's disguise and knew that it wasn't an umbrella—never had been.

It was a great staff. Six feet long or more, it had been crafted from golden wood and capped and shod with the same pale, alien metal as Han's sword. Carved runes along its length shone golden, and streams of silver-white power ran through the wood like blood through veins. At that moment, Lucky would have bet both feet that the wood breathed and throbbed to the ancient beat of the Wizard's heart.

The light-serpent drew back hissing its anger, coiled near the door, and then shattered. Billions of shards and splinters flew outward like exploded glass, or like a newborn universe. Thurlock was a vision of pulsing, golden force, but Lucky found that small comfort. He was as much afraid of the Wizard as he was of the unfathomable power that assaulted him. The two forces fought, and the house filled with sound and light and movement, and soon Lucky lost even the sense of what was up and what was down. A gust of wind came from nowhere, born inside the room, and it swept him back a step.

Then Han spoke, his voice soothing and still soft, but strong and heartening. Lucky locked his eyes on the Warrior.

Even with his strange new powers of vision, Han looked the same. He was a man, no more, except that he burned with a steady light like a lone candle in a fortress holding off the dark. He spun his sword before him, and the pale blade echoed the Wizard's bright staff. The shards of deathly blue light, still hissing like the demon serpent they had been, flew into the spinning blade and shrieked like things with living pain. They recoiled and crashed back against the walls and windows and then into the path of the Wizard's staff, where they vanished.

All the while, though sweat poured down his temples, Han stayed strong as oak, solid and calm. "Luccan," he said again, unhurried despite his labors. "Don't give in. You have strength you don't know about. Try to find it. Resist." It seemed like good advice to Lucky, but he couldn't follow it. He was stuck in some kind of hellish limbo. He didn't know even whether to trust his eyes, or whether he wanted to believe them.

If this isn't real, I'm crazy. If it is real, the world is a hundred-zillion times too scary.

He was living a nightmare. He thought it would never stop. Then suddenly it did.

Maizie let go a howl that shrieked above all the other noises, neither shrill nor deep but piercing everything. It stopped with the sound of glass shattering in the night in the direction of Han's cottage. Then dark fell, everywhere, as thick and black as grave dirt.

The only things Lucky could see then were a flickering of Wizard flame in the hearth, no bigger than a struck match, and an almost invisible white-gold sheath over the Wizard's right hand. The silence weighed down every effort at thought; the only sound Lucky heard was the faint whistle of his own wary breath. Biting cold raked against his skin and wrapped around him like dead hands, locking down his muscles so tight he couldn't even shiver.

He jumped at the sudden crash of something heavy hitting the front door hard enough to send a crack snapping through the oak. Immediately that was followed by a whining, snarling growl from the porch. The lights came on, and at the same time Lucky said, "Maizie!" Not fully believing he'd found the power to move, he ran for the door.

Thurlock and Han were stunned for about a millionth of a second, and then in unison they yelled, "Luccan, no!"

But Lucky wasn't listening. Maizie was outside the door and she was hurt, again or still, and he was going to help her. Thurlock had his staff raised, and Han was in motion, but it wasn't without cause that folks that knew Lucky from the streets of Valley City sometimes referred to him as, "the blur."

He was fast. He was already there. He threw the door to the Wizard's house wide open, and immediately saw his mistake.

Maizie snarled and bared her teeth. Her eyes blazed. She bunched her muscles, ready to leap for his throat. Ten feet behind her stood a tall, gaunt woman in blue robes, eyes blazing with that same cold color, and she laughed, a familiar sound. "Yes," she said. "Yes, dear boy, come out to play."

With his altered sight, he could see that she was but a shadow of life, human in form but wasted and eternally hungry. Where her heart should have been darkness swirled, as if drilling away her soul. That blackness was the presence at the heart of the storm, the thing that wanted him, and he felt its malice like a bellyful of ice.

An image of stars leapt to Lucky's mind, galaxies burning hot at their core, spinning off streams of heat and clusters of light. If that black spinning wind that stood in place of the woman's soul resembled anything, that was it, but it was all backward. It spiraled inward sucking light and heat into its blackness, and Lucky understood that if it touched him he would fall into it and never stop.

And it was cold. And it was less alive than death. But it was living, anyway, and coming closer.

Maizie sprang at Lucky, and so did Han. Han won, plowing into boy and dog at the same time. The impact sent Maizie flying back out the door, and Lucky sliding sideways, not stopping until he slammed into a leg of the dining room table, whereupon he heard a snap that he hoped was not a rib. Thurlock shouted, *"Head!"* and Han ducked his, just in time to avoid being hit by the Wizard's giant fireball as it rocketed out the door. The flaming sphere of magic zinged straight into the Witch's face, and knocked her back at least thirty feet, and the Wizard spelled the door shut.

But not before a man came in.

The stranger might have believed himself a Wizard, too. Or something. He muttered ugly-sounding words and flicked his hands about. If he was a Wizard he seemed rather dark, but that could have been because of the black robe and the curly blue-black hair sticking out at the edges of the cowl.

Han and Thurlock both looked at him, then at each other. Han raised his eyebrows inquiringly toward the Wizard, who shrugged in response. Han grabbed the man, easily pinning his arms behind his back.

"Throw him out, Han. It's time for some rain."

"Sir," Han said, with obvious concern, "are you up to that?"

"Piece of cake. Besides, listen to them out there." He put a hand behind his ear, and Han tilted his head to listen, too, but the man he was holding was cackling noisily, interfering.

Han shook him, gave him a barbed look, and said, "Shut up, man—"

"Mordred Brede."

"Whatever. I'm trying to hear." Apparently Han did something that caused discomfort, because the man grunted and did shut up, and then Lucky heard, too. Outside, almost but not quite lost in the wind, a thousand voices yelped and cried and hissed and moaned, chains rattled, ropes creaked, fog horns blew, ships' bells rang, and something kept saying, "boo."

"You see what I mean," Thurlock said. "There's so many of the blasted things. It would take us all night to get rid of them any other way."

Han nodded, then lowered his shoulder and, with a grunt heaved the black-robed man off the ground. Thurlock waved the door open and Han dumped his living load outside before he waved it shut again.

Another thunk rattled the oak, and a muffled "Ouch" came from the porch, followed by plain old cussing.

Thurlock raised his eyes and his arms and his staff and said, "Behlishan? Thurlock here. If you would please?" Rain poured immediately, pattering against roof and shingle, and all the other sounds ceased. The shadows fled from the window, Wizard flames surged in the hearth, and Han reached out a hand to help Lucky stand.

Over the Wizard's head, stretched like a rainbow from palm to palm, arced a golden light so beautiful Lucky could neither bear to look at it nor to turn away. It dispersed on the Wizard's breath and settled down into the corners and crannies of the old house driving out the last of the shadows, a comfort to follow the storm. Lucky leaned into Han, seeking strength the way a child will after a bad dream.

But the Wizard stood alone, sinking at the knees as if about to fall. His voice was low and rough and gravelly. "I need to reset the wards," he said, wobbling. "I could use some support."

In shock, Lucky came near the Wizard and saw him unimaginably old, frail, and thin, with parchment skin and blood pumping blue through tortuous veins at his temples. Lucky feared for himself and for Thurlock. But more than that, he wanted to help. With every sense he searched, wanting to find some small thing to give back to this man who had—in protecting him—so obviously given too much.

He started to say, "There's nothing I can do," but pain flared in his skull, and he realized that those words would have been a lie.

He took a long, slow breath, cornering some wild, neglected thing inside himself, and knowing suddenly that it had always been there, waiting to be tamed. At first he didn't recognize his own voice, so deep, so near that of a man. "I wish," he began, but he didn't know how to finish. This wish would make a difference. What should it be?

Finally, he said, "Safe."

Thurlock lifted his crinkled face and smiled, surprised. "Well," he said, "it's done, then. Isn't it?"

Lucky barely heard. As he'd spoken his wish, a fist of heat had formed at his solar plexus, then unfurled and pulsed out with his words, leaving him hollow, sick, and dizzy.

"Han," he croaked, and the Warrior's stalwart hands caught him. Swirling stars, then silent dark, then nothing.

11. No Rest for the Wizardly

Two hours after the storm, Thurlock sat at the table under the blazing chandelier, wearing an old grey robe, with a well-used purple blanket draped over his shoulders. His hair sprang out in a chaos of sweat-stiffened curls. Han, stepping into the room from the stairwell, was relieved to see he no longer trembled.

Thurlock pushed away the remains of his chicken soup and toast and asked after Luccan. It started a series of little conversations stuck together like beads on a string. While Han cleared the table, they discussed plans to go to Luccan's shack to retrieve his belongings.

"And while we're on the subject, Han, what exactly is he using for pajamas?"

"Yours, sir, of course. He was reluctant, but I assured him that Wizard's pajamas won't cause permanent damage, and that you're happy to share."

Thurlock snorted. "It's not as though you have any pajamas to loan."

"I knew you'd understand, sir."

"Fine," Thurlock backed down. "Get his clothes while you're there, and the Amber Knife."

As Han started washing up, Thurlock's tone turned grave. "I can't go with you and the boy tomorrow. I'll be going home. Again."

"Sir, with all this back and forth you're going to wear out the Portal," Han said, which was absurd. Portals could be collapsed, or lost. They could drift or invert, back up or kink, even freeze or overheat. Nobody had ever worn one out.

"Lili wants me to assure the Clan Leaders we'll clear up the problem with those cursed Blue Ice-drakes."

"So they'll stop the sacrifices."

A silver curl had fallen across Thurlock's face. He blew it away. "We like to believe we've changed since the Peril, but most Ethrans are just as superstitious now. She fears that if panic brings back Blood Ways in the North, others will follow suit. If she's bending her neck to ask for my help ..."

"It's serious."

"Precisely."

"And you can scold L'Aria, while you're there. Put the fear of the Wizard in her."

"The girl's been sassing the Lady Grace, if you can believe that."

Han smiled as he lit the burner under an old copper kettle. "You'll have tea in a bit."

"Extra sugar."

"Extra sugar, what, sir?"

"Please. Extra sugar, please. After the Clans I'll go to Nedhra City, do a bit of research in the University Archives. Willock's *World Windings*, in particular."

Han's hand halted a half-inch from a box of Lemon Sunrise tea. Willock was a name so infamous in the Sunlands that it had become synonymous with foul temper. *She's really got her Willock on today,* a student might say of a sharp-tongued schoolteacher. Or a parent would warn: *Don't you get all Willock with me, young man!*

He said, "Aren't those scrolls cursed?"

Thurlock clucked his tongue. "Nonsense. People are afraid to read them for fear of being thought grouchy—guilt by association. Even if information could be cursed, Willock couldn't have done it. As a Wizard, he was a charlatan. Had about as much magic as you've got in your big toe."

"I've got two of those, sir," Han said, and felt ridiculous for looking at one of said culprits where it tried to hide in its assigned sock.

"Fool that he was, though, he was observant, downright brilliant on astral influences and time flux ..." He drifted off, gazing beyond the dark M.E.R.L.I.N. "What else did you and the boy talk about?"

"I explained that, though unpleasant, recoil is expected after powering up and releasing a spell."

"Did he seem to understand?"

Han stepped into the dining room to look Thurlock in the eye. "He looked at me as though I'd grown three heads." The Wizard laughed heartily. "But," Han added, "it was you that scared him the most."

"Because of my awesome power, or because he saw me looking my age?" Thurlock wiggled his eyebrows, and his toothy grin was comical.

Han smiled at the clowning, but didn't laugh. "You scared me too, sir. You seemed ... drained."

Thurlock sighed and gathered his soft purple blanket closer. He rose from the table, joints popping. "It's because we're here, in this world. Behl is distant. Simple things like Wizard fire and parlor tricks remain easy; but calling so much light against such a foe, drawing down the rain, that kind of magic never comes cheap. Here in Earth, I had to spend enormous sums of energy to do it. But I'm alright," he said, and collapsed into an armchair, groaning. "Spry as a kitten." Raising his voice over the kettle's whistle, he said, "About Luccan, he'll master it in good time."

Lemon-scented steam bathed Han's face as he poured hot water over the teabag. "Lessons, sir? I should think it will be better once he's taught to focus his power through his tools."

"You're right. He'd learn best by starting at the beginning just like anyone else. Considering everything, though, there won't be any lessons just now. His tools are tied up with his identity; it would be dangerous to use the one without the other." He scratched roughly at his beard as if to roust a pest. "And because he is Suth Chiell, if he does put the two together ... Well, you saw what happened with the Key."

Han slapped his forehead. "I can't believe I'd forgotten that, sir. I didn't even salve the burn."

"No need for salve; it may leave a mark, but the injury will already have healed." Thurlock leaned sideways, eyeing Han in the kitchen. "He needed protection in that storm, and he got it. The Key of Behliseth burned him, but I'd wager my knee caps it saved him from worse."

Han brought Thurlock his sweet tea and joined him by the fire.

Thurlock sipped, smiled his thanks, and then grew somber. "Am I right in assuming that you used all your skills to examine Maizie this afternoon?"

"Of course."

"Then you know what was done to her."

"I don't, sir. I've told you that," Han said, and though he wondered what the Wizard was getting at, he jumped at the opportunity to talk about his frustration. "It was as if her thoughts had been coated with something slippery. And I don't know why my talent failed. It's never happened before."

"Yes it has."

"No. I mean—"

"I know what you mean, and yes it has. Your talent failed in exactly this same way before."

Han's face wrinkled with puzzlement. "When?"

"Two-hundred odd years ago? You were seventeen. You'd always dug into your brother's mind as easily as your own. Suddenly, every time you tried, he sent you a clear 'no,' but you convinced yourself you didn't hear it."

"I remember," Han said, keeping his tone calm despite a blaze of anger. The old man knew very well that if there was one subject that was always a sore one for Han, this was it. He resented the old man raising it. "This isn't the same," he said, picking at a loose thread in the chair's upholstery, sullen like the seventeen-year-old he'd been.

Thurlock nagged, "Don't pick at that, Han, you'll make it worse." Han chuckled, and a smile flickered over the Wizard's face. "It wasn't a question, my friend. You *know* what's wrong with that dog. I saw Maizie for two seconds while she was leaping for Luccan's throat in a power storm, a thousand things going on, and I'm not a mind reader. Yet I saw clearly what had been done.

"There's one magic with that profile, one person with that signature. *You know them both.*"

Han knew Thurlock, too, and it was plain that his patience had about fled. Yet, he persisted. "Sir, you're not suggesting—"

Thurlock slapped a hand down on the chair's arm. "Behl's whiskers, I'm not suggesting anything. I'm telling you to admit to yourself the simple truth."

"So if I don't say what you want to hear, what will you do, use a Command on me?"

"Don't insult me Han! Can I compel *even you* if need be? Yes! Will I if I must? Yes, again. This is far too important for me to allow you to hide from the truth." He paused to draw a breath and blow it out. The red that had suffused his face faded. In a quieter tone, he said. "I rather hope you'll face this on your own. Less painful in the long run."

After a heavy pause, Han's voice came out half-strangled. "Sir, it's not possible." He closed his eyes and let his shoulders fall, his sigh an admission of truth. "Okay, it is."

Silence followed, and Thurlock's voice scarcely broke it. "Would you like some coffee, Han?"

"Yes," he said, and though he felt drowned in weariness he added, "I'll make some."

"No. You sit, for once. I'll see to it."

Han looked up in surprise. Thurlock's eyes twinkled mischief. He wagged a crooked finger and a glass pot full of steaming, aromatic, brown liquid hovered before him. Another twitch brought a mug gliding from the kitchen, and a wave directed the pot to pour. It topped off the brew just below the mug's thick brim and then went off to the kitchen while the cup came over to Han, who took it in two hands and laughed. "Sir, you shouldn't have."

"I had a good reason for that magic," Thurlock grinned, "A friend in need of something to smile about. Besides, parlor tricks don't take anymore out of me than a flight of stairs—less probably."

Han blew on the hot liquid and sipped. The billowing steam and familiar bitter taste offered comfort. "I wasn't lying," he said, "not deliberately. I didn't want to see it. I still don't." He shook his head. "What is it about the idea that ... that Lohen Chiell is back ... alive ... that he's done this to Luccan's dog ... . Why am I so desperate to deny it?" The question would have been rhetorical if he had posed it to anyone but the Wizard.

"No mystery, Han," Thurlock said, "And no great failing. He's your elder brother. You don't want to see him as someone who could work dark magic at all, never mind harm Luccan. You want always to remember him as that brave young man that saved you from worse than death when you were helpless."

Han sipped his coffee, still wonderfully hot, and watched the flames dance in the hearth. It wasn't until he turned and met Thurlock's eyes with his own steady gaze that the Wizard spoke again.

"Nothing your brother is now," he said, "or ever will be, will change what he was in the past. You don't have to relinquish your right to love him."

***

Silence blanketed the house as Lucky stumbled down the stairs, half-awake. The stairwell was as dark as a gravestone's shadow, but moonlight draped the archway at its end. The glowing arc framed a monster with hair standing out in silver-limned coils like a twisted halo.

When Lucky caught sight of that giant he gasped in sudden, wide-awake terror. Shuffling backward up the stairs, he stumbled, but instead of crashing to the bottom, he was pulled up short in that nightmare's iron grip.

"You're alright, Luccan," Thurlock said, setting him upright.

Lucky's knees melted and he plopped down on the nearest step to recover. A moment later, he said, "I had a dream." He was astonished. He hadn't intended to say anything.

"I'll listen, if you'd like to tell me," Thurlock said.

"Yes, sir," he answered, surprising himself again.

Thurlock scared him even when it wasn't the dark of night. Yet, the old man had spoken softly, and now that Lucky's imagination had settled the stairwell seemed warm, small, safe. With robes whispering and stair treads creaking, Thurlock eased his long-legged frame down to sit three steps away and tilted his head to hear, perhaps kind, perhaps concerned.

"I dreamed I was a little boy," Lucky said. "I dreamed of having a father."

For a moment, Thurlock said nothing, and Lucky heard the house creak as if leaning in to listen. "Was it a bad dream," the old man asked, "Were you afraid?"

"No, I wasn't scared. We were playing some kind of game, I think." Lucky tried to remember the pictures in the dream, but nothing much came to him except a feeling of being protected and happy. He recalled his own childish giggle and a husky laugh from deep in his father's chest. "It was a good dream, I guess."

"But you're troubled by it."

"It's just that I never dream about a father." Lucky's words rushed out and echoed in the stairwell, striking him, on their return, as peculiar. "I dream about my mother—at least a woman I think is my mother—all the time." But the truth was Lucky never thought about his father even when he was awake. In three years it hadn't crossed his mind to wonder about the man except in rare times when someone had asked, and then he'd only felt mildly curious.

How odd that seemed now, and incredibly painful. A wave of grief swept over Lucky, as if his emotions were trying to make up in one swoop for having forgotten about the man. For an awful second he felt the press of tears. He shoved his hair back ruthlessly and whispered, "I don't understand."

Lucky heard Thurlock stirring in the shadows, heard the rasp as he chafed his beard and a sound like bellows as the big man filled his lungs and then sighed. "I don't understand, either, Luccan." His hand fell on Lucky's ankle and gave it a friendly squeeze.

"But I believe," he said, "that it must be a good thing that you dream of him now. To lose your father was a sad event in any case. To have lost even the memory of him ..."

Seconds trickled by, and then Thurlock cleared his throat. "But then knowing what you've forgotten may be a step toward remembering. That's the bright side, if there is one."

"Wow," Lucky said, unable to bite back sarcasm. "Really, thanks." Thurlock made a funny noise, and Lucky's cheeks burned, ashamed of his rudeness and afraid of its consequences. He'd mumbled, "Sorry, sir," before he realized the Wizard was laughing.

"Oh, don't fret, Luccan. You're right. A rather dimwitted response, I'd say, coming from a Wizard as old as stone." His low laugh rumbled again, and then he said, "I'll tell you what. To make up for that stellar wisdom, ask me one good question, and I'll do my best to answer it well. A 'why' question, I'd suggest. I'm told Wizards are especially good at those."

Lucky pondered and shunned a hundred questions, and then it struck him. There was only one thing to ask, here in the close safety of night. "Why can't you just tell me, Thurlock," he asked. "Why can't you tell me the things that you know, that I've forgotten?"

"Excellent. Like all the best questions that one has a simple answer. Here it is: I want you to get home safe. I'll explain," he said, and scooted up the two intervening steps.

Lucky made room on the stair and they sat side by side, facing the veil of moonlight. The Wizard's warmth felt solid and welcome.

"You see," Thurlock said, "there are a few ways for us to get from here to Ethra, but it's complicated, because Ethra and Earth occupy more or less the same space. And then, too, there are other worlds, other times, other possibilities." He stopped talking, scratched his beard, shook his head, and made a noise that sounded like, "Umph."

Lucky hoped that a more coherent explanation would follow.

"I suppose that sounds pretty strange," Thurlock said, and Lucky narrowly avoided responding with the ever-useful term, *duh*. "For now, perhaps we'd best leave it at that. What I want to make clear is that the ways to get home aren't like boarding a train or driving a car. They're the strongest magic we Ethrans know, and yet, at the same time, not magical in the least."

"Wait," Lucky said, scratching vigorously at his scalp. "What?"

Thurlock chuckled. "Sounds convoluted, doesn't it? It isn't really, but I invariably find describing and explaining problematic—thus I'm a Wizard and not a scientist." Lucky felt another squeeze on the ankle and found it curiously comforting. "Let's try this," Thurlock ventured. "It's not possible for a person to travel from world to world if they have no magic in them. But magic, as we usually define it, doesn't work at all on the way."

"Just tell me," Lucky exclaimed. "What does work?"

The Wizard's voice carried a teasing smile. "It's simple Luccan," he said. "You only have to know who you are and where you want to go."

***

Han stumbled in through the front door, thinking about a figure of speech Earthborns use, *the wee hours of the morning*. The present hour must be the most 'wee' of all. He rarely got so tired that he woke up groggy at any hour, but last night had been an exception. By evening's end he'd been asleep on his feet. He'd fallen into bed and resolved not to get up before daybreak, no matter what.

Except in the unlikely event of emergency. Such as, apparently, this.

He flipped a switch and the chandelier lit up just as Thurlock tripped off the bottom stair into the living room. Though muted, the light shone too bright for bleary eyes and both men brought an arm up as a shield. After their eyes began to adjust, they stood on opposite sides of the room and blinked sleep-deprived looks at each other.

"A call," Thurlock said.

"Yeah."

"An emergency."

"Uh-huh." Han hitched up the too-large pajamas he wore and, keeping the legs off the floor shuffled to the kitchen. He ran tap water into a cup for a quick and lazy version of Thurlock's tea. For himself, he poured cold coffee from the Wizard's magic pot. He stuck both cups in the microwave.

"The boy's okay." Thurlock announced, standing in the kitchen doorway. He leaned on his umbrella and hugged a frayed orange terrycloth robe around his middle. "And," he added, demonstrating keen powers of observation, "you've stolen my pajamas again."

"Borrowed," Han said, over the microwave's final beep. In brighter moments he thought of the appliance as a little miracle of Earth-made kitchen technology. Now he muttered curses, poking at it blindly trying to open the door.

Thurlock watched him fumble for a while and then rolled his eyes. He said, "Han, you're a disaster of apocalyptic proportions, begging to erupt. I'll get my own tea." Reaching for his cup, he said. "Whatever the problem is, it must be important or they wouldn't call in the middle of the night."

"It's morning, really."

"If you say so." In the dining room, Thurlock fumbled in a pocket for his spectacles, and then laid them on the table. Standing behind his chair, he pointed the golden tip of his umbrella at the M.E.R.L.I.N. "Receive." The device crackled and the glass swirled with color, and then ordered itself into a scene. In a sunlit, spring-green room in Ethra, the sisters Liliana and Rosishan stood side-by-side near a table of golden wood. The curtains puffed with morning breeze, the ancient pine floor shone with centuries of polish, and multicolored vases overflowed with blossoms.

"Ladies," Thurlock said, creaking into a bow.

"Yeah," said Han, holding up his PJs, drinking coffee, and bowing too.

"Oh," Liliana gasped, "What time is it there?"

Thurlock cleared his throat, but didn't answer. He was attempting to clean his spectacles with the hem of his robe.

"Too-bloody-early in the morning," Han muttered. He swished coffee around in his mouth and, while scrunching his waistband to keep his pants up, suggested they be seated. He ignored the sisters' shocked expressions, believing them insincere. Chair legs scuffed over floors in both worlds.

Thurlock called the meeting to order, senatorial despite his orange garb. "Shall we proceed? You request formal Council, I take it, Ladies?" Lili and Rose nodded. "And it can't wait for full Conclave?"

Rose muttered, "Obviously."

Or perhaps she only thought it.

"Alright, then," Thurlock said. "Called to order, etcetera." He primed his voice with a gulp of tea, made a sour face—clearly having forgotten the sugar—and addressed his niece formally. "Lady Grace, Liliana, begin please."

Lili was all business and wore a prim expression to prove it, but she started with a digression, mentioning the storm. The shock waves from all the power set loose in that conflict had disrupted magic in Ethra. "For an hour or so we found even a simple charm impossible." She believed it boosted her argument that Luccan should come home, "ready or not."

"Save it, Lili," Thurlock said, ignoring the formalities. "For your sake, I hope this isn't the reason you disturbed my sleep." He put an elbow on the table, and leaned his head against his fist.

Lili stuck her bottom jaw out and said, "Well, this is Council, where we vote, and my vote is—"

"We're wasting time," Thurlock said. "Let's assume everyone votes yes, even those who are absent. Now it's my turn, and I say, 'Overruled.' The nays are thus victorious, having absolutely creamed the opposition." He drained his cup of bitter tea and allowed a moment's silence. Then he spoke again, leaving sarcasm out. "That wasn't, I assume, the matter you wanted to bring to Council."

Lili took a rainbow colored shawl from the back of the chair and pulled it across her shoulders. "It's about L'Aria," she said, with the moue of someone who'd just eaten lemons whole. "The other day when she ran off, she apparently hiked up to Tiro's Eye to do some scrying."

At first, Han was surprised. Tiro's Eye was a seer's pond in the Greenwood, the forest that covered the northwestern Sunlands. Though the pond was situated so that weather never disturbed its glassy surface, the slightest unrest of a nearby human spirit would mar its smoothness with ripples. Most seers never mastered the stillness it took to put the pond to use. *But perhaps it's to be expected,* he thought. L'Aria was, after all, the daughter of the being—only partly human—for whom the pond was named.

Thurlock said, "I'd wondered how soon she would figure out she could do that."

"Well, good for her," Lili said, and everyone else traded amused glances. "That's not the point, though. She says she's found Lohen Chiell; that he's alive, and he's there in Earth."

Thurlock said. "Well, if anyone could find him, it would be her. And she's right; he's here; he has the Black Blade and he's used it. He worked a possession on Luccan's dog, set a nasty hex. She's raving mad, and whenever she sees Luccan she goes for his jugular."

Liliana's face went so pale that her freckles seemed to float, so Thurlock hurried on. "Don't worry; he's in no danger now."

Han interjected, "You know, I didn't mention this before, what with one thing and another, but she may be less of a threat to Luccan than it seems. Except for last night, in the midst of the Witch's worst, she's been fighting that curse." He stared at his hands, chewing his bottom lip and lost in thought.

"Explain," the Wizard said, impatient.

"The hex drives her to attack Luccan. Something inside her refuses."

Thurlock reflected. "Perhaps the maker of that curse didn't have his whole heart in it."

Lili made a small noise of derision, "We'd be fools to believe that," she said, and ignored the Wizard's glare. "More likely the Blade itself resisted. It might have been fashioned with the magic of the void, and it's certainly deadly, but it was never meant for his kind of cruel—"

Thurlock held up a hand that effectively forestalled the remainder of Liliana's diatribe. "Perhaps we're trying to unlock a mystery that doesn't exist," he said. "Maybe the dog simply loves the boy." He smiled under arched brows, daring anyone to argue.

"All right, fine. Love, unexplained mystery, or blind luck, it doesn't matter. Right now, you said, he's safe. That's what counts." Lili put the prim look that said 'business' back on her face. "We were talking about L'Aria."

"We were talking about Lohen Chiell," Thurlock corrected.

"Both," said Rose.

Liliana let her fist fall against the wood with an annoyed thump. "L'Aria tells us that Lohen is disturbed. She thinks we should help him. She wants us to allow her to go to Earth to find him"

"And I say she should go."

"And I say, Rose, you are as mad as the girl."

111

"And I," Thurlock said, defusing the coming explosion, "am surprised that she asked permission. Rose, why do you agree she should come?"

"You know how she is about him, Thurlock. She's always insisted he wasn't guilty. Of anything." Rose sat back and ran both hands through her mane of shining black hair, exposing the spear of silver-grey over her left brow. "She's been devoted to him since she was a toddler."

"Old news," said Lili, drumming her fingers.

Han cringed, expecting Rose to lash out at her half-sister. The two never harmonized on anything except the magic they worked together with their strange, spiral wands.

Rosishan only shook her head. "To tell the truth," she said, "I think Lili's right. He's lost. No one can save him. But L'Aria's always had—"

"A mind of her own," Lili said.

"—a stabilizing affect on Lohen. He's never harmed her—he protects her. Maybe, she can disarm him, so to speak." Rose shot a look at her sister, knowing but not unkind. "She's more capable than Lili thinks. Her power doesn't equal her father's yet, but her song gets stronger every day. And she's sassy, but not bad. I say, let her do what she can."

They talked about it for a while, at both tables, back and forth. Then Rose said, "Lili votes 'no'. I say 'yes.' Han, what's your vote?"

After a long, uncomfortable moment, Han said, "I can't sort this out, Rose. He's my brother. It clouds my thinking. I'll defer to Thurlock."

Perhaps Rosishan had counted on Han's support, thinking their long friendship should guarantee it, because her world-renowned temper flared. She slammed a hand down and shouted, spitting daggers from her dark eyes. "You *always* defer to Thurlock."

Rose was probably the only person alive that could dependably cause Han to lose his cool and now, by force of habit, he raised his own voice. "There you go again, pulling a Willock. And I'll be darned if it doesn't always turn out—"

"Bicker later, children." Thurlock's tone was exactly the one he had used to stop their fights when they'd both been six years old, and they went silent as quickly as they had then. "Rose," the Wizard said, "you and L'Aria are right in a way. She might be able to help him, and if she could bring him somehow back to his true self … well, we all know it would be a boon for Luccan, and for Ethra.

"Yet," he continued, shifting his gaze to meet that of his niece, "Lili, you have my vote on this one, and I guess that means you have Han's as well. That's three to one."

He pushed his chair back from the table, signaling to all that he was about to close the meeting. Rose leaned forward as if to protest, but for the second time in the last half-hour Thurlock held up his hand. He said, "I'll be at the Sisterhold tomorrow—or I guess that's today.

"As for L'Aria, I'll tell her myself to stay put, not that she'll listen. If she decides to leave all she needs is her own voice and a knee-deep pool of water. Still, if we can, let's try to give both of these young people a chance to survive to adulthood, shall we?"

***

In the dream, Hench stands under a wide blue sky, a breeze cooling his face. He sees a woman with golden hair and green eyes like jewels. She turns toward him smiling; surprise sparks her eyes. "Do you hear him?" They watch a toddling boy with hair the dark red of cedar bark and skin like heartwood.

"Papa," the child says, his first word. He reaches, asking to be held and Hench bends low to gather him up, long-forsaken smile tugging at the corners of his mouth.

"Wake, Lohen Chiell." Another voice speaks in the dream, a voice Hench has known all his life. He doesn't wake but the bright child vanishes and Hench's lame hand grips only the Knife. "Blade Keeper," the voice chides, and then calls him again by his true name. "Lohen Chiell, did you believe me lost? My faith never failed. It was your oath that was broken."

Hench flies, then, to another place and time, another world. He sees mountains painted purple and umber with dawn, marching into grey distance.

He stands, brown curls blowing wild in the bitter wind, at the rim of the never-fathomed canyon, Mardhral.

He listens, searches that wind, his last hope. He prays to hear in its moaning a single word, a name the loss of which is so painful he can bear it no longer. The name of the son that he cannot reach, cannot find, cannot help. The name of the son he has betrayed.

The wind doesn't speak, and the crevasse yawns wide and black and bottomless at his feet. He heaves the Black Knife over the edge. As it falls, it catches a sunbeam and turns the brilliance back on him. The light pierces his eye and burns it to dust and fume. Still the wind is silent, and he throws himself after the Blade into the bottomless canyon.

In the dream Lohen wishes the deed could be undone. In the dream, the Knife falls into his hand and they plunge together into darkness. The Blade speaks, in the dream, telling him how he might have his wish.

"Make right the last wrong you have done, so that we might begin again."

12. A Fine Time to Rebel

There had been a wreck on Meridian. Red and blue lights flashed against wet, mid-morning clouds, and traffic was jammed to a stop. Lucky was about to suggest to Han that they get off and walk. Though it would be a long trek through the rain from here to his shack, where they hoped to find Maizie and collect his things, walking would be better than being stuck on a bus between a bass-booming low-rider and a moving van. But traffic unsnarled, the bus moved, and he reconsidered.

He looked sideways at the man sitting next to him, took in his carefully placid features, his eyes which avoided meeting Lucky's, and the muscles which, even at rest, proclaimed raw power. The cords of his jaw rippled, a tiny, repeated motion—he wasn't truly tranquil. Like the Wizard's umbrella, he was more than he appeared.

With a note of challenge, Lucky said, "You're not a servant."

Han glanced at him, then looked away and chewed his lip for a moment. Quietly, he said, "Han Shieth is my name, but it's a title, too. Han Rha-Behl Ah'Shieth; that's the long form, the old language. Rough translation: Wizard's Left Hand." He settled back into his seat and crossed his arms. "It refers to a Warrior's shield side. I'm the Wizard's shield."

"Wizard's Left Hand," Lucky whispered, liking the sound. Exciting, like Knight of the Round Table, Cheyenne Dog Soldier, Captain of the Starship Enterprise. "But what do you do?"

"Sometimes it's about fighting, but Thurlock doesn't need a bodyguard. Basically, I deal with things I can handle, so Thurlock is free to do things only he can do."

"Like in that storm, what you did with your sword?"

"Yes," Han said slowly, "like that." He turned to Lucky, grinning, and it changed everything about him. "More often, I make sure he remembers to eat, has clean clothes, and can find his socks."

Lucky couldn't help but smile back, and then for a time he could ask questions easily.

He asked about Maizie.

Han explained, "Not demons, it's magic that possesses her, fills her mind with an idea and forces her to act on it."

That seemed less hopeless.

He asked why Han had come with him, why not Thurlock. "I mean, he's the heavy, right?"

A perplexed look came over Han's face. "I'm a cream puff?"

"Sorry," Lucky said, flaming with embarrassment.

"He had to be elsewhere for Wizard work." The last two words seemed to deserve quote marks.

"Like?"

"Reading," Han said. "He went to a very large library." They laughed together and when they'd stopped, a friendly silence sat between them on the cracked cushion.

"I have other questions, Han, several serious ones."

"Start with one."

Lucky blurted, "Who am I?"

Han shook his head. "Try again, lad."

The bus lumbered forward and stopped again, and now the strobes from the accident scene bounced off the faded, rain-soaked walls of the old Projects. Lucky hugged his bare arms against seeping chill, his ease gone. In the streets, a ragged man tipped up a bottle-shaped paper bag; a skinny dog nosed under heaps of garbage. Lucky recalled the times he'd taken shelter there, so many people hid behind those condemned walls. Yet the nights he'd hidden there had been his loneliest.

On the bus, he leaned a bit toward Han. He rocked and tilted around corners and breathed exhaust, but instead of the engine's whine, he heard Han's words in the storm. *"You have strength you don't know about."*

He asked, softly, "Could I have stopped it?"

"No," Han answered, not asking what he meant.

"Could I have helped?"

"You did."

The next question, Lucky whispered. "Was it magic, Han, what I did at the end?"

"Yes, it was." Han spoke low and steady as always, but it seemed to Lucky that the words ricocheted through the bus like three cartoon bullets.

No, he insisted. *I did not do magic. I don't know any Wizards or people with swords. It's a dream. No, it's a nightmare, but I'm going to wake up.*

His head began to throb. He gripped his elbows like life ropes, and slid down in his seat. Han watched him through narrowed eyes. The bus seemed to revolve, and on its third turn, Lucky croaked, "Han, I'm going to be sick."

Desperate to stop the wave of nausea, he resorted to old tricks. *Normal, normal,* he mentally chanted his calming mantra. *Normal, normal, normal ...*

And if I could just wish things and make them true, why am I here? All the times I've wished—

Han answered. "All powers have limits, lad. Yours, too."

Lucky shoved his hands through his hair and scratched at his scalp, painful and vicious. *I just want to undo it. I wish I could go backward five days. I wish ... I WISH it would all go away.*

He said out loud, "I wish—"

Before he could say more, that he wanted to be left alone and never see Han and Thurlock or anything magic again, Han grabbed Lucky's arm hard enough that it hurt. He flinched and immediately Han loosened his grip, but his eyes burned and his voice turned gruff— pleading and angry at the same time.

"Don't." he growled. "Don't say it." He looked straight into Lucky's eyes, and dropped his voice to a hoarse whisper. "Be careful. *Be very careful what you wish.* Your wishes may not have unlimited power, but they aren't trivial. *Don't play with them.*"

Han's warning lingered, taking up space on the seat between them, and VC Transit Sixty-six seemed all of a sudden a very crowded bus. The familiar landmarks of 12th and Main came into view; The Quick-Shoppe, Fail-safe Bail Bonds, the rusty VW in the third curbside parking space. *Normal,* Lucky thought, and he was glad they'd be getting off. He reached for the buzzer.

Han touched Lucky's hand, and whispered, "Wait."

Every nerve jangling in response, Lucky froze.

He followed the direction of Han's gaze to the Quick-Shoppe parking lot, where the pavement crawled with strange people who milled about like bugs suddenly exposed by a kicked-up rock. Dressed in black, they hunched shoulders and lurked in shadows. Way in the back of the lot, alongside a windowless wall, under neon that flickered weak in the daylight, the Crown Victoria brooded.

"We won't get off the bus, Luccan," Han said. "I'll take you back to Thurlock's house."

Lucky watched the black-clad group wander aimlessly until the bus pulled away, and then he sat back in his seat. He remembered the awful power in last night's storm, and he told himself, *Han is right, it isn't safe.*

But ice-cold energy rolled through his limbs as if someone had whipped his nerves into a milkshake. Sitting still ceased to be an option. As the bus neared the First Street stop, he snapped upright. "I'm getting off the bus, Han, whether you like it or not."

Han reached past Lucky and pulled the buzzer.

***

Five minutes later, the rain had disappeared. The summer sun burned bright, but not sweet. Standing with Han in a square of hot shade under a green canvas awning that smelled of grease, Lucky again tried to ignore the anxious twitch of his calf muscles. He pretended to blame the muggy heat, and the sweat rolling down his ribs for the antsy way he felt.

Han seemed not to notice Lucky's distress, or the heat, or the noise of cars, trucks, and bicycles splashing through the sea of rainwater pooled around the clogged run-off drain.

"Go back to Thurlock's," he said, his voice hard but not frantic. "I'll find Maizie, and I'll get your things."

"No."

"Lad, you've picked a fine time to rebel."

That's not it. But how can I explain? I can't help it. I have to move!

Across the street, a motion caught his eye, people in black again, and he realized he wasn't safe anywhere on the streets. Though the least safe action he could think of was to separate from Han, he started walking down First Street toward the Ravine. It might have looked bold, but he shook inside.

He thought about the trail he'd have to take from here to get to his shack via the Ravine. First Street dead-ended at an old mill yard, and that ended in a sharp drop to Black Creek. Poison Oak crowded the forest that ran along the top of this part of the gorge, and snake holes riddled the area like Swiss cheese. The slippery, almost vertical wall of the Ravine offered the only passable trail, a fold in the basalt a few feet below the canyon rim a hazardous venture, best not taken alone.

Han whistled, a single note, and hope jumped up in Lucky's throat. He stopped walking and turned, and when Han caught up with him, he resisted the impulse to dash for the gorge.

Han spoke loudly over the rush of traffic. "Luccan, I've got three choices." He ticked them off on his fingers. "I can let you go alone. I can take you back by force. I can go with you. Each choice could have consequences I don't want to name."

A Freightliner roared by on Main, accelerating through several low gears, and Han tugged at Lucky's elbow, urging him down First Street toward the old mill. A block-and-a half from Main, where the street's noise faded, he pulled Lucky around to face him. "You want to go into that Ravine, or maybe, you think you have to go. We can go together but, by all that's good, lad, *you must abide by my terms.*"

"Thurlock would be ..." Lucky let the words trail off; they felt defiant and disloyal. He finished the sentence silently. *He'd be mad if you let me go alone.*

"Thurlock might be mad," said Han, "that I let you go at all. But the terms aren't about that. They're about safety, possibly about staying alive. Here they are: One, stick with me close. Two, if we get separated, go back to Thurlock's. Three, if trouble comes, do what I tell you to do, no matter what you see, hear or feel. Agreed?"

Lucky did agree. It seemed a fair trade for having the strong man at his side, but Han's warnings and ground rules had set his heart galloping again. Part of him wanted to say, *never mind, run away*, and he feared that if he opened his mouth, the words would blurt themselves. He shut his lips and nodded.

Lucky felt Han's eyes burning through his skull. He started to look at his feet to escape the painful scrutiny, but Han said, "No." So, he summoned his resolve, raised his eyes to Han's, and held them there.

Finally Han nodded. "Good enough, let's go."

Past the mill yard, a mound of grey-black basalt guarded the entrance to Black Creek Ravine, smooth and round like the helmeted head of some enormous watchman. A single pine towered at each side of the stone hill, marines at attention, sentinels bracing the gate.

Feverish sun beat down, soaking up remnants of rain like a hot rag. All around, not even a whisper of a breeze disturbed dandelion or dust. But a phantom wind rushed through that gate and beyond it the air over Black Creek writhed, smoky with twisting plumes of mist, grey and black and electric blue.

Lucky's brain screamed, *that's not normal. Go back!* But in the same instant his feet broke for the gate and ran, pounding the earth so fast his steps beat into a single long sound. He heard Han shouting as if from far away, and he should have cared, he knew that, but he couldn't stop and he couldn't slow down or even make himself swerve. He felt like a fish, hooked and hauled on a taut line.

The stone mound was eight feet high, but Lucky leapt and landed only two footfalls before he flew over the summit. He was still airborne when the world cracked around him like a silent sonic boom. Before that concussion, he could hear Han shouting, see the sun and taste its heat. After, he was alone in a blue-grey soundless world and the sun's orb had stopped in the sky, black and cold.

Sound rushed in as hard wind squalled from the east, blasting Lucky with sand and hurling pebbles. He raised an arm to shield his eyes from the blinding grit but he still couldn't see. He came down too hard, too fast on the crevice in the rock that formed the trail and his feet stopped there, but the rest of him didn't. His arms reeled in open air. He was about to plunge a hundred yawning feet to the hungering rocks below.

A great bird swooped in with a shrill cry. Its wings spanned twice Lucky's height or more, and its black feathers shimmered every color against the dark sun. Lucky teetered, seized by fear that he would fall or that he wouldn't and the predator would pluck him off the slope and carry him away to feed its young. The raptor flew closer until Lucky could see himself reflected in its bright black eye, and its wings thrust air against him with enough force to counter the wind. He regained his balance.

Then the east wind stopped as suddenly as held breath. For that quiet moment Lucky's fear and shock abated, and he could hear himself think. Sensibly. Smart thoughts.

This is crazy. I'm going back.

He pivoted instantly to make good on that pledge, but the east wind snarled anew and threw itself at him with such force that it propelled him westward along the trail. Hunched against the blast, shielding his eyes, he fought but he was losing ground. Driven back step by step, he put out enormous effort just to land each footfall solid on the trail and not over its deadly edge.

In the throes of the struggle, he stumbled on a quiet place inside his mind. He wondered what had become of Han, wished the man was there to help. Eventually Han appeared some distance back on the trail. Again, as in the storm, he shone like a candle against darkness, but this time the flame sputtered and flashed in the wind. He struggled, but never faltered, and when he drew close enough, he reached out.

Just as Lucky was about to grab hold, the ground shook so hard it felt as though the world would crack wide open. With no time to adjust his stance and nothing to catch onto, Lucky toppled and started to slide. He tried to hug the stone, clawed at it, but it was silky smooth and offered nothing to grasp. A long way down, loosened stones splashed into the creek. The sound conjured pictures, news photos, grainy images of Hank George fallen. Shattered. Killed.

For a moment, Lucky's right foot hung unanchored in empty air, his left shoe jammed into a tiny crack in the stone. Then that shelf gave, and there was nothing left to halt his slide. He knew he would die. As he slipped slowly down the stone he grew calm, thinking farewells. *I wish I'd had a chance to say good-bye to Maizie ... I really should have told Thurlock thank you for letting me borrow his pajama pants ...*

Han slapped a rough grip on his wrist.

Rude interruption.

He regained his senses quickly and with immense gratitude latched his other hand around Han's wrist.

"Hang on, Luccan," Han coaxed.

But the ground rolled and stones rained down on them from above and the wind thundered, slapping at them over and over, striking impossibly hard. They couldn't win. They couldn't prevail against such relentless force. Lucky decided to let go, sure that if he didn't he would pull Han down with him.

He heard a growl and looked up to where Han knelt awkwardly on the narrow path, struggling for purchase. The man's eyes were shut tight against the wind, which had stung them to tears. Salt had left tracks on his brown cheeks, the only softness in a hard, angry scowl. Suddenly, the copper eyes snapped open and locked on Lucky's. "NO," Han shouted. "No! Don't let go. Remember the terms, Luccan—you gave your word."

Han's grip couldn't possibly get tighter, but it did, until Lucky expected bones to break.

"This is trouble, and I'm telling you what to do. *Hold on.* Don't you *dare* let go."

So Lucky held on, and when Han flattened himself in the crevice, dug his elbows into the rock, and told him to tighten his arms and shoulder, he did his best to make them rigid. Han had enormous strength in his arms, but they needed leverage and it just wasn't there. Every time he tried to pull Lucky up, Han started to slip down. Lucky grew certain that though Han's sweaty fingers might not fail, his own eventually would.

"Gods," Han rasped. "Gods help us, I can't ..."

Out of the opaque sky the bird appeared again, big and black and loud, and stretched its talons toward Lucky's back. And it grabbed him by the seat of the pants. And Han tugged, and the bird thrust upward, and Lucky's feet and knees indulged in frantic, bug-like scrabbling. The next thing he knew, he was laid out flat along the rock-fold footpath, definitely not crying.

Han lay flat on the rock too, head to head with Lucky, one hand still gripping Lucky's arm. After a few minutes, even though the ground still felt a little shaky, both of them breathed slower and Lucky felt the heat of overexertion fade to the chill of emotional shock. Han sat up and silently helped Lucky do the same. He had composed himself considerably, setting his face into its habitual, between-smiles, stoic mask.

Using his hand as a visor to shield his eyes from the leaden glare, he scanned the skies. After a minute or so, he dropped the hand and stared straight ahead, doing some serious lip chewing. More time passed thus, and then he turned his head slightly and squinted out of the corner of his eye.

"Tell me Luccan," he said, "do you *know* that bird?"

Lucky still shook but he was pretty sure the ground had stopped. He answered Han with a shrug, a shake of his head, and a wobbly smile, concentrating on fortifying his knees to stand. Once he felt secure in the upright position, he asked, "Was that an earthquake for everyone, or did it happen just for us?"

Han opined that the quake and the wind and even the strange, dark sun had indeed been conjured for them. "Although," he said, "we won't know for sure until it doesn't show up on the five o'clock news." He smiled, and Lucky finally stopped quivering.

But then Han stepped back to study Lucky's condition, and his face lost all traces of humor.

Dark red globules of blood seeped through the dust that coated Lucky from head to toe. On his left side, which had taken the brunt of the abuse, patches of color showed at elbow and knee and on top of his foot. Judging from the pain behind his ear, Lucky figured that was probably bloody, too.

Han's voice sounded hoarse. "By the gods' grey whiskers, lad, your hands ..."

Flexing them open and closed to show Han, he answered, "They're fine, see?" They hurt, but it didn't matter. What were bruises and shredded skin, compared to the gaping wound in his conscience? *It was my fault. I should have listened. I almost got us killed.*

"I'll go back," he said, searching for a way to soothe his guilt. "I'll go back, if you think I should."

Han squeezed Lucky's least-scraped shoulder. "No point in going back, now. We're half-way there, and if there's more trouble headed our way, I'd bet Thurlock's pajamas it'll find us regardless." He pointed west with a bob of his chin, toward Lucky's shack. "Let's just go."

Lucky followed blindly and despite Han's assurances, remorse grew heavier with every step. He blamed himself for what had already happened; he worried about what would happen next and blamed himself for that, too. The more he mulled it the bigger it got until he felt like he rolled a giant red ball of shame and anxiety in front of him along the narrow trail.

Hoping to deflate it at least a little, he whispered, "I'm sorry." When Han didn't answer, he said it again, louder. "I'm really sorry."

Han stopped, pivoted, and crossed his arms. "I heard you the first time," he said. "Honestly, I heard you before you said it. I'll say this because it's true and you need to know it. What's happening here is not your fault. Got that?"

Han stood poker faced, staring, and Lucky didn't know what to say, so he nodded.

"Good," Han nodded back. "Now I'll say this because it's even truer, and you need to know it even more. Letting guilt run away with your brain and your courage between its big yellow teeth never does any good, lad. You might need those things."

They hiked the tortuous trail for half an hour and advanced maybe a half-mile west as the crow flies. Overhead, a steel grey sky gathered up the sun's heat and pressed it down on them like a crusher, squeezing sweat from every pore. The trail broadened to a yard-wide, not-quite-flat shelf of loose red soil and crumbling shale.

Laboring behind Han, Lucky kept his eyes on the man's straight back and sure stride. By force of will he kept own his head high and his shoulders unbent, struggling to emulate the self-mastery of the man he followed.

Han's words had stung, but they'd rung true, and now Lucky's twin habits, honesty and mule-headed tenacity, asserted themselves. He might not manage quick-witted and brave, but he could at least avoid dull and chicken-livered. To that end, he let the salt-sweat trickling in his wounds clear his head, and soldiered on.

Han's step slowed as the trail flattened and passed into a corridor leading through a grove of ancient myrtle trees. Waxy leaves turned the light and even the ground amongst gnarled roots emerald and silver. Protected here by a bend in the gorge from the winds that often stunted their kind to shrubs, the myrtles had achieved their towering, eighty-foot potential, and overhead, their branches stretched across the road to clasp hands with kin. Through their million laced fingers peeked a clear sky, free of the day's iron haze, blue and dazzling.

Lucky drew up next to Han and they stepped into the grove together. As Lucky crossed that threshold, he remembered how it felt, just two days ago, the first time he entered the Wizard's house. Magic abided here, too, though not the kind that could be cast with a spell or summoned with a staff. Pure magic, here, life and light. For Lucky and Han it conjured five hundred yards of blessed respite.

The instant they began to trod the leaf-padded ground a breeze whispered the sweet-bay scent to Lucky's nostrils. "I've been here before," he said softly, remembering that the grove sat almost exactly opposite Grandpa Hank's cabin across the Ravine. On rare days when the wind blew out of the south, the scent of this sanctuary would come with it over the creek, and Hank would sit on his porch, close his eyes, and drink it in.

Lucky lifted an arm to point. "There's a spring over there, back in the trees," he told Han, "and the water's good—sweet and cold."

Han met his eyes and Lucky saw something in the glance, appraisal, or perhaps appreciation. Han returned Lucky's smile and said, "We'll stop."

The niche was a short jaunt from the path, but those few strides plunged them into deep, cool shade. The water bubbled, astonishingly, from a cleft in a freestanding stone, smooth basalt and almost spherical stone. From its underground roots, the rock swelled as high as Lucky's shoulders.

Below the spring's egress, the rock wore green moss like a scraggly beard, and it bathed its round foot in a clear, leaf-littered pool. Lucky and Han followed suit, leaving Lucky's worn shoes standing in the shadow of Han's still-shining boots.

They laughed at nothing in particular and made trivial comments about how good the place felt. They rinsed their hands and took turns cupping them under the bubbling flow to slake thirst that suddenly seemed to Lucky as vast as the Mojave Desert. Then Han splashed his face, shook his hair loose and retied it, padded a few steps away and, to Lucky's astonishment, lay down full length on the aromatic ground and slept.

By the time Lucky had soaked off the caked blood-and-dust, he felt perhaps a year or two older and wiser and a great deal more human. He waded out of the pool, and sat on the ground to don his shoes. For the first time he caught sight of the pale, slender knife strapped to the inside of Han's boot. He stared at it with a shudder of premonition, and when he raised his eyes he found Han standing near, watching him.

"I'm a Warrior, Luccan. I'm never without a weapon."

Lucky nodded and finished putting on his shoes. He looked back only once as they left the shady niche behind. The sweet-scented gallery looked as bright, pure and good than on the way in, but Lucky's heart weighed him down. "You'll use it," he said. "You'll use the knife before the day is over, won't you, Han?"

"It seems likely," Han said, and there was no joy in his voice at all.

13. Stone Knives, Twins, and Strangers

Lucky and Han came to a place where the rocky path turned to muck beneath their feet, and there they stopped. They couldn't see the sun anymore, but behind dense grey clouds they could feel the hidden heat source arcing west. Lucky remembered the cool green of the myrtle grove with longing.

At the edge of the grove's shade, Han had stopped and offered Lucky a choice. "I don't think our enemy will come here," he'd said, "not yet. You'll be safe, if you want to wait while I go on."

Lucky declined, and he knew he'd made the right choice. He had Maizie to think about. And it was *his* life torn up for new construction. He wanted to have some small say in the end result. He couldn't do that lollygagging in the shade.

They stood on the edge of a broad oval of flat land where the rock shelf that had been a narrow footpath widened out to create a bowl colonized by centuries of wayward soil, seed, and rain. To Lucky's left a wall of smooth stone pushed out to make Black Creek bend its elbow, far below. The rock pushed up into a lip two feet higher than the ground, and then descended in palisades, a frozen waterfall of stone.

The last time Lucky had seen the place, it had been a green meadow dotted with sweet peas and daisies. He'd come here with Grandpa Hank to hear stories and picnic on smoked fish, saltines, and Coca-Cola. In the afternoon, they'd napped in the sparse shade beneath gnarly, aged red elders.

Now the elderberries had ripened to the color of blood. The green grass had been churned to black muck. The sky sagged, dimmed charcoal grey and weighted with the smells of sulfur, ash, and rot. The wind had stilled, but now the earth gave rise to a frail, cold breath that teased at littered papers and rags. Near Lucky's foot, a square of white shifted in the restless air, weighted on one kinked corner by a rune-embossed coin from another world. He bent to retrieve it and found his most treasured photograph, a Polaroid of him laughing with Hank. The faces had half peeled away.

A deep voice called out from the center of the field. The man who spoke wore a black cloak and a cowl pulled back to reveal coarse, curly black hair, pale skin and paler lips, and a heavy blue-black shadow where his beard strained to sprout. His smile only made him look morbid. His eyes, like black coals, emitted an icy gleam.

"At last," he said. "You're here. We've been waiting."

At the word 'we' Lucky noticed another man standing ten yards from the one who spoke. They looked identical, except for the slack-jawed expression on the second man's face and the fact that he held a captive. He grinned, but all the while kept a tight grip on the rope that wrapped his prisoner's neck and held a hood of black fabric over her face.

"Perhaps you remember *me*," the first man said, drawing out the last word as if it was very important. "I am Mordred Brede. Boff, here," he gestured with a snap of his fingers, "is my brother, as you no doubt guessed."

"We're twins!" Boff's gleeful exclamation earned him a rock to the kneecap, aimed expertly by his perhaps not-so-loving brother.

"As you also doubtless see," Mordred went on, "Boff is stupid, but strong. Unfortunately," he addressed Han, "Boff has this girl at his mercy. Our employer, the Witch-Mortaine Isa, thinks you might know her." He let the suspense hang for a few seconds, then snapped, "Show him, Boff."

While Boff worked the hood free of the rope, Mordred turned to Lucky with feigned sadness. "I, on the other hand, only have a silly stone knife."

Boff revealed the girl's face, or at least her eyes and nose, since the rest was hidden behind a gag.

Mordred held up the Amber Blade.

Han sucked in a startled breath. "L'Aria."

L'Aria flipped her sable hair free of the rope, eyes blazing. She strained so hard against the cord that tied her wrists that the muscles along her neck stood out.

Lucky registered her saucy attitude and her serious danger, but his eyes locked onto the amber in Mordred's hands. In strange fascination, he said, "My Knife." The amber glimmered in his eyes as if bright sun shone through. He could almost hear the stone call his name.

But what about the girl?

He charged like a bull, bent head aimed for Boff's ribs. Beside him, Han broke at the same instant, running at Mordred, extracting that nine-inch, pale metal blade from his boot while on the fly.

Lucky had covered half the twenty yards distance when a half dozen people wearing black cloaks popped out of the shadows and blocked his way. He pushed and kicked, swung fists and elbows, but they moved like robots and acted like they didn't feel a thing.

They had him hemmed in, but he tore an arm free and on momentum smacked his fist into someone's jaw. The unintended blow knocked the man it hit into the woman behind him and sent them both sprawling. The success surprised Lucky, but he wasted no time taking advantage of the breach it left in the enemy line. With balled fists he dove through and prepared to assault the mountain of a man called Boff.

"Luccan, stop!" Han's order rang with authority, and Lucky slammed to a halt so sudden that his shoes left skids in the mud.

Han's charge on Mordred had been a ruse. He ducked around Mordred's defensive crouch, whirled toward Boff, and—still running—raised his blade. It whispered past Lucky's nose to sever Boff's rope, slicing clean through and setting L'Aria free.

The folks in black cloaks were back on their feet and they crowded around L'Aria while she tried to work her wrists loose. Lucky wanted to help, but he took a clout on the head, and for seconds the world went dark.

When daylight returned, L'Aria had tugged off the hood and tossed it aside. Lucky reached her just as the five conscious Black-cloaks started throwing punches. Soon, Lucky and L'Aria stood back-to-back, surrounded by a gang with hands as cold as zombie-flesh and eyes like glass.

When Boff finally registered that the rope he held was attached to nothing, he roared and began to throw fists about like a blind madman. L'Aria and Lucky twisted and dodged and managed to miss being hit most of the time. But Boff wasn't really aiming and the people in black acted like they didn't know they should duck. Before long, three of them had gone down under friendly fire.

Mordred entered the fray, yelling his brother's name and cursing non-stop. He took hold of L'Aria's hair, yanked her head back, and raised his fist to haul the hilt of the Amber Knife down on her nose.

No, not her nose was an absurd thought. Lucky ignored it and focused on doing something about it.

The something he came up with was to dive at L'Aria, taking her down to the muddy ground beneath him. She survived the crush with only a squelching noise, and Lucky rolled quickly away. Lying on his back, he saw Boff stumble over L'Aria's legs and come crashing toward them both like a slain giant. Instinctively, he brought his feet up to take the brunt of the man's weight, expecting a two-hundred plus pound disaster.

It never came.

Mordred must have seen that with L'Aria's nose out of the way his brother's curly head would take the blow, but he didn't stop. If anything, he drove the hit home with a little added force. On impact, Boff's head made a sound like a thumped melon. His nose crunched when it struck the ground before the rest of his skull. He went completely still, but his breath rippled the blood from his nostrils like wind on a tiny red lake. *Proof of life.*

Lucky and L'Aria scrambled to their feet, L'Aria spitting mud, and the enemy charged. Lucky gave out as much as he got, slapping, kicking, and punching. L'Aria did a little punching, too, but when an attacker came at her face to face, she stiffened, leaned toward him and…

She's singing him to death!

The Black-cloaks seemed a bit dull to begin with, as if their own brains weren't in charge. Though L'Aria's song didn't actually kill anyone, it left them more confused.

Now and then during the fight, the black hoods moved out of the way and Lucky caught a glimpse of Mordred and Han.

Han retrieved his metal blade, and Mordred had the amber. They squared off, ten feet apart. Mordred crouched on wide-planted feet and rocked like a Sumo wrestler, but Han moved more like a butterfly, or a bee, or a middleweight champ. He danced around his opponent jabbing and stinging and luring him away from Lucky and L'Aria.

Floundering, holding a meaty hand to his bloodied cheek, Mordred backed off. He hawked and spit, and as soon as he had enough breath he bellowed, "Set the creature free!" To Lucky's horror, a familiar snarl followed the shout, and Maizie bounded across the ruined green, teeth bared, hackles up, eyes beaded on him.

Fortunately, most of the Black-cloaks had been dropped, dazed, or confused, but it didn't look like that mattered now. Lucky had about three seconds before Maizie would get to him, and he had no idea what to do with it.

L'Aria's voice crept out into heavy, damp air over the field. High-pitched. Really high-pitched. Maizie slowed, stumbled, dropped her head and shook it, but then caught sight of Lucky again and came on. L'Aria's song trailed off.

Lucky shot a desperate look at Han.

Just as they made eye contact a high-low hum halfway between power lines and microphone feedback pulsed across the field. Maizie froze and then backed off. All heads swiveled toward the elder trees near the cliff, where the sound came from. A barrel chested man with a ruined left arm, a twisted left leg, and an impossibly fast rolling gait shot out from the brush.

He held his right hand high gripping a stone knife by the blade. The raised hilt somehow drew light from the hidden sun and returned it in a thin crystal beam.

That knife ... It's like mine. Exactly like mine, except black.

The stranger spoke and the Blade shot out indigo fire. The thin ray of light raked over the field and locked onto Maizie's eyes. She spun around and a low, panting growl sounded deep in her chest. He spoke again and jerked the knife back. As if tied to it, Maizie jerked sideways on stiffened legs, and then she followed it toward the cliff, snapping at air the whole time.

As she neared the meadows edge, she broke into a run, and then suddenly leapt to clear the up-thrust stone of the palisades. Her howl fell through emptiness toward the creek. The splash that ended it echoed in Lucky's brain sounding like the word "dead."

The light fell back into the stone dagger's hilt and silenced it. The stranger retreated, but kept his eyes locked on Han, whose stare in turn followed him. He edged into the shadows under the trees.

Though Lucky would have sworn Han had forgotten everything but the crippled stranger, in that instant he backed into Mordred, crouched down, and reached up to grab Mordred's head. One hand pushed against the bigger man's stubbly chin, and the other twisted a hank of black hair at the back of his skull, applying sideways torque. He rolled, pulling Mordred over with him.

The heavier man hit the ground hard, flat on his back, and took a second blow as Han slammed his own body down. Han kept rolling and sprang up while Mordred still struggled to re-inflate his lungs. He stopped, metal blade balanced in his hand, poised in a fighter's crouch, waiting.

Lucky waited, too, and sensed L'Aria beside him doing likewise. Both of them watched the men fighting so intensely that they almost didn't notice when four new Black-cloaks came out of the trees. One of them held a choke chain. Lucky seethed thinking they'd been using that on Maizie. The anger gave him enough energy to duck as the man swung it at his head and then rushed in to tackle him.

Unpleasant surprise, the guy didn't fall. Lucky did, though, after he bounced off the guys muscles. These four Black-cloaks acted like they ran under their own power. Instead of fighting like zombies, they fought like they meant it. Lucky rolled to his feet just in time for the next swing of the chain to connect with his temple, a glancing blow, but hard enough to make him cross-eyed. Then he heard a loud smack and L'Aria grunted in pain.

She yelled. "Lohen Chiell, help me!"

The lame man who had slowed down to stare at Han had almost disappeared beyond the edge of the field. He pivoted and stormed back across the mucked-up grass. As he came near where L'Aria fought, he lowered his head, roared, and rolled in like Neptune on a tidal wave, throwing punches with his mean right fist. Ribs crunched, small bones cracked, and bad guys fell like broke-winged flies.

Lohen Chiell took some blows, too. He ended up with bruises, a bite-mark, and bloody knuckles. He didn't seem to notice. He stepped over to L'Aria, wrapped his good arm around her and crouched down to hoist her over his shoulder.

When he straightened and steadied himself, he and Lucky stood eye to eye. He said, "Luccan."

Lucky's guts gripped in pure fear, and before he could think about why, he reacted, raining fists on the stranger's head for all he was worth. The man stood stock still under the assault for a moment, trying to talk but not fighting back. Then he shook his head, spun around, and stalked away.

Some yards off, he set L'Aria on her feet and snarled out a few gruff-sounding words, hooking the thumb of his right hand toward the creek. L'Aria's fists settled on her hips, and she leaned in like a harpy preparing for a good scold, but before she could speak, the man narrowed his one seeing eye and growled, "Go!" She spun around, dark sheet of hair flaring out behind her, and marched toward the cliff.

Lucky almost set his feet in motion to run after her, but one of the black-cloaks formerly confused by L'Aria's song stood in his way. Lucky pivoted to face him, and in the process cracked him in the nose with an elbow, accidental, but effective. When he turned around again, he looked for L'Aria. She stood on the stone lip at the edge of the cliff. Before Lucky could move, she leapt, and was gone.

Lohen Chiell still stood only a few yards from Luccan, and after L'Aria jumped, he cast a glance back over his shoulder. Lucky gave him the best glare he could muster. The stranger holstered the Blade at his belt and moved toward the cliff, his limp more pronounced, looking suddenly weary.

With no one left to fight, Lucky's supply of adrenaline dried up and he sank to the grass. Ten yards away, Han and Mordred continued to struggle. Mordred's elbow struck Han's left brow with a crack, bone on bone. It split the skin over Han's eye, but he managed to land the kick he'd aimed at Mordred's knee. When the leg collapsed the beefy man landed face down in the mud. Han twisted Mordred's knife-arm straight up behind his back, pinning the other arm on the ground under his boot.

With one hand freed, he swiped away the blood that was already trickling into his eye. He held tight to Mordred, but stared at Lohen Chiell as he limped by. Lohen flung the look back at Han. Something, a challenge, Lucky thought, glinted in his dark eye like steel.

Taking advantage of Han's divided attention, Mordred squirmed with sudden energy until he got his feet under him to stand. Han jerked against the meaty arm he still held and Mordred's shoulder popped loud enough for Lucky to hear it twenty yards away. The Sorcerer howled in pain, but somehow kept hold of the Amber Blade. He shoved his weight against Han, knocking him off balance, and then he snaked around to lock his undamaged arm around Han's neck.

Lucky scrambled to his feet, thinking he'd rush in and try to help, but the battle cry of Han Shieth curdled his blood and stopped him in his tracks. It froze Mordred, too, and even Lohen Chiell stopped and turned to watch before he followed Maizie and L'Aria over the cliff.

Han twisted, spun like a top, and slammed an elbow into Mordred's ribs. Still in the spin, he jabbed two fingers of his other hand into the cluster of nerves under Mordred's jaw. A measured blow, but it left his opponent blind with pain. Mordred reeled backward, stumbled and went down.

His head smacked against the ridge of stone atop the palisades. He was knocked out instantly, but his arm swung up and over with the momentum of the fall and the Amber Blade flew from his grasp. The Knife arced over the ravine and tumbled, singing, through sudden blue sky and into the depths of Black Creek.

The strange twins were both out cold. All the others had fled. Han caught his breath and walked over to where Lucky waited, half in shock. He looked him up and down with hard eyes, turned him around, checking cuts and bruises.

He asked, gruffly, "Are you alright?"

Lucky could only nod, too overwhelmed to trust his voice.

Han swiped the blood from his own face with the back of his arm. He stared at Mordred for a long minute.

"Help me with this," he said.

They drug Mordred across the field and laid him next to Boff. Han turned both brothers onto their side—Boff almost gently, less so for Mordred.

"Han," Lucky asked, "why are you doing that?"

"So they don't choke on their own spit."

Startled by Han's growl, Lucky's eyes went wide, and without thinking he took a step back.

Han turned his eyes away, and though his voice quieted, there was no softness in it. "Go home," he said. "Go to Thurlock's."

"But I can help—"

"Go."

Lucky's eyes followed Han as he took off his boots and placed them carefully, side by side, on a rock. He stripped off his shirt and hung it over the boots. Then, like Maizie and L'Aria and the man she'd called Lohen Chiell, he leapt from the cliff into Black Creek's pools.

14. The Wizard's Question

On the way back to Thurlock's, Lucky ran into the Langdon brothers. For some reason, as if the day hadn't already been evil enough, they saw him from across the street and took out after him. They chased him past houses and churches and playgrounds and car lots, blocks and blocks before he finally escaped by diving under a rusty fender in a vacant lot. He was almost grateful; here at least was a threat he understood. But he ended so exhausted that he considered staying in the corroded shelter until he felt stronger or died.

He closed his eyes, but pictures of Han and Maizie and even L'Aria seemed to be tacked to the backs of his eyelids. *The Wizard*, he kept thinking, and though he wasn't sure what he meant, he rolled out from under cover, stood, and started his long shamble to the foothills. Instantly, the sky blackened and opened wide, and Lucky trudged the entire way in a downpour that surely set the record for world's longest cloudburst.

By the time he reached Thurlock's back stoop, his hair clung to his head like thick, red-brown plaster. His shirt hung in shreds. Mud, grass, rust, and blood painted him in broad strokes from head to toe. He raised his hand to knock, but the door swung wide with Thurlock looming on the other side of it. Without a word, the Wizard pulled Lucky out of the rain and onto the bare floor of the mud porch.

Lucky stood there, shell-shocked.

Thurlock stood next to him, scratching his beard. "I'm not very good at this sort of thing," he said. "Han's usually the one that takes care of people." He pursed his lips, and then, seeming to make a decision, pointed a finger to the floor at Lucky's feet, conjuring a thick, shaggy rug. Lucky automatically began to wipe mud from his bare soles, not stopping until Thurlock said, "That's enough, boy. Be still."

The old man dropped his spectacles in an inside pocket of his robes and palmed his tired eyes. "Where are your shoes?"

Lucky didn't answer.

"Okay, then, we'll try another question. What happened?"

Lucky sighed, pushed his hair back, and said, "Han sent me home."

Thurlock raised his right eyebrow and shot him a curious look before leading him into the dim kitchen.

The last time Lucky had been in the kitchen, with Han that very morning, it had been a cheerful place smelling of cinnamon. Now it seemed dark and hollow and dank as a cave, and he had a feeling that creepy things were hiding in the corners. It didn't feel normal. Nothing felt normal. *There's no such thing as normal.* Lucky began to tremble.

Thurlock sighed again, gathered Lucky under his arm, and ushered him into the bathroom. He started the water in the shower and adjusted the temperature. "You stink, Luccan," he said, and pulled the door shut on his way out. "Wash."

Under the hot water, Lucky's scrapes and scratches burned, but the heat soothed him and the soap smelled good. He stayed until the water went cold. When he stepped from the shower, all the events of that day fell on his shoulders like a lead shirt.

His brain felt swollen with painful thoughts that didn't make sense. Try as he might to straighten them into some kind of order, he couldn't. He wrapped himself in two fluffy towels and sank down to sit on the side of the tub, head hanging from hunched shoulders. Water ran into his eyes and he wiped it away over and over again.

Thurlock knocked on the door and passed him clean sweats and a tee shirt. Lucky recovered enough to dress and to wonder half-heartedly whose clothes he was putting on. When he came out of the bathroom, he saw the Wizard seated in his favorite armchair near the unlit hearth, but he didn't go to sit beside him. Instead, he plunked down on a hard chair in the dining room, laid his head on the table in the glow of the chandelier, and slept.

His own shout woke him. "Wait!" He panted, as if he'd been running. He looked around the room and saw nothing in particular. Nevertheless, he was afraid of everything he saw. And what he didn't see, too.

Thurlock put a hand on his shoulder. "Let's go up to the Tower," he said. "We'll be more comfortable." He started up the stairs and Lucky followed, shuffling close on the Wizard's heels because at this juncture being afraid of Thurlock was more bearable than being afraid of everything else.

At the top of the stairs, yellow light streamed under the Tower room door like sunshine. Thurlock fumbled with the doorknob and muttered words Lucky didn't recognize, and nothing happened. The Wizard heaved a sigh, rolled his eyes, and thumped the door with the palm of his hand, and the door creaked open. Lucky walked through, the door shut behind him with a firecracker bang, and a six-month ration of adrenaline flooded his bloodstream.

Then he saw the window.

"Oh," he said.

Framed in a west-facing window, brilliant sunshine blazed. All the other windows in the tower—which was round from inside out, though it was square from outside in—all the other windows framed rain falling in sheets from blustery skies.

"Don't worry about that," the Wizard said, and indicated the odd aperture with a wave. "I often get the most out of every little sun break through that window. The light is welcome, at a time like this, don't you agree? And rest easy. This room is never where it seems to be, so it always makes a poor target."

Not where it seems to be? "Where is it, then, sir?"

"It's just Thurlock, Luccan, please. Before long you'll be sounding like Han; sir this, sir that. I appreciate the respect, but it's not required, not appropriate." A heavy-legged oval table stood against the wall to Lucky's right. Thurlock pulled out a chair at the end of it and gently pushed him toward it. "Sit, please," he said, so Lucky did.

A fireplace occupied the west wall—a smaller version of the stone bulwark downstairs. Thurlock flicked his right hand and it blazed. He puttered about, humming and fussing with a black, lidded pot. He filled it at a small, possibly fossilized sink and then hung it from a hook in the fireplace.

Lucky felt confused.

"Instant cocoa," Thurlock announced, displaying a packet as if it were the Nobel Peace Prize. "Wonderful invention—one of the things I'll miss about Earth." He turned over two mugs. "Join me?"

"Yes, please," Lucky said, although just a few days ago he would not have wanted anything a known Wizard had to offer. For a time after Thurlock plunked down the steaming cups, there was no talk, only crackling flames, and quite a lot of blowing, stirring, and slurping. The chocolate tasted sweet, and the square of sunlight had softened to a comforting glow, and Lucky began to relax.

"So," the Wizard ventured, leaning back in his chair apparently to get a better view of Lucky's condition. "I'm no doctor, but I can help if you have injuries that need attention. Is there anything still bleeding?"

Lucky shook his head.

"Anything feel broken?"

"No, sir."

"No terrible headache, don't feel dizzy when you stand up? Not sick at your stom—"

"*No!*" Surprised by his own impatience, Lucky quieted his tone. "No, sir, I'm fine. It's only more bruises and scratches. They'll go away."

Thurlock smiled and shrugged. "I'm sorry. Han would have known without asking." His eyes twinkled and he seemed then so human, so ordinary, that for a moment Lucky forgot his worries and just liked the old man.

Seconds later, Thurlock straightened the lapels of his Wizard's robes, donned his spectacles, and aimed a serious gaze over the gold rims. "If I had been here today," he said, quiet and business-like, "I might have known what was happening when it happened, but I've been away. Please, if you can, tell me."

Lucky didn't answer right away, didn't even think about the question. He focused instead on the un-Wizardly drip of chocolate in the old man's beard. But when he looked up and met Thurlock's grey eyes, he found them as calming as sunlit seas.

He began to recite, attempting to navigate a sensible course through the day's events. He spoke at length, but his tale emerged neither coherent nor complete. He answered a few questions along the way — especially about the big, black bird, and about the myrtle grove — but mostly he stopped, backtracked, and started again until, at long last, he got to the end.

"Han was ... I think he was mad at me. He didn't smile, not even his eyes."

Thurlock shook his head. "He wasn't mad at you."

Lucky shrugged. "I had promised, so I did what he'd told me. I came here."

"I'm glad you did."

Lucky leaned over his still steaming chocolate, relieved that Thurlock let silence fall around them. After a time, he asked questions of his own. "Will I see Maizie again? Will she ever be alright?"

"It's not impossible."

"What about Han? Will he come back?"

Thurlock nodded. "Certainly."

Other questions hounded him, but just thinking them through left him exhausted, so he dropped his sore head in his battered hands, and only asked, "Why?"

Thurlock gave no response, but sat eyeing him, tugging at a stiff strand of grey beard. He grunted, suddenly, and pursed his lips. He reached over and patted Lucky's hand. "Let it be, for now, Luccan. Drink your chocolate. Rest. There are always questions, and almost always another time will come for asking." He turned away to gaze into the hearth.

The Wizard's tower was filled with ordinary things: a narrow four poster bed, a ragged quilt and a bedside rug both checked in purple and gold, fragrant tea and tiny oranges, books and a Rubik's cube; and jigsaw puzzles, lots of them, their boxes piled high and leaning against a credenza.

The place also harbored things that did not seem ordinary at all. Stacks of yellowed scrolls crowded into cubbies. Strange instruments occupied corners and counters. Mystifying implements sat side-by-side with luridly painted decks of cards. Shelves were crammed with bottles of powders and liquids of every color, small rocks, and desiccated insects, and every sort of Wizard's whatnot. And, of course, the Wizard himself.

A portrait of Lucky's mother hung on the west wall in a plain oak frame.

Lucky knew it was his mother, without doubt. The golden curls, the smile, and the green eyes, all of which he'd dreamed about on Midsummer Morning. *Like mine, those eyes.* And he'd dreamed about them again just moments ago while sleeping off his terror beneath the chandelier.

He and his mother had been laughing, in that dream, and then his mother had smiled sadly and called him by his name. Next, though, she'd spoken unfamiliar words, *"Suth Chiell,"* and a flock of invisible voices had repeated after her. An icy darkness chock full of scary sounds had come howling in, just as it had in the Midsummer Morning dream. But, in today's dream, his mother had put a hand on her hip, stomped her foot, and rolled her eyes.

"Not again," she'd said, *"I don't believe this."*

Lucky had shouted, *"Mom, I don't understand."*

Her green eyes had flashed, and her tone had become vexed. *"Ask Thurlock,"* she'd said. Then she'd pivoted and stomped away, muttering under her breath.

"Thurlock?"

"Luccan?"

"I dreamed about my mother. Just a while ago. She said ask you."

"Did she now?"

"She stomped her foot and yelled, 'Ask Thurlock.'" He laughed to hear himself say it, and the Wizard did too, and then they both lifted their mugs of cocoa, newly refilled, and drank. Lucky spilled a drop and looked around the table for napkins, but he didn't find any. "She really did say that," he said. And then, since he'd gotten started, he kept talking. "I've dreamed of her before, but I always thought it was imagination. She's beautiful."

"Yes." Thurlock scratched at his beard and discovered the drying chocolate lodged there. He got up to rummage in a drawer and came back with a handful of napkins from a taco stand. He put them down on the table, apparently forgetting about his beard, but he did offer one to Lucky.

141

Lucky took it and dabbed tidily at his spilled drop. "You know my mother."

"Yes."

"Will you tell me about her?"

"Perhaps."

"Now?"

"Soon."

"That's her." Lucky pointed at the portrait, amazed that he felt so calm.

Thurlock beamed a smile at him, clapped him on the shoulder and said, "It is."

"She called my name—Luccan." Thurlock watched Lucky over the top of his cup as he sipped, ignoring the steamed up spectacles at the end of his nose. Lucky went on. "She said another name, too," he said, just remembering. "Eli? No. El... Elieth."

Thurlock nodded calmly, but color shaded his cheeks. "That's right," he said. "In Ethra, it's what we would call your milk-name, the name a mother gives her child at birth."

"Then she said 'Suth Chiell.' What does it mean?"

Thurlock put his mug down and took a deep breath. His eyes narrowed and his brow furrowed, intense, until suddenly a smile broke out. "Now that," he said, "is the crux of the matter. It's the Wizard's eternal question. What does it *mean*?"

He waved at the parchments and books. "Nine-tenths of a Wizard's work is learning, studying, taking in the facts. But the part that matters is putting all the factors together and figuring out, or guessing, most of the time, what they mean." He pursed his lips, bobbed his head, as if conceding a point. "And then, yes, you've also got to decide what to do about it."

He walked over to a cluster of parchment rolls, and plucked one from the center of the stack. "I've seen some odd things, recently," he said as he took a seat. "And I've been alarmed. We already knew that we were in a precarious position, Luccan, but now I realize we have a tougher opponent than any I'd imagined."

Thurlock went silent again, rolling the parchment out inch by inch. Lucky could see round charts with lines connecting dots of various sizes, and deduced that they were star charts. He stayed quiet, trying to be respectful, but he became convinced that Thurlock had forgotten him. So, following up on the Wizard's last words, he asked, "Who?"

"Not who, my boy," Thurlock said, snatching the spectacles off his nose. He pointed them at Lucky and said, "Not who, what. It's time, Luccan. *Time* is against us. The day we met, Summer Solstice happened in Earth and Ethra at precisely the same moment, an extremely *rare* occurrence. We knew it was important, and we were right. We found you.

"But I hadn't understood how profound a change would follow. I now see that these two worlds have begun to unfold in patterns precisely opposite one another. Look, look here." He unrolled the parchment a bit more and held it out.

"You see? Ethra last night, on this side, the view from latitudinal and longitudinal coordinates matching the location of this tower in Earth. Sagittarius is shooting at the scorpion, as he should. On this side, here in Earth last night, the view from this tower. Sagittarius, on my oath, is shooting at his own hindquarters. Outrageous! And there's more ... moons, anomalies, fluctuations. I can't explain it all now, but you get the idea."

Truthfully, Lucky didn't get the idea at all, though he did understand that star clusters didn't, as a rule, shoot at their hindquarters. He opened his mouth to make a joke about it, but the Wizard's expression had changed to just plain worry.

"I've been around a while," he said, and Lucky had to listen close to hear the soft words over the sound of drumming rain. "I've not seen anything like it. And I can't find any record anywhere, here or at home, that anyone else has witnessed such a thing, either. Not even old Willock." He paused to drain the last of his cocoa, dribbling a spot on his robes.

"Willock?"

"But I've done my job as well as I can," he said, "and I think I know what it means. In a nutshell ... the long and the short of it ... to cut to the heart of the matter—"

"Thurlock, get to the point." Lucky covered his mouth, abashed, but the old man laughed.

"Well said, my boy. The point is this: The roads between Earth and Ethra have endured longer than history can tell. But now, things change. Our twin worlds pull against each other like frightened horses linked in the harness. I haven't learned why, but what it means, Luccan, is that our window of opportunity to get you home safe is smaller than anyone knew. We are nearly out of time."

Having voiced that ominous concern, he rose and stowed the parchment away, calm and seemingly cheerful. "As to what you dreamed," he said, "and what that means ... Simply put, it means you have a memory. And that's a start, isn't it? Certainly, it's more than we had before."

PART THREE: Revelations

15. Who Is He and How Does He Know My Name?

After three cups of cocoa, all the little oranges in the basket, and a plateful of bite-sized cookies shaped like leaves and filled with maple crème, Lucky wasn't hungry. He thanked the Wizard, watched while Thurlock slammed a palm into the stuck door to let him out, and tramped down three flights of stairs to the little room he'd come at some point to think of as his.

Exhausted, but sick with the memory of the morning, he tried to sleep and fought it at the same time, afraid to find out what images shared his bunk in dreamland. But the sun coming through the window warmed him and the maple tree made shadow-leaves on the wall, and somewhere in its branches a couple of birds warbled. He did sleep, surprised himself by awaking refreshed after only a couple of hours. Even more surprising, he stepped out of his bedroom and met Thurlock, face to ribcage, on the landing just outside his door.

"Ah," the Wizard said, "Good, you're awake. That's a nice coincidence. I've a chore for you."

"Chore?"

"Yes, a chore. You can pretend you're a normal teenager, for the moment. Clean the attic."

Of course, "normal" was as good as a magic word to Lucky. He liked the idea, but he felt a *'you're not the boss of me'* rise up in his throat, anyway. He opened his mouth to say it, looked up to meet the Wizard's steely gaze ... and changed his mind. Rebellion might be normal for a teen, but he wasn't ready to risk it with this particular old man.

Instead, he asked, "There's an attic?"

"There is now. Upstairs, just off the third step from the top." Thurlock rattled off a set of instructions and then started down the stairs, calling the last few words over his shoulder, "And if you find anything you want, keep it."

Lucky folded himself through the half-sized door, and found a room that could better be described as a hidey-hole. The gabled ceiling hung too low for Lucky to stand, even at its peak, and if he stretched his arms out he could almost touch the walls on either side. Wide gaps in the siding let in striped light from the sun outside, along with a crop of spiders and bugs that skittered out of sight when Lucky pulled the chain to light up the single glaring bulb.

The cubby begged investigation, chock-full of crates, bins, boxes, and one paper sack. All wore a deceptive coat of ancient dust, as if they and the attic had been there forever.

He worked a full hour, sweating and sneezing and sorting things out the way Thurlock had instructed. It was a task calling for organization, and he was happy to do it. He had a penchant for order. In a weird kind of way, the chore made sense, which hadn't been true of anything for three days.

He started with a row of four small chests made of dark wood, each with a rounded top and fitted with a golden hasp and hinge. The first three were empty; the fourth held small paintings so precisely rendered that he at first thought they were photographs. One pictured a younger Han. Two were of Lucky's mother. One depicted a little girl with a nose that reminded him of L'Aria. He pushed away thoughts of the afternoon's fight, but he chose to keep that picture along with the others, setting them all in front of the door so he wouldn't forget to take them out when the job was done.

"Make a pile," the Wizard had said, "of things you can identify but don't remember." That pile grew into a tall mound, a veritable tower built of everything from baby clothes to tennis rackets, horseshoes to flower pots.

"Make another pile of things about which you can't even begin to guess." In the end, that group held only four objects. The strangest was a conglomeration of gears and pulleys and bells in a glass housing that reminded Lucky unpleasantly of Thurlock's brain-teasing clock.

There was supposed be a pile for "things you remember from your childhood but don't want." As Lucky could have predicted had Thurlock asked, no such pile developed.

Finished with the sorting, Lucky stood up as straight as the ceiling would let him, wiped sweaty hands on dusty sweats, and surveyed the results. His collection of keepers held only the portraits and one additional item, the thing that had hid in the brown paper sack. Lucky bent to pick it up and closed his hand around soft, red-and-yellow plaid fabric.

He *didn't* remember the blanket. He had no idea why he smiled, thinking he might.

That's what he mused on, later, as he sat in the wing chair in the Wizard's living room with the red plaid spread on his lap. He ran his fingers over the silk binding, and it seemed to smooth everything out. The chandelier rang soft tones in the almost-still air. Lemon lay curled on a corner of the blanket, purring. Even the tick of Thurlock's clock seemed lazy. If he hadn't been so baffled by his mysterious fondness for a blanket, he might have fallen asleep.

The front door opened with a shocking rush, and Han came streaming in along with the late afternoon sun. The creek or the rain had washed him clean of blood and grime, and he'd tethered his hair back into its perfect queue. Only the gash over his eyebrow, some cuts and bruises, and a swollen right hand testified to the day's trials.

"You're okay, lad?" When Lucky nodded, Han smiled. "Good." Perhaps his step lacked some of its usual spring, but he took the stairs three at a time to Thurlock's tower.

Lucky wanted to follow, but a little voice told him to mind his own business.

"This is my business." He said it out loud to show the little voice who was in charge. "This is all my business."

He started up to the Wizard's tower, but on the third step from the top, where the attic door had been an hour ago, sounds escaping Thurlock's door stopped him. Unbelievably, Thurlock and Han argued in the tower. He knew eavesdropping was despicable, disloyal, and dishonest. His stomach hurt just to think of it, but he crouched into the shadows, wished himself quiet as spider feet, and settled in to listen.

The sounds increased as if someone gradually turned up the volume, and then suddenly Thurlock's voice boomed, causing Lucky's innards to leap skyward and cutting off Han's voice altogether.

"Han Shieth! I've told you already, I do not hold you responsible for that mess at the Ravine, nor am I upset that you didn't force Luccan to come home. I have every faith in the decisions you made. Now—"

A sharp crack punctuated his speech, and Lucky pictured his big hand smacking the table.

"—stop apologizing, before I do get perturbed!"

Complete silence followed, and Lucky kept every muscle still, lest the stairs creak. He didn't even breathe until it became unavoidable, and then he plugged his left nostril, which tended to whistle. He heard shuffling and clanking inside the tower room, and then the rising sound of water filling cups. He unplugged his nostril and caught a scent of chocolate wafting by.

More quietly but still loud enough for Lucky to hear, Thurlock said, "And no, to answer your question, I haven't yet decided how or what or how much to tell the boy about Lohen Chiell."

"He has a right—"

"I know that."

"It might help—"

"I know that, too."

A long silence followed that sharp exchange, filled only with tiny slurping sounds. "So," Thurlock asked, no-nonsense, "he drew the Blade, set it humming ... and then the dog ran? Tell me what you saw, exactly. Had he come with the Witch's people?"

Lucky had a hard time imagining Han so disturbed that he would pace; yet he found himself tracking the man's voice back and forth across the room. He spoke quietly, and Lucky could only decipher the bits he uttered as he passed near the door. "... couldn't tell sir ... his mind was closed off ... L'Aria as always ... the look on his face ... the dog is mad ... can't read her thoughts at all—"

Silence.

Then Thurlock: "Luccan! Either come in or get away from the door."

As soon as Lucky finished choking on air, he got away from the door. No-brainer.

A short while later, Lucky lay on the bed he now thought of as his, feigning sleep. He hadn't seen Han after fleeing the stairs. Thurlock had knocked on Lucky's door, come in, glared for two minutes or nine-thousand years, and swished out again, banging the door shut behind him.

Lucky tried to work up resentment, but he could only get angry with himself. Besides, he'd never had much practice at sulking, and it soon proved too boring to keep him awake. He drifted into a troubled sleep filled with stone knives, twins, and strangers.

***

The interruption caused by Lucky's eavesdropping had broken the tension between Han and Thurlock. As they passed on the stairs outside Lucky's door, Han said, "I'm starving."

He went to the kitchen and started a roast in the microwave. "I just love this thing," he said. He assembled a pie and stuck it in the oven, peeled potatoes into a pot of water, set biscuit dough to rise in the bowl, snapped green beans into a colander ready for steaming at the last minute.

Carrying two glasses of tea, he went out to the front porch, where he knew he would find Thurlock in the rocker, watching the shadows change as the sun began to fall.

"Sir," Han said, handing Thurlock a glass and sinking into the vacant chair at his right.

"You must have been reading my mind," the Wizard said, and they both smiled. "But since I can't read yours, tell me. You never found it?"

"The Amber Knife?"

"I assume that's what you were after when you dove into the creek."

"I found no trace, not even a tingle of the Blade's magic."

"L'Aria's doing, perhaps. She didn't have it on her when she got home to the Sisterhold, or Lili would have known, but she could have hidden it on the way. Given enough water, her magic nearly equals her father's, aside from Tiro's ability to shapeshift."

"She stays in human skin, but she may as well be in otter fur." Han held his cold glass up to the cut on his brow. "It's convenient, the way they travel. They can go anywhere, if there's a river. Or even a pond."

"They're called *'Tir'* for a reason. It's the old language, but roughly it means 'river song'. But they can only travel by water in Earth or Ethra, between these two worlds. The magic may have survived from before the worlds split. Some people think it's what binds the worlds together, as well."

"Power like that ..."

"Tiro holds great power, surely, and L'Aria's likely will grow as she grows. But it's limited, for practical purposes. They can create Portals in water. They can tinker with an unprotected mind or heart, since so much of our matter is water. Tiro, unique in all of Ethra, can change shape. But no parlor tricks for either of them, no household spells, no wizardry, and they can't read minds, either. Still, I wonder how Isa's people managed to capture her."

"We were lucky to find her."

"And luck can't be counted on."

"Did Lili and Rose tell her to stay home, once she got there?"

Thurlock rolled his eyes and snorted. "Oh yes, they told her. About five minutes before she left again."

***

Han rapped on Lucky's door. "Wake up, lad, and wash. Feast in five minutes."

In the dining room, the chandelier blazed even though summer daylight still stretched in from the west. In the glow, the round table sagged toward its center under the weight of platters and bowls and baskets of food.

"Is it a holiday?"

"It's just Han," Thurlock said, rolling his eyes.

He waved at the table, mumbled "fortify," and nodded in satisfaction as the tabletop snapped to attention. Turning back to Lucky with a wry smile, he said, "You can always tell when he's had a rough day; he produces more food than we could eat in a week."

151

Lucky didn't mind. He smelled beef and gravy and biscuits. His stomach growled, gearing up for the job ahead.

When Han finally had the table fully loaded, he sat across from Lucky and pushed a platter of roast beef under his nose. "You handled yourself well in the Ravine today."

It took Lucky a full minute to realize there was no "but," "however," or "although" attached to the end of Han's sentence. He knew he beamed at the unexpected praise, and that made him blush, but he breathed his thanks and set to filling up the vast uncharted territory under his ribs. When his mouth stood briefly empty, he asked, "L'Aria ...?"

"Home," Han said, also squeezing words between bites. "She's safe, in Ethra."

Lucky was confused about how that might be, and swallowed a bite early preparing to ask, but just then Thurlock looked at him sideways and said, "She mentioned that she thought you were rather gallant."

Embarrassed, Lucky stuffed a biscuit in his mouth and moved on to other questions.

"Maizie?"

"We don't know."

"My Knife?"

"Missing," Han said, and then, pre-empting further questions, "and by the time I got back to the field, Mordred and his poor brother were gone, and no one else was around either."

Aside from the scrape of silverware and polite requests to pass the pepper or the butter or the beans they ate in silence for some time. Han seemed focused wholly on his plate, but Lucky could feel the Wizard's eyes on him. He tried to ignore it, but when Thurlock cleared his throat and placed his fork at the edge of his plate, Lucky forgot how to chew.

Thurlock said, "You have more questions."

It was true; he did, although these questions made him nervous. He took a huge gulp of water to wash down the beef and drown the heebie-jeebies, and decided to ease into it by starting with generalities. "What is that black stuff?"

"Black stuff?"

"I don't know how to describe it ... smoke? I saw it in the Ravine today, and I saw it before, during the storm."

Han raised his eyebrows, nodded vigorously to Thurlock. "It's just like I said, sir. He sees. Didn't I tell you?" He shook pepper over his potatoes and gravy with self-satisfied emphasis.

"Alright, so you told me. How would I know?" Thurlock stopped to sneeze, and then said through a wad of purple hanky, "You're the mind reader."

"And I'll wager he sees a lot more than that. He's got the Sight. And no, frankly, I've had very little success reading his mind except when he's calling me. He's blocking it already, I'm sure of it."

"With no training?"

"I'm as amazed as you, but he seems to be—"

"I seem to be what? What sight? You're talking about me like I'm not here!" The house became very silent at Lucky's words, and then Thurlock and Han stumbled over each other trying to apologize.

"We're used to being alone," Han finally explained. "The Sight," he said. "You could probably describe it better than me. What you want to know is where it comes from, whether you can control it, and what you're seeing when it's working. Am I right?" He waited for Lucky's nod.

"It's a talent, like my thought reading. You can learn to call it up, to refine it, and to shut it down. As to what you're seeing ..." Han paused for thoughtful lip chewing. "You're looking beneath what's usually visible, like lifting a veil, seeing the nature of things." He shrugged and flashed a brief smile. "Maybe Thurlock can tell you more."

"No, that was well said. But Luccan, you asked about the 'black stuff.'"

"I did, sir."

"Not sir, to you, just Thurlock." He sat back in his chair pulling at his beard, and then launched into a discourse explaining what Lucky saw as *"black stuff"* in terms of Earth science, which he hoped Lucky would better understand.

But when he'd finished comparing the ghostly, swirly substance to a black hole with a personality that can break itself into pieces, appear in many places at once, and act through others' minds and bodies, and then said that it was really a god whose name was Mahl, Lucky just sat staring.

Han got up and brought back a huge, crumb-crusted, cinnamon-dusted apple pie. He hummed as he quarried them each a huge slab.

Lucky couldn't think of any way to ask for more information about the black-hole-god-thing-Mahl that wouldn't involve the word *evil*, which sounded far too melodramatic. So, when Thurlock asked if he had more questions, he decided to ask the one that had lodged itself in his brain the moment he'd first laid eyes on the subject, that afternoon in the Ravine.

"That man," he said, "Lohen Chiell. Who is he, and how does he know my name?"

No one answered, except for sadness darkening Han's eyes and concern flashing in Thurlock's. Lucky opened his mouth to repeat the question, but it froze in his throat when a howl of canine bloodlust shattered the peace.

Lucky jumped up and flew to the wide front window, where he got a clear view of scarlet-rimmed eyes and slavering jaws. Although he imagined teeth ripping his throat, he shot toward the door to rush to Maizie's aid. The Wizard clamped an iron hand on his arm, holding him back, and Han flew past him and outside.

In the same beat, the Black Blade's siren song hummed through the yard, and as abruptly as Maizie's howls had started, they stopped. Her claws clicked off the porch and into the distance on the paved road, and the blade's note faded into the dusk.
Lucky turned away from the window and started up the stairs to go to his room. Maizie had fled, and so had the time for questions.

16. A Lesson from Ophiuchus' Serpent

As cozy as Lucky felt wrapped in his new/old plaid blanket, as grateful as his bones were to be snuggled up warm and relieved of duty, his eyes wouldn't close. He lay awake in the normal bed in the ordinary moonlit room on the second floor of Thurlock's house for what seemed like forever. Thoughts rushed by, drained away, hit the uptake and ran again, like water in a recycling fountain.

He kept replaying the scene at the table, and he couldn't stop thinking about that last question, the one he hadn't asked again after Maizie had come and gone. *Who was that man?* He racked his brain, trying to think of a time when they'd met before that day, some way to explain why the man would know him, and even know his real name.

And, in case that didn't disturb him enough, he thought about what Thurlock had said in his tower? Crazy things that never should have been spoken in a room bright with sunlight and smelling of oranges and chocolate. *"Time is against us ... shorter than we knew."* The words echoed back and forth in Lucky's skull—left brain, right brain, left, right—always getting scrambled in the middle but meaning the same frightening thing on every repetition.

He flopped onto his stomach, irritated. *How am I supposed to sleep with that going on in my head?* He flipped onto one side, and then back onto the other, but no matter which way he twisted, his brain cells refused to leave off playing ping-pong with worries about time and stars, and Maizie gone mad, and the Key of Behliseth, and a sassy girl with a cute nose, and stone Knives, and muscled-up strangers in matched sets.

And, he added, *a scarred man with one eye who had one of the Knives, carried off the girl, controlled Maizie, seemed to know Han, and called me Luccan.*

"So much for sleep," he said, not caring that he spoke way too loudly for the middle of the night. He rolled out of bed, hopped around until he lost the tangled sheets, hiked up Thurlock's pajamas, and left the room.

Seeking the Wizard's counsel required getting to his door, but at the uppermost landing of the stairs, Lucky found his way blocked by a small mountain glowing in silver light. He stood wondering whether to go around or climb over until he realized that the whistling wind was only Thurlock's slow breathing, and the mountain was only his robe-covered knees. In the small space of the landing, Thurlock lay on his back with his knees drawn up and his hands clasped over his chest.

"Welcome."

The Wizard's voice was quiet but as always it filled the entire space between Lucky's ears. Startled off balance, Lucky teetered on the very edge of the top step, listing dangerously backward. Not seeming to hurry at all, Thurlock reached out a hand and latched onto the cloth of Lucky's borrowed pajamas at the knee. It steadied him until he regained his balance.

"Welcome," the Wizard said again, "to my observatory."

Lucky peered up into the space that he was sure had been occupied by an ordinary, boring ceiling the last time he was there. He saw a wide circular glass dome, and behind it a sheet of star-filled midnight so brilliant and close that Lucky reached up a hand, half-expecting to pluck stars like picking berries. "Thurlock," he asked, "What are you doing?"

"I'm stargazing, of course."

"All this weird stuff going on and you're staring at the sky." It wasn't until every one of those sarcastic words had escaped his mouth that Lucky remembered he'd taken the no-rudeness pledge just two days ago. And, of all the people to whom he could have mouthed off, he'd chosen the only full-fledged, staff wielding, with-one-word-I-can-fuse-your-tongue-to-your-shoe-laces Wizard in town.

Thurlock let silence hang between them in the dark, but when finally he spoke, his words seemed formed around a smile. "I learn a lot this way. Sometimes things that will be important begin in the heavens. At other times heavenly bodies shed new light on old puzzles, or open our eyes to new possibilities." He shifted to one side of the landing, making room. "Would you care to join me?"

Lucky breathed, wiped his sweating palms on his borrowed pajamas, and stepped over Thurlock's middle to the space the Wizard had cleared for him on the floor. Lowering himself to sit, he asked, "How do you know what's important, in all those lights?"

Thurlock shook with quiet laughter. "You do have a way of asking the right questions, young man. That's the problem with stargazing, exactly."

Lucky shoved his forelock out of his eyes, and spread himself on the floor alongside Thurlock. He felt like a dwarf next to the giant-sized Wizard, and foolish for having attempted to chastise him. He half expected to squeak like a mouse, so it startled him when his voice emerged almost normal.

"Why am I acting so strange, lately?" He didn't explain. The Wizard would know.

"That," Thurlock said, "is another right question." After a pause during which Lucky heard him rasping at his beard, he went on. "Probably, it has several right answers. You are fourteen, first of all, and people do act in ways that defy explanation around that age."

Without thinking, Lucky clicked his tongue, dismissing that idea as rubbish.

"Though typically," Thurlock went on, "they refuse to admit it." He raised his arms to put his hands behind his head, in the process smacking Lucky with an elbow. "Sorry. Close quarters, eh?"

After he settled back again, he said, "Also, it's been a shock—all that's happened to you in the last few days." In a sudden rush of movement, he thrust a knuckly finger at the heavens. "There. Do you see it?"

Lucky had looked at that spot before the Wizard pointed. A burst of light had caught his eye, followed by a cluster of falling traces like fading fireworks. "Meteor shower."

"So it would seem, Luccan, but—" He came down hard on that word and repeated it, "but, there are no meteor showers to be seen in that part of the sky at this time of year. Look at the sky around the bursting lights. There is the constellation Sagittarius to one side, Scorpio to the other, and Ophiuchus, the Serpent Holder standing above. Where those falling stars are, up until just seconds ago, Ophiuchus' foot was there. It's as though the Scorpion stung him with its tail, and smashed the foot to bits."

"Wait ... Thurlock, is this for real? I mean, stars don't do that, right?"

"Well no, of course not. Or maybe. I suppose it depends on how you look at it."

Lucky snorted, deciding that he wasn't likely to get a straight answer. "Well then, what does it mean?"

"Hm. That's more to the point, but I haven't a clue. I would guess, though, that the Serpent Holder feels about like you do, like your feet have been knocked from under you. It'll be interesting to see whether he keeps his balance and keeps the snake under control.

"And then too," Thurlock said, as the light show faded, "there have been spells."

"Spells?"

"Yes, of course. That woman you've seen a few times, the unattractive one, her name is Isa. She's a Witch. Quite a powerful one at the moment. She's done a crafty job with her spells, these past days, and I suspect that has influenced your behavior."

"I never thought it was for real."

"What?"

"Evil Witches."

"Oh, there are evil Witches alright, though certainly not all Witches are evil. Your mother—since you've remembered her a little, I think I can tell you this. Your mother is a wonderful Witch. Her name, by the way, is Liliana."

Thinking about his mother reminded Lucky of his dream, the one he'd had that afternoon when he'd slept off his terror under the chandelier. "Elieth, you said it's another name? Is Suth Chiell my last name, then?"

"No, no. It's a title. We don't use last names in Ethra the way they are used in most places here in Earth. But, on your mother's side, if it's of interest to you, your family name is Ol'Karrigh, the same as mine."

"What about on my father's side?"

"On your father's side," the Wizard said softly, "you are a descendant of the Drakhonic family line, like Han."

Lucky lay silently beside the old man so long that his eyelids half-closed and Thurlock's long steady breaths almost lulled him into sleep. Then something flashed in the sky, a brilliant light cutting across the handle of one of the Dippers. "Is that a satellite, do you think?"

"Hmm," Thurlock considered, tilting his head. "That, or possibly a dragon."

Lucky laughed before he realized it wasn't a joke. "You mean ... are dragons real?"

"In some worlds."

"Ethra?" Lucky hadn't said the word before, and it felt both strange and familiar on his tongue. Thurlock grunted in a way that seemed affirmative, and Lucky asked, "Do they breathe fire?"

"The green ones do," Thurlock said, "quite a lot of it. And they're the biggest, too, about the size of City Hall."

Lucky just barely stopped himself from asking if they hoarded treasure and had jewel encrusted under-bellies. He was getting off track. "Some time, will you tell me more?"

"Some time, but that isn't what you came up here to talk about. What would you ask next?"

"I must have other names."

"Why do you say that?"

"You asked me, that first night, if I remembered any more of them. Plural."

Thurlock laughed, and raised two hands to shoo away a thickening silver mist that had gathered in the hall. "Stardust," he explained, "useful, but it's a nuisance for visibility." He wiped his hands on his knees, causing his robes to glitter. "Not much gets by you does it, my boy? You're right, you have more names. The third is Perdhro. It was passed on to you from your mother's mother's father, I believe."

"Luccan Elieth Perdhro? That's my whole name?"

"No."

"What else."

"I don't know, more is the pity."

Though no one could see it in the dark, Lucky rolled his eyes at that answer, imitating Thurlock without realizing it. Then he scratched roughly at his scalp, considering his choices. It was either try to figure out what to ask to get the Wizard to explain his answer, or just let the whole thing go. As tired as Lucky was, the choice made itself. That line of questioning had reached a dead end.

Pointing up as another light streaked across the sky, Lucky asked, "Dragon?"

"Jet."

"It's a title you said."

"Jet?"

"Suth Chiell. What … What exactly is a Suth Chiell?"

"I'll show you," Thurlock answered. "Scoot up." He did so himself, propping his back against the wall. When Lucky sat beside him, the Wizard pointed his right index finger toward the far wall, and a square of light appeared there, as if from a projector. Color swirled and then composed itself into a picture, a full-length portrait.

"There," Thurlock said. "There's a Suth Chiell right there. Lustrex was his name, poor man."

The man looked old fashioned and a bit stuffy, to Lucky's mind, but on his head he wore a burnished circlet of pale metal, with a flashing jewel set in the center. Lucky's eyebrows shot up when he saw that the Suth Chiell Lustrex also wore a Key around his neck, either the same one Lucky had or another just like it. And the Amber Knife was sheathed at his belt. Many questions and observations vied for Lucky's tongue just then, but in the end he said, "I don't have a crown like that." He felt silly to have said it, but Thurlock didn't laugh.

"Yet," the Wizard said.

"Uh … can't you tell me what this Suth Chiell thing is all about?"

"I could. No reason why I couldn't. But before I do you'd better be sure you really want to know. No," he waved a hand to disappear the portrait, and laid back down flat in the starlight. "No, don't get all upset because I said that. I can practically feel you rolling your eyes.

"The thing is, Luccan, the more you know about what it means to be Suth Chiell, the more you will feel compelled by your nature to live up to the responsibilities. The requirements of the office are both grave and great, for many people will depend on you. To do those duties honorably and well, you must have strong faith in the truths of your own heart.

"Before you ask me to tell you more, ask yourself, are you ready, truly, to live up to that? Are you prepared to examine your heart at every turn and act, for the welfare of others, on what you find there?"

Lucky had it in mind to say, *I wouldn't have asked if I didn't want the answer*. But his native caution flashed warning signs, and he took a lesson from Han, biting his lip to stop the words. *I'm not*, he admitted, startled at the truth of it. *I'm not ready. I can't even take care of myself now that the world's gone whacky. How could I possibly take on responsibilities that are "grave and great?"*

"No." He couldn't hear himself over the pounding of his heart, but he must have said it aloud. Thurlock relaxed beside him, and gave him a familiar, comforting squeeze on the ankle.

Lucky lay down and let his thoughts drift until the floor began to get noticeably harder, at which point he thought about leaving for the soft bed in his room on the second floor of Thurlock's house.

"He's your father, Luccan."

"What," Lucky said, reaching up to finger the jewel in his non-existent crown, "Lustrex?"

Thurlock snorted as if the question was more ridiculous than the rest of the conversation. "No, not Lustrex. Lohen Chiell. You asked who he was and how he knew your name."

Lucky's eyes burned, suddenly, and he wondered if he could be allergic to stardust, all the while concentrating on squeezing them tight to keep them dry. Once he could safely speak, he tried to ask everything at once. "What does he ...? Why did he ...? Where ... Thurlock?"

"Easy, Luccan. I'll tell you a little. I wish I could believe it would make you happy. It won't, but you'll want to know, and as Han—may Behl bless his scolding tongue—reminded me, you have a right to the information. Here, get up. Come sit with me. Nobody wants to hear these kinds of things lying down."

The Wizard stood, snapped his fingers, and the stars went out. The door to the tower room swung open before them and the lamps flamed to welcome them. Lucky followed Thurlock to the small space before the hearth, and when the old man dropped into one of the chairs, he took the other. He felt so at home, for once, that without thinking he tucked his bare feet up on the seat cushion.

Thurlock wagged a finger and rainbow flames crackled in the hearth, but even the warmth in the Wizard's voice didn't stop the chill that raced down Lucky's spine upon hearing his first few words.

"The truth is, Luccan, your father left you a long time ago. You were very small, four, maybe five years old the last time he came home for any meaningful length of time. He was a troubled man, had been for years, and he fell into some bad ways. We thought ... This will be hard to hear," he said, and reached a hand across the intervening space to squeeze Lucky's shoulder. "We thought he had killed himself."

Lucky drew in a breath that shook audibly. He wasn't sure why those words punched him in the stomach, but it hurt. Some people had tried to say the same about Grandpa Hank. That had nothing to do with Lucky's father, but somehow it did.

He was grateful for Thurlock's silence. He needed a moment to think. He tried to remember everything about the man he'd seen in the Ravine that day. He saw his hand wrapped around the Knife, his scars, his blind eye. He heard the man say his name. What did that expression on his misshapen face mean?

"Your father has always been a dangerous man, Luccan. He hasn't always been mean, or bad, or on the wrong side. But he's always been dangerous."

Lucky recalled Lohen Chiell's dragging left leg, and at the same time the way he'd fought through the Black-cloaks, and the incredible ease with which he'd hefted L'Aria over his shoulder. The Wizard's words sunk in.

"And he remains dangerous, withered limbs and all."

Lucky swallowed. "Thurlock, should I be afraid of him?"

"The fact is, I don't yet know."

The silence that followed did not separate Lucky from Thurlock. If anything, Lucky felt himself draw, in spirit, closer to the old man. He'd asked his questions; he'd received answers. He didn't like what he'd heard, but that didn't seem as important as he would have guessed.

They sat in the comfort of the Wizard's room long enough for Lucky to feel at peace.

The chimes of Thurlock's clock on the mantel downstairs rose through the chimney, striking twelve. "Ah," the Wizard said, yawning, "it's already tomorrow. How do you feel, now, young man?"

"Sleepy," Lucky answered, surprised by it. He rose, flashed a smile, and headed out the tower room door mumbling thanks and good night.

Words followed him on the stairs, whisper soft but close and clear.

"Spells and stars," the Wizard said. "Lost fathers, and being fourteen—those things are reasons, Luccan, never excuses. Ophiuchus has lost a foot, but I expect him to keep a firm hold on his serpent. You've lost many of the things a young person usually leans on, yet I expect you to find your balance. Act carefully, be wise, and trust your heart to know your friends. Even more than others, Suth Chiell, you cannot afford poor choices."

17. A Farewell Cup for Uncle Han

Lucky stood at his bedroom window, listening to the faint shuffling sounds the Wizard made in his tower three stories up, and wondering if there was something he should be doing. Across the yard, Han's little white house gleamed under a blue sky that felt impossible. Lucky pushed up on the window and it readily opened wide. He took it for a sign, slid out, and made his way down the maple.

Han's front door swung open before he knocked. Han stood square-shouldered in the flat yellow light of late morning, his unstrung bow resting in his hands. Behind him, sword and shield glittered from the wall.

"You don't have to knock," he said. "Just come in."

"I thought it would be locked."

"It's always locked," Han laughed, "But you can always come in anyway."

He must have seen Lucky's eyes steal to the bow in his hands. "Tell me lad," he said, eyebrows arched, "as far as you remember, have you ever shot a bow?"

They gathered up arrows and filled a small pack with apples, cheese, and canteens of water for breakfast. Han showed Lucky how to position the quiver at his shoulder for easy reach, and dropped in a bundle of yellow arrows with bright pink feathers.

"It's so you can find them easily," he said.

Lucky pointed to the other arrows, the ones with feathers patterned like fire. "What about these?"

"They're flame arrows. When they strike their target, they ignite, and they burn much hotter and stronger than ordinary fire. The birds who give the feathers are rare, and the arrows have to be enchanted one at a time by a wizard. Usually apprentices do it, but the three with golden shafts and feathers were done by Thurlock. We never use flamers for practice."

Han led him to a small valley just over the hill from Thurlock's, where a streamlet flashed in the sun. The grass was as green as the banks of Black Creek. The sky stretched shoulder to shoulder, a wide blue field with one woolly cloud grazing near the horizon.

Lucky stopped in his tracks. *It's too beautiful.* "How could a day like this happen, right now?"

Han seemed to know what he meant. "Sometimes, it's coincidence," he said. "There might be an hour of quiet in the middle of a battle, a week of peace in a year-long war." He glanced up to where Thurlock's tower loomed against the blue sky, chewing his bottom lip.

"I suspect this is different, though. I'd bet Thurlock's clock the old man bought us a little time so we can rest. Or maybe to keep us out of his hair. Either way, it probably cost him dear." His eyes dropped sideways to meet Lucky's, full of his sudden smile, and he gave Lucky's shoulder a squeeze. "It won't last, but we'd be ingrates if we didn't enjoy it while we had the chance."

Simple enough, Lucky thought, when Han showed him how to string the bow, but when he tried it he discovered he had three feet and two left hands. Han stopped him, patient, but perhaps teasing just a little. "To start with," he said, "you've got your feet backward. This one goes behind the bow, that one in front, so you can bend it toward you. Equally important, you've got to hook the string to the bottom end *before* you start."

It was humbling.

Later, though, practice draws went well, and Han said, "You're stronger than you look, lad." The praise patched Lucky's pride, and he smiled even after his first arrow fell from the string and bounced off his toe.

They followed the stream's green twists down through the foothills, away from people and houses and roads. They took turns shooting at long abandoned wasp hives and birds nests, a few rotting hay rolls, hollow logs, and once a cracked blue bucket. Han always made his shot in a single fluid motion, "look, draw, release," and he never missed.

Thurlock's tower stayed in view, a constant reminder, but they were clear of its shadow and they didn't talk about trouble at all until late afternoon. They retrieved arrows, and Han congratulated Lucky.

"Look," he said, "you've got a nice grouping here. It means you're consistent. That's good, because then you know what to fix." Shouldering the bow, he said, "We'll work on that next time. For now we'd best get back. If I keep you out here any longer, the Wizard will likely skin me alive."

Lucky stopped abruptly, staring at Thurlock's square-eyed tower.

Han stopped too, and turned to him with on eyebrow cocked. "Figure of speech, lad."

"It's not that," Lucky said, running two hands through his hair. "It just ... everything's so crazy."

Kindness and sorrow mingled in Han's voice. "It is," he said, "and I expect it will get crazier."

***

With no lights on, the tile in Han's neat, tiny kitchen shone with a slow gleam reflecting a half-moon sky. Han leaned a hip against the counter, looking out the open window into the summer night and fingering the runes marking his bow. The touch took him back to his own youth, and the memory of wood smoke tickled his nose.

"You've made a beautiful bow," Lohen had said. "Let's not take chances. Burn the runes in, instead of carving; it will keep the fibers strong." He could still feel Lohen's rough hand fall on his shoulder. "You're going to be a powerful man, Han. You'll need a worthy weapon."

The memory had remained fresh; he relived it with the first arrow he nocked every time he used the bow. That time with his brother had been a rare day. *Like today with Luccan. Respite in troubled times.*

He leaned on the tiles of his countertop to gaze up at Thurlock's tower, all its windows ablaze as the Wizard doggedly pursued answers far into the night. Suddenly, in the dark patch above the roof's peak, silvery lights burst and then blossomed like far away fireworks. "Falling stars," Han said, trying out the words Thurlock had told him Earthborns used. *Though scientifically,* the old man had explained, *they're meteors.*

"No." Han shook his head, and then named them as Ethrans always did. "Wizard's tears."

Thurlock had not slept more than a few hours in three days. He hadn't left his tower all day except once to fetch a book and once to quiz Luccan on the progress of his memory, which had taken little time and left the lad nervous and the Wizard disappointed. Han had left trays laden with sweet tea and the old man's favorite foods—even maple bars—by Thurlock's closed door, and worried when he picked them up again hours later, cold and untouched.

Now, Han filled a tall amber glass with water from his kitchen tap. He drank deeply, washing down his anxiety. *I'll find out soon enough what's troubling the old man.* He put the glass down and started to turn, but glanced across the yard to the tower one last time. From the Wizard's high window, a square of paper drifted down like an autumn leaf, coming to rest in the grass afloat on moonlit dew.

By the time Han crossed the yard to pick it up, his sandaled feet were wet and cold. "Come upstairs, Han," the message read. "Now. We need to talk."

Since Han had last seen it, Thurlock had transformed his tower into a fire hazard. Ancient Ethran charts papered the walls, many now spotted yellow with sticky notes. The Wizard adored sticky notes. He'd also developed a fondness for broad-tipped markers in rainbow hues, which explained the feast of color amongst the heaps of paper crowding floor, table, and every flat surface.

Books five inches thick perched where they could, open to dog-eared, underlined pages. Hovering over a few of these tomes, golden lights with no visible source of energy or support scanned the print, placing an arrow here, a question mark there, turning the pages as if with a wet finger. None of what he saw was new to Han. He'd just never seen so much of it at one time. "What's happened, sir?"

Thurlock's spectacles hung at the very end of his nose, and he looked over their tops at Han. "Nothing new has happened at all." He walked over to the table and rifled around, digging to the bottom of the centermost heap. He extracted a page, paced back and forth along the only clear path in the floor three times, then put the paper on the table unexamined and laid his glasses atop it. He palmed his eyes, sad or weary or both. "Sit down," he said.

Han did so, and waited.

Thurlock opened his mouth several times as if to speak, but only cleared his throat. Finally, he rolled his eyes, reached a magically gloved hand into the fire, and hefted the kettle to pour water over the instant cocoa in two cups. Taking a seat before the hearth, he asked, "Luccan's okay?"

Han knew that wasn't the question the Wizard had been building up to, and he almost said so, but thought better of it. Relaxing into the other armchair, he crossed an ankle over the opposite knee and took a thumb to a scuff on his sandal. "He seems fine, had a quiet day." He took the cup Thurlock offered, meeting his eyes. "Thank you," he said, referring to more than cocoa. "I think he's starting to trust me."

"An uncle's just reward," Thurlock smiled gently.

Han matched the smile with a sad one of his own. "I suppose; but he still doesn't remember?"

"Getting close, I think."

"Did you see what he brought out of the attic?"

"No, I was working. I meant to ask—"

"He came out carrying that old blanket he had when he was a baby—the red plaid." This time Thurlock smiled thoroughly enough to crinkle his eyes.

Han grinned back. "He took it with him to bed!" In his mind's eye, he could still see a copper-toned two-year-old trailing that same blanket everywhere he toddled.

Soon the smiles slipped off their faces. In the golden light, Han felt Thurlock's eyes on him, and he decided to make things easier. "Do you want me to leave tonight, sir?"

Thurlock snapped his fingers at each of the magical lights around the room, killing all the flames but one. In shadow, the Wizard's face looked somber. "Morning will be soon enough, my friend," he said. "Come an hour before dawn, if you would. We'll share a Farewell Cup?"

***

By the time Han left Thurlock's tower, time had crept close to midnight. He yawned as he started down the stairs. Busy mulling over all that Thurlock had said, the creak of a footstep on the stairs startled him. He looked up and froze, his own foot halfway between one riser and the next. For a painful moment he had mistaken the shadowed face looking up from the landing for his brother's, so similar was its shape.

Luccan spoke. "You're going to leave."

Han stood mute, blinking.

He said it again. "You're leaving."

"Yes," Han answered, but he didn't try to explain everything that Thurlock had told him—about time compressing in some places and stretching in others, wormholes in the fabric of the worlds, reversing poles, shrinking vortices, and uncertain endings. He didn't understand it, anyway.

He did understand that Black Creek Ravine had become a deadly place, and that someone had to go there and do what could be done about it, but he didn't say that either. He didn't explain that he remained the only someone that might do the job. He didn't tell his nephew that, having chosen long ago, he couldn't be anything but Han Shieth, Wizard's Left Hand, now that need had arisen.

He especially didn't tell Luccan that the Wizard had plans for him, too.

He only said, "It's important, lad."

Luccan's whisper quivered. "Don't go."

Han caught his lip between his teeth, afraid to try to speak.

"Or let me go with you."

Han had no answer.

Luccan looked at him for a long time, his young face growing hard, his dry eyes gleaming in the blade of moonlight that slashed the stairwell. Han remained silent and still until Luccan turned and closed the door of his room firmly between them. They hadn't said farewell.

***

Two hours before dawn, a cool spear of moonlight pierced Han's eyes and woke him from a dream of dragons, swords, and drums. He sat up sweating, eyes darting to the corners of his familiar room, furnished only with the bed and a single stand, which held a small chest and a green-glass reading lamp. In accord with habit, Han had kept the white walls free of decoration save for a crest above the light switch, three inches high and five across. A Flame Eagle.

Wrought of sun-metal, its fiery breath curled over its head like a wreath. A shock of arrows rode in the grip of its talons, and its wings were spread. The tip-most flight feathers each ended in a blade. This was the crest of Behlishan's Guard, the premier infantry of Ethra's Sunlands. Among them, Han had become the most premier of all. He'd chosen a Warrior's path at nineteen, quite young by Ethran standards. It had been easy to choose, and since then he'd never doubted, never once answered a call to arms with reluctance or regret.

Until last night, no one had ever asked him not to go.

Han shook away the troubling memory of his midnight encounter with Luccan and set about his preparations.

Dawn was barely a hint in the east when he stepped into Thurlock's room, but hearth and candle gave sufficient light to see that Thurlock had restored the tower to order. Han knew the Wizard had seen to the clean-up for his sake.

In his honor, Thurlock had closed his books and stacked them, rolled his charts and tied them, gathered his papers and bound them in portfolios with neatly penned titles. Han valued order, and because the Wizard valued him, he'd spelled the windows spotless, chased dust from the mantle, made the bed, buffed the floor, and laid straight the rugs beside his bed and hearth. Han loved beauty and color, so Thurlock's flames threw sparks that bloomed into lilies and roses; red, orange, and gold to mirror the blossoms filling the green vase centered on the table.

Beside the vase dwelled two earthenware cups without handle or stem and a slender bottle half-filled with the amber liquid known as Shahna's Gold, elixir of the Farewell Cup.

Warriors and Wizards of Ethra did not take the Farewell Cup lightly. By tradition, it cleared the mind and shored-up the heart for battle. By tradition, it assured that friends would be united when the fighting was done. By tradition, any cause would be thwarted if the Farewell Cup was shared by hearts not allied in peace and united in purpose.

Thus, when Thurlock stood in crisp robes, silver hair newly tied, and asked if he should pour, Han said, "Not just yet, sir. Please, sit with me by the fire?"

Han had things he would have liked to say, but they would be fruitless, he knew it. Why tell Thurlock he didn't want to go? Why say that leaving Luccan, after the boy pleaded with him to stay, was just too hard? He couldn't beg to be excused.

He'd come knowing that, fit for the mission. His hair was tight in a top knot; a sun-metal band protected his brow. He wore the uniform of Behlishan's Guard: kilted sun-cloth tunic over breeches banded over the knee; sash and belt of dragon hide fitted to secure weapons, provisions and kit; shin-strapped sandals of pliable, durable, northern sealskin.

He sank his teeth into his lip, said nothing and tried to think of the greater good, to bring his heart into harmony with the needs of the moment, and with the Wizard—who wasn't to blame.

In the end, after a silence so long the sun passed through dawn and on to breakfast, Thurlock said, "You are the only one I can send. You won't be abandoning the boy, Han Shieth."

"Do you think that he will come to understand that, sir?"

"I hope so."

Han got up suddenly, and for lack of a meaningful destination, went to the door and let Lemon Martinez in to curl up on the hearthstones. "It's getting late, sir," he said. "Orders?"

Thurlock let out a sigh heavy enough to jostle his magic flames. "Do what you can to hobble the Witch," he said. "Try to disable whatever tools she's got on the loose in that ravine. The things I've discovered in my studies these last few days ... I believe she knows. Her window of opportunity is closing too, and she's desperate."

The Wizard stood and began to pace in the small space before the hearth, curving around Han who stood motionless in his path. "While she had plenty of time, she would have done what she could to keep him alive as long as possible. The longer he would live under her control, the more of his strength she could steal, and the more effectively she could utilize it. But now ..."

He stopped, pivoting to meet Han's eyes, standing silent until his swaying robes fell still. "She'll make a move, soon. If she takes him and can't subvert him quickly, she'll use faster means to extract what power she can from him. In that case, he won't long survive."

Their eyes remained locked for a long moment. Then Han nodded, and Thurlock turned to sag against the mantle. "I'll do what I can to prepare Luccan, and I'll try ... I'll take him home. I'll come back and join you here as soon as I can.

"Meanwhile, try to find the Blades. Help the dog, for kindness sake, if you find her and you can." The old man paused, and his eyes softened. "And, whatever it might mean at this point, you'll have to deal with your brother."

***

A solitary bird sang outside Lucky's window, but he lingered on a gold-lit island midway between sleep and wakefulness. Red and yellow plaid lay close to his face, blurring in his half-open eyes, and the fabric's softness soothed his cheek. With two hands he clutched the blanket by its silk bound edge. He let his eyes close again and in that instant he saw other hands clutching that same shiny binding.

There had been four strong hands holding four corners, lifting the blanket to toss a small boy, screaming with delight, toward the sun. The colors of the plaid swirled around young Luccan as he'd fallen laughing back onto the brushed wool, then he'd flown again into the joy of blue sky. The two men had laughed with him, and the sound had echoed from distant cliffs.

Lucky sat up in his bed in Thurlock's house, scarcely breathing. He hugged the blanket tight to his chest and closed his eyes, afraid to lose the picture in his mind. He was awake; it was not a dream; it was a memory.

Four brown hands had held the blanket, two men. One man was his father, but that face he couldn't see. The other face belonged to his uncle, Han Shieth.

Blanket flying behind him like the cape of a low-budget super hero, Lucky crashed up the stairs. He lifted his fist to bang on the Wizard's door, but it swung open at his first touch and he tripped on the Wizard's pajamas and fell through. On his way to the floor, his vision swept past Han's sword and bow leaning against the wall, and as he picked himself up, he saw Han, Warrior clad and rock strong. An unfamiliar pride welled in his chest. He let it explode in a shout.

"Uncle Han!"

For once, he must have taken both men by surprise, for they stood in front of the magic fire, staring at him.

Thurlock's open mouth shut itself and then spread into a first rate smile.

Han's smile played over his lips, cautious. He almost whispered, "You remember, lad?"

Lucky said, quieter, "Uncle Han ..." He took a step toward the man, but before he could take another, Han reached him and wrapped him in a hug a bear would have envied.

Thurlock said, light in his voice, "Be careful, Han, you'll break him," and Lucky secretly agreed. Han only pulled the surprised Wizard inside the hug, too.

Lucky started to feel like sandwich meat, and said "Mmmmmppphh." Han let go, laughing, and for a while they all stood at loose ends in front of the fire. Lucky folded and unfolded his blanket, the cat looked daggers at Lucky and swatted at the cloth, and Han smiled and bobbed his head. Thurlock scratched his beard, mumbling, "Good, very good indeed."

The silence started to feel permanent, so Lucky said. "You're leaving now, Uncle Han."

"I am, but it isn't good-bye."

Thurlock said, "It's necessary, Luccan."

Lucky pushed his hair back, then crossed his arms over his chest and took a firm stance much like Han's. He said, "Be careful." Both men seemed to breathe easier.

Han gave Lucky a nod and a smile. "I'll do my best."

"Join us," the Wizard said, "for the Farewell Cup," and he told Lucky the story of Shahna, a Warrior woman from the mists of Ethra's past, and the liquid gold that had sealed her oath to the Flame Eagle.

"And so," he finished, "we take a cup of Gold together, at partings like these. It's tradition."

Lucky stepped up to join in the toast, and Thurlock conjured a third earthenware cup. He poured, and passed out the drinks. He had lifted his own cup and seemed about to say something profound, but Han interrupted.

"Don't you think it might be a little ... fiery ... for him, sir?"

"Oh! Well, yes. Sorry." He tapped the side of Luccan's cup, and smiled. "All taken care of," he said. "No stronger than apple juice."

The Wizard's toast didn't seem so profound after all. "Here's to a good end," he said.

Lucky agreed heartily with the sentiment, but found that even without its flame, Shahna's gold tasted bittersweet.

18. A Young Person's Guide to Making Sense of It

At breakfast, Lucky and Thurlock occupied opposite ends of the dining table and between the two of them polished off six maple bars, two cinnamon rolls, and a half-gallon of chocolate milk. Lucky had chuckled, thinking, *by the time Han comes back we'll both be round, toothless, and stuck in the doors trying to get out for groceries.*

He had grinned at the image until Thurlock shattered it. "Brush your teeth," the Wizard said, leaning around the chandelier. "Then clean the basement."

Lucky was not unwilling, though for the sake of form he wrinkled his brow and protested as if Thurlock had told him to break all his own toes. Teen angst, Lucky realized, came naturally when living with an adult that assigned chores. Truthfully, he hoped the basement would be like the attic. Maybe he would find some kind of touchstone, something like the plaid blanket.

The cellar door opened like a vault from a raised concrete frame hidden in the pansies behind the mulberry, though Lucky was sure no such thing existed when he had crouched in that spot four long days ago, to hide. At the bottom of a flight of narrow stone steps he found a cavernous space, so still he could hear the dust settle. The bare bulb overhead lent a shimmer to the falling particles, but otherwise illuminated only four quarry-stone walls, a dirt floor aged as hard as concrete, and the goose bumps prickling Lucky's arms.

Other than dust and air, the space held only a few underfed spiders and a horrendous amount of dirt. Lucky ignored the spiders and attacked the dirt with broom, mop, vigor, and determination, but the effort was doomed. If Lucky swept, the dirt went airborne, then precipitated; if he mopped, it clumped, then dried. He tried wishing it clean, but nothing changed even a tiny bit.

He gave up and sat in the corner to think about Han.

Han had said Lucky could walk with him, "To the top of the first hill, no farther." When they'd reached the hilltop, Lucky had stood next to him, knee-deep in grey-green grass saying nothing until a hot, harsh wind blew from the east and stung his eyes. Then he'd asked, "Will you be gone long?"

Han had shrugged. "Not if I can help it." Chewing his lip, he'd glanced up to where the windows of the Wizard's Tower winked in the sun. He seemed, for once, at a loss for what to say, but then he caught Lucky's eye. "Remember, I have all of Thurlock's pajamas in my chest of drawers. Don't bother asking him if you need clean ones."

Lucky rolled his eyes, a skill he was getting better at.

Han smiled and stepped away.

"Wait!" Lucky had fidgeted trying to find words. "Uncle Han, I'm sorry," he said, shoving his hair out of his eyes. "If I could remember home, we could all go there and you wouldn't have to do this."

Han had stepped back near Lucky, taken his drooping shoulders in his hands, and given them a small shake. "None of this is your fault," he'd said, the gold in his eyes blazing. And, if you go home now, I'll be glad because you'll be safe ... safer, but there will still be things that have to be done here, and I'll still be the one to stay and do them."

Now, Lucky sat in the cellar's dust, sneezing, sniffing and wiping his nose with a neat square of tissue he took from his pocket, wishing he hadn't started thinking about Han. He'd prefer not to think about anything, it was all too strange. Scratching his head angrily, he spoke loud enough to shake dust clouds from the walls. "I just wish I could make sense of it."

Instantly, Lucky felt a small explosion in his belly. Though he didn't remember passing out, he came to with an aching head and dust coating his eyelashes. His hand, he found, cradled a miniature book. The title glittered in the dim light, embossed in gilt runes. Though the runes looked as strange as ever, and though Lucky could not account for the sudden knowledge, he knew exactly what they meant.

"The Revelations Regarding the Suth Chiell in the Last Days of the Mark of the Sun," he read aloud. He lifted the book to the light to make out the smaller, English print below that. "A Young Person's Guide to Making Sense of It."

He read it again, twice. He cracked the book open and popped it shut. His heart had turned to butterflies and his hands shook. Dare he believe he was holding the answers in his hands? What if he didn't like what he read?

I'll have to take the chance. A shiver ran through him as he opened the book to the first yellowed, onionskin page. *Perhaps tonight I'll be home.*

Yeah, right.

On the first page, in small, plain English typeface, were the words, "In darkest night dwells brightest light." On the second page, "When friends cry, the loyal fly." These were not revelations; they were proverbs, or fortunes from Chinese cookies. Some of them had a nice ring. Lucky especially liked the sound of, "When hope fails, love sails." Still, if they meant anything at all, Lucky had no clue what it might be, and they didn't strike him as momentous. He flipped through the pages, shaking his head, sorely disappointed.

Until he got to the end. The last two facing pages were cryptic, yes, but important. The hints were not subtle.

When Lucky opened to those pages, a choir of voices accompanied by a full symphony orchestra burst forth in a hyper-angelic crescendo. If that wasn't enough, the bold, black typeface was aflame, burning the words into the page as if pressed with a hot iron brand.

"Like Bonanza," Lucky said, remembering Grandpa Hank's smile every time the re-runs came on TV with the Ponderosa Brand burning through the map. The flaming words in the book seemed to say, "See here, this can't be all bad."

And it wasn't, he decided, once he'd read the messages. The first, at the top of the second to the last page, read, "The broken lamp may yet shield the flame." It was impossible to grasp; its meaning seemed to hide in Lucky's thoughts like rain in a river. Yet it was like a parent tucking warmth around a dreaming child, unseen and barely sensed, but a comfort all the same. Lucky breathed deep and, for the moment that fit inside that breath, felt safe.

Halfway down that same page, still-smoking letters read, "A Gateway may be hidden, but never truly closed." *Whatever that means.* As soon as Lucky finished that thought, an asterisk flashed next to the words, and another down at the bottom followed by this in fine print: "Some scholars, notably Willock III, have argued that this passage refers to the fabled Suth Chiell's Gateway, of pre-modern times." Lucky still had no clue what the words meant, but they seemed to hold out some kind of promise, and his mood continued to rise.

The last words in the book, scrawled large on the final page, were spoke directly to Lucky. Or so he surmised, since he was the Suth Chiell who'd conjured the book. "Though all other hopes should fail," he read aloud, "Suth Chiell, you will prevail."

Feeling the prediction reinforce his backbone, he lifted his eyebrows. "Okay, then," he said in that on-again, off-again deep voice, that man's voice that was starting to sound familiar.

He admitted that it was hard to give full faith to a prediction that burned itself onto a page in a book he'd wished into his hands while cleaning a cellar that didn't exist beneath a Wizard's house. Still, he saw no reason to quibble.

***

The golden-globe handle of Thurlock's umbrella flamed in the sunlight, sparking return flashes from the chandelier's prisms. Thurlock picked it up and let it thump the floor in time with his right foot as he paced behind the table, robes chasing him like a worried dog at his heels. Lemon sat with his back turned, snapping his tail against the floor, disturbed by the Wizard's unease.

"Uncle," Liliana said from the M.E.R.L.I.N., "Can't you be still? You're making me seasick." She did look ill. Her hair looked brassy, her eyes heavy, and her complexion paled nearly snow white against the azure wall of her dressing room.

His pacing wasn't causing all that, but he stopped anyway, leaning on the windowsill. He wished he could escape his troubles by climbing out. "Liliana," he said, "I'm worried, more worried than a Wizard should ever be."

He came back to stand where he could meet his niece's gaze but, struck by the realization that her capacities were stretched thinner even than his own, he clamped his mouth shut. He'd been on the verge of confiding all his concerns. Now he wondered if it might be better to tell her nothing at all. But she'd be anxious to hear about Luccan, and she had a right to know about Lohen.

"I've sent Han into the ravine," he told her. I'm not certain what else he'll meet, but I know he'll have to deal with his brother." Thurlock started to pace again. "I've never seen Han so unsure."

Lili ignored the remark about Han's state of mind. "What do you mean, 'deal with' Lohen?"

"Good question. I don't know the answer." Truthfully, Lohen's actions in the ravine, the day he'd charged in on Maizie's heels and then flown to L'Aria's rescue, bewildered Thurlock. He hadn't tried to hurt Luccan or engage Han directly, but Han had said he wasn't one-hundred percent certain whether Lohen had been part of Mordred's bunch.

"You know Lohen better than anyone, Lili. What do you think he'll do now?"

"When I married him, I never imagined I would say this, but—" Her voice caught in her throat and she looked away, breathing deeply for a long thirty seconds. When she spoke again, her voice had cleared, and only the white handkerchief she clutched and crumpled told how hard the words came. "Lohen has been troubled and at least a little insane as long as I've known him, but it's different now. He's too far gone."

Her voice fell to a whisper, as if she passed a death sentence. "He's past redemption. Whatever he does next, it won't be good."

Thurlock stroked his beard, as if smoothing its kinks would straighten his thoughts as well. "Lili," he began, and then stopped, looking out the window and absently fingering the roundness of his umbrella handle. It began to glow and hum, the disguised staff so much a part of Thurlock that his distress called its magic to the ready.

"Put it down, Uncle."

He didn't put it down, but he stilled his fingers and concentrated on thinking as clearly as he could about the threat of Lohen Chiell. *Am I certain,* he asked himself, *that he means harm, that he is, as Lili says, not redeemable? If so, I can stop him, easily enough.* But, in plain words, stopping him meant killing him, and everything that defined Thurlock as a Wizard and as a man rebelled.

Liliana broke into his thoughts. "He's beyond hope."

Thurlock raised his grey eyes, steadier now, more certain. "We don't know that."

"He's done horrible things, Uncle."

"Some, yes, but not half so many or so horrible as the storytellers make out." He rose from his chair and went to the window again, thumping his umbrella beside him like a cane. "I think that ending up in the service of the Witch was the last thing he would have wanted."

"He joined up with her, didn't he?" A bitter laugh punctuated her words.

Thurlock whirled around to face her. "*Willingly*? You feel *sure* of that?"

It was less a question than a rebuke and Lili's eyes sparked, but she stayed silent, waiting.

Focused on something far off, Thurlock pulled the tie from his hair and shook it out, a silver halo. "A thousand years is a long time to be alive, niece. It gives one a lot of opportunity for mistakes." He fixed his gaze unflinching on Lili's eyes. "The last thing Lohen did that we all knew about was jump into Mardhral Canyon meaning, I'm sure, to take his own life. Do you know what he did just before that?"

Lili shook her head, mute.

"I do." Thurlock said. "He came to me and asked to join this mission, to help find Luccan. I couldn't bring myself to trust him. That, I think now, was one of the worst blunders I have ever made."

"Uncle—"

"Hear me out!" Thurlock's weathered visage reddened. "This is not easy for me to admit, even to myself. As I said, it was a mistake. Yes, bitterness and anger had taken him, but I should have looked deeper." He shook his head in regret. "At the least I should have taken the opportunity to keep him close, where I might have prevented him from doing more harm."

"You couldn't have—"

"I could have, and I should have, but I did not, and he jumped." He worked his jaws around a bitter taste. "While we all thought him dead, I could almost live with it. I told myself that it was better, that his misery was over, that Luccan and Ethra and all of us were safer." His eyelids fell closed. When he looked up, only the twitch of the tic beneath his eye betrayed his remorse.

"Uncle," Liliana pleaded. "He's lost."

"No," he said, but then hedged. "Maybe."

"*Maybe!*" Liliana's wide eyes and shocked tone said clearly she thought his mind had snapped at last.

"Yes," he said, with a bit of sauce. "Yes, maybe, as in perhaps, as in I'm not sure. I've recalled what Han said when I debriefed him about the Ravine, about the moment when Lohen called Luccan by his name. He said that his brother's face 'shone as if with hope.'"

Liliana stood silent, twirling a long golden lock around her forefinger, then sat again at her dressing table, laid her arms on the wood, and rested her head there. After some time, she pushed herself up. "Good day then Uncle," she said with no trace of emotion. "Keep me posted."

"Wait, child. There's something I want you to do."

With a tired look and a heavy sigh, Lili turned back to Thurlock.

"Talk to your son," the Wizard said. "Tomorrow, I'll try to bring him home."

19. A Story of Brothers with Blades

The June sun was only more punishment to Lohen. He trod the heart of the Ravine, the banks of Black Creek, blind to its beauty. The rainbow-flanked fish, the golden lilies, the sun-caught red of a dragon fly—they were no more than a trial to be borne like the sucking black mud beneath his feet. Anger turned everything ugly, blazed back at the sun from his eyes. He hated the rushing demands of rage, but he'd lost all hope that he could stop it.

He had tried. In the chill dawn mist, he'd built a lively fire between the sheltering cedar and the singing creek. The slow healing of his limbs, surely wrought by the Black Blade's touch, had given him hope that his heart could be healed, too. That the wrong he'd done could be redeemed. He'd trembled with fear that this slender thread of hope would snap if he tried it, but he'd thought of Luccan and resolved to act.

He'd cleansed the Blade in the flames, bathed in the cold creek, sent up a smoke of cedar and herbs to clear his mind, doing everything he knew to make sure this magic would be unpolluted. "I never meant to hurt my son," he'd said, swearing "by Behl's Light," though it had been so long since that name had passed his lips that the shock of it hurt. He'd repeated the oath until his throat had gone dry.

This would be his last chance at even a small measure of mental peace. This would be his only chance to help his son, the boy whose first word had been "Papa," the boy who'd grown now to the size of a man.

"Make right the last wrong," the Blade had instructed.

He'd called Maizie, using the magic's hold one last time to compel the dog's obedience. Then, finding a surprise of relief at the kindness of it, he set about doing what must be done, so that he might, as the Blade had promised, begin again. Hours had washed by since he'd countered the hex and released Maizie, yet she'd followed on his heels every step, eyes alight with devotion.

Nothing else had changed.

In the past few days, Lohen had become stronger, but his face remained a scarred mask, his left eye socket remained an empty pit. The scab where his soul had once tethered still itched and burned, and his red-fisted heart still pounded his breastbone demanding, if not justice, revenge.

His mind still circled, searching for a word, that single name that might render him worthy once again to be called 'Papa.' That secret stayed hidden but a memory surfaced, a memory he'd held submerged for two centuries, the memory of what a soul blacker than his had done.

The stream spoke as it hissed over rocks and choked in the shallows, and the rasping taunt bit into him like a surgeon's saw, slicing bone with every stroke. He tried to shut his ears against the story he heard in the rushing water, the story he hated most. The story of his life, of the day he'd lost his youth, his home, and his hope. The day hate had dug its seed into his heart.

He smelled smoke, striding down the hill toward home. He'd visited Nedhra city, fifty miles from the family's stead. In addition to news and letters for his parents, he carried a gift for his brother's eleventh birthday—a sling that wound up and would toss stones an incredible distance. He looked forward to seeing Han smile when he put it in his hands.

The smoke disturbed his happy thoughts. It didn't have the flavor of a cooking fire, or the pungency of the smokes used for curing meat or fish. It was the wrong time of year for the fields to be burned off, and the smell seemed wrong, dirty, contaminated. He stopped when he rounded the bend and had a clear sight of his parents' stead.

And then he started running.

Remnants still burned, but only low ridges where the walls had stood, huddled pieces of resistant furniture, and in one place a blazing doorframe leading on both sides to nothing.

The first corpse he saw, as he stood with the heat of flames and coals on his face, was his uncle, an old man whose skill with horses had taken him to work in the far north long ago, and whose devotion to an orphaned girl had reaped him no reward of love. Abandoned in old age, he'd come to stay with his sister's family, bringing a kind face, a sad smile, and grand stories of winged horses and starry northern skies.

He'd not simply been killed, nor had Lohen's mother and father. Everywhere he looked, Lohen saw evidence of torture. He couldn't bear seeing it, but he couldn't look away. He stood, not moving or thinking, until night crept in and the flames around him hissed into silence.

Mindless, Lohen turned and took a step back toward the road, and that's when he heard a faint sound. He followed the breathy cry and found Han hidden in a holly thicket, hugging his knees and sobbing. At first Lohen was only glad, relieved to see him alive. Then the truth dawned, and he fell to his knees, the wind knocked from his lungs by a new horror.

Han Shieth had seen his family murdered.

Lohen struggled to choke back nausea and pulled Han out of the shelter, shielding him from the holly that tore at his own skin. Ignoring the stink of vomit, he carried Han to the brook where they had fished and played, and where the remains of their parents and uncle were mercifully out of sight.

It seemed to him that the stream should run hot with ash, black with filth, or red with blood, but it was cool and clean. In moonlit summer stillness, Lohen bathed his brother's face, cleansed and soothed the fist he must have bitten to keep from screaming, and let Ethra's sweet water wash him clean.

When he'd done all he could, he sat with his back against a willow and held Han under the crook of his muscled arm. He sang their mother's songs in a low, steady voice until Han slept, and then he kept singing until, against all odds, the sun came up.

***

Already glazed with sweat in the afternoon sun, Han made the summit of a rocky, thistle-grown ridge to find Lohen in plain sight at the bottom of the descending slant. Unbelievably, he kneeled at Black Creek's edge, choking on sobs and slamming his hands into the rough, pebbled ground again and again. Han's heart fisted in his throat to see his brother's pain, and without thinking he called out.

Lohen leapt to his feet and whirled to face him, grief translated instantly to rage, eye blazing a challenge. He moved swiftly, crashing through thin ranks of trees to claim possession of a level clearing just inside the forest that studded the slope like a rough crust. Feet planted wide, he lifted the Black Blade in an arc over his head and with a word transformed that implement into its alter ego, the Sword of Light.

Han would have to fight, but reluctance born of old love and new pity gripped him like barbed wire shackles. If his life was all he would wager, he might have left his sword sheathed and met his brother's blade with bared neck. But the stakes were far higher, and when the Wizard had said, "*Deal with your brother,*" he'd made a claim on duty and a Warrior's honor.

Before descending the slope Han secured his bow, quiver, and pack out of the way of his sword arm, strapped on his shield, and adjusted his knife in the sheath bound to his leg. Then he clipped the two-inch-wide sun-metal circlet on his head, slipping it over the crown piece that made it a fair helmet.

Finally, he loosened his sword and whispered its name: "*Chiell Shan.*" Child of Light, that meant, and for all that it carried death on its shoulders, Han knew it had always fought for Behlishan. Forged of sun-metal, an alloy with no Earth-made match, the strong, light blade never went brittle though sharpened to an edge so fine it almost could not be seen. It had drawn its first blood in battle over five hundred years ago. Han's grandfather had carried it to war, great-grandfather before that.

The legendary weapon had rested over the mantelpiece in Han's childhood home. Thurlock had plucked it from the ashes after the fire, when Han was eleven, and presented it to him when he'd started weapons training at fifteen. The Wizard had told him the sword's stories and its name. "Never," the old Master had said, "use this blade with hatred or vengeance."

When he stepped into the clearing and drew his weapon, it felt good in his hand and the metal rang out a call to duty. Yet even that music, a Warrior's song, could not subdue his whispering hope that he and his brother might find another way.

Han stood upslope from Lohen, and that should have given him an advantage. He was stronger, less damaged, and more practiced. His sword had been crafted with magic at the forge, and he knew the weapon better than he knew his own hand. The odds, it would seem, should be in his favor.

But Lohen put the sinking sun at his back and in Han's eyes. Though shorter in stature, he'd always been brawny and tough. Most of what Han knew about fighting, he'd learned first from Lohen. A hunter, not a Warrior, yet all of Ethra renowned him for his skill with the blade. And his weapon was not made *with* magic; it was made *of* magic. No part of Han was fool enough to think this fight would be easily won.

"Han Shieth," Lohen said when they faced off, his tone casual as though they met for coffee.

"Brother," Han answered, the word sticking in his throat.

Lohen whispered, and indigo light flared along the Blade, pulsing from hilt to tip. The sword looked solid, one minute gleaming like polished iron, the next like blue steel. The light was real; the steel and iron weren't. It didn't matter. Real or illusion, the sword could kill.

Lohen's first savage swing came overhand, meant to cleave bone. Han dropped into a defensive crouch, gripped his sword with two hands and raised it from his shoulder, sliding Lohen's strike off the flat of his blade. Lohen struck next at Han's left flank, but Han pivoted and blocked with his shield. Shifting his grip, he reversed his sword and smashed the pommel into Lohen's face like an iron fist, crushing skin over bone beneath the empty eye socket. He'd bought a moment to breathe.

Lohen stepped back and swiped his hand over the gash. He glanced at the scarlet smear on his fingers, the red of it like flame, like rage. Han met Lohen's ever-faster slashes and thrusts with shield and blade. Once he even knocked away his brother's sword with the back of his hand. He hit the flat of the blade, but still the edge nicked the back of his knuckle, and Lohen pressed harder, seizing advantage from Han's pain.

Still Han held back. He danced away from Lohen, parried his powerful moves, feinted but never tried to drive his sword home.

He couldn't win the way he was fighting, and he knew it. *If an opponent means to kill, and one does naught but defend, the defender will certainly die.* Those words made up the Warrior's First-Learned Premise. As he pivoted and ducked and danced his defense, the axiom sang through his mind, always in the voice of the man who'd taught it to him—Lohen.

They battled on, Lohen without the protection of a shield, but also unencumbered by it. The Black Blade fell as heavy as a two-hander, but handled as light as a rapier, and Lohen wielded it with great speed.

By the time Han began to slow, anyone with less skill and strength would have long since been slain. Yet, dripping sweat, chest heaving, the moment came when Han's reaction lagged a fraction of a second. He raised his shield in time to take the blow, but stumbled back, off balance. Lohen saw advantage and bulled in aiming a two-handed thrust.

He veered at the last second, bellowing as if in agony, and threw the Black Blade down into the churned mud and trampled grass at his feet. His head hung down, brown curls flung wild, like a man tied to a stake. His shoulders heaved as if racked by sobs yet he made no sound.

He lifted his face and screamed. "Kill me!"

The words were so thick with venom that it took seconds for Han to understand.

Lohen snarled again, vicious and impatient, "Kill me now." He turned away, body bent around some wound that Han hadn't given him and couldn't see. Over his own labored breath, Han barely heard the next quiet words at all.

"Han, I want to die."

Han stood, sandals rooted in slick mud, searching but finding nothing to say. His silence seemed to anger Lohen all over again, and he hauled himself around to face Han, his look both defiant and pleading. Han shook his head from side to side, more bewildered than he'd ever been.

Lohen might have taken the motion as refusal, or contempt. "Fight, then," he spat, picking up the Black Knife. "You came to do the Wizard's dirty work? Do your job." Transformed, possessed of absurd calm, he flicked his wrist to bring forth once more the sword of steel-blue light. "Here is where one of us will die."

"I don't want to fight," Han said.

"Liar! You love to fight, love your weapons, love to win. Do you think I don't remember, warrior child? You *live* to fight." He laughed, low and easy, lifting his sword to the ready. "Let me tell you, little brother. This is the battle you've been preparing for all your life. I am the enemy you've been trained to kill." He stopped, half-smiling. "Do your best. You might win, eh?"

He crouched, blade held just above shoulder height in front of him, and taunted, "Live by the sword, die by the sword, they say. But you can't do both. Choose."

Han didn't move.

The seconds grew long. Lohen grew impatient, and when he moved his dance was amazing, beautiful, impossible with his weak leg. He bobbed, spun, quick-stepped side to side; he feinted, thrust, slashed, always a split second ahead of Han. He mounted a textbook attack, staged a master's demonstration. Impressive, but not pressing, he no longer fought to kill.

Han kept centered to his brother's sparring, dodged and parried. He thought he knew Lohen's mind, and decided to try to beat him at his own game. Words punctuated with the clang and clash of swords, he said, "It's true, Lohen, Thurlock sent me to deal with you. You know why. But," he broke off to dance around a stone, "maybe there's another way."

Lohen screamed, "Fight, curse you," and blitzed Han in deadly sincerity. They clashed until they both bled from dozens of cuts. The smell of fresh blood and salt sweat made Han want to wretch, but he fought on, defending—always defending—searching for that centered calm that had won him many a battle. It wouldn't come, that Warrior's mind. He cared too much.

Lohen lifted a sleeve to wipe watery blood off his brow. With an offhand tilt of his head, he said, "You think I won't kill you? I'll plow you into the ground unless you kill me first, brother." Suddenly, his face lit up with satisfaction, like a child that figures out the one taunt that will goad his playmate every time. Scorn saturated his words like poison.

"But you're not my brother, are you? You're the Wizard's creation; Thurlock's tool. My mother and father wouldn't even recognize you."

"*Fury,*" the Wizard had taught, "*is as likely to kill you as your foe,*" and Han had taken it to heart. He never gave anger a place in a fight.

But when he heard Lohen's taunt, he succumbed at once to rushing, mind-stealing, hurricane rage.

He attacked viciously, and for the next five minutes didn't care if he died. He didn't think about Luccan or Ethra or Earth. He didn't consider duty or honor, or remember anything sweet and good or precious or loved. He wanted only to punish his brother for those words.

Breathing in gasps, words pierced by the crashing blades, Han shot bitterness at the man who had once been his moon and sun. "Don't," he snarled. "Don't talk about our parents. Don't *dare* call them into this. *I was there! I* watched them scream while their skin smoked. *I* watched them die." Landing an arm-shocking blow against Han's blade, he let his voice fall into deadly, cold command. "Don't call them down to watch us betray them."

Lohen's face warped with emotion but his flagging fight surged. Even half crippled, with the Black Blade he almost matched Han's wrath and their grandfather's sword. Words flashed between them as sharp as blows, and they crossed into territory they'd never before tread.

We should have said these things long ago, Han thought. His rage crested and broke.

Lohen backed away, his voice came breathy and low. "Yes, you saw. I didn't. I was too late." He planted his sword point and leaned on the light as if it were steel. Something like a sob broke from his heaving chest. But he pulled air back into his lungs, roared, and came at Han like a mad wolf.

No more words, breath couldn't be wasted. Attention couldn't be spared, strength mustn't be squandered. Han at last found his Warrior's calm. In perfect rhythm he struck, blocked, slashed, danced, thrust, shielded, struck again, and again, and again. Lohen listed to the left, his weak limbs failing. He stumbled.

With Lohen's defenses wide open, Han rushed in hell-bent to deal a final blow, but as his brother had done, he pulled his blade wide a split second before impact.

He'd thrown so much force behind the swing that when he turned it, he was wrenched around. His foot slid in the ooze, and he went down. The mud grabbed his sword, tore it from his grasp as he fell backward.

The base of his skull struck stone. He sprawled under a spinning, black-edged sky.

The sound Lohen Chiell made, running at Han, could have been a scream or a war cry. Hearing it, Han believed he would die, and he had more time than he would have expected for regrets. He pushed them away, squinted in concentration, and refused the encroaching blackness.

He would wait; he would know when the sword struck.

***

After the fight with Han, Lohen had fled like a hit-and-run driver, leaving his brother unconscious and bleeding in the muck of the battleground. He'd stumbled over the treacherous ground, letting Maizie lead. She'd broken a trail through briars and thorns and night.

Now, hours later, she led him back to where Han still lay in the muck, silent as death, flies buzzing his wounds.

Lohen laid a hand on his brother's chest, felt his heart beating strong, and stood up in sudden surprise at the wave of relief that washed over him. He roughed Maizie's fur, looked into her calm black eyes, and said, "Thank you, dog."

He kindled a fire, brought water, moistened Han's lips, and cleansed the cuts and bruises. In moonlight, he killed two brindle rabbits with Han's bow and sent Maizie through the grass to retrieve them. He roasted the meat over orange coals, let Maizie eat what fell in the fire, and set the rest aside to stay warm for Han.

While stars stood still overhead, dripping seconds out one at a time, he fed the fire's small appetite and stood vigil. All the while he knew that none of this caretaking and nothing he could do would change what he'd become in his brother's eyes. *He won't want to see me,* he warned himself. *Not now, not ever.*

Past midnight, Han stirred and the pattern of his breathing changed to ordinary sleep. Lohen smoothed Han's hair in parting, whispered farewell, and left to wander again across the remains of night.

20. Plans and Contingencies

Lucky gave up all pretense of cleaning the basement. He sat on the hard dirt absently brushing at crawly things and studying the little book he'd wished into his hands. He was tracing his fingers over the embossed golden runes on the cover when Thurlock came down to the basement and laid an enormous hand on his shoulder.

"There's someone waiting to talk to you, young man."

For the first time in three years, using the M.E.R.L.I.N. planted in the Wizard's dining room wall, Lucky spoke to his mother. He didn't care that they spoke from separate worlds, that he couldn't touch her hand, or smell her hair, or feel her warmth. It made no difference that they found little to say. Every minute was perfect. Cloud nine.

"I miss you, Mom," he said after a long silence.

"I know, Son." The love and longing in her eyes had been so patent that Lucky felt she might drink him up, but it wasn't a bad feeling.

She introduced him to a sturdy, dark-eyed woman. "This is your Aunt Rose."

He smiled, but before he could make a polite reply, she shooed the smiling woman away. Then she started dishing out advice.

She told him to trust Thurlock, to be careful, to work hard and always do his best. He should be polite, brush the back teeth, too, and never run with his shoelaces undone. Early to bed was good. Chocolate milk for breakfast was not.

"And come home," she said. "Come home safe and soon."

Lucky didn't listen too close. When he first saw her face, the sun came up in his heart, and he was pretty sure that he'd never be cold or lonely again.

But when the magical window went blank, he felt like a bug trapped in the porch light after someone cut the switch. He could still crawl around in the dark, but there was no way out.

In the evening, the big house was dark and quiet, and it seemed emptier than the absence of one man should have made it. Thurlock sat with Lucky on the porch until night spilled its ink over the long summer twilight. Clouds walled off the stars. It would be hours before moonrise.

Out beyond the reach of light from lamps and windows, the whole night wore mourner's black.

Lucky and Thurlock retreated indoors and sat at the table under the dim chandelier, swatting occasionally at a party of flies searching the sticky table for sustenance.

Lucky flung a question at Thurlock like throwing down a gauntlet. "Why now?"

The Wizard arched his brows and frowned.

"Why did you have me talk to my mother now?"

Thurlock scratched his beard before he answered, his half smile making him seem unsure. "It seemed like the right time," he said. "I thought ... *hoped* it might help."

"Well," Lucky said, "it made things worse."

Days of struggle, of unbelievable happenings, towering fear and dreadful possibilities, fell like stones and pinned his courage to the floor like a moth in a landslide. Hope slipped away. *I'll never make it home, Han will never come back, and I'll die before my time due to the effects of chocolate milk for breakfast.*

Lucky wanted to sleep. He wanted to forget everything, possibly forever, and the only thing that kept him from heading immediately to his safe, soft bed was hunger.

"Pizza," the Wizard announced.

The pizza driver's knock surprised Lucky—he'd come to think of Thurlock's house as a place that wouldn't appear on any map—but he let it go without comment and they ate in silence, companionable but not exactly friendly. The intimacy of their late night conversations in the stairwell had evaporated.

While they cleared away the trash and crumbs of dinner, Lucky tried a couple of questions about his magical book.

"Yes," Thurlock, said, thumbing the pages. "They're prophecies."

But when Lucky asked for their meaning, Thurlock said one could never tell.

"They're not riddles, exactly; the meaning comes clear, eventually, but until that happens, they're rather open-ended. One can only watch and wait."

Lucky started up the stairs with the Wizard's heavy footfalls clumping behind him. He paused at his bedroom door, not feeling charitable, but not wanting to be rude. "Good night, sir," he said.

"Not sir," the Wizard said. "It's just Thurlock." His eyes sparked with humor, and they both smiled. "Good night to you as well," he continued, "but before you sleep there's something I'd like you to do.

"Gather in your mind thoughts of Ethra. The small things you've remembered, what we've told you, the little you've seen these last days, and even the places of your dreams. Keep your mother in your thoughts and practice building a picture of her face behind your eyelids. Will you do that?"

Confused, Lucky hesitated. "Y ... Yes, I will. But, why?"

"You'll need those thoughts for the trip home." He smoothed Lucky's flopping hair back for him, turned and continued up the stairs. "I'll wake you. We'll depart at three A.M."

***

When Thurlock woke Lucky at three in the morning, he was surprised that he'd slept, and still more surprised that he felt rested and calm. He dressed quickly and rolled Thurlock's pajamas, his magic book, and the pictures he'd found in the attic tightly inside his blanket. He stuffed that bundle in his ragged backpack, and headed for the stairs, doubling back for the Key of Behliseth. After slinging the key on its chain around his neck, he'd gone down to meet Thurlock in the dining room, as instructed.

His stomach growled. He hoped for another sweet breakfast before departure, but before he could even speak the Wizard rolled his eyes, mumbled "Not hungry," and suddenly Lucky wasn't.

The Wizard tilted his head toward the hall. "Restroom?"

"Huh?"

"Behl save me," Thurlock said, "from teenagers at three in the morning." He slid his hand over his eyes and tried again, enunciating clearly. "Rest. Room. Do you need to use it?"

When Lucky came back, Thurlock had just finished a cup of tea and he said, "Better now. Sorry for the impatience, my boy, I'm not a morning person." He produced a maple bar from a pocket in his robes and handed it to Lucky, saying "Quickly, now." Lucky downed it in three heroic bites.

"Did you do as I asked last night? Rehearse your memories?"

"I did." Lucky considered adding, *the best I could*, but he wasn't given time.

"Fine, let's go. Give me your hand."

Lucky held up his left, and Thurlock wrapped it around the staff, which had been stripped of its umbrella disguise. He placed his own hand over Lucky's, sheltering it completely, and then gave stern instructions.

"Hold firm, it will help you through the Portal. But beware. Once we're in the vortices you may lose awareness of the staff, my hand, and even your own body."

A shiver Lucky could not stop rattled him from soles to crown, and the Wizard abruptly stopped speaking. After a moment, he cleared his throat and spoke in a softer voice, reassuring. "I won't let go, boy. I'll be with you; I'll help guide you. But Luccan," he paused until Lucky met his eyes. "You must *want* to get there. You must *want to go home*. Do you?"

Lucky swallowed, said, "Yes," and hoped dearly that it was true.

***

Hurtling through the vortices at greater than the speed of light feels exactly like floating in nothing at a complete standstill. But humans, confronted with the absence of tangible reality have an odd habit of making one up.

Thurlock knew the strange sensations well, the prickle of cold air that wasn't really there moving over flesh that had lost its substance, vistas from a roadside that existed only in the mind, calls of birds from remembered treetops, the scent of imagined grasses, and the rustle of a ghost breeze.

Fellow travelers, beyond the Portals, would usually feel about as substantial as a new idea. If they'd travelled a lot and had a grip on where they wanted to go, they might feel as solid as a well-pondered theory. Thurlock had learned to expect such ghostly company.

But Luccan faded to less than a wisp of a dream.

They had stepped up to the M.E.R.L.I.N. and through the Portal, and in a wink that slender, all-important strand of person slipped out of Thurlock's grasp. Struck by fear, anger, and blinding self-doubt, Thurlock nearly lost track of himself, too. He had to struggle to keep from being strewn piecemeal to the farthest corners of Naught.

His staff helped. Magic was useless in the vortices, but there was so much of Thurlock in the wood and metal, after all these years, that he could use it as an anchor. He felt like a tattered flag, but he gathered his intentions and reached his destination in one piece but a little askew.

He made landfall in Ethra in a rolled-up position that would have been convenient for knee sniffing. It wasn't altogether bad, for it allowed his metal-capped staff to precede him. That, along with the thickness of his nearly petrified skull, protected him when he hurtled out of the Portal and bumped to a stop in a cave-like niche in an outcrop of feldspar.

"Behl's fiery whiskers," he said, but he silently gave thanks that he'd arrived at night, when the Ethran countryside slumbered. Anyone could access Home Port since it lay not more than a hundred yards from Sisterhold Manor and right off the road. In daylight, a crowd often gathered; after dark, no crowd. He didn't have to defend his dignity, field questions, or explain his scowl.

Convinced of solitude and preoccupied with un-kinking his spine and shaking out his robes, the sound of a soft, baritone chuckle startled him. He whirled toward the orchard shadows that surrounded the Port, sparks ready at his fingertips.

"Hold, Wizard!" The voice sounded deep and light at the same time, rich with laughter flowing just beneath the surface. Despite the apparent youth of the compact man that stepped forward, his half-smile and lively eyes bore witness to a love of life that, through loneliness and every kind of tragedy, had endured uncounted ages.

Thurlock's grim face softened to a smile. "Tiro! I can't begin to tell you how good it is to see you." He embraced the dark, rough clad man. Hope made seeing his friend even more joyous. Perhaps his appearance at this particular time boded well for Luccan and the outcome of the peril in Earth.

"Aye, Thurlock, well met, though I wish it was in untroubled times." Tiro's old-fashioned, formal diction took nothing from either the warmth or the urgency behind his words. "I was hoping to see the Suth Chiell emerge from the Portal in your wake. I'd hoped also that you would bring my daughter, or at least word of her safety."

"I'm sorry."

Tiro stepped back into the trees, and Thurlock followed, knowing that the reclusive changeling would be more comfortable where they wouldn't be seen should anyone pass on the road. They sat together on an old log, the remains of an ancient cottonwood that had fallen decades ago alongside Orchard Creek. The stream, sifting over its sandy bed, sang gently of ease. Fireflies lazed among reeds on the opposite bank. An owl made its usual inquiry, calm and dignified, "Who?"

"I am afraid for L'Aria, Wizard."

Thurlock shook his head. Tiro's words in the midst of the peaceful night chilled him to the marrow. His own steady voice surprised him. "You couldn't persuade her to stay home?"

"As you might expect, she gave me no opportunity. She well knows how and when to avoid me." Tiro said it with an indulgent smile, but it didn't erase the worry from his eyes.

"And what news of Luccan?"

"I failed," Thurlock said, and then clenched his jaw tight. When he could speak without his fears rushing out, he continued. "I couldn't hold on to him. He slipped away."

"Back to Earth?"

Thurlock scratched his beard, considering. "I think so. Yes, very likely back to Earth."

Beside him, Tiro sighed and ran his hands through the mane of dark hair that stood out from his head in soft bristles. "I've brought something."

He stood and walked to a spot among the reeds and willows lining the creek's bank, shouldered two large, fur-clad water-skins. Dropping them by Thurlock's feet, he said, "From Kindled Springs. Might it help?"

"Certainly it will. Thank you."

Water from Kindled Springs refreshed body, mind, and soul like no other food or drink known to Ethra. Many speculated, but no one knew whether magic produced that quality, or if the flame that eternally skimmed its surface somehow changed the water.

For an ordinary human—even a powerful, skilled Wizard—to reach the Springs took days of travelling mountain terrain, and then more days through a maze of caves. Once there, a person could easily die in the attempt to fetch the water, either from breathing the gases in the cavern, or in passing through the scorching flames.

Waterways led to the Springs in a much more direct line, but it required the ability to stay submerged through long tunnels beyond the capacity of ordinary lungs. Tiro, shifting shape and swimming as a king of otters, could make that trip and fetch the water without ever surfacing in the dangerous cavern.

"I wish I could offer more of it," Tiro said, a slight smile touching his eyes, "but this was all I could tow back through the tunnels."

The journey hadn't been easy, even for Tiro. Thurlock laid a hand on the smaller man's vest-clad shoulder. "This will be enough," he said. "It may well save the day."

"Fare well, this mission," Tiro said, and then he waded into the shadowed stream and vanished from sight.

***

Lights burned in all the downstairs windows of Sisterhold Manor, though the summer dawn would be waiting in the wings for another hour. It seemed likely the household hadn't slept at all, awaiting Luccan's return.

Thurlock mounted the steps to the verandah, lifted the brass-stag striker, knocked three times and went in.

The furniture and the polished floor shone in the glow of candles and lamps. A long table groaned under the makings of a feast. Platters piled with fruits, baskets spilling sweet rolls and spice cakes, griddlecakes waiting for butter and syrup milk, juice, coffee, tea, and even a small keg of golden ale. From the kitchen came the clank and clatter of pans, the sizzle of meats on the fire, and a tapestry of smells that set Thurlock's stomach clamoring for attention.

But Liliana, Rosishan, and a handful of others stood silent, facing Thurlock with their reactions etched on their faces. Surprise. Disappointment. Fear.

"I'm sorry," he said, scowling to hide self-doubt and forestall questions. "Luccan isn't with me."

He tightened his grip on his staff and his confidence, and made no further apology. He regretted the new, heightened fear Liliana must have for her son, but this wasn't the time for bickering, blame, or 'I-told-you-so.'

He needed speed. He'd formulated a contingency plan for this situation before he'd ever stepped across the Portal with Luccan in tow. With Tiro's gift, the plan had more chance of succeeding, but L'Aria's danger added to his concerns. No certainties; even magic can't guarantee success, but the quicker his plan could be put in motion, the better the chances.

He spoke quietly, not wanting to cause panic. "Lili, Rose, I'd like a private word in the library." He stopped to survey the crowd and settled his gaze on a tall woman with laconic eyes who seemed to melt into the walls a few feet away. "Please join us, Gerania.

"The rest of you, a feast awaits, and we'll have angry cooks if it goes unappreciated. It's a tough assignment, but perhaps you'll give it your best effort?"

Thurlock smiled, and it seemed to brighten what had become a gloomy room. A few chuckles answered him and people shuffled away. Thurlock made for the stairs in the back of the spacious hall, the three women following close.

Small leather sandals pounded across the floor, and two high-pitched voices called, "Mama, wait!"

The little girls with dun-colored heads looked a lot like Gerania. Thurlock spoke up before their mother could answer. "Trista, Glayda, two of my favorite and shortest neighbors." He went down on a knee to wrap one long arm around the both of them as they rushed in for a giggling hug.

"Girls, listen, we four adults are going upstairs to the library to talk, and talking always makes me thirsty. And, the smell of all that food is making me hungry. Would you sneak a tray of rolls—sweet rolls, mind you—and a pot of tea from the kitchen and bring them up to us? I'll owe you a favor."

The girls, whose eyes had flown wide at the idea of being owed a favor by the great Wizard, rushed off in a flurry of ribbon-tied braids and flowered skirts. Despite his worries, Thurlock smiled.

The smell of leather, dust and ink greeted Thurlock as he walked into the library. Surrounded by books, scrolls, and parchment, the Wizard breathed a little easier. Chair legs whispered over the carpeted floor as everyone took a seat at a round table in the center of the room. Lili took her spiral Spring Wand out of a deep pocket of her gown and tapped the chandelier over their heads, setting it ablaze.

Thurlock met Lili's green-gold eyes and laid his hand over hers on the table. "Niece, I've done some probing, and I believe Luccan isn't lost."

Lili's look brightened a bit, hope crossing swords with fear and anger.

Thurlock took a deep breath and forged on. "He's returned to Earth, which is better than Naught, but yes, he is in grave danger there."

"I'm going to him, Uncle! Don't try to stop me this time—"

"Yes," Thurlock interjected. "Yes, Lili, I will need your help in Earth, and Rose's as well."

When the blank look faded from Lili's face, Thurlock knew his words had sunk in. He told them all what he'd guessed about Luccan's situation, and Han's. They asked a few questions and he answered when he could. When they were as up-to-date as he could make them, he sat back, smoothing his untidy beard as if it would help order his thoughts.

He nodded toward Gerania and asked, "How long before day breaks?"

The second-in-command of Behlishan's Guard, ranking officer in Han's absence, had a reputation for impeccable precision belied by a lackadaisical manner. "Fifty-three minutes," she drawled, "and uh, twelve ... no, ten seconds, sir."

"That's not much time. Let's get down to specifics. Lili, how many of the Mounted Guard do we have that can make it through the Portals with us, with their mounts?"

Lili shook her head. "Not many, at the moment."

Thurlock waited for more, but it was Rose who explained.

"We've sent troops north, as you suggested, trying to hold down the disturbances. Last week—my idea, I'm afraid—we doubled the size of the mission when we got reports of Ice-Drakes—"

"Winged Blue Salamanders," Thurlock corrected.

"That's right, sir, Ice-Drakes. Some incidents involved Wights and Glacier Wolves, too. We had four reports in a day."

Seconds ticked by.

"What is it, Rose? Please, drop the other shoe."

"We don't know where they are, sir."

"The Salamanders?"

"Those too, but I meant the troops. They're not killed, so the Seers tell us, but no one can find them."

"I see ..." Thurlock said, tugging at his beard. Suddenly he nodded, perched his spectacles on his nose and peered over the rims at each of the women. "It's Isa's work," he said, "a trick. She's brilliant at times. But then, if she were incredibly stupid she wouldn't be the 'Witch-Mortaine,' would she?

"Come to think on it, though, it makes little difference. We need speed, I think, not numbers. Southport is the only Portal within fifty miles big enough for horses, and even there we can only travel through a few at a time."

"What about at the other end?"

"I don't think that will be as much of a problem, Lili. There's a very large natural Portal in the Ravine that will work fine as long as we can emerge in the cavern proper, and not the caves behind it. It's manageable."

They discussed how many soldiers to take, and finally settled on six, all professionals; members of an elite squad of the Mounted Guard known as Shana's Rangers. Liliana commanded the Rangers, and she trusted her troops.

"Rose," Thurlock said, "I want you to get in touch with Ghriffon. I'll feel much better if we have a few Eagles with us."

A light knock announced the two little girls, come with a well-cozied teapot, sweet rolls, and smiles that were not shy at all.

Thurlock thanked them for saving him from starvation.

When they'd off-loaded their goods, Gerania straightened braids, dusted skirts and tied a loose sandal. "Go eat, girls, and then you can play, but don't have any fun." They giggled all the way out the door, obviously used to their mother's teasing. Everyone smiled, but faces went grim once more when the children had gone.

Nabbing a cinnamon-sweet roll and a cup of tea, Thurlock continued laying out the plans. "Gerania, you'll have the Regular Mounted here to support Behlishan's Guard."

"That'll help, sir. We'll be spreading the troops pretty thin covering the Sisterhold, Nedhra City, and the Ports."

Swallowing the last of the roll, Thurlock wiped crumbs from his beard. "It will be enough," he said. "The real battle will be happening in that awful Ravine, which is certainly not what or where it seems in the first place, and is completely skewed now that Isa's planted her cursed Tower at the east end."

Gerania, who had less experience of the Witch-Mortaine than the others, shook her head. "What about the people, sir, the Earthborns? They tolerate her evil-doing?"

Thurlock shook his head, arched his brows, chewed. Mouth empty, he answered. "If there's anything Isa has become very skilled at, it's concealing her presence and the damage it does. She has that Tower so well hidden I had trouble pinning it down myself. And, of course, she's managed to twist some Earthborn minds.

"So, you're in charge here, Gerania, and you can put together a search party to go north. We three and the six Rangers will head for Earth. Rose, let's pray Ghriffon still likes you. We'll need those Eagles."

He paused to wash his third roll down with tea, then pushed his chair back. "Now, if I'm not mistaken it's nearly dawn."

"Just under nineteen minutes, sir," Gerania offered.

"I've got to get to the Oakridge. Meet me at Southport in two hours."

Rose objected. "That's not enough time."

Lili shot back her reply wearing a scowl. "It's *too* much time, when my son is in harm's way every passing minute."

"I'm sorry, Rose, Lili is right this time, and in fact it's worse than that."

The women all looked back at him with questions in their eyes.

"You see," Thurlock said, "the balance is disturbed, and growing more so, thanks to the Ice-Lord Mahl. Time is ... perhaps wobbling is the word. It can't be counted on at all."

21. Mordred Brede

Isa sat at the glass worktable in her chamber, surrounded by potions and powders and horrid things pickled in brine. Pale blue fire lit the room beyond, sending tints and shadows to dance over her pallid hands. Exhausted, she raised a steel chalice to her cracked lips with shaking hands.

She had delivered Mordred to Mahl, as she had promised. Time had been short, so rather than drag him along the usual twisting path to sorcery, she'd sustained him with her own tainted blood and drilled him non-stop. When he'd learned enough Dark Chant, when he'd gained the skills necessary to stifle and bend the mind of a pre-conditioned mob, then she judged him ready to meet his Master.

She'd nurtured Mordred's cold heart, fed his quest for dark knowledge, bequeathed to him the core of her morbid sorceries. All that remained was to give him power. That, he would get from the Ice-Lord, just as she had long ago.

For the last hour, she'd watched him writhe while the Master possessed him, infected him with the power of the void, the essence of Naught. As it ended, his tortured body arched painfully and collapsed, falling hard on the stone floor. A long, smoky breath escaped his lungs. Then, for a moment, nothing ... until a gasp started him breathing again.

His eyes had been as deep and richly black as raven stones. Now, he looked back at her from discs of blue ice, shallow, pale eyes that mirrored her own.

"Mordred," she called.

Mahl had forced him, she knew, to the very brink of death. When she beckoned, he struggled to stand, but couldn't. In the end he crawled, a show of obedience that she was pleased to see. If he had not obeyed, if he had thought to challenge her, she would have had to destroy him, and then all the energy she'd spent on him would have bought her nothing but Mahl's wrath.

"You've done well," she told him. "You will be rewarded." She offered him her chalice, with the remains of her fortifying potion.

Trembling, he took the cup. "Thank you, Witch-Mortaine. I'm honored." He raised the cup and swallowed, and after a moment his breathing slowed.

"Rise, now," she said, knowing the potency of the brew she'd given him. "Listen."

She set Mordred over her followers as Captain and put most of her resources at his disposal, assigning him the task of taking Luccan. "Alive if you can," she told him. "I'd prefer for him to die later, after I've made use of him. Apply all of your tricks and powers. Use our black-cloaked slaves. Let the boy think he'll die. He'll run blind, right into your trap."

Mordred smiled, a cruel expression.

"If the girl gets in the way, kill her if it pleases you."

"Yes," he answered slowly, clearly savoring the prospect.

"Just don't forget, apprentice, which child is your prime target."

His feet fell heavy, rattling the stone as he left her chamber.

As for Thurlock, Isa thought, *if that old trickster shows up, he's mine.*

***

Home. Lucky thought that single word over and over, clenched it in the folds of his mind as hungrily as a wolf clamps a rabbit in its jaws.

Home. That's where he was going. The Wizard had told him so. "*I won't let go ...*"

But he was alone now. He'd lost Thurlock. And if it was home he was heading toward, he seemed to be taking a long time to get there. He struggled to hold that home in Ethra in his mind as Thurlock had instructed, but too many people he cared about remained in Earth. They popped up in his thoughts like bubbles, one after another.

He remembered Lohen first, which seemed odd, and then Han and Maizie and the shack. That had been home, too, where he and Maizie had lived, walked in the pines and played by the creek. He'd played by the creek with Grandpa Hank, too, and Henry.

He became aware of something soft and smooth, but powerful, brushing against him. Great wings beat noisily and whipped a wind into the empty space. He breathed deep and smelled sage, cedar, wood smoke, perking coffee, and birthday candles burning on maple syrup pancakes.

He slammed to a stop. In the dark. Making full body contact with rock.

He used his hands to examine the space around him. Rock below, packed earth above and on the sides.

He recognized the sounds outside and guessed where he had landed. Nettle Brook babbled off to his left, tumbling down into Black Creek, which hummed a deeper note down below. As regular as a ticking clock, one stone clunked and slid in the middle of the brook, perched right at the edge but never falling. It had floated there at least as long as Lucky had been in Earth.

His fingers clamped around a familiar object, a GI Joe he'd left in this 'foxhole' two years ago, when he'd still thought of himself on some days as a child. He knew this place. He laughed, relieved to be alive and not stuck in nowhere — or wherever he'd gone after stepping through the M.E.R.L.I.N.

Reaching his arms out past his head to the den's entrance, he found the root he knew would be hanging there. He pulled himself out, climbed to the ridge, and headed up to Grandpa Hank's familiar front door.

The log house was dark and cold, and once Lucky had lit the hurricane lamp on the mantle, he saw dust balled so thick in the corners he expected it to sprout legs and whiskers and skitter away. He shrugged off his pack, amazed that it had come through the journey intact. He took out the little portraits and studied them briefly, one by one, and then he dropped the blanket over his shoulders, both actions done in an effort to ward the wintry chill.

The blanket helped, but he still shivered.

Layers. He still had clothes there in Hank's house, if they'd fit, but he looked at the dark doorways to other rooms and quailed at the idea of going through them. He rifled through his pack, found the Wizard's pajamas, and pulled them over his jeans. At last he was warmed.

The firewood he'd carried in, the kindling he'd split, and even the newspaper Hank had read on the morning of his death were all still neatly stacked by the river-rock fireplace. Lucky was no Thurlock, he couldn't make magic flames, and he had only one match to light the fire so as he struck it and held it against the tinder, he added a fervent wish. He wasn't sure if it was the wish that did the trick, but the fire blazed and he held up a fist in victory.

For a while, he didn't think. He just stood in front of the fire, wrapped in red plaid and Wizard's pajamas, absorbing heat and light and growing hungry.

When he heard the first thunk from Grandpa Hank's hand-drum, which still hung next to the mirror above the mantle, he didn't think the noise was odd. The warming skin would often "talk," as Hank would say, as it grew taut over the drum's bones. Lucky felt glad to hear it, and he caught himself thinking, *I've missed you*, as if the drum was an old friend.

But it wasn't at all usual for the drum to *keep* talking in a rhythm matching exactly the pattern of Hank's song. He thought, *ghost*, but he didn't believe it until the drum began to shine like a small sun forging through night. Fascinated, he stared at that white luminous hide so hard that he saw it happen, witnessed the moment when the standing bear, painted there in red and black, began to dance.

"You need sleep," Lucky told himself, tearing his eyes away, "or food, or heavy medication."

He pushed his hair back from his face, shrugged away the dread slinking up his spine, and even forced a laugh. But when his gaze swept past the dim-lit room behind him in the mirror, his eyes grew wide and he forgot to breathe.

The face in the mirror hid in shadow, but Lucky could read the smile. Cold fled before a landslide of pure relief, and he wondered why he'd thought the log house empty. The light was on in the kitchen and the herbed stew Lucky could hear bubbling on the stove filled the air with a steamy, savory promise of a full-bellied goodnight.

The stew smelled like Grandpa's, but the man in the mirror wasn't Hank George. Lucky knew that. Hank was dead.

Lucky turned, smiling. "Henry, I—"

But the room was deserted.

The drum rumbled like thunder and dropped off its nail to land, silenced and dull, in the dust at Lucky's feet. *A warning.*

He took a fortifying look at the picture of his mother, stripped off the Wizard's pajamas and stuffed them both in his backpack. He looked around one last time in the golden light of the fire, doused the lamp, and turned to leave.

Sudden frost blighted the room. Every calorie of heat fled so abruptly that the mirror cracked. The imagined glow of the kitchen bulb and the soul-nourishing smells of food vanished completely, replaced by the bleak, hard smells of glacier ice and carbon vapor. The empty house teemed with life, or with its terrible opposite. Ghosts, monsters, living dead.

"*The Sight,*" Han had said. "*You can learn to control it ... to send it away.*"

Lucky shut his eyes again and concentrated on remembering the steady beat of Hank's drum, drawing his racing heart down into its strong rhythm. He started for the door, not needing eyes to know the way. A draft of ordinary night air whispered over him, rattling the frost-coated strands of his hair. The sounds spirits stilled. The breeze brought in the brook's chatter and pre-dawn's tentative birdcalls.

He sighed, relieved. He'd reached the door, and a summer day was ready to come alive.

He opened his eyes and they widened in shock. Mordred Brede blocked the exit. Outside, a swarm of Black-cloaked followers held torches to wall and post and eave, setting Hank's house aflame.

"I've a car waiting," Mordred said, and seized Lucky's arm in a titan grip. "Come on out now, Luccan. I wouldn't want you to burn."

PART FOUR: When All Others Fail

22. In the Light of a New Day

Han forced his crusted eyelids apart a fraction, but then squeezed them shut against the million stars that blazed back. Their brilliance hurt, and the constellations confused him.

These are the wrong stars ...
I'm camping in the Greenwood with Lohen, and he keeps me safe ...
No, I've been dreaming ...

He opened his eyes again. *I'm not a boy; this isn't Ethra. It's been a lifetime since we camped in the Greenwood. And it was Lohen I was fighting when I fell.*

As that same brother had taught him, he lay still, trying to get his bearings, to discover what might be waiting for him to move. The treetops waved black against the graying east near dawn. The creek muttered downhill, and behind him he sensed the looming rock slope. He smelled, as expected, grass, dew, mud, pine, river moss, and even fish. He also smelled, not expected, campfire ash and roasted meat.

He let his eyes close again, wondering if those surprising aromas lingered from his dream. A heavy shoe fell, nearby, crushing grass; then another step and another, closer.

He waited, and when the time was right snaked out an arm, grabbed a thick ankle, and gave a twist, laying his assailant face down in the dirt. He jammed a knee into his kidney, twisted both arms up against the shoulder blades, and clenched the big man's stubbly chin in a rock-hard grip, poised for that final, fatal snap.

The pre-dawn sky bore down on him heavy as lead. Sweat ran in his eyes, tinted with yesterday's blood, and they burned like flame. His breath sheared through flared nostrils. He bit his lip bloody in clenched teeth and raged, silent and nearly mindless, at the man he held pinned in a high-torque wrestler's grip. A slight movement with one hand, a half-inch twist, would snap the man's neck.

For half a minute, it was all Han could do to keep that hand still. Almost too late, an old voice in his mind cut through the rage and made itself heard. *"The least degree of force,"* it insisted.

He shuddered, released a rattling breath, relaxed his hold but kept it secure, and struggled to clear his mind. The man on the ground tried to talk. The light had grown, and Han saw his captive's face. "Mordred?"

"Nggoo Mmmfff."

To Han's surprise a whimper followed. What's more, in the inch of skin showing between dark eye and wiry beard, gleaming in the grey light, were runnels of tears. Han let up a little more on the chin. "What did you say?"

"Boff," the man said, but he was also thinking about Han, so Han heard it loud and clear in his mind. *Scary man, like Mord.*

Han didn't mind being scary when a situation called for it, but he didn't want to be like Mord. "I'm going to let you up Boff. Please don't run and don't fight." He helped him to his feet, watched him wipe his dripping nose on his sleeve, walked him to a rock and told him to sit. He didn't seem likely to move, he and the rock being equally inert.

Han took a deep breath, shrugged the tension out of his shoulders, and tried to decide what to ask first. "Where's Mordred, Boff?"

"He killed me."

"He killed you?"

Boff was a man of few words, but by aiming his questions carefully Han gleaned some key facts. Mordred had pushed his brother off a cliff. Boff had missed the rocks and fallen into the creek.

And L'Aria had pulled him out.

"Behl's Whiskers," Han said, borrowing the Wizard's epithet. He said it again after Boff told him who he'd seen making the fire and shooting the rabbits that roasted in the coals.

At that point Boff screwed his face into a pout and volunteered, "You killed me."

Han, thankful to have avoided switching from Warrior to murderer, apologized. By way of making amends, he passed half a roasted rabbit to Boff. The big, childlike man tore into it, eyes wide with joy.

Han smiled, but after his first careful bite he joined his guest in ripping meat off bone in glorious abandon. They finished the first rabbit, then the second. Han sighed and cleaned the grease off his face, hands, and arms to the elbows with a bunch of grass.

His cuts and bruises had been washed. Looking around, he found that his water-skin had been filled and his tunic had been rinsed and laid over the top of a juniper scrub to dry. His bow and quiver leaned against a boulder beside his sword, which had been cleansed of blood and polished to a shine.

Lohen had come back, tended his wounds, hunted and cooked his food. Sometime soon, Han would have to think about that.

But now is not the time. The sun is climbing, and I've still got a job to do.

***

The sun flashed off Black Creek a hundred feet below, blazing into Lohen Chiell's grit-scratched eye. A grouchy crow mumbled in the shadows and jays shrilled from the treetops. The scents of hot pine and shale dust thickened the air. Weary, Lohen prayed for an hour of silent dark or even cloud cover and a sling shot to shut the scavengers up.

He'd climbed slowly, cutting diagonally up the slope of the gorge for the last half-hour, though not mindful of any purpose. His legs had begun to ache with effort, yet he'd kept on, step after step, following Maizie, who'd been his guide through dark morning, comfortless dawn, and hours under a sun hot enough to wring sweat from stones.

West of the Blue Tower and east of the clearing where by now, he prayed, his brother would have awakened and enjoyed his rabbit, he came upon the Myrtle Grove. He marveled that in all the days he'd wandered this canyon, on the Witch's errands and then lately on his own, he'd never seen this stand of ancient trees. But there was more to Black Creek Ravine than met the eye; the place harbored secrets in every shadow. Why should this one surprise him?

A hint of green-laden breeze, barely cool, blew over the myrtles and rattled their papery leaves, carrying their sweet-sharp scent and promising refreshment. Maizie trod the path into the tunnel of cooled, dim shade, and as Lohen followed, just for a moment he felt as though he'd walked out of Earth and into Ethra.

He chuckled, realizing how unlikely such a thing was. *Although, where there's a Wizard like Thurlock, and a Witch like Isa involved, one can never be too sure that anything truly is where it seems to be.*

Deep inside the grove, Maizie led him away from the road, and then stopped beside a pool where clear water bubbled out of a globe of black rock. He dunked his head in the freshet, hoping the cold would dull the ache between his ears. Sitting back on his heels he slicked water off his hair and tried to quench his burning eye, pressing a wet hand against the lid.

He was looking for the energy to stand when Maizie bounded back from her brief exploration in the brush, and nudged him under the arm with her big, bony nose. In his exhausted state, it was enough to knock him flat. Sprawled and muddy, his only defense was to raise an arm, shielding his face from her pink slopping tongue.

He decided he was too worn out to get to his feet, and instead scooted out of the mud like an upside-down inchworm. He had to stop, breathless and laughing at himself, glad no one could see his ungraceful effort. When he recovered, he slid back until he found a hollow in the thick leaf mould, a place that felt ready to receive him, as if someone else had lain there recently, with him in mind.

"Dog," he said, "watch over me. I have to sleep." He expected slumber to drop like a stage curtain. Instead, the backs of his eyelids flickered in video replay of the last sixteen hours blow-by-blow.

The fight with Han, his flight and his return to his brother's side. The pain of having to leave before Han opened his eyes for fear of the hatred he would see in them. After, he'd roamed the dark Ravine, following Maizie's lead through the remains of night and too far into morning, not stopping for food or sleep or even to rest his blistered feet.

Now, in the cool of the grove, his eye began to burn again, and he blinked away the salt gathered in its corners. He sighed, turning the tail of it into a yawn. "Watch over me, dog," he said once more. Blessedly cooled in the shadow of green leaves, darkness fell behind his lids at last, like benediction.

Minutes later he heard singing, a distinctive song, a singular, unmistakable chiming voice.

L'Aria.

This strange, magical girl had loved him since she toddled. Sometimes, for Lohen, it was a bloody nuisance.

Unable to keep exasperation from his voice, he asked her before he even opened his eyes, "Why are you here, Spitfire? I'm sure your aunts told you to stay home after your last adventure?" He opened his eyes then and saw her throw her head back in laughter, a gesture that lived up to her nickname.

She answered the second question first. "They told me not to cross the Portals. If there's water, I don't need a Portal. I have my song. And what I'm doing here is finding you, because it's important."

Her saucy tone and lopsided face brimmed with defiance, but Lohen was way past wanting to argue. His eyelids hung so heavy he wished that if he must keep them open, he could tack them up with glue. No reply seemed worth the effort. He spent the last of his energy to sit up, tossed his wild hair out of his eye, and waited to hear what L'Aria deemed so urgent.

"Your son needs you," she said.

"Oh," Lohen responded. He gave the word no emphasis, and said nothing more.

"I have the Amber Knife." She didn't offer to explain how that came about, and Lohen didn't ask because he knew he would wish he hadn't. What mattered was that she wanted to hand it over to him.

She also had the woven-reed pouch she'd given Luccan on his eleventh birthday, filled with old coins. The same coins he'd last seen scattered in the trampled meadow. He watched her shake them out into the pool, using the last one to anchor the pouch atop the stone globe. He didn't wonder why she did it; it seemed the sort of thing any young girl might do.

He did wonder what would prompt her to want to put Luccan's Blade into his hands. He was a traitor and a madman—a murderer, most Ethrans believed. L'Aria knew all about that. The thought crossed his mind that perhaps, by some unimaginable means, this unique,

213

troublesome but innocent girl had fallen under the Witch-Mortaine's influence.

But when he looked into her well-deep black eyes he knew Isa hadn't touched her. There was no evil there. Weary as he was, his eyes flew wide with surprise at what he *did* find in her gaze. Something he'd not seen in human eyes for many years. Something more magical than any Blade or Staff, curse or spell or song.

Trust. L'Aria had chosen to believe in him.

Absently, he rubbed at his left hand, still damaged, though healing since the Black Blade's return. He wondered what part of him was whole and good enough to deserve L'Aria's faith. *But how can I refuse what she asks when she looks at me like that?* He took the Amber Knife and he tucked it, safely sheathed, into his belt opposite the Black.

"I know you'll do what's right," L'Aria said, hand on her hip. "*You* don't know, *Thurlock* doesn't know, but *I do.* You will."

Overpowered by fatigue, Lohen shook his head and sank back into the soft fragrance of rich soil and fallen myrtle leaves. The breeze didn't touch the ground, but he heard it sighing through the trees' crowns. It whispered syllables, like a remembrance of the Gods' Breath, Behlis Ethra's fair dawn wind.

"Go home now," he told L'Aria, having found himself once again on the sweet edge of sleep. He cut her protest short, touching the Black Knife once to remind her that, though her aunts couldn't make her stay, he could make her go. And it might be unpleasant if he did.

"Fine, then," she said, pouting, and she waded into the pool. Lohen had to smile, watching her disappear beneath the surface. He hoped she would go home where she might be safe, but he was under no illusion that her obedience was a sure thing. Fading at last toward dreams, he let that thought go, along with all others but one.

Please, he begged the wind, *whisper my son's lost name.*

***

By the time Han rose and prepared himself to move, Warrior clad and armed, the sun had moved well past noon. He put his tardy start down to having been injured, but he admitted that he'd been reluctant to go searching for the new trouble. Now, he stood at the edge of the clearing and called his thoughts to order.

Alright, first things first, he started, and for some reason it reminded him of Luccan.

At the same instant, his nephew's call for help slammed into his brain, full of fear and fight and an image of Mordred Brede shoving Luccan to the floor in the back of Isa's big white Ford. In seconds, Han shouldered his bow and his pack and hooked his quiver at his belt, preparing to run to Luccan's aid.

He headed east to Isa's keep, the only place Mordred would take his captive. Chills and heat, fear and anger battled in him at the thought of Luccan at the mercy of the Witch-Mortaine.

***

When Lohen woke up to the touch of Maizie's wet nose, the sun was spinning down through thin clouds toward the western peaks. White rays sliced into the heart of the grove between the trunks of the sheltering myrtles, their touch on Lohen's skin like cold steel.

He gazed toward the east, squinting as if he might peer through magic veils and miles of trees and rocks.

Maizie *whuffed,* seeming anxious to be on the move.

Lohen nodded and scratched her ears. "You're right," he said. "It's time to go. We'll hunt something to eat on the way."

She set off through the trees and he let her lead, but this time he knew where she would take him. And he knew what he had to do. He took a last deep breath of the grove's sweet air and told the wind what he'd come at last to understand.

"My son," he said. "My son needs me."

23. Let Auntie Isa Take Care of You

Lucky remembered the ice touch of Mordred's hands as he shoved him into the Crown Vic, but he didn't remember the ride. It was almost as if it hadn't happened, as if he'd fallen into the car at Grandpa Hank's and fallen out in this cold, damp corner of stone and dust.

His eyes refused to close on the blue light seeping from the walls, though it stung them like sleet. No sounds reached his ears except a faint echo of his pulse and, high above, a distant howl like ghosts of long dead wolves. His lungs rebelled at every breath of rancid air, and his stomach was so empty it made a fist. He had what he wore and nothing else, no red blanket and Wizard's pajamas to block the creeping chill, no small portraits to warm his heart.

He had no way to know how long he'd been curled in that corner hugging his knees. It felt like such a long time that everything that had ever gone before was lost. And if by chance it was night now, he was sure it was going to stay night forever.

A moment of comfort came, a small golden light and a fluttering like tiny wings against his chest. Lucky looked for the source and found the Key of Behliseth humming at the end of its chain. It felt like finding home, and he cupped both hands around it. For that small moment he felt warmed.

Then a door Lucky had not before seen slammed open. He dropped the Key behind his shirt to keep it secret.

Two women and two men entered the room, all with whitish hair, pinkish pale skin, and lightless indigo eyes. They dressed alike in short tunics and loose trousers of a cloth that seemed sometimes white, sometimes blue. Their torches sputtered and cracked with blue flame, yet their eyes stayed dim.

Crowding around Lucky in his corner, they started in kicking and beating him, never uttering a word, never showing any emotion—which made them seem all the more vicious. They hit him so many times that his muscles cramped and he hurt everywhere. But it was their frigid breath, like poison gas, that laid him low.

Lucky imagined his brain slowly coating with ice. It was hard to think about anything but heat, and after a while he forgot even to defend himself. That's when two of his attackers dug their fingers into his hair and dragged him out the door and down a dark, slanting corridor, the other two following behind.

At first it was a relief when they left him on an ice-slick cobbled floor in the center of a vast circular dungeon. But the only light in that place fell from a single bright dot of open sky so high it seemed miles away, and horrible sounds came through the dark from everywhere around Lucky, begging terrifying explanations. Immense breath rattled, something squished and slimed, teeth chomped and crunched. Closer now, but still coming from above, the same ghostly wolves howled their hunger.

Lucky huddled in his fears for minutes or hours or forever, wishing for anything but dark. When a door opened in a distant, shadowed wall, he welcomed the burst of blue light. His relief died immediately as the Witch-Mortaine Isa strode in, chrome-blue robes shining like a housefly's carapace, chilling eyes wicked with hate. The four servants that had dragged him from his cell carried the hem of her robe, bowing so low Lucky was amazed they could walk.

Together, they spoke in hollow, apathetic tones. "Fall on your knees before the Demon Queen."

Lucky just stood there, thinking how stupid that sounded and shaking in fear. Isa pointed at him with a claw-like finger, and his legs started to fold under him in obedience. He fought it, struggling to stay on his feet and muttering over and over, "No."

The Witch started talking, at least Lucky assumed the sounds were words, and her slaves picked up the refrain as if they were having some kind of monster sing-along. The sounds invaded his brain, so ugly he felt them crawling through like worms and bugs until the chant broke off. Once again Isa jabbed a sharp finger at Lucky's face. Shrouded in sudden pain, he dropped. His knees hit the stones.

"Ah," Isa said, "that's better. I see you're not so unreasonable after all, Luccan." Looking down her long nose at him, practically drooling contempt, she said, "Come, dear angry boy. Let Auntie Isa take care of you."

It was a magical Command, like Thurlock's, but mean. Something like air filling a balloon unfolded Lucky from the floor and stood him on his feet. Something like wires moved his arms and legs. A breezeway wound upward along the keep's blue-glass walls, its inside edge kissing open space. Lucky clambered up the steep ramp, following the Witch in mindless obedience.

Torches mounted in steel brackets along the way stained the walls and stone ramp with splashes of luminous blue. The flames burned cold, stealing Lucky's body heat, and the walls wore a hard coat of frost. He stayed as far from them as possible, avoiding their icy touch even though that meant treading inches from the deadly drop into the Tower's central well, an open space so deep it seemed to have no floor.

At last they stopped, having climbed for so long that Lucky imagined he'd find himself eye-to-eye with the pinnacles of Death of the Gods if he could look out. They stood on a narrow landing, he and the four pale people waiting silent and still until a steel panel slid open at Isa's command.

They filed into a chamber shaped something like a slice of pie with the tip cut off. Large, but not cavernous like the vast round hall he'd just come from.

White marble slabs tiled the floor, and on a broad stone shelf at the back of the room, thirteen pole-mounted torches flared and hissed. Their fire lent only icy light, but a pit near the center of the chamber held a brazier crackling with orange flames. Lucky flew toward that bright, hot blaze like a moonstruck moth.

Isa stood at the front of the room on a platform of blue stone. To each side of her a steel column supported colorless candles burning blue and throwing shadows in waves. Beneath them Isa seemed to grow taller and more terrible and Lucky heard again in his mind the words, *"Demon Queen."* He turned away, but the Witch's stare prickled at the back of his neck.

He remained silent but for his shivering breath. Uneasy with Isa at his back, he pivoted to face her, and then moved to put the flames between them. For comfort and courage he leaned as close as he dared to the heat, but it wasn't nearly enough to cut the Tower's arctic chill.

Isa stared at him unblinking, lids half-lowered, and Lucky felt as though he was being measured, or recorded.

Finally, as she turned to leave, she instructed her slaves. "I've things to attend, a nuisance at our doors, I'm told. See to the boy's comforts. Find a way to warm him. He's frail; he won't survive the cold. I want him alive, for a while. Keep him that way." She slithered out of the room dragging a cold wind in her wake.

Cold slave hands pushed Lucky back to sit on a heavy black cloak they had taken from a niche in the wall and laid on the floor near the brazier. They placed another cloak over him, and he was dully grateful. He hardly noticed the rank stench wafting from the fabric.

Someone pushed a cup at him, and he wrapped his hands around the heat. The dark liquid steamed, clouding Lucky's eyes, and he didn't resist when told to drink it. After he swallowed, warmth spread to his toes and a bag of lint enveloped his brain. He didn't like the fuzzy feeling, but felt so relieved when he stopped shivering. He stared at the bright flame in the brazier, and for no reason he could name, he took it as a promise.

As long as it burns I'll be all right.

***

Isa left her four Ethran servants to tend the boy until she could return, and summoned her recent Earthborn recruits. She gathered them in the vast circular Sanctum, the better to show them their insignificance, to inflame their need to serve the Demon Queen. She preferred dimness and shadow, but weaker, ordinary eyes needed light. With a dark word and a flick of thin, sharp fingers, she set a ring of torches burning behind them, blue and cold.

She stood tall in the center of the space, robed as always in blue. Acolytes surrounded her, all Earthborn and easily enslaved by magic. They numbered fifty-two, and huddled in kneeling quadrants of thirteen each. Not as many as she would have liked, but a fair number considering the limitations of time.

Mordred waited in the dark outside the circle, bearing a small stone dagger and a mirrored tray holding four large, crystal goblets. Each cup contained a potion brewed of red elder, skullcap, bindweed, and rue. As Isa had taught him, Mordred had, in each cup, drowned a wolf spider and weighted it with moonstone and jet. The final ingredient, the one that would bind them to Mordred, and through him to her and to Mahl, would be added later, in ritual sacrifice.

Having earlier cast a glamour to mellow her voice, Isa lifted her draped arms and bade the supplicants raise their eyes. She began to speak, preaching with a rhythm and flow designed to mesmerize. As eyes glazed in the audience, she blended her words into Dark-chant, low and guttural, sending shadows into their hearts to bleed them of heat.

The last syllables of the spell echoed into the vastness of the Sanctum. From the slaves, no sound, no movement.

"Mordred," she called, and all heads turned to follow him as he came forward, placed the tray at her feet, and went to one knee. He turned the knife and offered it. She took it, and then pulled him to his feet, raising his hand to present him to the gathering.

"Here is your Captain," she said. All bowed their heads, and a slow smile of satisfaction twisted Mordred's face. His eyes glittered in anticipation of new power.

After a moment, Isa instructed the Earthborns to stand in their places. "As is proper, your Captain will fortify you with his own strength, through his own sacrifice.

"Behold his gift."

He knelt again before her, and she drew the knife three inches down each of his forearms, turning the knife to slide under the skin and increase the flow of blood. The smile didn't leave his face. He uttered no sound. He held his arms over the tray and let his blood, dark with the taint of Mahl, fall into the cups drip by drip.

Quietly, Isa said, "Sufficient."

Mordred stood, bearing the tray, and waited while she instructed the supplicants.

Isa had named a leader for each quadrant of thirteen, a person with some small portion of magic underlying their greed. To each of these four, while his tarnished blood still flowed down his arms, Mordred entrusted a crystal goblet. They did not drink first, but passed the cup each among their twelve.

When all the others had partaken, the leaders took the cups again and drank, draining every drop of potion until stone and spider fell upon their pallid lips, a sorcerer's kiss.

***

Clouds, dark as coal against the three quarter moon, swirled and sparked around the Blue Tower's spiked peak. Han lingered just inside a narrow strip of forest, a bony claw of the pine barren that edged Isa's domain. The mat of needles at his feet was still green and pungent, but the grey branches overhead had been laid bare. The ghost forest testified to the Witch's stock-in-trade. Death.

Stripped trees supplied sparse cover, but with silence and the almost magical camouflage of sun-cloth, Han hoped to avoid watchful eyes from Isa's lair. He chewed his lip. Tender though the flesh was after his fight with Lohen, indulging the habit helped him think. He focused all his senses on finding any flaw in the Witch's stronghold, which thrust from Earth to sky a hundred yards away, but a hopeless distance across her moat's abyss.

He blew a hard breath out his nostrils and growled low in his throat. Dismay and frustration, mounting since dawn, drove his heart a notch faster, and ire hammered at his temples. Search as he might, using every skill he possessed, he could neither see nor imagine any way to sneak or break or fake his way into the Tower.

And what would I do if I could get in? Seize the Witch's Keep by my lonesome?

But he wasn't alone. Emanating from somewhere close were thought echoes from four familiar minds: L'Aria (which shouldn't surprise him), Boff (whom he'd left behind hours ago), Maizie (which seemed somehow natural), and (most astounding of all) Lemon Martinez.

Han caught sight of them and laughed. They seemed so unlikely, standing together on the blighted ground craning their necks skyward.

Han shook his head and sighed.

Well, that's just great. Though happy to see them, they complicated his dilemma. He would hold himself responsible for them. He couldn't help it, and his mind played previews of a thousand threats that could make it impossible for him to keep them safe.

He followed their collective gaze, searching the sheer walls up to where they met the clouds. Sharp as his eyes were, he found only glass, steel, more glass, and more steel. *What in the name of the Wizard's pajamas are you all gawking at? And what are you doing here, anyway? What in Behl's blazes am I supposed to do with you?*

The Wizard's voice chimed in, an echo of a frequently given scolding. "Han, there are things beyond your control." Han grimaced, enjoying the thought like heartburn, but bowed to the inevitable. He stepped out of the dead pines to greet what would surely be his army. The strangest, teensiest, most mix-matched strike force ever to do battle.

As he approached, L'Aria looked at him, and pointed up. He followed her finger's direction. Finally he saw, and it stopped him cold.

Lohen.

He had ascended the tower despite its sheer walls, so high that he seemed no bigger than a fly. He struggled along a narrow crow's walk with only a thin steel rail glinting between him and the wind-whipped clouds.

"How did he get up there?"

L'Aria quirked one side of her mouth and shrugged.

Lohen tugged a hatch open against the wind and disappeared into the Tower. The hatch slammed shut with a report like a gunshot. A chill shivered down Han's spine. It had nothing to do with weather.

24. And the Witch is Glad

Lucky became aware of a beautiful, golden light shining in all around him, golden and dancing with the rhythm of his heart. A smooth road of rich earth lay before him, lined with fragrant trees and roadside pasture studded with wildflowers. He traced the spiral rise of a robin's lilt. He feasted his eyes on morning. At the end of the road, like a beacon of all that is right and good, stood his mother, arms spread in welcome.

The steel door slid back; the Witch stepped in. Lucky's eyes flew open, and Liliana vanished along with all the promise of the golden road. Pale hands snatched the cloak away. Lucky sat groggy and afraid, chafing the goose bumps on his bare arms. The servants bowed, foreheads to the floor, one of them shoving Lucky on the way down, trying to make him bow, too. He steeled his spine and got to his feet instead.

Isa planted her feet wide, directly in front of him. In her hands she held a many-tailed scourge unlike any weapon Lucky had ever seen or imagined. Its glass-tipped lashes squirmed as if alive. Lucky worked up his sluggish courage, tore his eyes from the terrifying weapon, and raised them to meet Isa's glowing orbs.

She stared back at him, but spoke to her slaves. "I have called two Cairnwights with their Wolves from the Wolf-hold to replace you here. You four shall proceed to the nether gate. The enemy at our doors—"

She broke off, making a strangled coughing sound, and Lucky wondered whether her servants knew the Heimlich maneuver. Then he realized she wasn't choking, but laughing. She caught her breath and resumed her instructions.

"Where was I? Oh yes, the enemy at our gates (chuckle) is motley and ridiculous (snort), but battles are by nature unpredictable (sigh).

"So, heed my command. If the war drums die, raise the gate. Let the Ice-Drake fly."

For the first time, Lucky thought he saw a sign of life in their faces—eyes widened in fear. Still, they filed obediently out the door, and Isa turned her attention to Lucky.

She smiled, though Lucky was not sure that was the right word for what happened to her face, and waved a hand at the brazier, extinguishing the flame.

"Do your best to hold up in the cold," she said. "Glacier Wolves can't abide heat and neither can the Cairnwights who keep them, and they are useful to me."

With the flame doused, Lucky felt as though his last friend had died, and his guts tied themselves into a knot. He shivered, having nothing much left between him and the cold.

Isa spun on her slipper-clad heel and leaned her weapon against the wall, as if disarming for peace talks. The whip continued to writhe and clatter and hiss out black smokes, standing in its corner.

"We should get to know one another, boy. You have no way to know this, yet, but you stand to gain a great deal by virtue of my acquaintance."

As she spoke her tone sweetened, but Lucky felt sure it was part of her magic. He wasn't strong enough—or he didn't know how—to hold off the spell she cast with her voice, but he struggled, trying his best to do it anyway. He wasn't to find out if it would work, at least not yet, because just then the steel door at the front of the chamber slid wide.

"Enter," Isa said without looking behind her. "Take guard positions."

The Cairnwights appeared almost human, but they had no hair and skin like parchment. Black veins webbed what Lucky could see of their arms, legs, and faces, pulsing through the pale skin. They wore sleeveless short robes, belted at the waist with thin steel chains. Their eyes and robes shimmered, a blue so pale and cold it held not even a memory of sun.

The Wolves resembled large Afghan hounds at first glance. White shaggy hair. Curled up tails, noses too long for their faces. Their limbs were long and their bodies narrow—the same shape as the dog painted on the side of a greyhound bus.

Definitely, they wouldn't have made good pets. They snarled through rows of razor-like teeth, double sets of gleaming three-inch canines. Their lips and noses were the only places not shrouded in pale fur; the bare skin there was so pale Lucky could almost see through it. Their eyes pearled ghost-white except for the pupil, dart-sharp and burning red.

As they crossed the room, the Wights' flat feet slapped the marble floor, but the Wolves' paws clicked and scraped, sporting claws like hooked knives.

The Cairnwights controlled the Wolves with whistled commands, two beasts to each Wight. They stationed themselves and their animals each to one side, so that every eye was trained on Lucky.

"Luccan, pay them no mind," Isa said.

Lucky thought that would be a tough order to follow even if he wanted to. But she went on speaking, and she seemed to draw closer even though she was still standing in the same place on the platform at the front of the room. It became harder and harder for Lucky to resist her mesmerizing voice.

It felt like her magic strangled his thoughts, clamping down tighter and tighter. It hurt, but Lucky bent over his knees and clutched his fists to his chest, determined to hold on to his mind.

Just when he thought he might break, the Key of Behliseth pulsed under his hands, a tiny throb next to the crazed beat of his heart, and he wished he could put all of himself inside it. He couldn't, but behind his eyelids he saw the golden light again, and the road with his mother waiting at the end of it.

"Mom," he croaked. "Help me."

"Stupid child," Isa snapped. "Your Mommy isn't here." Her voice changed again, becoming a demon's growl. Hearing it grate against his ears was agonizing. Lucky cringed, dreading her next words, but they didn't come.

"No, Isa," said another voice, deep and masculine. "His mother isn't here, but I am."

The Cairnwights seemed to stand even more still. The Wolves growled, but so low it was hard to hear. Isa spun toward a small door at the side of the room, and Lucky's eyes followed.

Lohen Chiell.

Surprise broke Isa's concentration, and Lucky's pain lifted. His mind cleared. The trouble, now that he could think, was that a hundred thoughts shot to the surface all at once, and close on their heels came a hundred fears.

"*He's always been dangerous,*" Thurlock had said.

My father ... Lucky tried the sound of the words in his mind ... *my father, Lohen Chiell.* The concept was foreign. As far as he could remember, this man had spoken only one word to him. "*Luccan,*" in the midst of a brawl in Black Creek Ravine.

Now Isa honed her voice to an edge so sharp Lucky wondered if it might draw blood, but she wasn't speaking to him. All her attention went to Lohen Chiell.

"You *dare* to stand before me? Perhaps you expect me to protect you from the Wizard?" She snorted a rude laugh and shook her head as if disbelieving. "*Slave,* if you hope to draw breath for another minute *you'd best bow low* and you'd best bring me something that will buy *your* life."

Lohen didn't smile, but something flickered in his one seeing eye that seemed part humor and part threat. Very quietly, he said. "My knees are tired of floors. As to what I bring, perhaps it's death."

Lucky had no context in which to fit those words and his mind raced. *What does he mean, he brings death? Whose death?* He hoped the man—he couldn't think *my father,* just yet—he hoped Lohen meant to kill the Witch, though he doubted anyone could accomplish that. Except perhaps Thurlock.

Lohen advanced straight toward Lucky. In his right hand he carried the stone Knife Lucky had seen at the ravine, the Black twin to his own Amber. And amazingly, *that* Knife, the Amber, hung in a sheath on Lohen's belt. His left hand rested on its hilt. Lohen didn't look at Lucky, but the scowl on his face scared him anyway.

Lucky turned to face him. He didn't see a father. He didn't see a rescuer. He saw a scarred, hard-muscled, rough-talking man brandishing knives and threatening death. He saw a man who had "*always been dangerous*" steps away and coming closer, with two Stone Blades in his hands.

Fright galloped in fast and fierce and Lucky forgot about Wights and Wolves, and even the Witch. Every cell he owned was riveted on his father.

He panicked, and he had no way out, so he attacked.

"Luccan," Lohen said, "Son," but Lucky could hardly hear it. His blood was rushing loud in his ears like liquid fear. He stormed at Lohen, hailing punches with all his strength.

Surprised, Lohen let the Black Blade clatter to the floor and seized Lucky's hands. "Luccan, wait."

Lohen's voice sounded choked, and Lucky twisted around to see his face. Tears trailed over Lohen's scarred cheek from a brown eye that seemed familiar, and far too gentle for a madman.

By now Lucky was caught up in the fight body and soul, so he didn't stop to wonder what those tears might mean. He focused instead on the advantage it gave him. He jerked his arms free and pressed it for all he was worth. Just like that day in the ravine, Lohen tried to stop him but never hit back.

All at once, that sank in. Tears, the gentle eye, the way Lohen nearly choked every time he said, "Luccan." Lucky added all like two plus two plus two, and he finally got it. Jolted to his senses, he stopped his fists.

I've made a mistake about this man, a bad mistake—

Across the room Isa leaned on the steel candelabra, her smile both cruel and smug.

And, Lucky thought, *the Witch is glad.*

25. Wolves, Wights, and Heroes

Faint sounds had begun to escape the tower—calls, commands, footsteps echoing against the cold walls. Han and his unusual troupe took cover amidst a hill-sized stack of boulders and twisted deadwood. They remained within yards of the empty moat, but shielded from the wind and the Tower's glare.

A horn shrieked from inside the Witch's Hold.

Peering between stones, Han watched a sally port open where nothing but blank glass had been before. Mordred, visible but protected behind a shield-curtain of blue light, stepped out onto a granite ledge. Two young women rolled a huge drum past the sorcerer and into a niche in the Tower's glowing wall. A young man followed, cradling a huge battle horn.

The deep voice of the drum began to beat a cadence. His upraised hands crackling with power, Mordred began to chant. He conjured a ghostly construct, a thin grey mist that arced fifty yards across the moat. Particles appeared within the cloud and started to swarm like excited gnats. They multiplied, clustered, and then condensed to form a bridge. In the crossed light of moon and glowing tower, it gleamed as black and slick, as demon's blood.

Hope, like a tiny balloon, quickened Han's heart. He pictured the conflict to come, remembered the clumsy, bewitched slaves in the Ravine a few days ago. He drew Chiell Shan with his right hand, drew the sun-metal knife with his left, and drew a breath to send L'Aria and the others back into the pines to find better cover. Only two or three Black-cloaks could come off the bridge at a time. He could hold them off alone, at least for a while.

But instead of Black-cloaks, a Cairnwight emerged, followed by six more, each handling a pair of Glacier Wolves. *This changes things. A different story altogether.*

Han turned to survey his volunteers and saw L'Aria climbing toward the top of the mound. When she reached the summit, she started to sing. Han had little magic of his own, but he could, at least, see it. The girl's chiming song flowed shining over the rocky ground in waves.

Interference, something to mix up Mordred's spells and befuddle some minds, no doubt.

Boff stepped out from the rocks, picked up a stone the size of a skull and hurled it across the moat. It didn't break through Mordred's shield, but the sorcerer flinched. Boff threw another stone, and another ...

Between the two of them they'll likely make a fine thorn in Mordred's side.

But the Wolves, with two-inch fangs and razor claws, had no need of Mordred's attention.

They were by no means invincible, but they were tough. The weaker link, the Wights carried only hobbles and short crystal knives. They had frail bodies, even compared to humans, their distant kin. At home in the Ice-fields, the Wolves helped them hunt, and in return received shelter and food in the harshest season. In battle, Wolves served as shields and weapons, and took payment in enemy blood.

The narrow bridge meant only one pair of wolves could come off at a time. The best bet would be to stop them there.

"Piece of cake," Han said, but the sarcasm tasted sour. He swallowed it as the first Wolf team reached the near side of the bridge, then dashed out from behind the rocks and came at them from the side. With a two-handed sweep of Chiell Shan, he slashed through a Wolf's neck before it could dodge and dropped it where it stood.

The Cairnwight stumbled over its slain charge, and Han brought Chiell Shan down in an overhand strike that laid the Wight's pale skin open from ear to hipbone. It fell, bloody arm collapsing beneath it, and knocked the next Wight in line back into the ranks.

Han spun quickly to meet the slain Wolf's battle-mate, a fury of claws and teeth. The beast danced side to side, and Han danced, too, using moves so well practiced they'd become instinct. He twisted away as the Wolf leapt for his throat. Claws raked his shoulder, but he landed a bone-cleaving blow to the creature's head. It fell in a heap.

Defending, buying time to assist their comrade and move the dead beasts, the Wights stationed two teams of Wolves in a snarling half-circle at the end of the bridge.

Boff moved in closer and targeted them with his stones. Han couldn't see Lemon Martinez, who was probably napping, but Maizie lunged and snapped just close enough to add a little harassment. L'Aria's song had no noticeable effect on the Wights, but to Han's surprise, it clearly unsettled the Wolves, making it a bit harder for the Wights to maintain control.

With his three comrades keeping them confused, Han had time to step back, switch weapons, and fire three arrows.

Another Wight fell and both its Wolves.

They'd made a dent, Han thought, and apparently it set the enemy back. The remaining five Wights whistled their Wolves into an orderly retreat.

Giving chase would be suicide; the bridge would probably disappear underfoot. Han considered spending more arrows, but he had few, and he had a gut feeling that the real battle hadn't begun.

"Well," he muttered, "we've got a reprieve." He strode back to the rocky hill, signaling the others to follow into the shelter of the boulders. Lemon met them there.

Han took stock. No injuries yet, aside from his own. That was good. His little squad seemed in good spirits. *Perhaps too good*, he thought. *They don't know what's yet to come.*

He imagined his nephew locked in the Tower, facing the Witch alone. The thought made his heart skip. And in that moment he let himself admit a painful truth. *I'm not going to be able to get inside. I can't help him.*

The image of Lohen disappearing through the hatch into the Tower popped into his mind. He thought about yesterday, felt Lohen's light-sword bite into his skin as they fought. But, then, he all but tasted the roasted rabbit.

"My brother," he said to L'Aria. "Whose side is he on?"

She looked at him with the most level look he'd ever seen her wear. "He'll do what's right," she said.

He wanted to believe her. He lowered his eyes, nodded, but bit his lip, refusing to let relief flow unchecked. What if the girl was wrong?

"By all the gods, let's pray that 'Lucky' is more than a name. What happened just now out here ... that was mostly luck."

"But not *all* luck, Han." L'Aria leaned forward as she spoke, standing in the shadows of the stone shelter with clenched fists at her side.

Han flashed a smile, marveling that she cloaked herself in defiance even at a time like this. "You're right, Spit. Your song helped. But from now on I want you to stay back here. Sing your magic from out of sight."

She sighed, "I can't."

Not sass, for once.

"My magic's not strong. I'm not like my father."

The admission clearly pained her. "You're young," Han said. "It will grow."

She half-smiled, but otherwise ignored the reassurance. "I can already do a lot with water," she said. "Move it, stop it, use it to make a portal for myself. But other stuff ... not so much. I can confuse people a little and make them feel like they're swimming against the current. But if I can't *see* what I'm fighting, I can't focus on it. The magic sort of ... drifts away."

While she spoke, she'd torn a shred from the hem of her skirt and poured a bit of water on it from Han's canteen. She hummed, dabbing at the striped wound on Han's shoulder.

Surprised at her action and at how much it soothed the icy pain, Han closed his eyes for a second and let go a tense breath. "Thanks," he said, looking up.

Despite her kind touch and apologetic tone, determined fire still burned in L'Aria's dark eyes.

"Okay." Han nodded, giving way to the unavoidable. "Do what you've been doing. They haven't had time to train archers, but watch for stones and things flying your way. I'll have Lemon stay with you. He can be pretty mean—"

The cat growled. Han didn't interpret. It wasn't fit for L'Aria's ears.

"—or distract someone until I can get to you."

"She saved me," Boff said. "I'll help."

"Good, thanks. And Maizie," he said, giving the dog a good scratch, "will guard at the base of the hill."

Having settled their defense as best he could, Han rationed out half his remaining supply of water—not enough, but no one complained. He cinched his essentially empty pack and stowed it in the rocks. "It won't be long before we'll have to fight again. Stay here until then, rest if you can. I'm going out."

"They'll see you," L'Aria said, saucy, but concerned, too.

"Likely they won't. I've got skills and sun-cloth. But *you* stay here," he repeated. "When it's time, I'll signal."

Moments later, he stood more or less concealed inside the margins of the ruined forest. He narrowed his eyes against the Tower's glare, scanning. Nothing moved but the evil wind, a frigid blast that could not be natural in the summer night. He stooped to yank up a handful of dead grass, and began to clean his sword, scraping away half-frozen blood. Gory, sticky, and it stank.

"Now this," he said, "is *fun*." He laughed, but there was a bitter edge to it. The break in fighting had already lasted longer than he'd expected. He needed a plan, he needed it now, and he had no idea where to find it.

In the glow from the Tower he peered through the night that had fallen over the forest, searching amongst the ghostly trees. "What," he asked himself in a hushed voice. "Do I think I'm going to find a strategy tied to a branch? Perhaps a battle plan will fall from the sky."

Something fell from the sky, not a battle plan but something huge and black. It had wings, it smelled like a birdcage, and it settled neatly to the ground ten feet away amidst a flurry of black feathers.

Han lifted his sword ready to lunge, but stopped when the giant winged thing became a man. Tall, dark, lean, wearing black jeans and a tee, holding both hands in the air, and saying, "Don't shoot."

Han looked at his sword. "Shoot?"

"Slash, thrust, whatever." The man dropped his hands to his long black hair and re-banded his ponytail, then smiled and held out a brown hand. "Henry George, Hank's nephew, if that means anything to you."

"I've heard of you, yes," Han said. Politely, he returned Henry's smile.

But the smile vanished instantly, as did Henry's, when they shook hands. Pain flared in Han's undamaged shoulder, burning as if the Mark of the Sun was being branded into it. When he met Henry's eyes he found his own surprise and pain mirrored there. Han remembered what Hank George had told Luccan about the Mark of the Others.

"My nephew is the last."

The pain vanished when they pulled their hands apart. Each shrugged his shoulder and cleared his throat, but neither said a word about what had just happened. After a time, Henry's slow smile found its way back. "I'm pleased to make your acquaintance," he said.

"Likewise." Han sat on his boulder and gestured to another, as if inviting Henry into his parlor. Then he listened while Henry told his tale.

He'd been at home in his city apartment, sitting at the table with a cup of coffee ...

"Suddenly, I was struck by a bolt of fear about my Uncle Hank. It didn't make sense; Hank's dead. Still, I couldn't shake it. I flew up to Uncle's place, but the worst thing I found there was dust mites."

"So you're a changeling?"

"You mean a shape-shifter?"

"That's strong magic."

"Oh, not so much. It's a talent I was born with, like my grandfather. I practiced a lot, so I got pretty good at it." He smiled. "It came in handy in the army."

With a twinge of hope, Han asked, "You're a Warrior, then?"

Henry shook his head and waved a hand. "Just plain Henry." He crossed his arms and chafed his biceps. "It's warmer in the sky than down here. Strange weather for June. Gives me goose bumps."

Not goose, Han thought. "What kind of bird?"

"Condor, basically a big vulture. I'm a little bigger than most, twelve-foot wingspan. Prettier than most, too, if I might say so myself."

Han smiled a little, and huddled into his cloak. "You followed Lucky here?"

"No. I had to get back to work, I'm a firefighter, when I'm not a bird, and I had duty for the next couple days. I got back to Hank's at daybreak this morning, just in time to see his house burning. Heck of a note. I got that taken care of but it set me back hours. Eventually, though, I flew out this way, and caught sight of that blue tower."

"You can see it?"

"I can't now." He swiveled his head this way and that, like a bird looking for a worm. "But I can see it fine when I'm wearing feathers. Strange. Like magic." He arched his brows to make it a question.

"Yes," Han said.

"Thought so," Henry nodded and continued. "Anyway, how can I help?"

Han opened his mouth to speak but then snapped it shut and stared. Suddenly, he laughed. *He's not Thurlock, but he's more than we had before.*

"Here's what you should know," he said. "There's a sorcerer, goes by the name of Mordred. He's powerful, but he's new and his boss has given him a bite that he can barely get his teeth around—"

THROOM, THROOM, THROOM ...

The sudden thunder of the northern drum shook the last dead pine needles to the ground and jolted Han to his feet. The horn blasted from within the keep, answered by the yaps and snarls of Wolves and muffled footsteps.

Han cinched up his belts and secured his bow on his back. The quiver at his hip still held a handful of plain arrows and five flamers. Shield in place, sword in hand, he turned to signal L'Aria and the others, but they'd already come out. They didn't look prepared, but they did look stubborn. He smiled, but his fondness was laced with fear.

The time for explanations had fled. Taking Henry by the elbow and meeting his eyes, Han said, "If you want to help, just fight for all you're worth."

The sally port gaped and Mordred emerged. Safe behind his force field, he conjured the black bridge anew. This time when the buzzing mist clotted solid, the bridge split into two spans. Han wished he could split himself, too.

Mordred's chant got louder and the drumbeat got faster. Blackcloaks, jerking like puppets, began to quick-march across the bridge. On the parallel span, the five Cairnwights kept pace. Their Wolves slathered for blood.

Han sent an arrow through the neck of the lead Wight, and the creature fell to its knees and toppled to the bridge deck. Instantly, the loose Wolves lunged, all teeth and gleaming claws, and turned their bloodlust on their own pack-mates, even tearing into the corpse. The Cairnwights' usually placid, luminous eyes flashed alarm.

That's not right, Han thought, even as he nocked his next arrow. *Glacier Wolves are pack animals. Their survival depends on loyalty. Why would they turn on each other?* The flash of insight came as he drew back his bow for the second shot.

It's the magic.

The Ravine was swimming in it: the massive power that Isa expended to maintain her presence in Earth, to hold the Blue Tower there—or at least make it seem to be there—and yet keep it hidden from the world at large; the spells and enchantments she'd laid on her Earthborn servants; Mordred's steady chant to direct those slaves and hold the bridge. Add to that L'Aria's song, probably Henry's thing, and maybe even Han's small skills.

It's driven the beasts mad.

Even so, the Wights commanded amazing skill. They whistled and gestured in perfect coordination, their pale forms liquid shadows against the blue light of the Witch's stronghold, dancers moving to some fantastical, hypnotic song. By the time Han gave himself a mental shake and loosed the second arrow, the Wights had begun to bring the half-crazed beasts into order.

The second arrow flew true and took a Cairnwight through the lung. This time the newly orphaned Wolves rushed at Han. He barely had time to stumble back, shoulder his bow, and tear Chiell Shan from its sheath. Arm and blade outstretched, he swept it in a wide arc. He connected with nothing more solid than the tip of an ear, but for a split second he kept the snarling beasts at bay. The maneuver bought him just enough time to shift his stance and gather his strength.

Without discipline, the keeperless Wolves flung themselves at Han with unchecked energy. He used it against them, letting one impale itself on his thrusting sword and seconds later slicing open the belly of the second.

But his moves had been desperate; his success, at least in part, had been luck. His timing lagged a thin shade behind his intentions, and the Cairnwights seized their moment. Keeping their fragile selves out of Chiell Shan's reach, they played two teams against him at once in a deadly, teasing rhythm. Feint, dodge, stalk, lunge. One beast and then another.

Han could never predict where the next Wolf would strike or exactly when. He was forced over and over again to defend on one side and leave the other exposed. Like a castle besieged, he inflicted small damage where he could. Doomed, he supposed, to fail in the end, he fought even harder, determined to take his last chance to cripple the power these creatures served.

Claws slashed his right leg, and it burned and ached as though immersed in dry ice. Han noted the injury, took it into account, shifted his weight and altered his moves to allow for it. But he didn't retreat. He thought of Luccan, the Wizard's laugh, the warm golden shine of Behlis Ethra's spring.

He found it then, the Warrior's Mind. He began to fight with cold purpose. His moves felt to him like slow, smooth motion, though his weapon flashed lightning fast. He didn't gain the upper hand, but he held on and whittled away at the Wolves' numbers.

A true Captain—even in combat, even in pain—as he fought he gave a corner of his mind to his troops. A stolen glance, the sound of a cry or footsteps, now and again a shred of someone's thought.

The Condor landed, transformed, and pulled a mean-looking club from the hands of a Black-cloaked corpse. Positioning himself at the end of the second span, Henry took on the enemy two-by-two as they stepped off the bridge. Many fell; blood soaked the ground.

Most of those who slipped by didn't make it ten feet before they met the sharp end of Maizie's madness. Maybe the same magic-sickness that had affected the Wolves got to her, too. Whatever the reason, the driven rage she had previously turned on Lucky swelled again. This time, she turned it on the enemy.

The few Black-cloaks who made it past the dog's teeth headed for the hill of stones where L'Aria sang and Lemon, unmoving but for his flicking tail, feigned indifference. Han wondered why Mordred would direct so much energy toward L'Aria. Perhaps he wanted to silence her magic, lighten his load. But Han couldn't help but think the sorcerer's motive might be something more twisted.

But the would-be assassins couldn't match Boff's strength. He planted himself in their path and blocked their way with hammering fists and unshakeable determination. L'Aria's song flowed on unbroken.

Fierce pride in his comrades swelled Han's heart. It gave him strength, but also fed his fears. His soldiers fought hard. Brave, resourceful, and strong, they amazed him, and he was grateful. But they were so few.

L'Aria's voice grew hoarse. Maizie's tongue lolled and dripped as she panted between attacks. A stone slipped from Boff's bloody grasp. Henry swiped stinging sweat from his eyes. And even the Warrior mind can't hold a body up forever. The claw marks in Han's shoulder burned more, not less, as time passed, and his injured leg became a slow, heavy burden.

And as long as the drum would beat, as long as Mordred would chant, the bridges would hold and Isa's slaves would march across.

Mordred is the key.

Han had to find some way to deal with the sorcerer, but he could think of nothing that didn't require more strength, more speed, and undeniably more magic than he could hope to find.

A laugh escaped him. Gallows humor. *Why,* he asked himself, *are Wizards never around when you need them?*

Courting resentment for Thurlock's absence, Han stumbled heavily out of a desperate two-handed slash. He took down the attacking Wolf, the blade slipping through the skin of its throat like a knife through cream, but his momentum took him too far. He landed heavily on his injured leg and went down.

He had killed four Wights and eight Wolves. Three teams remained. Six beasts

I'm finished.

***

Most of the Mounted Guard joining the expedition to Earth had already gathered in the hall on the lower floor of the Sisterhold. Most of the others present at the feast counted among those who needed to know the plans. Lili and Gerania headed down the main stairs to set things in motion.

Rose went up, rather than down, to the small, thatched belfry, where she would blow her eagle-whistle to send its piercing note off to ride the winds. The call, as always, would be answered within minutes by one of Ethra's colorful, horse-sized Flame Eagles.

Thurlock took the back stairs. Down one flight past the armory, another past basement workrooms, and down a long ramp into cellars carved from rock and dirt and shored up with rough-cut timbers. Thurlock, who long ago had been imprisoned in a dungeon built in much the same manner, whispered to himself, "You won't be trapped, you old fool."

He kept up the self-talk as he continued through a long corridor lit by glowing stones. He passed by all the doors, turned three times at intersections, came to a blank wall, knocked it with his staff, and fell through the trap door that appeared beneath his feet. He landed on his feet, hard and stiff-legged.

"Behl's hairy teeth," he growled, "I am getting too old for that." He headed for the back wall, thinking longingly of Earth devices such as escalators, elevators, and convenience stores. He ducked hanging bundles of herbs, feathers, and sundry whatnots. He dodged tables, benches, barrels, and a central brick chimney over a fire pit, complete with cauldron on an iron hook. He banged his knee, stubbed his toe, and got dust in his eye.

He blew more dust off a shelf holding various glass vessels, and coughed vigorously while attempting to sort through the goods. Finally, he selected three vials, all with brassbound corks—two large, one small, tempered for heat, frost, and light, and pre-treated with an infusion of cracked-shield lichen and creeping sandwort.

He went back the way he had come, complaining, "All that trouble for three empty bottles," and dashed out the back door. His long strides ate up the distance to the Oakridge, and he arrived with about five minutes to spare until dawn. Just enough time to let his horse know he needed her.

West of the ridge, rolling pasturelands lay cradled between the twin ranges of the Sister Hills. Somewhere in the miles of grass, Sherah, Thurlock's famous silver-grey mare, awaited his call. Thurlock stuck two fingers in the corners of his mouth, just as his cousin Thor had taught him when he was seven years old, and sounded a loud, sharp whistle. He smiled, just as proud of that whistle as he was on the day he first mastered it.

He turned to face east, and when a faint grey light began to shimmer at the world's edge, he raised his staff to the heavens. Just as the sun charged the horizon, blindingly bright, he shouted, *"Behl-Eth Dahn,"* *Behl* has given. Chanting a repeating psalm, he called the light into his outstretched left hand.

Slowly the fire spread through him until he stood like a torch in the wind. He channeled Behl's light from his right hand, through his staff, and from there let it pour into the three vials.

When they were full he said, "Thanks," rather casually, then capped the bottles.

"Now, Behl, the wind?"

In much the same process but without the pyrotechnics, he gathered in the dawn wind, the Gods' Breath, and filled it with his own strength, goodness, and valor. As an afterthought he added in a little *joie-de-vive*, and then with a magical word he locked that wind into the fibers of his shining staff.

"Done," he said, and climbed down to greet his waiting horse. "It's time, Sherah," he said. "Be swift."

***

The instant Lucky stopped fighting Lohen, Isa's loathsome voice echoed in whispers around the blue-lit chamber. "Luccan, you are lovely when you're angry. We may yet become friends." She laughed, and it chilled Lucky to the heart. She strode to the wall and hefted her weapon. "Alas, you didn't finish the job. It's my turn."

To Lucky's right, Lohen dove into a roll, retrieved the Black Knife as he passed, and snapped to his feet lightning fast, smooth despite his stiff left leg.

"Stop him!" At Isa's command, Wights whistled and Wolves moved. In a blink, all six beasts circled Lohen, a loose, snarling hoop of glittering teeth.

Lohen twisted the Black Blade in his hand, and a sword-shaped beam of indigo light sprang forth. It was an amazing thing to see and at that moment Lohen seemed an amazing man. *My father,* Lucky tried the idea again, and it started to fit.

One of the Wights whistled a short trill, and its Wolves leapt. Lohen spun with the sword, dodging one and slashing the other with the magical blade. The sight of all that blood, scarlet even in the awful light, left Lucky startled sick. Before the slain Wolf even hit the ground, the Wight sounded a note and the other creature lunged again, snapping teeth.

Lohen turned his head slightly side to side, apparently to compensate for his one-eyed field of vision. He stood otherwise still as if unsure. But when the beast leapt, he moved just enough, just in time, shifting his blade to impale the Wolf.

The sudden weight of the dead Wolf tipped him off balance, and he stumbled back. But he recovered, stepped sideways, and sliced the shoulder of another beast, shallow but damaging.

The Cairnwights' stiff features remained unreadable, yet their surprise was almost tangible. They delayed an instant before giving the next command, and Lohen seized that shred of opportunity to slide inside the protecting Wolves. He cut through a Cairnwight's throat.

Lucky sensed the other two Wights' alarm. The Wolves seemed almost out of control, crazy with bloodlust. Even the wounded Wolf snapped and tried to lunge on three legs.

Then, with a sharp whistle, the Wights set all the Wolves on Lohen at once. To Lucky it seemed as if they'd just given in to the Wolves madness. Whatever the reason, it changed things. The Wolves no longer worked together, guided in a coordinated assault, and maybe that's what kept Lohen alive for the next few minutes. He spun and dodged with hardly time to do anything but react and defend himself, and when seconds had become long minutes he'd only been able to kill one more beast.

Scratched and bitten in a dozen places, with every step he left a bloody print on the slick marble floor, an image Lucky couldn't shake from his mind.

He's fighting alone, Lucky thought, *for his life ...*

For his life! His father had finally shown up and could very possibly die right before his eyes. That reality struck Lucky like a stone, and he balled up his fists. *I have to help.*

Isa roared, "*No!*" The magical Command latched onto Lucky like claw-fingers in a death grip. He couldn't move. "That's not to be, boy," she said, "I'm enjoying this sport."

Lucky pulled against her magic with every ounce of strength he had. To his own surprise, he began to gain ground. He could feel the Witch's hold begin to weaken.

Isa screamed, "Stand, child!"

Lucky's eyes and ears were chock-full of Wolf snarls and hairy white bodies and claws and teeth battering the man he now thought of automatically as *my father* into a corner. Panicked, and encouraged by his own slow progress, he kept struggling to break Isa's hold.

"I will teach you obedience, boy." The lashes of the Witch's scourge writhed as she cocked her arm back for a blow, and the weapon sliced through space hissing a warning.

Lucky turned away at the last hairs'-breadth instant and the blow struck across his back. Pain he couldn't have imagined until that moment blazed through the tendrils of every nerve. He heard a blood-curdling, terrified cry and then realized, *I'm the one screaming.*

The whip flashed upward in preparation for another strike but Lucky hardened himself against it, dredging up every ounce of stubborn will. *I won't,* he vowed. *I won't scream like that again.* He held his breath, waiting for the scourge to whistle through the air, waiting for its cruel tails to rip his flesh.

"Not my son!" Lohen Chiell's bellow rang through the cold chamber like a battle cry. As if it powered him up, Lohen went as wild as the Wolves. He slashed, cleaved, and thrust, killed one more Wolf and sliced a bloody gash down the length of a Wight's back.

Each Wight still commanded one Wolf, but Lohen's mad rush left them startled, injured, and bewildered. They withdrew their beasts, stepping back toward the corners, away from Lohen.

Isa stared at Lohen, stunned, her mouth hanging open as if her jaw had come unhinged. But it looked like Lohen had spent what energy fury had lent him, and now he sagged, chest heaving and losing blood. Isa recovered her wits quickly and ordered the Wights back to their task, threatening them with her scourge.

Lucky started toward Lohen again, still determined to help, but he was exhausted by hours of pain, effort, and terror. He stopped, dizzy, teetering on the edge of the now cold fire pit. But his movement had drawn Isa's attention, and she once again turned to strike him.

After a desperate struggle, Lohen took another Wolf out. Then he stumbled across the chamber and rooted himself between Lucky and Isa's lash, spreading fatherly arms out like the shielding wings of an angel.

The whip came down on Lohen once, but then he pivoted, raising his light-blade. When the whip fell again, he slashed through its tails. The damaged weapon sizzled and flared like cut power lines, and the room clouded with stinking black smoke.

By then blood and sweat poured off Lohen like rain, his breath came hard, and his voice worn to a rag. Still he insisted, "You cannot have my son."

Isa fixed him with a stare, then turned her back and walked across the chamber. The surviving Wolf, amazingly, was the one Lohen had wounded early on, and now blood loss had weakened it so much it could barely stand. Isa rasped a Command at the Wights.

"Take that useless beast and get out."

Vicious scowl pasted in place, Isa turned to face Lohen and spoke very softly. "You stupid slave. Fool, you are, to think you've already suffered the worst that I can do." She muttered strange words, and waved her hand in a quick gesture. Like spider legs, the severed tails of the whip grew back, glass-shard tips and all.

This time, when Isa snapped her weapon, she muttered a spell behind it, and it struck Lohen so hard that he slid across the floor. He put his arms under him to rise, but the Witch struck again. Lohen's clothes were shredded, and blood beaded on his flayed skin.

Whatever parasite—fear, exhaustion, pain—whatever had held Lucky back, in that moment it lost its grip. Strength reared up inside him, part wish, part rage, part terror, maybe part compassion. Without thinking he set it loose, and it drove him in a headlong, roaring rush, straight at the Witch.

Isa wheeled around to face him. For the tiniest moment, her ice-blue eyes widened in shock or alarm. Then she raised the scourge as if to strike again, but stopped, looking at it as if considering whether it was truly the best tool for the job. She shook her head and laughed, her smile an ugly slash.

She raised her hands and began to chant.

She seemed to be calling down some awful power, turning the air between them thick and foul and drawing every last shred of warmth out from the stone and steel of the bloody chamber.

Lucky felt a warm comfort at his side and he knew it was Lohen before he looked. His father was bloody and bruised, but on his feet. When he took hold of Lucky's hand his grip was sticky with blood, but warm and strong and impossibly steady.

Turning Lucky's palm up, he slapped down the hilt of the Amber Knife. The two of them stood at the same height and he met Lucky's eyes with a level gaze. "It's what I came here for, to give you what's yours. It's more than a knife, Luccan, more than amber."

243

Lucky's hand curled around that Blade as if it had its own mind, as if it had waited, biding time for the touch of this very stone.

"Luccan," Lohen said, calling Lucky's attention back. "It's dangerous; great magic always bears risk, and there's no time to teach you. But, if all else fails, this Blade can stop Isa."

The Witch kept up her chant, the harsh sounds swelling and repeating in a tangled echo. A flash from the dais where she stood was followed by a grating sound, like a train braking to a stop on rusty rails. The massive spell she'd created, a hissing ball of blue flame and ropy black smokes, began to spin in her hands, looking like a mass of sparking electric eels trapped in translucent skin.

Lohen released a ragged breath and gulped another. He took hold of Lucky's arm and pulled him around so they were face to face. When he spoke, he sounded as if he believed the words would be his last. "Son," he said, "maybe you'll forgive me in the end."

The child inside Lucky demanded explanations, wanted to shout questions. *Who are you? Why did you leave me? Why come back now?* But, said a smarter voice, *now isn't the time.* He put kindness, not forgiveness and not love, but all the kindness he possessed into his eyes. "Papa," he said, his voice deep, like a man's.

Lohen nodded, showing Lucky a smile, small and sad, but honest. Lucky pushed his hair back and locked eyes with his father, and then they turned together to face the Witch.

"Lowly slave," Isa said to Lohen, the last echoes of her chant falling away. "You've caused nothing but grief since the day that Black Knife was returned. It ends now." Without even a blink of hesitation, she hurled the spell.

But the floor was bloody, and she slipped.

The spell flew off-course, rocketing not toward Lohen, but toward Lucky. For an instant, the entire chamber held its breath. Isa froze with her pale brows arched, her mouth slack. Then she shouted, "Not the boy, I want him!"

Lohen stepped in front of Lucky, setting his feet wide and raising his magical sword into the path of the spell.

The explosion of clashing magic shook the Tower to its foundations, knocking Lucky sideways with a force that felt like a speeding truck. Miraculously, when the initial shock passed, Lucky found he could move. He rolled to his knees and stared for a moment at his empty hands bleeding scarlet on the white marble floor, then he raised his head to see.

Death.

Carcasses of Wolves, a Wight's torn corpse, shapeless piles of debris stained with blood, both red and black.

And a scarred man in torn clothing, hand still clutching a black stone Knife. *Broken candle ... shield the flame.* The words had comforted Lucky when he'd read them in his strange little book in Thurlock's basement. Now, they tore at his heart.

26. Black Hearts and Flames

A breath of strange silence, and then an explosion cracked the sky around the Tower's steel spire. The world shivered in Han's eyes as if about to dissolve and shook beneath him. The blue glare of the Tower, for an immeasurable fraction of time, failed. Mordred's chant faltered; the drum skipped a beat. The bridge vanished, and the team of Wight and Wolves stationed at the span's end fell to their deaths in the deep emptiness of the moat.

Something happened inside!

In that moment even the Wolves stalled, and Han scrambled for his sword and then for meager cover behind the root mass of an upturned tree. For a moment, his heart soared, lofted on hope like wings. His thoughts went immediately to Luccan, and he tried to shoot a thought-message past the Tower's wavering magic. But in no more than a blink, a low sound like humming power lines arose and the eerie blue began to shine again.

The drummers beat the cadence with fear-born fervor. Mordred's chant snaked on. Mordred's shield re-formed and crackled as the sorcerer powered it once more to full strength. And Mordred's army, though tattered, fought again.

The sally port began to yawn open in the Tower's wall.

More Black-cloaks, reinforcements.

More thralls to be thrown against Han and his allies. More pawns to the will of Mordred. Who could only be stopped with a Wizard's power.

Watching it begin again, Han's emotions traveled a dark road. Mordred, Isa, and the empty-hearted Lord of Ice, he hated as he had never hated before. But worse, so bitter was he to be left here with little power and less hope that it was on the tip of his tongue to curse gods and Wizards, too. All of them.

But ...

Perhaps by accident, his fingertips brushed the feathered arrows at his hip. As if the touch had tripped a switch, a memory tumbled forth.

Dawn. The sweet tang of Shahna's Gold on his tongue. He gave Luccan's shoulder a squeeze and turned away to leave the Wizard's Tower.

"Wait," Thurlock said.

Han stopped in the doorway.

"Remember, Warrior. Flame will sometimes find a path where even your strength and skill cannot take you."

Cryptic, but now Han understood. All this time he'd spent bemoaning his lack of power, the Wizard's own magic had been riding his hip, waiting for him to set it loose.

***

"Sit up!"

Isa spat the Command from across the death-littered room, and, without any contribution from his mind, Lucky's sore body tried to obey. Hands and feet slipped on stone slicked with blood and sweat, and he finally stopped, exhausted, when he'd scrabbled onto knees and elbows. From that humiliating position he stared at the Witch-Mortaine in disbelief.

Her skin hung loose, glimmering with graveyard sheen, a semblance of flesh that hardly covered her bones. The ice-blue shield she'd thrown up just before the blast had protected her from the spell's worst impact, Lucky suspected, just as his father's intervention had protected him. Still, to look at her, it was hard to believe she was strung together well enough to stand.

In fact, she wasn't. She leaned against the wall, and as Lucky watched, she began to tremble. She fixed him with a look that clearly dared him to say anything, and then she took a flask from a deep pocket of her blue-shine robes.

Steel, slender as two fingers, as long as a hand, the bottle was capped with a black plug bound on by thin red threads. In one motion the Witch sliced through the bindings with a sharp thumbnail, popped the cork, and lifted it to her upraised, gaping mouth.

She didn't swallow, but rather sucked the smoky black substance into her lungs, looking at Lucky sideways the whole time. She inhaled for so long that he began to hope she would burst, but all she did was cap the bottle, hide it in her robes somewhere, and let her breath out real slow.

Something horrible happened then, something Lucky knew he would wish for the rest of his life he had never seen. Her eyes flickered. Her skin faded, or more accurately thinned, until Lucky could see through into the sick, blackened organs and veins within. And then Isa was gone, and a shadow, a kind of witch-shaped nothingness took her place.

The whole weird transition happened in less time than it took Lucky to do a double take, and when it was over, he wondered if he'd really seen it. Because, by the time pure shock got knocked out by a giant wave of fear, she was back.

As horrible as ever.

Laughing.

"Sit up," she yelled again, and crossed the cavernous room in ten strides. She grabbed him by the shredded back of his shirt and dragged him to the nearest corner. "Sit," she repeated, but instead of putting magic in the words, she yanked him upright and drove the order home with a hard shake that slammed his head against the wall.

She brought out her steel bottle. "Perhaps you need a sip of my special tea to shore you up?"

He pasted his hands to the walls, ignoring the icy surface, willing himself to stay upright at all costs. He retched at the thought of that horrid ... stuff ... fuming into his body.

She chuckled. "I'll take that as a no. Now, don't move."

Lucky doubted that he could.

She walked to the center of the room, then pivoted, waving at each of the thirteen torches and killing the flames. She left the triplet candles burning on the platform, then stood beneath those eerie lights, one hand pressed against each of the steel pillars that held the candles aloft. For a long time she stayed there, silent and still, her tattered blue robes draped from her outstretched arms like wings on an angel's ruined corpse.

Lucky pulled his eyes away from her, and looked again at his father. Lohen's body hadn't been torn or crushed. He'd simply gone still. Lucky tried to convince himself that he saw Lohen's chest moving up and down, very slightly. Then he shook his head hard enough to wake up its knocks and bruises.

He's dead, he told himself. *And I'm a fool. I never know when to quit hoping, quit believing.*

Suddenly, the smoldering anger he always pretended wasn't there flamed out of control. He stared at his father's brown, bloody, lifeless hands and demanded, *how could you do this? How could you leave me again?*

But in the fifteen short years of his life, Lucky had been left or lost a bunch of times. To be honest, he was mad at everyone. He started ticking off the list, *Hank, for dying. Henry, for letting me leave. Thurlock for losing me on the way. Han, for leaving me. My mother for not—*

Wait.

There was the Witch-Mortaine, only yards away, hanging as if suspended by her own evil. She was the cruel one, the dark one. She was the root cause of Lucky's trouble.

Once he put his mind to it, tacking all his hatred onto Isa's tail came easy.

***

Han's moment of enlightenment cost him dearly, for in the scant seconds he spent immersed in golden memory, blind to the blue-lit night, the last remaining team of Wolves crept up silent behind him. They'd launched themselves at him before he knew they were there. He whirled, swinging Chiell Shan two-handed in a desperate arc with the beasts in mid-leap.

He caught one Wolf across the hindquarters and flank, and it fell to the side, where it scrabbled helplessly on the blood-slicked rock. The second Wolf escaped the blade and leapt. Han stumbled backward off the rock and thought he was done for, but the fall saved him. Instead of tearing into his throat, the beast rocketed over his head.

Han had curled up as he fell, so his head didn't smash on the rocks, but his back hit hard. His breath rushed out. And try as he might he couldn't suck a new one in. And the Wolf would return. And until Han could breathe, he couldn't move.

The sky went black overhead and Han expected the worst, *for the umpteenth time this week*, he told himself. Gladly, he realized he'd thought wrong again, the shadow was Henry, the Condor, coming to rescue him. The great bird raked his talons across the Wolf's belly and opened a pair of gashes, long and deep. The beast thrashed on the ground, howling in pain.

The Condor prepared to strike again and finish it, but pulled up suddenly and circled overhead. Han rolled to his feet, but soon saw that this fight was over.

With movements so quick and small they were hard to follow, the last Wight standing slit the throats of each of its wounded Wolves. Each time, it covered the beasts' eyes with a gentle hand, and spoke—the only words Han had ever heard a Wight utter. Then, the pale almost-human creature from the north of Ethra reversed its slender dagger, held it with two hands, and plunged it into its own belly, twisting for a fatal cut.

Henry had already altered his course and flew to the hilltop, where a knot of black cloaks tried to get past Boff and Maizie to L'Aria, who hadn't stopped singing yet, though she sounded a bit hoarse. Han thought that with Henry's help, the others could keep her safe, and he had another task. This might be his only chance.

Stumbling, bleeding, and sweating, Han climbed again to take cover behind the huge spread of the upturned tree root. He drew three arrows from his quiver, two bearing rainbow flames, the third fletched in sun yellow and painted gold. He took aim beyond the shield curtain, beyond the heavy black of the sorcerer's robe, on a spot deep in the cold center of Mordred's heart. He loosed all three arrows in rapid succession.

The first arrow sent a shiver of sparks through the shield. The next strike lit the whole force field with rainbow flame. He nocked the third arrow—Thurlock's golden work—to the bowstring. He drew it back, and set it loose.

Clarity.

A moment spaced within heartbeats, moving so slowly past Han's senses that it might have held a lifetime. The bowstring thrummed, and force punched his shoulder like a slow fist. All of the light in the blue night drew close in to brighten a slender tube through which Han watched the Wizard's arrow fly.

The sun-metal point shattered the shield and struck home. So tuned were Han's senses that he heard the black threads of the sorcerers robe snap under the point, felt layers of skin stretch and tear. Finally, the dense, determined tissue of the sorcerer's black heart sucked the arrow in as if welcoming death, and exploded in a burst of golden heat.

Han watched Mordred's eyes widen, soften, even smile in surprise. Then, the animal smell of fear. No longer was Mordred a sorcerer, an enemy, a fiend. He was simply a man, someone's child. In striking him down Han had done nothing evil, only a job that must be done. Yet for that instant he wished with every shred of his soul that he could take it back. The slow stretched seconds snapped.

Wild night rushed Han from every direction, everything happening at once, none of it what he expected. Before Mordred's knees even crumpled, Boff shouted in dismay. He tensed, head to toe, and then ran onto the bridge holding his arms out as if to catch his brother, or break his fall.

The port in the Tower wall opened wide behind Mordred, and it seemed it would swallow him whole. But Mordred fell forward, not into the Tower's heart, but into the abyss that held its roots. The black bridge vanished under Boff's feet, and Boff, too, plunged to his death.

In that instant, Lemon screeched, a blood-curdling alley-cat's yowl. L'Aria screamed a half-beat later, ending her song in a cry so crammed with anger and fear that Han could taste it. He leapt from his perch to go to her aid, scanning the bloody battle yard on his way.

A few Black-cloaks ran for the pines. A few milled in confusion with no sorcerer to drive them. But some were fighting, and now they fought as if they meant it, as if they had just woke up to their own bitterness.

A dozen of them, led by a brutish blond woman, swarmed over the mound toward L'Aria. Before Han had finished his first step, Lemon

Martinez leapt, transformed into a snarling ball of claws and teeth. He sprang straight into the big woman's face, dug his front claws into her scalp, and slashed with the hind claws again and again.

She killed him, of course. She tore him from her face, dashed him to the rocks, and then stomped with her heavy boot until his tiny, secretly loyal heart split wide open. Her vengeance was blind; Lemon had shredded her eyes. And it was futile. L'Aria let go all of her youthful rage on the woman and pushed her back so hard that she fell, tripped up two of her followers, and landed broken on the rocks, spitted on her comrades' spear.

The other Black-cloaks came on, and L'Aria fought back, young hands curled into determined fists. Maizie reached her side and darted at the attackers, snapping and tearing their flesh. The Condor landed, and transformed, and Henry used his long reach to take charge of the hill.

As Han reached the foot of the hill, he caught sight of L'Aria's face, bruised and bloody.

The truth struck home.

She'll die here. Why didn't I send her away?

A sound startled him out of his lament, a sound like the roar of wind in an ice-cave. Every motion ceased. Fear froze hearts good and evil alike and the battle stopped, posed like a museum tableau. Han knew the sound, and he forced his head to turn toward the Tower, where the door gaped wide.

"Ice-Drake," he said, and he couldn't suppress a shudder, both of fear and revulsion. In Han's opinion, Ice-drakes, mutants made from dragon's eggs and foul magic, were Ethra's most abominable mistake. Their frigid breath killed with horrible efficiency, and everything was prey. And if Dragons—mutant or not—could talk, the one thing they would never say is, "I'm not hungry."

The beast emerged and spread her majestic, glittering wings.

Most Drakes were small and flawed, often flightless or blind, mistakes produced when bungling sorcerers mishandled the dark magic designed to transform natural beasts into evil creatures.

This was not just any Ice-Drake.

This Drake was legend.

"Sahlamahn."

As Han whispered her name, scenes from stories his great-uncle had told him of this cruel, wondrous northern beast played out in his mind's eye. He heard again the cadence of the old man's voice, just as it sounded when it fueled his childhood imaginings.

Sahlamahn, the first Ice Drake ever transformed, and the only one ever to rise flawless. *Sahlamahn*, eerily beautiful while her cousins were horrid and clumsy. Sahlamahn outsized other Blue Drakes by half, and she had it all: flight, armor, claws, and breath that could freeze-dry blood still in the veins.

She bore no riders now and never had. She'd never done the bidding of anyone except the Sorcerer, long since dead, whose evil had made her what she was.

So why will she do Isa's bidding now?

Clearly, Han wasn't the only who wasn't sure the Drake would pick and choose her prey. A stream of black-cloaked figures broke for the trees, seeking cover. Han thought that wasn't a bad idea, but he saw Henry atop the hill, supporting the sagging L'Aria against his hip with one arm and pointing with the other.

Following that gesture, Han saw that the fleeing Earthborns had stopped in their tracks. What could have given them a scare to rival Sahlamahn? Then, on the high ridge just beyond the trees, Han saw what approached, and smiled.

Liliana, at the head of a mounted column that ranged along the ridge. Her steed, Aedanh, led easily, his gait proud, his hooves fleet. His coat shone like spun gold even in the Tower's foul glow, and he and Lili both boasted the gilt and silver colors of the Sunlands. Just behind rode six of Shahna's Rangers, the Mounted Guard's elite, bedecked in burnished mail and the diamond patterned green of the Sisterhold, their horses' tails and manes streaming in a wind raised by speed.

Five Flame Eagles sailed the sky above them—massive birds plumed in white and crested black, saffron, and red. Rosishan rode upon their battle-wise king, Ghriffon. The wind lifted her cloak, flashing the stark red of the Eagle Alliance, the diamond green, and the bright-sewn rainbow symbols of her magic.

"On your left!" The shout came from the tail of the column of horse soldiers, accompanied by the ring of an extra set of hooves, falling fast and light. Again, the deep voice, "Passing on your left."

As the others moved aside to let the rider by, Han smiled. Relief threatened to flood his eyes. He'd stopped believing this moment would come.

Thurlock had arrived.

***

Lucky sat in his corner, vaulted in darkness, and glared at Isa, letting rebellion build like a mudflow behind a dam. *She's ignoring me. She thinks I can't hurt her.*

His nostrils flared at the awareness of her casual disregard. He recalled his father's instruction. *"This Blade can stop her."* He sucked at his cheek, tasting blood. He'd lost his hold on the Amber Knife in the blast, but he spotted it now on the floor across the room, close to Isa.

I'm fast enough. He tensed to spring.

But Isa heard something, or she felt it, and pivoted to point a finger at Lucky. She conjured a fist-sized bullet of blue, crackling light and hurled it streaking through the fumes to stab through his skull. Instantly, he writhed in pain, unable to control his movements or the mewling sounds he made. A million years later, when Isa dropped her hand, as suddenly as it had started, the torture stopped.

"We'll try once more to have our talk," she said. "Before we do, let me compliment you. Defiance looks good on you. Or was it hate?" Her lips twitched and she chortled in glee. "You gave me a little boost, and I do appreciate it. But we've things to do. Forget the Knife. Leave it lie."

She turned on a heel and began to pace, robes trailing. Stopping in front of Lucky, she locked her death-blue gaze on his eyes, and her bloodless lips twisted. She held her hands out toward Lucky and slowly unfurled her fists. Something flowed out of them, some kind of magic that smelled like cheap wine and felt as thick and deadly sweet as molasses in a flytrap.

"Luccan," Isa said, in hypnotic cadence. "I'm sorry about your father. I couldn't let him continue. I was afraid he would kill you."

"You lie, Witch. It was you that almost killed me." The words were bold, even brave, but to Lucky his voice sounded small and senseless like the last buzz of a dying insect.

"Luccan," she said again.

Lucky felt magic fall around him like chains.

"You've been misled. In no way do I desire your death. Quite the contrary, these regrettable events today were not my wish, not my doing. All I want is a chance to *help* you. I brought you here to show you your potential, the vast power you could choose to embrace." If Lucky's attempt at defiance had angered her, she kept it secret. She spoke in rhythm, hypnotizing. Words oozed from her lips in globs.

Lucky tried to stay strong, but Isa was very skilled at Sorcery. Being evil didn't mean she couldn't be subtle, and being subtle didn't mean her magic couldn't be strong. The spell she laid over her speech had all of that. He was going under, sliding into her words, drowning in lies like syrup.

Calling up all the strength he had left, he put his feet under him and stood. He gathered in the corners of his mind and focused, struggling to complete one thought: *I wish—*

Isa raised her voice, spinning a spell in a voice like thunder and diamonds. She held her hand up and her long fingers squirmed like spider legs. Lucky's thoughts got stuck, caught in her glittering web.

"No one has told you the whole truth about that Key you wear, have they, Luccan?"

Lucky lifted his hand, touched the Key where it rested beneath his torn shirt.

"No one has told you what that Key will unlock. They don't want you to know what you hold, what you are. They let out knowledge like fishing line, keeping you on the hook until they can reel you in. They make choices for you, and make you think you've done the choosing."

Threads made of words and magic clung to Lucky's brain, hung in the doorways of his mind, studded with treacherous beauty like wintry ropes coated with glittering frost.

She captured him, pulled her web tight, dropped her voice to a sly whisper.

"The truth is, Luccan, power is beautiful, and those that hold it need not apologize. And your power ... *your* power is endless. All people are at your command. Their lives belong to you. The power to make, *and to unmake, is yours.*"

Lucky stared straight ahead, straight into the Witch's eyes. He wanted to turn away, break free, disappear. He pictured himself charging the blue glass walls, head down like a bull, launching himself through in a burst of shards. But he couldn't move, couldn't even shift his weight, and in seconds those last self-made thoughts vanished.

"Luccan, I can help you," Isa said, promising the reward she'd schemed to make him want. Her voice grew urgent, and she lowered herself to one knee. Eye to eye, she leaned so close that her cold breath ruffled the fine hairs on Lucky's lip. "I can give it all to you. But one thing *you* must do first. *You* must remove a single obstacle; the one man who has the power to oppose you. You will have to kill him."

She fell silent, letting the words circle like buzzards before swooping in to strip the meat from Lucky's last resistance. "He is outside, fool enough to come to our keep, where the Lord Mahl has fortified every inch of stone and steel, and where his own master will surely never come."

Slowly, never breaking her gaze, she drew the slender flask from her robes once more. She held it up between them and flicked off the cap with a thumb, allowing the greasy smoke to billow out. When a tight, dense cloud had formed above the bottle, she blew a long, putrid breath into it, sending the haze swirling toward Lucky.

He didn't want to, but he couldn't help it. He breathed.

"Yes," Isa said. "That's good. The Essence will help you see, Luccan, make you strong for your task."

As cold flooded Lucky's lungs and became part of him, or he became part of it, she rose to her feet. Stepping over Lohen's body, picking her way through scattered debris, she went to the door. Before opening it, she stopped.

"Rest now," she said. "When I return, I'll lay your nemesis at your feet. We'll join together, Luccan. We'll rule the worlds, *once Thurlock is dead.*"

27. Sahlamahn

Sahlamahn swooped out from the Tower, flying low and causing everyone on the battlefield to cringe. When she lifted away toward the dark, pre-dawn sky, her wings catching the Tower's glow and glinting like sapphires and ice, the collective relief seemed almost an audible sigh.

The Black-cloaks turned their attention back to the coming riders. A handful of them broke for a getaway. Han let them go. The rest, to Han's amazement, seemed prepared to take a stand. Perhaps twelve remained. Even if they'd all been fresh and none tired or injured, they would have posed little threat to six Mounted Guard.

Thurlock sped past Ethrans and Earthborns alike, bent low over Sherah's mane. Even at night, the mare's silver coat flashed as they passed through shadows. Her hooves, shod with sun-metal, sparked with every stride.

Liliana passed the Earthborns by, too, a sweep of her sword pointing her soldiers to the fight. Han limped as quickly as he might to the base of the hill, and got there in time to grasp Sherah's bridle as she skidded to a stop. Aedanh crowded in, and Ghriffon perched on a boulder.

Only Thurlock dismounted. Time was short.

Han said, "Sir, the Drake ... It's Sahlamahn. I've only two of your arrows left."

"Where's your shield, Han? We can use that."

Han opened his mouth to answer before he realized he didn't know. It had been struck from his arm in the fight, and he had no idea when or where.

Henry, who had propped the exhausted L'Aria on a boulder and stood aside from the Ethrans, panting and bleeding a little, spoke up. "I know where it is. Let me catch my breath and I'll fly for it."

"You're the Condor," Thurlock said, and though it wasn't a question he waited for Henry's nod before continuing. "Lest there be no time to say it later, sir, thank you for what you've done. But you're exhausted and injured. He stopped to look at L'Aria, Maizie, and Han. "All of you are. I've brought something that can help a little."

Thurlock called down one of the Eagles, a she-bird named Fiera. At the Wizard's direction, Henry told the bird where to find the shield. As Fiera flew to her task, Thurlock took a fur-covered water-skin from his saddle and stepped toward Han, the most seriously wounded.

Han shook his head and pointed to L'Aria.

The Wizard nodded, "Yes," he said, "of course."

When all the others had received their share, Han poured a swallow on his tongue, and recognized it instantly.

He smiled at Thurlock. "You've seen Tiro."

Thurlock only smiled back.

Though the Kindled Springs water didn't heal Han's injuries, it helped him find strength in spite of them. Not a night's sleep, but at least as refreshing as a long nap.

"Lohen went in—"

Thurlock held up his palm. "It's no surprise."

"Lemon is—"

"Later," the Wizard said. "Right now we've a Blue Salamander to deal with. You're okay to ride, and shoot?"

He acknowledged Han's answering nod, and then turned to Ghriffon. "We'll need you and your crew to help with the Drake."

In reply, the Eagle King lifted his beak and blew a column of furious scarlet flame ten yards high into the night. Flame Eagles and Ice-Drakes had a list of grievances between them centuries long. It took no convincing to get them to fight.

With a few words—and some squeaks and head-tilts that no one else save possibly Henry understood in the least—the Wizard told the King what he'd planned. Then, while Han strapped on the shield Fiera had brought back to him, he lifted the protesting L'Aria onto Ghriffon's back behind her Aunt Rose.

"You'll be safest here."

He said something in Sherah's ear, mounted up, and reached out a hand to help Han up behind him.

"Lady Grace," he said, "and Rose, Sister Witch. I'll need to go into the Tower, so I have to cross the moat, and we may as well kill a

Drake with the same stone, so to speak. Can the two of you give us some ground to stand on?"

"Yes," Lili said.

Rose added, "Be quick, though. We're too far from home to keep that up for long."

"All speed, then," the Wizard said, and looked to the sky. "Sahlamahn is on her way in to find breakfast. Let's begin."

The four riderless Eagles took off, circled around and got into position behind Sahlamahn. Staying carefully clear of her deadly breath, dodging her whipping tail, they drove her in like avian cowhands. Blasts of flame charred her scales and nudged her toward the moat as if it were a cattle chute.

On the ground, the six soldiers tidied up the last loose ends of battle with the Black-cloaks, rounding up the die-hards and offering them a single chance to flee into the pines. All but two took the deal, and the crew quickly subdued them.

Lili dismounted, handing Aedanh's reins to one of the guard. "In case something happens," she said.

Ghriffon airlifted Rose to the ledge where Mordred had made his stand, and then perched on a high ledge, wings half-spread for balance, while L'Aria clung to his neck.

Liliana and Rosishan, Sister-Witches, began melodic chants that spanned the moat and echoed one off the other in ethereal counterpoint. Each Sister held a Spring Wand, a slender coiling branch the length of a woman's forearm. Lili's was formed from a pale green bough, Rose's dusty red.

Small globes of light formed near their hands, then climbed the length of the wand one after the other, blossoming from the tip. In seconds, their voices entwined and grew strong, and a long garland of light-blooms roped from each wand. Then the Witches swung their wands forward, pointing them toward one another. Their magic met, spliced, and broadened into a bridge cobbled from stones of rainbow light.

Mounted behind Thurlock, Han felt curiously small, but under the circumstances he thought that was fine. Sherah's patience seemed thinner than either his or Thurlock's; she stamped and snorted, while they did their best to relax and still keep their seats. Everything was ready, and they'd said the few words needed to cement their plan. Now, they only waited for the Drake to be jockeyed into place.

Sahlamahn had other ideas, though, and made her move so fast that probably no one saw it coming; certainly not Han. His jaw dropped. He choked out, "Sir!" He pointed.

Thurlock said, "Oh," seeming just as surprised.

The Drake had suddenly swooped straight up with a single push from her great wings, an aerobatic move even the Eagles couldn't match. Their efforts to follow, fast as they were, looked placid next to her Mercurial climb. In a flash she escaped the reach of their flames.

Sahlamahn repeated the swooping maneuver with ease again and again, each time falling into a slight curving drop then rocketing upward. Soon she had risen so high that even the jewel glitter off her wings disappeared in the distant dark. Ice-Drakes on the hunt liked to fly in the high, cold winds to give an added chill to the air in their auxiliary lungs, the ones they used to kill.

Thurlock said quietly, "Han, tell the Witches to save their energy."

Han conveyed that to Rose by means of thought, and Rose signaled Lili. The Sisters lowered their Wands and the volume and speed of their melodic chants, but kept the glowing magic ready.

Sahlamahn returned in a nosedive, wings pinned flat to her sides. Falling bullet-fast, she aimed for the cluster of soldiers and captives that had taken shelter in the trees. Thurlock reined Sherah around and signaled with his knees, and the mare dashed ahead full speed. When they were within range, he lifted his staff, but Sahlamahn flew fast and very close to her intended prey. The Wizard couldn't set the full force of his magic on her without endangering the people he wanted to save.

He swung his staff out in front, holding it like a jousting knight, and sent a single white-hot blade of flames across the Drake's path. She swerved, using the reverse thrust from a blast of super-cooled air and a tweak of her wings to power into a labored climb. It cost her speed and agility, but she froze both captive Earthborns and an Ethran soldier with just the edges of that breath.

The Eagles had been circling overhead and now they dove, but the Condor got there first. He flew straight toward the Drake, coming at a right angle toward her long, toothy snout—a reckless move. Sahlamahn had expended much of her killing air, but a Drake is never defenseless. She turned her head toward her bold assailant. Han, watching below from too far away to help, expected the Condor to freeze and fall like an iceberg. Just in time, the black wings splayed and swiveled and propelled him upward an essential few feet.

Fly, Han mentally urged, but Henry perched on the monster's head. Digging his talons into tough hide and curling his neck at an impossible angle, he pecked at Sahlamahn's white dinner-plate eye. She screeched, bucked, twisted in the air as vitreous fluid spewed out, then pushed into a desperate climb.

Henry hung on, scraping talons and beak wherever he could find something soft enough to scratch until she rolled so sharply that he lost his hold and tumbled down. He pulled himself up just short of the pines' spiky tops, then braked with his wings and descended into the branches.

Han scarcely had time for a sigh of relief.

The Condor's rogue attack held the Drake close in and left her half-blind, unsure of her course without dual vision. It bought time, and now the Eagles caught up. They flew as close as they safely could to her good eye, knowing she'd dodge away from their flames to protect it.

Ghriffon, though avoiding recklessness with L'Aria still clinging to his back, swept off from the Tower's wall. Riding the air between Sahlamahn's vast wings, he raked his talons over her back time and again, keeping her close to the ground. Bit by bit, they herded her closer to the Tower until she flew over the moat. She dove, and the Eagles let her go, pumping their wings to keep from being dragged down in her tailwind.

Thurlock once again lifted his golden staff. Sherah reared up, and burst into full, flying stride.

"Hang on," Thurlock shouted. He and Han leaned toward Sherah's neck as she bunched her haunches and leapt. A true leap of faith, for when Sherah's hooves left the edge of Earth, nothing spanned the moat beneath them but blue-lit air.

But the Sisters had their magic in hand, and even as Wizard and Warrior sailed out into nothing, their linked magic hardened again into the rainbow bridge. Sherah came down nimble and sure on stones of light, her sun-metal shod hooves blazing gold.

In the Tower's cruel light, Sahlamahn's ice-blue scales sparkled like diamond knives. Han had expected that she'd stay low in the moat, but instead she shot up suddenly, fifty yards to their right. Her sapphire wings raised a dark steely wind. When she trumpeted, ragged fringes of her breath laced the Wizard's beard with frost. Like a serpent, she curled into a tight, twisting turn, then flattened her wings against her flanks and bulleted into a deliberate dive, driving hard at Han and Thurlock.

Thurlock never flinched. He raised his voice over the howl of her monster wind. "Shield!"

Han raised the dragon hide buckler, thrusting it toward the right as if that small disk would stave off the monster's onslaught. Thurlock pointed his staff toward her and spoke. A spinning ball of white light and concentrated power shot from the staff's sun-metal tip like lightning and passed through Han's shield. Fire blasted from the far side of it, a thunder-flash of superheated, golden magic.

Sahlamahn's great, beautiful wings burst into gem-bright flames. Reeking smoke coiled from burning hide. In agony, she screamed and dove in a futile attempt to escape the blaze she carried in her flesh.

The Sister magic beneath Sherah's hooves began to pulse and vibrate. The Witches were near their limit. Thurlock swung his legs over Sherah's head and jumped to the bridge deck, tossing the reins to Han. "Trust Sherah," he called back over his shoulder, and then ran, planted his staff, and vaulted onto the granite ledge at the Tower's hidden door.

As Sahlamahn neared her next pass under the bridge, Han strove for calm. Thurlock had given him what he needed—two remaining sun-fletched flame arrows and a crippled dragon. It was up to him to finish her. He'd have one chance to do it.

The Drake ducked to pass under the bridge. As Sherah struggled against the wind and the faltering magic to give him a steady seat, Han nocked the Wizard's arrow and pulled the bowstring back into a full draw.

Sahlamahn's great head emerged beneath him. Chewing his lip mercilessly, he struggled to take aim on the tiny, moving target. There, just behind the Drake's armored skull, just above the reticulated scales of her back, a sickle of pale, pulsing, unprotected flesh.

He fired.

He missed.

The arrow bounced off the Drake's hard skull and fell unlit into the moat.

For an instant, the Sister's magic broke down. Sherah stumbled, but the Witches made it solid again before she fell. The close call set Han's heart thumping. When the fright passed he finally relaxed, and almost laughed.

Die later, fool, he told himself. *Right now, aim, fire, kill the Drake before it's too late.*

He sensed the continuing strain on the magic that held them aloft over the moat, felt Sherah quiver as she wrestled with her instinct to flee before the road vanished. He watched his small target pull away until it became a tiny blip in his vision, an idea more than a sight.

Somehow, the distance, the difficulty of the shot, the impossibility of survival, made it easier. Nothing existed in any world except this single bowshot. With his mind, he rode the arrow as it flew.

The shaft ran fast and true and plunged deep into the beast's brain. Paralyzed, Sahlamahn began to plummet, Wizard's flame wreathing her skull and bursting from her eyes, nostrils, and mouth.

"Behl eth Dahn," Han whispered, incapable of another thought.

Sherah moved, not ready to die now or later, and not willing to let the Wizard down. He'd entrusted Han to her care, and care she would. Trumpeting as if calling to the wind for aid, she muscled into a leap. She landed her hooves once just as the bridge vanished. With one more great stride she bounded to the safety of solid ground.

Han slumped out of the saddle and, hugging the mare's frothy neck, turned to face the Tower. The Wizard, grey robes shining, stood at the edge of the granite and looked back at him.

A smile. A wink. Thumbs up.

Han laughed and, he felt certain, so did Sherah.

Thurlock took a deep draft of the water from Kindled Springs, pivoted on his heel, and rapped his golden staff on Isa's door.

28. Mannatha

Thurlock. Lucky heard the name, and even spoken in Isa's hollow voice it stirred his memory, chiseled bits from the ice that had encased his heart. The door to the chamber slid open, and the Witch said the name again, but this time with a note of surprise, or perhaps alarm.

"You were perhaps not expecting me?" Thurlock's voice chimed into the chamber as mellow and rich as struck gold. The haze over Lucky's eyes thinned, and he saw the Wizard framed in the dark doorway, staff gleaming with its own light.

"How did you get up here?" Isa sounded both angry and incredulous.

"I followed my nose, Isa. Unmistakable scent."

The cold in Lucky's bones still held him stiff, but the Wizard's quip made him want to laugh and cry all at once. He did neither, but his voice scraped loose. "Thurlock."

The Wizard responded with a businesslike nod. "Hello, Luccan."

Lucky's heart thumped.

"Luccan!" The Witch cast his name at him on a growl, all wrapped up in power again. In the same moment, she drew from her robes the slender steel flask and sent it flying toward him with a jet of magic.

Lucky flinched but it would have been too slow. Thurlock swung his staff like a bat and intercepted the missile. The flask shattered in a flash of light. The remains of the smoky black substance sizzled in the air and evaporated.

"Isa. Leave the boy alone."

Isa's reply hissed through the chamber. "You, Thurlock, have no power to Command in my Tower and no power at all over me."

"But I do."

"You're a weakling, soft. Sentiment and self-doubt cripples you. You cannot prevail."

"It's true, I'll grant it. I'm but human, and I can't stand against you in your master's house. But I've brought along some things that might help."

Isa stared at him, a look so cold Lucky thought it might freeze fire. She spoke very softly.

"When I've finished my work here today, Wizard, when I have given *that* child's power, to Mahl ..." She paused to gaze at Lucky. "You and your weakling god will be like ants at the feet of my Lord Mahl and ... Well, he'll be interested in the boy, but I'll ... dispose, let's say. I'll dispose of you myself."

She thrust her hands overhead and screeched out sounds so foul they could only be a curse. Bringing her hands down in front of her like judgment, she jabbed all of her fingers toward the Wizard, blue lightning streaking from their tips. The Wizard's head jerked back, and then he stood frozen in place, glazed in icy flame.

All of the dark doubt the Witch had tried to plant in Lucky withered away. He tried to stand, but the Essence had not yet let go of his limbs. They felt stiff and painfully cold. He wanted desperately to help the Wizard, but beyond wishing it, he could do nothing. He finally managed to move his right hand a few inches and take hold of the Key of Behliseth.

Thurlock's hands tightened on his staff, and a thin white-gold shield expanded inch-by-inch to surround him, holding the blue force off of him by the slimmest margin. His face contorted with effort and slowly, slowly he lowered his left hand to his robe and drew a heavy glass vial from a pocket. He opened his hand and the vial clattered to floor, but it didn't shatter.

Against the force and weight of Isa's magic, he raised his staff knee-high, and then brought the sun-metal tip crashing down on the vial. The glass disintegrated and light exploded, creating a sheet of golden flame that battled Isa's fire. Freed, Thurlock raised the staff again, higher this time, and held it with two hands low on the shaft. "By Behl's light and the Gods' Breath of the Sunlands," he thundered, "*you will not have him!*"

This time he brought the pommel down, striking sun-metal globe against the blood-smeared marble floor with a loud *crack!* A wind rushed forth from it, a great undying gust that blew the Wizard's robes and hair back, and then circled him as if he, Thurlock, was the very heart of a whirlwind. With a broad sweep of his arms, he threw the staggering force of the wind toward the Witch-Mortaine.

The force of the wind quenched Isa's magic and hurled her against the hard, icy walls. Her skull crashed against the glass block. She remained standing until the wind let go. Then she slid to the floor and sat with her back propped crookedly against the wall of her fortress, glass-blue eyes wide open and empty.

Thurlock's wind, smelling of new hay, salt breeze, and sunshine, had driven the last traces of Isa's smoky evil from Lucky's lungs. His mind cleared, warmth filled his chest and spread all the way to his toes and fingers. He still hurt just about everywhere, but at least his body felt like it belonged to him again.

Better yet, the Witch was dead. He said, "*Yes!*"

But Thurlock, after stooping for a moment to catch his breath, had walked heavily over to Isa's body, and now he knelt beside her corpse, shaking his head slowly. He whispered something Lucky couldn't hear, and then closed her eyelids with a gentle hand.

"I'm sorry, Isa," he said. "I wish it had been different."

Lucky gaped in disbelief. "You're sorry! Don't you want her dead?"

"My wants don't much matter at this point, do they?" Ire flashed in Thurlock's eyes, but he spoke calmly. "Since you asked, you should know. Isa wasn't always the creature you've seen. Once she was ... I loved her, long ago."

Lucky started to object that it wasn't possible for Isa ever to have been someone that could be loved, but he shut his mouth when he read a warning in Thurlock's face.

"We'd better go," Thurlock said, back to business.

He might have said more, but again Lucky interrupted. "But we're safe now, aren't we? I mean, she's dead ..."

"We are for the moment, but you forget, or perhaps you never knew, that Isa was but a servant, a tool. I have no doubt that her master can still make use—"

A thin wheeze and a weak cough came from across the chamber.

Lucky nearly tripped over his still-aching legs, trying to run toward what he had thought was his father's dead body.

"He's alive!"

Thurlock's huge strides got him there first. He knelt by Lohen and raised his head to ease his breathing. Two steps away, Lucky stopped, finding himself too anxious and afraid, happy and angry to move, or even breathe.

Lohen's eyes were open, glazed as if with fever, but not blind. He met the Wizard's gaze. "The God's Breath," he rasped, and a flicker of a smile crossed his bloody lips. "I remember, Wizard. I heard it in the wind. The Oakridge ... my son ..." The words trailed into a fit of coughing.

Thurlock waved Lucky closer. "Here, Luccan, help me. Hold his head up." From his robes, he fished out a water-skin covered with fur; he uncapped it and held the spout to Lohen's mouth.

After a few drops had trickled past his lips, Lohen breathed easier. He nodded at Thurlock, and the Wizard gave him more. He seemed to relax then, as if the pain eased, but he said, "I don't have much time."

Thurlock took hold of Lohen again and eased him back to rest, propped against his shoulder. "It's you he wants, Luccan. Come around where he can see you."

Lucky bent over Lohen, willing tears not to fall, wanting desperately to find words of reassurance.

"Son," Lohen breathed.

"You're going to be okay. We'll get you out of here and—"

"No!" Then, more gently, "No, son. I'll die."

Lucky swallowed a protest. "Papa."

That brought Lohen a smile. "Listen," he said between labored breaths, "*Mannatha*. It's who you are. *Luccan Elieth Perdhro, Mannatha, Suth Chiell.*" He lifted a hand and smoothed Lucky's hair off his brow. Seconds later, he was gone.

Thurlock put a hand on Lucky's shoulder, and a long silent moment went by. Just as it seemed Thurlock might speak, a strange, hollow laugh came from across the chamber ...

Near the wall ...

Where they'd left Isa's corpse.

The Witch's broken remains still lay skewed crookedly against the wall, but her eyes had popped wide open. In life, the irises had been so pale that Lucky had feared he might see through them, but now they'd gone blue-black and dull. And they never blinked. Her dead lips moved. Her voice erupted unlike that of any living human soul.

"You are impressive, Wizard Thurlock, certainly more durable than this pathetic Witch presently at my service."

A foul voice, certainly foul, but it carried the accents, patterns, and closed-mouth vowels of a person highly educated at an English University. Lucky arched his brows and stepped back in open-mouthed shock.

"An idea strikes me," the voice continued. "Borrowing a phrase from this world, we might say my 'star is on the rise.' On the other hand, your master, that conniver Behl, is well past his day. Why don't you cut your losses, join up with me? You can live forever, second in power only to me. Quite an offer, eh, old boy? What do you say?"

Thurlock rolled his eyes. "I won't even grace that with an answer, you old fraud."

The thing laughed, in that restrained "huh, huh, huh" of the English upper crust, and Lucky's jaw dropped even further. Then a shadow, a transparent yet solid blackness, oozed from Isa's body and hovered around her like a smothering cloud.

Lucky knew that blackness.

Mahl. The evil god Thurlock had tried to explain that night a million years ago over apple pie. Lucky wondered if he could will himself blind, turn off "The Sight." But as horrible as it was to see a talking, dead Witch possessed by an ultra badass shadow, he didn't dare look away.

"Well," the dead mouth said, "I had to try, you know. A matter of form. I must admit, old man, choosing you was the smartest move your boss ever made. I say, though, what about a compromise? Give me the boy. I'll take him and let you live for now. Surely you won't miss him much, he's only a pup. You can train up another."

"As generous as that offer is," Thurlock answered, lips curled in sarcasm, "I refuse. Even if I was inclined to agree, which I am not, Luccan isn't mine to give."

"Well then." The voice dropped to a whisper, in that instant gone deadly cold. "Let the games begin."

The shadow wrapped around the Witch and raised her body to stand loosely on its dead feet. Then, it swelled around her until it filled the chamber, straining the glass Tower's seams and leaving only a shrinking circle of light where Lucky and Thurlock stood over Lohen's body.

The darkness flashed and crackled, bristled with bolts of blue fire. It started to swirl around the little circle of light, picking up speed until it whirled so fast Lucky felt dizzy. The noise of it shook the floor, cries and howls and crazy laughter. Thousands of tiny, tormented souls, that's what it sounded like, and all of them hungry.

The shadow deepened, intensified, and a wave of blue flame, low to the floor, rolled through it thundering like a freight train. As it passed over and through each of the dead Wolves and Wights littering the chamber, they started to move in a sick imitation of life.

Alien zombies. It seemed like the last straw.

Whatever grit Lucky had found in recent moments, whatever hope Thurlock's return had brought, whatever secret faith Lucky had nurtured that he might win free, it fled before this devil's carnival.

Raised like an unholy Lazarus, a Cairnwight emitted a choked whistle. The other Wight joined in, and the Wolves howled. The beasts had turned blacker than night now, though in life they'd been white as snowfields. The ruby flames of their eyes had died. The only things that hadn't changed at all were the glistening teeth and steely claws.

The blue flame broke through the thin curtain of light, and rolled toward Lohen's body.

"No!" Lucky shouted, throwing himself down to cover the corpse. *"You can't have my father!"*

But the blue fire crept on, and though it seemed to move at a snail's pace, Lucky had scarcely drawn another breath before he felt icy flames licking at the skin of his back. Hunched over Lohen, clutching the

Key of Behliseth against his chest, he said it again, this time barely a whisper.

"No. You cannot have my father."

Maybe that was one of Lucky's potent wishes, or maybe it was because the Key of Behliseth was pressed between Lucky and his father. Perhaps there was another explanation. Whatever the cause, when the blue flame rolled through, Lohen wasn't raised. His remains vanished in a flurry of sparks, Black Knife and all, there one instant and gone the next.

Lucky lay on his back, drenched in pain, struggling to breathe and stay conscious.

Thurlock shouted, a huge sound with no words, and Lucky turned in time to see him crash his staff down on another vial. Again, light exploded. This time Thurlock spun in place and swept his staff in a circle, carrying along a fountain of gold-bright stars.

The brilliance conquered the bits of shadow that had encroached and walled off the dark, enclosing Lucky and Thurlock in a cylinder of light.

But Thurlock wasn't done. He concentrated, worked so hard he began to sweat, chanted until from somewhere he raised a golden fire that engulfed his staff and the hand that held it. Then he lifted his face and said in a loud, clear voice, "Hold! I, Thurlock Ol'Karrigh, Rha-shi Behliseth, Premier Wizard of the Ethran Sunlands, bind this light in balance against the void."

He drew his hand across the space, spouting flame, and emblazoned the golden wall with the familiar runes of his name. At once, the light-shield hardened. And the blackness outside of it, though it seethed and whispered, fell nearly still.

Thurlock leaned over his staff, dripping sweat and laboring to catch his breath. Glancing toward Lucky, he gestured, waving him closer. Lucky got to his feet, a painful process, and took a couple steps to stand by the Wizard.

The old man pulled out the water-skin and passed it to him.

"Drink," he said.

Lucky took a short swallow and started to hand it back, but it was so good, so *refreshing*, that he brought it back to his lips for a good long draught. When he came up for air, he noticed the Wizard—the tired, thirsty Wizard—looking at him with brows raised.

"There's some left," Lucky said, passing the skin back. Thurlock tipped it up over his mouth, but only a few drops fell to his parched lips.

Chagrinned, Lucky said, "I'm sorry, sir ... I, uh, I wasn't thinking."

"Oh, it's fine Luccan," Thurlock answered, and the twinkle of a smile gleamed in his eyes. "It's fine. I'm glad you drank it, and I'm glad it's done you some good. A few drops are plenty for me. I'm better already, and I need you to be strong."

"Me?"

"I'll need your help."

It was the last thing Lucky expected to hear. Hadn't the Wizard come to rescue him? Flabbergasted, Lucky shook his head, pushed his hair out of his eyes, started to tremble.

Get a grip, Lucky.

"Luccan, listen. This can't last. This—" Thurlock broke off to wave a hand at the light-shield. "This is all I've got. I have no more vials of light, no more dawn wind stored in my staff. My strength isn't gone, but neither is it endless. And Behlishan, the god who can make me stronger, won't come. If you want to get out of here alive, you must help."

"Won't come? Won't come! What kind of god is that? That thing out there," he jabbed a finger at the blackness beyond the shield, "that's a god isn't it? Mahl? Isn't that what you said? If that thing can be here, why not this ... this Behl?"

"Please calm yourself," Thurlock said.

Lucky tried to loosen his clenched fist and jaw. But he turned away from the Wizard's eyes.

"No Ethran god belongs in Earth." Thurlock said. "Mahl destroys Earth's balance just by being here. But he's always hungry, empty. That's what he is, a living void that can never be filled. He doesn't care a whit about balance. He feeds wherever he can.

"But, just as Mahl has his nature, Behl has his. He *is balance*. If he came here to Earth, it would only tilt the tables farther. He won't do it. He loves you; he is my greatest friend. But nothing will make him betray his nature."

Lucky heard. Brain-wise, he understood. Heart-wise all that came through was, *you're on your own, kid.*

Again.

But this time was different. All the times he'd felt alone before—even in the cave Hank called The Road Between, even when Grandpa Hank died, and even, especially, here in the tower before his father or Thurlock showed up—always some secret part of him had believed that help would come.

Now, his mind strayed to Han, but he sensed nothing that might have been his uncle's presence, and that little twinkle of hope died before it was born. Thurlock would fail, was failing already. *And my father ... dead and gone.*

"Luccan, you must help," Thurlock repeated.

Lucky glanced at him. Once again he'd planted his staff squarely in front of him. The shadow outside had begun to quiver and bend, though the dead still stood unmoving as if pickled in black formaldehyde. Thurlock worked hard to hold the light-shield firm a while longer.

Lucky wanted to say, stop. Forget it. What's the use?

He stared at the spot where his father had lain in his final moments. Remembered how he looked in that moment of death. His features had relaxed, and despite the scars Lucky had seen for the first time how alike they were.

Lohen had looked young. He'd looked *peaceful*. But even at his last breath, he'd gripped the Black Knife with two hands. Lucky thought of that Knife's twin, the Amber, and his right palm began to itch for the weight of the hilt.

"This Blade can stop her," Lohen had said.

Could it?

It was about a yard beyond the wall of light, practically at the feet of the zombie Witch. But the shadow didn't touch it. A bubble protected the Blade; shadow surrounded it but didn't make contact.

Maybe ... maybe Mahl is afraid to touch it. If the Amber could stop the Witch, maybe it can hurt him.

He gauged the distance. *I'm fast,* he thought. *I could get it.* But he'd have to go through the fires that battled at the barrier, both gold and blue. And then he'd have to go through the shadow. All the horrible things inside it would touch him.

What would happen to me?

But what did it matter? He might die, but he was pretty sure dead was the only way he'd ever make it out of this nightmare, anyway. He caught sight of the Witch's face, and felt his lips curl in a snarl. He thought nothing of it when she grinned in return.

He hated her, dead or alive, now as much as ever. All her malice was still there, all her selfish glee in the power to destroy. He wanted to slash her so bad he could feel the Knife in his hands. It might be worth it, even if he died in the instant afterward.

"Luccan," the Wizard said.

Lucky dove for the Knife. His right arm went through the curtains of flame.

Thurlock shouted "No!" He grabbed hold of Lucky's ankle and dragged him back, and at the same time swiped his staff through the breach. "Hold," he panted, and it almost sounded like he was pleading with the magic. "In Behl's name, hold."

"What did you do that for?"

"Luccan—"

"I wanted to kill her! Why did you stop me?"

The Wizard seemed tired. He may have been nearing exhaustion. But when he shouted there was enough power behind it to raise hackles on Lucky's neck.

"You cannot kill what is already dead!"

He had Lucky's full attention.

In a more normal tone, he said, "Your anger, your hate is a gift to Mahl. He feeds on it. He revels in it."

The hideous noises had started up again outside the Wizard's circle. Horrible laughter, a deep, hollow sound doubled by the screech of the Witch's dead larynx. Zombie Wolves howled. Zombie Wights whistled. Echoing voices from things hidden in shadow cried and moaned. Isa's empty voice started a chant. The living dead began to circle the chamber, like twisted children in a playground dance.

Goose flesh prickled on Lucky's skin. It became clear: Thurlock could not keep the shadow and its creatures out forever. Mahl would win; he only needed to persist.

"I'm sorry that all of this has happened so quickly," Thurlock said, "and you're being asked to help though you've had no chance to learn how. It's patently unfair." A trace of his usual humor sparked in his grey eyes, but then it died.

"I can't fix that," he said. "The best I can do is to offer a few words and ask you to listen with your heart open."

Not too sure, Lucky only nodded.

Thurlock pursed his lips, as if concerned about the adequacy of that response, and then took a deep, resigned breath. "I cannot do this alone," he said.

"Then we're going to die, Thurlock." Even as he spoke he thought, *so much for listening with an open heart*, but he couldn't stop. "We're going to die, and that monster out there is going to win because I can't do it. I thought I could, but I was wrong. I can't. I'm sorry, but *you're the Wizard*, not me."

"Yes," Thurlock said, patience sounding strained. "I'm a Wizard, but Mahl is a *god*, and we're on his turf."

"It's hopeless then—"

"Hush. Listen. Hate. That's his power source. Anger. Revenge. Those things make him strong. And when I say 'hate, anger, revenge,' I mean yours. It doesn't matter who you're hating—Isa, Mahl, me, even yourself—you're fortifying the very thing you want to destroy. Let it go, Luccan, before it's too late."

The words, *"too late,"* echoed.

Five yards away on all sides, a super powerful light-and-life-sucking shadow full of dead things waxed more wicked strong with every second. Blue and white lightning streaked through it a hundred times a minute. Ravaged faces grinned at Lucky; dead hands clawed at the wall between them. Zombie voices chanted and hissed; ghostly throats shrieked and howled.

The shield of golden light, the only thing holding it all back, had worn thin. Lucky felt Thurlock waiting for him.

I don't know what he wants me to do. Whatever it is, I can't do it.

"Luccan," Thurlock said softly. "Don't give up. Hold on to hope."

Lucky snorted. "My hope," he said, and thrust his burned hand out to point, "was that Knife."

"Luccan, the Knife is not the way." Thurlock's brisk tone drove the next words home. "We're out of time. Please, use what you've been given and take us home. This is *your* task. You have the key."

Oh ... the Key. Lucky reached to the place where it hung at the end of its chain.

"Not that Key. That's part of it, but it's the key that lies beneath it—"

Wrong again, Lucky. Frustrated beyond hope, up to his neck in things he couldn't believe and problems he couldn't solve, he closed his ears, clammed up, and refused to think. But inside his silent shell, thoughts found him. Memories.

In his strange book: *Suth Chiell you shall prevail.* A lie?

His father's dying words: *"Mannatha. It's who you are."*

Thurlock, speaking of a name given to Lucky that was lost, that even he, the Wizard, didn't know: *"More is the pity."*

Mannatha, the name his father had found in the Wizard's wind. That was the name the Wizard had wanted. A secret name. A powerful name.

"Use what you've been given," Thurlock had implored.

Well ... what exactly is that? Ever an orderly person, he started a mental list. To think, he pushed his hair out of his eyes; it hurt.

Make that number one, I've been given cuts, bruises, torn clothes, and a very painful burnt arm. Despite everything, he almost smiled. *But that's not what the Wizard meant.*

What else? Speed ... Tools and power I don't understand ... Magic I can't control ... A new name ...

But there was more, a gift wrapped inside his father's voice, tucked away in three small syllables. His father had died to give it to him, but he hadn't seen it then. Now it slammed him like a punch in the gut.

His father had given back to him what the Witch had stolen three years ago, the only thing Lucky had ever really forgotten.

He understood.

What was out there in the Witch's chamber wasn't darkness, but emptiness. And what he could use against it, what he had been given, was the power to fill it up. With light, joy, laughter, even with tears. With life.

Mahl could want, but he couldn't love. He couldn't hope. For all his god-power, he could never decipher the human spirit. That was why he had needed Isa.

That's why he wanted me.

Using Isa's corpse, he had her hands, but her soul, her *humanity*, had gone. Without that, he was blind to the heart. He would never guess that one person would fight or even die for another. He just didn't get it. That was the giant chink in his armor. Against Mahl, Lucky was armed to the teeth.

He had in his arsenal his mother's voice, her laughter, her breath brushing his cheek; Hank George beating his drum; Han's gentle words, *"Take it easy, lad;"* the taste of Thurlock's instant cocoa; the comfort of a lesson under the stars. Forever, he had the memory of his father saying, *"Forgive me."*

Love, brighter than a Wizard's magic flames.

Hope, all the strands of it tied together.

Those were the things he had been given.

And a Key. *"The one that lies beneath."* With a small, surprised laugh, Lucky put his hand over the Key of Behliseth. Buried but alive under that bright metal, thumping a beat steady and strong, he found the true Key. Yes, the Key to magic, but also to powers greater and more mysterious.

"Luccan?"

Lucky jumped, startled by the Wizard's voice. It had taken only seconds for him to wind through his thoughts, but time hadn't been standing still. The shadow had gained momentum. Evil screamed and howled out there, now, and the zombie Witch and zombie creatures circled so fast they were almost running. The relentless dark magic had weakened the light-shield, forced it down and bent it over so that now all that protected them was a small, lit-up dome. And it was shrinking. Time was up.

"Now," Lucky said. He flashed the Wizard a smile and took hold of the Key of Behliseth.

"I am Luccan Elieth Perdhro, Mannatha, Suth Chiell."

He spoke his names in a strong, steady voice, but when he finished he gasped in shock. His shoulders blazed.

Twisting his neck to see, he found that on his right shoulder a dark sun had erupted, the duplicate of Hank George's Mark of the Others; on his left burned its pale twin, the Ethran Mark of the Sun. The Marks spread like wildfire, central rays reaching toward each other.

When those beams joined over Lucky's heart and broached the Key of Behliseth, Lucky's bright magic was set free.

He wouldn't have known what to do next, but the Wizard guided his free hand to his staff. He closed his hand on the wood and it felt exactly right. Twelve rays of light beamed from the sun-metal globe in rainbow colors—all lively and warm, even the blues.

Without thinking about it first, he held his other hand out and called the Amber Knife. *Thwack*, it hit his palm. In a gesture of victory he couldn't hold back, Lucky thrust that hand up, the Blade clenched in his fist stabbing skyward.

A pillar of white light blasted from the Knife's point and up through the roof of the dome. Around them, the great, dark mass of the Ice-Lord Mahl fell away; the dead and undead thinned and dissolved to hazy mist.

For a slow motion instant, Lucky locked his gaze on Thurlock's ancient, grey eyes.

"Together," the Wizard said.

As one, they lifted the heavy staff and crashed it down. The stone floor vanished. Light sheeted from the heel of the staff and curved to form a glowing golden orb.

With Lucky and Thurlock safe inside, the magical sphere rocketed through the Tower's spire like a shooting star.

PART FIVE: Finding Home

29. Luccan, Let Go!

Lucky opened his eyes thinking he must have passed out. He didn't know where he was or how he got there. Trying to work it out, he searched through the crazy events of the last twenty-four hours like so many hyperlinks: <u>Horrors</u>, <u>Revelations</u>, <u>You Can't Be Serious</u>, and, all by itself on the imaginary webpage, <u>Magic</u>.

Yeah. No wonder his legs felt about as sturdy as a dishrag. One thing for sure, wherever his magic had taken him, he wasn't in Isa's tower anymore; too much light. Everywhere, three-hundred-sixty degrees. And it was all warm and golden. He liked it, but ...

Where's the floor?

"Let go, Luccan." Thurlock sounded annoyed.

Lucky woke up the rest of the way, and found that one of his sweaty hands clutched the Wizard's staff, and the other had a death grip on the Wizard's robes. He was standing so close that Thurlock's beard tickled his forehead and the smell of stale sweat was stealing his air. Far from pleasant, but still.

"If I let go, I'll fall."

"You won't." Apparently clinging fourteen-year-old boys were not tops on Thurlock's list of favorite things. And the Wizard was tired, looking older than stone again, though not nearly as bad as after the storm in his living room. But, he seemed way more solid than ... *light*. So Lucky argued.

"I will, too."

"Luccan, you'll be fine." Thurlock pried Lucky's fingers from his clothing and held him at arm's length. "Look," he said, "I'm standing, you're standing. We're not falling."

He's right, Lucky admitted. He breathed a little easier until two breaths later, when he suddenly remembered that he had been holding the Key of Behliseth in his now empty hand. He panicked. Then, patting at his chest like it was on fire, he found it on its chain around his neck.

Relieved and drained, he sank down to the ... *nothing*, and sat on it. "I thought it was over," he said, and dropped his head into his hands.

Thurlock bent creaking joints one at a time, and then, when he was down far enough, sort of rolled sideways and ended up sitting. He sighed. Or maybe groaned.

"Have faith, Lucky."

The sound of the nickname, for some reason, helped. He gave Thurlock a weak smile. "You called me Lucky."

"It's one of your names isn't it? And fairly apt, I'd say. That Hank George knew a thing or two."

Lucky nodded, pushed his hair out of his eyes, and swallowed hard. "Where are we? I mean ... what is this ... round—?"

Thurlock's exclamation cut the question short. "Look!"

Lucky's head jerked up, and his eyes flew wide. Straight out in front of them, slightly veiled by a skin of golden light, something loomed. Something that had five sides, stood in the middle of nothing, framed in stone, and hummed and vibrated like a turbine engine. Something for which, although he sorted through his entire vocabulary, Lucky could find no name.

A hole in the world.

The space inside it flashed, alternating black and white, faster and faster. Then it filled with steady light, so bright that Lucky had to squeeze his eyes shut. A heartbeat later he opened them again and saw a universe slowly spinning toward a black center. He gaped, mesmerized.

The blackness grew. The bright dots around it could have been stars or sparks or even fireflies, spiraling inward to drain into the dark—which seemed as hungry as a black hole.

Gradually, it took on a new dimension. A membrane grew over the emptiness to cover it like a lens. That only made it seem deeper, darker, more mysterious.

Like the Wizard's eye.
Odd thought.

30. The Twin Stars of Home

With a stomach-flipping jerk the sphere of light in which Lucky and Thurlock rode began to move toward the spinning darkness. Energized with a wave of panic, Lucky grabbed the Key of Behliseth with one hand, the Wizard's staff with the other, and sprang to his feet.

From nowhere the idea struck that this monstrous thing might be a Portal, though it bore no resemblance at all to the tame M.E.R.L.I.N. in the Wizard's living room.

"Thurlock," Lucky said, voice quavering like an aged soprano. *"Is that what I think it is?"*

"If you think it's a Portal of Naught, then yes." Thurlock struggled to his feet with the help of his staff and Lucky's belatedly offered hand. Brushing invisible dust off his robes, he went on. "No fear, though Luccan. Think of it as a road, or a gateway, perhaps."

Lucky's skin prickled head to toe. "A road," he said, treading with caution. "A gateway ... to where?"

The Wizard's eyes crinkled above his tattered beard, and he gently laughed. "Well," he said. "Not to answer a question with a question—I know how you hate that—but, where do you want to go?"

Worlds started to spin in Lucky's head. He felt the light-coach stumble as if its power source threatened to fail, troubling his queasy stomach. "Can't we slow this thing down?"

The Wizard leaned closer, the gathered wrinkles around his eyes spelling out concern. "I can't," he said, "but you probably can. This is your magic."

Lucky wanted to rebel against that idea one last time, but he said, "Okay," and to that simple admission the orb responded, slowing to a cosmic crawl. "Okay," he repeated, and tried to think.

Where do I want to go? That depends. "Thurlock, what about Han?"

"Hmm, well." Thurlock tugged at his beard. "I left him outside Isa's Tower not long ago, and he was alright. A bit worse for the wear, but he can deal with that, and he's quite resourceful, you know. He has little magic, but in a way that is his magic, if you get my drift. Why once I saw him—"

"Thurlock, the point!"

"Oh, sorry. I'm back to my old habits, aren't I? The point is Han will be fine—"

"L'Aria?"

Thurlock smiled and raised his eyebrows. "She'll be fine, too. You aren't the only young person with gifts, you know."

Lucky thought he should feel better, hearing that, but he didn't. It wasn't that he didn't believe the Wizard. Truthfully, he'd already known—somehow, sort of—that Han and L'Aria were both okay. He still worried about them, and Maizie, and a million other things, but that wasn't the trouble.

He pressed his palms against his eyes, trying to slow the whirling images in his head. Small improvement, though. When the chaos slowed, it settled into fearful visions of blood and death and evil. His stomach heaved.

"Thurlock," he whispered. "The things I've seen ..."

The Wizard went still and serious. His sea-grey eyes rimmed with moisture, the muscle of his cheek twitched to the rhythm of old, secret pain. He reached out a hand and tweaked Lucky's hair out of his eyes.

"I'm sorry," he said.

Lucky looked back at him for a long time, steady. Finally he nodded. "Yeah."

The visions scattered, broken up by bits of remembered childhood. His mother, his uncle, Thurlock, even his father. And L'Aria; she'd been his friend. A winter kitchen, a flowering orchard, a summer swimming hole. Moments, pieces of time frozen like snapshots.

Beyond the Wizard's threshold, Lucky had expected to find his way back to his childhood, but it couldn't be done. He knew that now. Three years and the last long week, crammed with things, people, terror, impossible events that had happened anyway, all of that hung between him and childhood like a curtain of stone.

So he straightened his shoulders, shoved his hair back, and set his sails instead for a bright star, a mirrored beacon that would always shine in twin places: his heart, and just beyond the horizon of the future.

Together those lights made up a single destination, and Lucky knew what it was called.

He turned again to meet his friend's age-worn eyes. A smile crept onto his face.

"Home," he said. "Thurlock, I want to go home."

About the Author

Loretta Sylvestre grew up barefoot and city-wild in Los Angeles County California, and now makes her home on the rainy side of Washington State, where stories push up from the leaf mold at night like mushrooms. She graduated from The Evergreen State College, with major emphasis on music, mental health, and cultural studies. She lives with a cat, Boudreau, and earns the money for his food and his hobbies (such as collecting ponytail holders) by working as a civil servant.

She writes a lot – because she loves it and because she can't seem to stop. Her stories have appeared in SN Review, Foliate Oak, The Battered Suitcase, The Linnet's Wings, and now – huzzah – Tales from the Moonlit Path. She has published one novel, a YA fantasy entitled Beyond the Wizard's Threshold, and is in the process of preparing another novel for Marion Margaret Press.

She loves to read, too, and leaves books in her path like a trail of crumbs. Cherryh, Butcher, Huff, Perry, Francis, Erdrich, Tolkien, L'Engle, Funke, Gaiman, Lovecraft, Brooks, Goethe, Collins, Bradbury, and Hobb, just to name a few authors. New favorites: Jason Rolfe – find his work in The Harrow and in The Willows; Tom Beck – find his work in Liquid Imagination.

Her blog is called Worlds Well Written (http://www.worldswellwritten.com).
The subtitle of the site is, A Writers and Readers Conversation, and all are invited to participate.

Her Live Journal page (http://worldsbyloretta.livejournal.com) has a few public posts and more for friends, and there aren't many things she likes better than a new friend.

About the Cover Artist

Ron Leming has been a professional writer and artist for over 25 years, with publications in markets such as Fangoria, Space and Time, Year's Best Horror IV, Outlaw Biker, Mayfair, Ironman, Gauntlet, several Chaosium role playing games, DVD covers for Zombiegeddon, Slaughter Party, Minds of Terror, book Covers for JF Gonzales' the Beloved, Victor Heck's Book of Legion and many others. His book, the Gutbucket Quest, co-written with Piers Anthony, was published in hardback in May of 2000 and released in paperback in May of 2001. He was also the editor of the Damnations anthology and of the infamous parody genre newsletter, the Daily Bonestructure. He's the co-author of the screenplay for the horror film Carnies. http://www.carniesmovie.com

His friends and mentors have included Erle Stanley Gardner, J.N. Williamson, Robert Bloch and Piers Anthony. Originally from Ventura, California, and homesick, he presently lives in Amarillo, Texas, being an old hippy in an unhip world, looking for honest graphics work, and looking for love.

About the Cover Designer

Stephen Blundell lives in Brisbane, Australia with his wife Joanne and three year old son, Michael. His illustrations have graced many book covers and interiors from horror to historical fiction. He is currently working on his own novel as well as his zombie comic "Before The Ashes". His art can be found at www.djdyme.deviantart.com and he can often be found on Facebook where he regularly posts new images.

The Still Life of Hannah Morgan
by Lora Deeprose

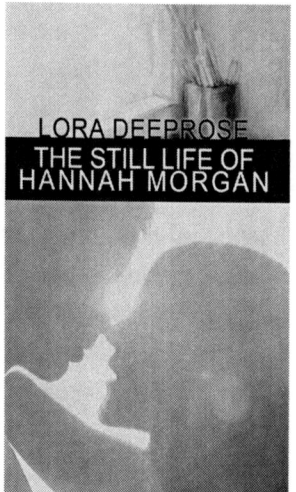

Cover art and design by Stephen Blundell
Edited by Loretta Sylvestre and Deena Mauldin
Genre: Romance (Mild Adult Content)
ISBN: 978-0-9829295-0-6
Length: 304 pages
Format: 6X9 Perfect Bound Softcover
Price: $12.99
Publication Date: September 18, 2010

"The longer you choose to play it safe, the more miserable your life will become. The universe rewards risk my dear; you know what you need to do."

Hannah Morgan's life is at a standstill. Her dreams of becoming an artist vanished with the sudden death of her grandmother and mentor. To appease her distant and disapproving mother, Hannah gets a respectable job at a high-end day spa. Instead of painting masterpieces, Hannah spends her days painting nails and giving facials to wealthy women. Her dreams for the future have become a hideous nightmare. And it just keeps getting worse. She catches her boyfriend cheating, loses her job, and has to watch from the sidelines as her best friend, Jasmine Blue, goes after her own dreams of owning her own salon.

Then she meets Aaron, a working artist, and finds in him a kindred spirit. And, to her surprise, she finds the courage to follow her dreams. When circumstances beyond her control threaten to destroy both her relationship with Aaron and her dreams of a bright future, Hannah fears her mother was right—that some dreams aren't meant to come true.

Now available through Barnes and Noble and Amazon.com from Marion Margaret Press.

The Piper
S.L. Partington

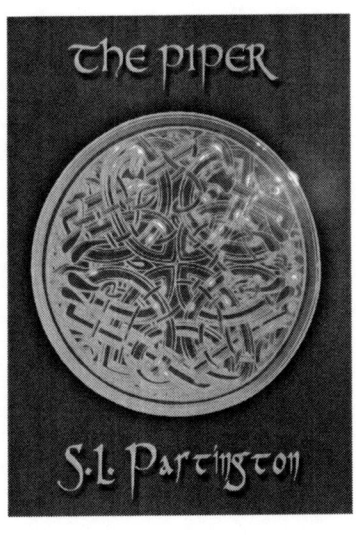

Cover art and design
by Stephen Blundell
Edited by
Loretta Sylvestre

Genre: Historical Fiction
ISBN: 978-0-9829295-2-0
Length: 76 Pages
Format: 6X9 Perfect Bound Softcover
Price: $6.99 USA
Publication Date: September 25, 2010

"It is agreed then. The piper will enter Duntrune and spy out their garrison..."

With those words, a man's fate is decided.

It is the year 1642. Colla Coitach, Chieftan of Clan Donald of Colonsay, seeks to wrest his ancestral home from his enemy, the Campbells and Duncan MacArthur, Colla's personal piper, is sent to spy out the enemy garrison in advance of Colla's impending raid. Young and inexperienced, tossed out into a dangerous world where every word from his mouth is either a complete or a mangled half truth, Duncan strives to keep suspicious Campbell eyes from his true purpose while he seeks to do his master's will.

Aided by Eileen Murdoch, the lovely highland woman who pretends to be his love, Duncan must overcome his fear and self-doubt and find the courage the information Colla has asked him to retrieve. Sent to accomplish an impossible task, Duncan finds himself torn between his love for Eileen and the knowledge that oaths, once spoken, are binding forever.

Duty. Honor. Love.

Sometimes a man must choose the harder road...

Available now from Marion Margaret Press through Barnes and Noble and Amazon.com

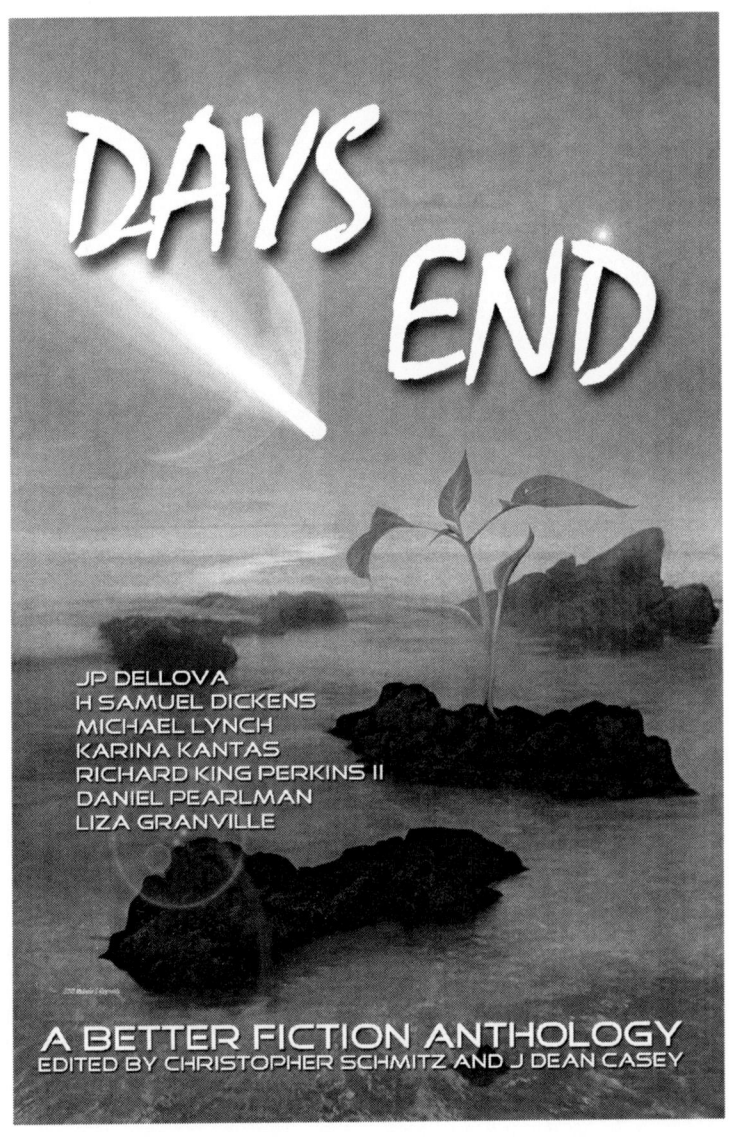

Available now from Marion Margaret Press through Barnes and Noble and Amazon.com